TOWERS'
PROGENY

For Carolyn,

Buck Brannon

BUCK BRANNON

outskirts
press

Outskirts Press, Inc.
http://www.outskirtspress.com

ISBN: 978-1-4787-9463-9

Library of Congress Control Number: 2019916834

PRINTED IN THE UNITED STATES OF AMERICA

DEDICATIONS

TOWERS' PROGENY is dedicated to the thousands of individuals that perished during the attack by Islamic terrorists on 9/11/2001 and those that are continuing to suffer from that heinous action.

...And also to my sister BARBARA J DORMAN. Barbara was my journalistic inspiration in my teen years. Barbara left a trail of civic accomplishments throughout the state of Texas. I miss her dearly.

ACKNOWLEDGMENTS

I wish to acknowledge Kathy L. Woodard for her efforts in editing both TOWERS' PROGENY and the first novel in my trilogy TOWERS ABOVE. Both of these works of fiction would not nearly be as enjoyable without her literary skills.

I would also like to acknowledge two "Beta testers" Donna Long and Barbara Taylor. Their proofing of TOWERS' PROGENY was indispensable, and my thanks goes out to both of them.

And, of course, the most significant "Thank You" goes to my wife Nancy! She has contributed countless hours of work and encouragement for these two ventures.

A big thank you to Outskirts Publishing for showing me how a polished novel is produced.

PROLOGUE

September 2, 2017....

Marty dared to broach the topic first.

"Rob, when Towers Above and Nidalas were sprinting stride for stride down Woodlands Park's home stretch, did you notice how much alike both thoroughbreds looked?"

I hesitated just long enough in my response that I got caught in a lie.

"No, Marty, I didn't notice," was my poorly disguised reply.

"C'mon, Rob, you know that's not true!" she shot back at me.

My mind flashed back to April 2016 and the night when Mark dragged me to the waffle joint for an early breakfast, where he revealed his secret relationship with one of our government's intelligence agencies.

I couldn't suppress my imagination any longer. "Did Mark somehow genetically mess with Towers Above's DNA?" And there it was! My darkest thoughts had spilled out and were no longer hidden in some of my deepest cerebral folds of brain tissue.

"Ya know, Marty, you're to blame for my evil thoughts. You and your damn conspiracy ideas! You started it when you brought up Juan's driving that sleek Camaro ZL1 out at the farm and then questioning where he got the money to buy it! And then the guy shows up on social media, in a Costa Rican video, no less!"

"Obviously posting on a social media site matches his affection for sport cars. Perhaps a South American benefactor offered him a job as an assistant thoroughbred farm manager in Costa

Rica and he jumped at the opportunity."

"Leaving his job as an attendant to Triple Crown winner, Towers Above, wasn't as difficult as he thought it would be. After all, Towers Above was finished with thoroughbred racing and was retired to stud, and that was enough reason to move on."

"I'm guessing when Juan was told that his Costa Rica wheels would be a Ferrari 488 Spider, he couldn't wait to turn zero-sixty in less than three seconds. Sure, his 'off the line' times depended on the conditions of Costa Rica's roads, but he was confident in his abilities."

Marty walked away from our discussion while I continued to fantasize. I visualized Juan rolling through each shift of the Ferrari's transmission while his Go-Pro recorded his 0-60 moments, until he finally broke the three-second barrier...and then immediately posted the video on Facebook.

So yeah, I mused, as one of the owners of Towers Above, I was filled with questions about Juan's exit from the Bluegrass State. And for my friend Tommy, as a CIA employee, I expected it to be a call to action. Once an operator, always an operator. Tommy never was fond of loose ends, and the 2016 terrorist turmoil at Woodlands Park in the Commonwealth of Kentucky needed to be tied up and finished forever.

Besides, social media postings can have unforeseen consequences...can't they?

# CHAPTER 1

Several months had passed since seeing the new Tommy, and I was still stunned by how different he looked. I accepted that while my old friend was figuratively dead out of necessity, a new Tommy was born after an amazing plastic surgery job. He also had a new name, Lanny. I kept this to myself, though, sparing Marty the details of the Challenge Cup Reunion Dinner seven days earlier. It didn't make sense for me to bring any of this up to my wife, as she had moved on.

Unlike Marty, who'd emotionally closed the book on that frightful day in April, the day when a man hell-bent on retribution threatened the lives of Towers Above and Nidalas, I was still struggling with painful memories. It was time for me to put those memories away, too. After all, the series of horrific events at Woodlands Park Race Track had ended months ago.

I was tired and crawled into bed, nestling against Marty, who was fast asleep and snoring lightly. It didn't take long for me to reach the same state and start dreaming. My sense of smell was strong this night, and I was dreaming in color.

The dream was vivid. I was kicking back, dragging on a Salem Light 100, enjoying the taste and rush of nicotine, even though I'd quit smoking twenty years ago. The Beach Boys were singing "God Only Knows" when I suddenly realized the song wasn't a dream – it was the ringtone on my cell phone. Now wide awake and hoping the phone wouldn't wake Marty, I quickly searched for and found the phone on the floor. I hurried into the bath-room to take the call. "Hello," I answered.

"Rob, tell me about Juan and the internet video--"

"What the hell, Tommy ... oh shit, I'm sorry. I mean Lanny!"

Hearing footsteps, I turned and saw Marty leaning against the frame of the bathroom door. Obviously she'd heard the phone ring. "Lanny? Who the hell is Lanny and what does he have to do with Tommy?" my wife demanded of me.

"Jesus, Marty, go back to bed," I said, while also trying to cover the phone so her angry voice couldn't be heard at the other end.

"I'm not leaving until you tell me who's on the other end of that call."

"Christ, Marty, it's Tommy," I told her. "Do I have to go out-side to finish this conversation?"

I already knew the answer, even as I asked the question. "You go outside half naked, and I promise you won't get back inside the house," she threatened. "Don't forget a house key and by the way, the police should be here in about five minutes once I set off the burglar alarm."

I knew Marty was all bluster and brushed past her, heading for the deck off the kitchen. Grabbing my coat to keep warm in the fall's chilly night air, I returned to the phone call.

"You still there, Lanny? Hello, hello?"

All I heard was laughter – a laugh I'd never heard before be-cause in all the time we spent together during the previous year, neither of us had a reason to laugh. I couldn't help it – I began laughing too.

"Rob, I'm sorry. I shouldn't have laughed, but you need to learn how to cover the microphone on your phone," Lanny said. "Wow, she tore you a new one. I didn't mean to wake both of you, or call this late, but I've hardly slept since the dinner. I've been thinking all week about what you said about the video. There's no damn way a stable hand who makes scratch for wages is able to save enough money to bet big on Towers Above. And to boot, he makes enough money to chuck it all, travel to South America, and buy a Ferrari?"

After pausing a moment to let me digest what he just said, Lanny continued. "I've searched the internet again and again and can't find the video you talked about. The best I can figure is that someone deleted it. So Rob, I need your help because the video means there's more to the Towers Above/Nidalas saga – and we need to figure out what it is. Do you have any idea where Juan was when the video was made?"

"No, I don't. Donnie showed that video to me. Let me get in touch with him tomorrow and see what he knows. How do you want me to get back to you on this?"

"Tell you what, Rob … you've got my phone number now, and that's the best way to reach me. And for God's sake, don't delete it! My phone's secure. And you can still call me Tommy. I know that you and Marty, and Art and Ted would be the last folks to give me up! Now you better hurry up and get back inside and tend to your woman before your nuts freeze and become useless!"

I heard laughter again, then a sudden silence. Tommy had hung up.

Returning inside the house, I headed back to the bedroom wondering where the confrontation with Marty would take place. I rounded the corner to the bathroom and she was waiting by the doorway, ready to pounce

"Well …?"

"Look Marty, I'm sorry. I didn't expect that call. It was a total surprise." It took a split second to realize that wasn't going to cut it with her.

Sitting on the edge of the tub, I told Marty what had taken place during the Challenge Cup dinner, and what had transpired with Tommy. I explained about his changed physical appearance and new name, then told her about the conversation I'd just had with him.

I saw a tear rolling down Marty's cheek – which she didn't attempt to wipe away or draw attention to. That would give away her emotions.

"What did I say to cause that?" I blurted out to her.

"My God, Rob, I can't go through any more of this! I want out! No more! No Tommy or Ted! No more clandestine crap. I want our humdrum life back. Please, I'm begging you!"

The single tear was now a tsunami. I reached for her hand and in an instant was holding Marty in my arms. She finally released all the pent-up feelings that had been brewing for over a year.

"Listen to me, honey. Look me in the eyes. I'll talk to Donnie tomorrow, get the information, and give it to Tommy. What he does with it after shouldn't involve either of us. I promise I will tell him that."

"I'll tell him that we can't be involved in anyone's international affairs anymore. Marty, I will, I promise."

Marty's hold on me grew tighter, but she didn't speak a word. I couldn't tell if she sensed that I was speaking a half-truth, but I knew what Tommy was thinking: There was a boatload of money floating around supplied by someone or some organization, and it landed in Juan's lap.

I knew that Juan had as much opportunity for physical contact with Towers Above, and conversely with Nidalas, as any of us had. I also knew that Tommy had to go through every door to find answers, then close and lock the door permanently. That's what intelligence people do, and Tommy had done it for years. I was pretty sure he was determined to do this one last time.

CHAPTER 2

Marty returned to bed while I grabbed my phone and texted Donnie. I knew he was probably asleep, and that he'd see the text the first thing in the morning.

"Will you be home in the morning? We need to talk … it's urgent!"

Heading to the bedroom, I heard the ping telling me I had a text. "Damn, Donnie, you keep crazier hours than I do," I said. The text confirmed that he'd be home in the morning, but I had to get there early since he was meeting with some prospective thoroughbred owners later that morning. He was setting up breeding dates with a couple of their mares with Towers Above for sometime in the late winter months.

"See you at 7:00," I replied, then set my alarm and went back to bed.

I was early, arriving around 6:45 and heading for TA's barn. No trip to the farm could happen without visiting our champ, TA. We played our game as always. I would put a peppermint candy in one hand, show it to him, and put both hands behind my back. Then I played the shell game with the mint – knowing the smell of it was on both my hands. Sometimes I'd tuck the mint in the waistband of my pants – then show TA my empty hands. He just looked at me, shaking his mane and calling my bluff. When we were done playing our little game, without exception, he always picked the hand with the mint. Donnie played the same game with the horse, and always with the same results. He swore TA's sense of smell was all part of the magnificent horse's genetic makeup.

"Why do you even bother, Rob? You don't stand a chance," I heard Donnie say from behind me.

"Donnie, there's always that one time," I answered back.

"That text last night--or should I say early this morning?--had a load of worry in it. What's going on, buddy?" he asked.

"Donnie, I got a call from Tommy last night. I'll spare you the drama that happened between Marty and me because of the call. But he wants to find out where Juan is now. It made me wonder too. I definitely remember Marty questioning how Juan could afford that late-model Camaro on his salary."

I saw a look of defensiveness flash across Donnie's face.

"Look, Donnie, you know I've never questioned how you pay your employees and Tommy never implied that you had a role in anything suspicious. When Tommy and I were together at a dinner last week, I happened to mention the Ferrari video that you showed me from the internet. You've got to admit, moving up from owning an American sports car to a Ferrari presents a lot of questions."

"Hold on, Rob. Juan was leasing his Camaro. It's none of my business how much someone's net worth might be. Hell, maybe he has a rich uncle ...."

"Donnie, the video has disappeared from the 'net. It's been deleted. You don't know Tommy like I do. That video was like waving raw meat in front of a starving tiger. I'm telling you, he's not questioning your actions! If you have the slightest clue where Juan is, please tell me now!"

I could tell Donnie was hurt by my line of questioning. He

walked some ten paces away from me, stopped, and paused for a good half minute.

"Geraldo originally showed me the video. He mentioned to me that Juan has some sort of extended family in Costa Rica. He's back there cleaning the stalls. Why don't you go down there and interrogate him yourself?"

"Donnie, that's not necess--"

"Screw you, Rob! You know I thought you and I had a trust, a special bond! You can go to hell."

Donnie turned and walked away.

"Donnie, stop. Hold on, please don't do this!"

"Oh God, please, fifty years of brotherhood and friendship, gone," I inwardly screamed. I started to run after Donnie, and just as quickly as I started, I stopped. The problem with thinking about a conspiracy is that it creates instant confusion. I hadn't seen the corporate accounting books. I had no clue how much Juan made. Maybe Donnie was Juan's gambling partner. Maybe neither one was.

I returned to my car and placed the call.

"Hey Rob, are you thawed out yet?" Tommy said, laughing.

"I'm more than thawed. I just got torched by Donnie. He thinks I'm linking him to Juan, and he basically told me to do something that's anatomically impossible to do. Supposedly Geraldo told Donnie that Juan has family in Costa Rica. You might start there. But I don't know Juan's last name. Oh, Donnie also said that Juan was leasing the sports car he was driving here in Kentucky."

"I don't need a last name. I'll find him. Thanks, and you understand, don't you, why I've got to follow this through to its conclusion?" Tommy asked, desperately hoping I understood.

"I don't have a problem with that, Tommy, but I need a favor. I don't want to know where this road takes you, where it ends, or who is involved. Marty and I need to get back to our normal lives. Do you understand?"

"Understood," Tommy said. "I'll see you at the track." The phone went silent.

Off on his own, Donnie texted Mark, who was halfway across the world. Unfortunately, Donnie didn't know that Mark's texts were screened by his girlfriend or that Mark would never see the message that read:

"Want to give you a heads up! Rob was just here and questioning Juan's finances. Apparently Rob's federal agent friend has an interest in the situation and wants to talk with Juan. Can you stop that from happening? You and I have too much to lose if the puzzle pieces are put in place! D."

# CHAPTER 3

"So, Geraldo is now part of this equation. I bet he has Juan's cell number, and I'm thinking it's time for Geraldo to take an unscheduled vacation," Tommy mumbled to himself, knowing he had to reconnect with the agency before he could do anything. Once an agent, always an agent. Anyone who has ever worked with the feds is never totally disconnected, but Tommy still had to get approval to re-engage and permission to execute his plan.

An operative is always part of the fraternity, and the only way anyone ever cuts the cord is by dying.

Danny's cell phone rang – and he immediately recognized the number. "I bet you're calling me because you're bored, aren't you?" he said.

"Danny, you have no idea. How's Stan doing? I heard he was in a car accident and just wondered how he was doing. If you get a chance, have him give me a call, please. Sorry, I've got to go. I'll talk to you later."

Nonsensical language always makes sense to other CIA employees. Tommy knew Danny understood what his message was asking him to do.

Even a phone call became a contest. That's how competitive Tommy was and always would be. After hanging up, he sat back and waited, mentally betting that a return call wouldn't take more than fifteen minutes. Staring at the hands on his watch, he began shifting uneasily in his seat. At the thirteen-minute mark, the phone rang, and a grin spread over Tommy's face.

"What the hell do you want?" he heard as Stan's voice exploded over the cellphone speakers.

"I've got some loose ends to tie up from the activities this past April," Tommy said.

"Okay, fill me in," Stan directed.

Tommy explained what was going on and asked permission to conduct a snatch-and-detain operation. If his suspicions were confirmed, the next phase of the plan would then be to get permission to travel to Costa Rica and do the same there.

"I'm going to have to climb the ladder and clean some gutters, but as far as I'm concerned, it's a go for us. I'll get back to you as soon as possible," Stan said.

It would take Stan a couple of hours to get approval from his superiors for what Tommy was asking him to do.

Later that evening, Tommy received a short text with four words. "The road is paved!"

It was nearly 24 hours later when Geraldo was roused from a sound sleep. He and his belongings were gathered up and he was quickly on the road to an agency safe house somewhere in the Bluegrass state.

Every member of Tommy's team was wearing a mask, which was good because Geraldo stunk. Whether his clothing was smeared with manure or personal hygiene was not his strong suit, Tommy wanted to hose him down when they reached the safe house. Once they arrived, Tommy talked to their guest in fluid Spanglish.

"What's Juan's telephone number and where in Costa Rica is he?" was Tommy's first question. Geraldo's back stiffened and he tugged at his restraints. It was clearly obvious that the relationship between the two former co-workers was more than that of casual acquaintances.

"Do you like pain, Geraldo?" was Tommy's second question. Geraldo's head jerked up and Tommy saw the fear in his captive's eyes.

It took just seconds before Geraldo began spitting out information. Tommy was stunned it was that quick – rarely did a detainee roll over almost instantaneously. Now with unbound hands, Geraldo asked for his phone and scrolled through his contacts, soon finding and pointing to Juan's phone number and address in Costa Rica.

Now that he had the necessary information, it was time to get to work. Tommy directed another agent to clean Geraldo up and get him in bed. Turning to Geraldo, Tommy told him to relax, and that he was going to be their guest for a while. He was taking no chances that Geraldo could warn Juan or anyone else that trouble was coming their way.

Tommy again texted Stan, requesting permission for Danny to go with him to Costa Rica. Stan gave his immediate approval.

Arrangements were made shortly after that for Danny. Tommy told him to meet the next day at noon, at the Greater Cincinnati International Airport. "I'll be at the Delta Airlines counter tomorrow. Only pack tropical gear."

Tommy's next call was a secure one to the station agent in San Jose, the capital of Costa Rica. Tommy gave his contact all the information he had on Juan, hoping that some basic investigative research could be done immediately. This would save both Danny and himself some time and legwork when they arrived in the country.

What he heard, though, was not what he'd expected.

"Sir, my name is Agent Diaz and I've got some bad news. There's been a lot of chatter down here in the last 24 hours about your target, and the origin of the communications is in America. Your person of interest was found dead this morning at an exclusive residence about 20 kilometers east of town."

Tommy fell silent. "Did you copy that, sir?" Agent Diaz inquired.

"Sorry about that, Diaz; I'm here. Would you please get going on my request from earlier and also find out what information the authorities already have?" Not pleased with this turn of events, Tommy ended the call and collapsed on his bed next to his half-packed suitcase.

"Murder, really? A stable hand has to be silenced? Over what?" Tommy ranted to himself. "I know Rob Becker didn't blab, and we snatched Geraldo as quickly as possible."

Lost in thought, Tommy came to his next conclusion. "That leaves Donnie as the probable leaker. When I get back, it's time for him and me to talk. And why is another American intelligence agency involved with this insignificant farm worker?"

These were Tommy's jumbled thoughts at that moment – thoughts that needed answers and explanations. He finished packing and retired for a fitful night's sleep, realizing he'd stumbled onto something far more involved than suspected just a few days earlier.

 HAPTER 4

Tommy and Danny arrived as agreed at the Cincinnati Airport. Each man was there 90 minutes before their flight's departure to Atlanta, where they would get on a connecting flight to Costa Rica. Neither man acknowledged the other in the gate area. Tommy finished the paperwork he'd started the night before and placed his yellow legal pad on top of his coat. Rising to stretch his legs, Tommy then walked a few feet down the terminal to get a cup of coffee.

Danny swooped in and took the seat next to where Tommy's jacket and yellow note pad lay unattended. He casually placed his jacket on top of the pad and bent over to re-tie his right shoelace before grabbing his jacket and the pad underneath. The heist was complete.

The plane was only half filled with passengers, and there was no one seated next to either Danny or Tommy. They were purposely distanced from each other. Danny began reading Tommy's primer on Costa Rica that was outlined in the legal pad.

Tommy knew this was Danny's first trip to Costa Rica and he needed to explain to him why so many people were drawn there. Not only is it one of four countries favored as a second home by citizens from other countries throughout the world, but it holds a special allure to American expatriates. The country's popularity is topped only by Panama, its southern neighbor, as a favored destination. A majority of the population speaks English, and octogenarians are plentiful. The average life expectancy is eighty years. Almost 10 percent of the population is foreign born. The country has no standing army and derives over 90 percent of its energy from renewable sources,

Costa Rica is a retirement paradise.

In bold letters Tommy had written in the notes: "How is a Mexican with supposed limited resources able to take up residence in this country? When we land, we need to visit Juan's home and look for answers there before we check in with Stan."

Tommy didn't write down the name of whichever US intelligence agency he thought was responsible for the hit on Juan. If it was by a fellow patriot, Tommy was convinced the intelligence agency best known as the DIA was somehow involved. As the right arm of the Department of Defense, DIA is responsible for implementing the DOD's military defense actions. The DIA is also the watchdog and protector of DOD's intelligence, including existing operations and any future dark operations. This wouldn't be the first time the DOD and the CIA butted heads. Tommy could readily recall many operations that resulted in conflicts between the DIA's Defense Clandestine Service and the CIA agents that the DIA often relied upon to do their scut work.

Finally, the flight was over, and the plane landed. After deplaning, the two men met their Costa Rican contact in the baggage claim area. Once in the car, Tommy wanted an update.

"Your guys down here seem pretty emphatic that our target was taken out by another patriot. How so?"

Their new friend, Dwayne, turned away from the steering wheel, looking directly at Tommy and said, "The guy that did the hit is also in the morgue downtown. My police sources tell me that Juan's residence has one of the most sophisticated security and alarm systems they've seen in the country. A silent alarm was tripped and police responded instantly, knowing the house had not been prone to false alarms. Upon their arrival, they found two bodies, Juan and the John Doe, who had made it to his car but died in the driver's seat. He was killed by a bullet to the neck. So, guys, where to?"

"Can we access the house easily?" Tommy asked.

"Way ahead of you. We've got an agent inside right now. I figured that'd be your first stop, since the dead guy isn't going anywhere."

Tommy was deep in thought. "This just gets better and better. A guy that mucks stables and cool-walks thoroughbreds lives in a residence with a premier security system? Are you kidding me? It's time to find out who's backing this operation!"

Tommy loved the hunt. He would have been a helluva detective if he had decided to work in the public sector instead.

Once inside the house, Tommy turned into a bloodhound, looking for and sniffing out the unusual. His initial read came from a quick visual scan of the basic contents in the house. He walked to the recliner and tipped it backwards. Sure enough, it was a La-Z-Boy. In the corner of the room was a hand-carved roll top desk. Hanging from the ceiling over the desk was a Tiffany lamp. And atop the desk was a bronze sculpture of a grizzly bear perched on a slab of granite, staring down at a miniature fish – probably meant to be representative of a salmon. Tommy turned the artwork upside down, hoping to find the sculptor's name. He wasn't disappointed. Not only was the artist's name on the bottom, but so was the name of his gallery in Montana. "Surely the gallery has a list of people who purchased this sculpture I'm holding," Tommy mumbled to himself.

Taking out his phone, Tommy snapped pictures of the sculpture with the gallery's name on the underside and texted them to Stan in Virginia. The quick pursuit of a list of buyers of the Grizzly Fishing artwork, as Tommy now called it, had begun.

After rifling through the rest of the contents in the home, the team headed for the morgue.

Once there, Tommy and Danny began to examine and photograph the body. Danny pried open the corpse's eyelids, placed a measuring instrument between the pupils of both eyes and snapped a picture. Now the Agency had documentation of the dead man's inter-pupillary distance. Then Danny grabbed a Dopp Kit from his briefcase, removed the fingerprint kit and applied ink to John Doe's fingers. It took just a bit of time to get satisfactory prints.

The deceased never cooperated during the fingerprinting procedure, but this time, Danny was pleased with how it went. He only broke two fingers during the process and completed the task in fifteen minutes. Danny then forced John Doe's mouth open to get pictures of any dental work that had been done. He always hated the cracking sounds made from stretching and tearing tendons and ligaments attached to the muscles and bones but was still able to successfully fight the effects of the body in rigor mortis. By bending nearly upside down, Danny photographed the upper teeth. Straightening back up, he then took pictures of the man's lower jaw and teeth. It took nearly an hour to get everything they needed before palming a hundred-dollar bill into the mortician's hand and leaving the morgue.

Thirty minutes later, they were at the safe house where within one hour, they'd emailed and faxed their reports and additional documents to the agency back home.

Now it was a waiting game while the wonks back in the states sorted everything out and came up with the identification. The wait would be long enough to give them time to head to the agency's ocean retreat and get in some deep-sea fishing!

CHAPTER 5

As soon as all the information from Costa Rica arrived at CIA headquarters, Stan directed every department involved to come up with answers ASAP! Juan's assassination in Costa Rica had elevated the priority of Tommy's case to the highest level.

The fingerprints were the easiest identifier to process and were immediately entered into the CIA's computer system.

Stan called his wife and told her not to hold dinner, as it would be another all-nighter at the agency. Every existing database, American and global, was going to be analyzed.

It was just past midnight when Stan received a call.

"Boss, we've got a roadblock. The computer didn't come up with an ID."

"I'll be right down," Stan replied.

After a quick elevator ride, Stan arrived at Jeff's office. Jeff had a look on his face that didn't bode well, was Stan's first thought. "Shut the door, boss, please. It's not only that we don't have an identity, but the computer won't allow us to access the information. We rebooted it and ran the analysis three times and all we get is 'This information is classified.' You know what that means."

Not unexpectedly, the investigation into John Doe's interpupillary analysis came back with the same results as the fingerprint analysis. Nothing.

Stan slumped into a chair and buried his head in his hands. "Damn, Jeff, we've got at least seventeen or more intelligence agencies in this country, and the assassin is an agent for one of them. If I go shaking the bushes, the word will get out and we'll wake up everyone involved. They'll shut down whatever they're protecting. Okay Jeff, let's check out the sculpture and focus on that."

Stan had realized the scope of the terroristic events of April was even larger than first thought. "Damn, Tommy, you do have a knack for sniffing out trouble," he mumbled to himself. Stan texted his men in Montana to confirm they'd be at the Thompson Gallery as soon as it opened the next day. Learning that the team had arrived at the cabin on Flathead Lake a half hour earlier and were on schedule took some of the sting out.

In the meantime, thousands of miles to the east, it was morning and the beginning of a new day in Saudi Arabia. The Four Horseman's Farm silent partner, Mark, had just received an encoded text from the Pentagon.

"Your father is ill. Suggest you head for home. E-tickets included in attachment. Safe travels, Mother."

Sometimes in the American intelligence community, all it takes are a few broken tree branches to produce an alarm!

Mark wanted to stay and help Nidalas finish his recovery therapy, but it was time to bid his Arab friends adieu.

CHAPTER 6

Hank and Rudy hoped Todd Thompson was a patriot. As long as he understood the importance of giving them names of individuals who'd purchased the Grizzly and Salmon sculpture, there'd be no problems. They also knew there was a good chance the man would lawyer up – and there wasn't time for that. They readied the cabin for an interrogation, if it was necessary, as Tommy had instructed.

Arriving at the gallery soon after it opened the next morning, the two wandered the store as any shoppers would, browsing and looking at the artwork on display.

"Good morning, gentlemen! Is there something in particular you're looking for today?" Todd Thompson asked the two men.

Hank responded, "Yes, there is. A friend of mine has one of your sculptures. It's a grizzly bear on a ledge and the bear is looking down at a fish just caught. I absolutely love it. Do you have another of that particular piece available?"

"I do have one – it's on display in another room. Please come with me. I do the sculptures myself. Do either of you know the lost wax technique?"

Shaking their heads, the men said "No." Stopping in front of the sculpture, Todd explained the process. "I wax the original design, and then invest it into a material that can handle high temperatures. Next I place it into an oven and increase the heat until the wax vaporizes. The next step is to inject molten metal into the cavity and I get a rough casting for a new sculpture. That then becomes the piece of art you're looking at now. It's a time-consuming process. However, I only start a new casting for a buyer after it's been ordered and paid for."

"Do you have records of people that have bought your sculptures? What I mean is how many of this particular piece have you sold?" Hank asked.

"Off the top of my head I'm not sure, but let me go look." As Todd headed to the office, Hank gave Rudy the nod, and they both went in the same direction. Rudy entered the office and closed the door, while Hank stood guard in case a customer came into the gallery.

Rifling through his records, Todd didn't notice the door closing. "If you order one today, I will have sold almost 500 of the Grizzly sculptures."

Turning around to face Hank again, Todd's eyes were immediately drawn to his customer's open left hand – holding a government badge. Hank's jacket was pulled back just enough to also reveal that he was carrying a weapon.

"Whoa, guys, I don't want any trouble! Who are you and what do you want?" Todd stammered in obvious fear.

Hank could tell Todd had just experienced a bladder problem.

"Mr. Thompson, we're with Homeland Security. Check out my identification."

Hank paused, reading Todd's body language and waiting for his response. If Todd says okay or nods approval, the chances of having to abduct him are pretty slim. But any objections and both of us will have to pounce immediately, the agent thought.

"Okay, again what do you want from me?"

"We'd like a list of the names and addresses of your customers that purchased the Grizzly sculpture. I see the printer there in the corner. Please just print out the list and we'll be gone," Hank said.

"It's not that easy. I ... I ... don't have my sales sorted by type and I don't know how to do that on the computer. My wife handles all that stuff for me. Let me call her. She can be here in a moment!"

Hank gestured for Todd to calm down. "Take it easy," he told the nervous artist. "Why don't you let me see just what your computer can do? Okay?" Todd nodded approval a second time and stepped back, allowing Hank access to his computer. Thirty minutes later, Hank had generated a list with names of every buyer of the Grizzly sculpture. The men sat silently while the list printed. Hank was amazed that Todd didn't ask more questions. He knew from experience, though, that a badge and weapon could go a long way in getting someone to cooperate.

With the list now in hand, Hank quickly looked it over, checking that the total number of buyers was right, and making sure there was an address with each name. Except for five names, every purchaser had a street address. The other five had a post-office box. Hank turned to Rudy and nodded his approval.

"Mr. Thompson, your country thanks you for helping us. You have no idea how important this information is, and when our job is done, I'll be back to order my Grizzly sculpture."

Todd's knees buckled. The last thing he saw before fainting was the two agents exiting the gallery.

Hank and Rudy headed back to the cabin and once inside, began photographing the list. An email with the encrypted names and addresses would soon be in Stan's inbox. Their assignment was now done.

Rudy couldn't keep it together any longer.

"Are you shitting me … your country thanks you! Where the hell did that come from?" Rudy asked, trying to control his laugher, but with little success. Hank couldn't help but laugh too.

Both men had performed flawlessly. Perhaps it was because they were skilled at the job, or perhaps it was because Todd Thompson was a true patriot.

CHAPTER 7

S tan was at his desk, downing a fourth cup of black coffee, and he was wired. He could feel his heart skipping beats and made a mental note – no more than two cups of caffeine each day. Tilted back in his chair, he heard his assistant knock and saw her peek around the partially closed door.

"We just got a text from the guys in Montana. It's time to get to work!"

"Thanks, Jan, I was starting to get bored," he quickly told her.

An email that corresponded to the text came through on the computer at that moment. It was a short missive with an attached spreadsheet.

"Hope this helps," the message read.

Jan printed out the attachment with the list of names and handed it to Stan. He quickly saw the total number of sculptures that had been purchased, shaking his head. "Crap, I was hoping for no more than fifty." He had Jan run another copy of the data and had the IT department sort the information by state, gender, and occupation.

This is going to take precious hours that we don't have! I hate having to run background checks on all of these individuals. Jesus, Tommy, you and those frigging horses, Stan thought.

For the umpteenth time, he pulled up the video of the race between Towers Above and Nidalas on his computer. He couldn't help himself. Stan silently wished he'd been present to watch the thrilling duel and the dead-heat finish on that Saturday in April.

Halfway through the video, a thought occurred to him. I doubt the Saudis would recognize any of these names, let alone be willing to help, but the handlers of Towers Above just might.

"Jan, get Tommy on his cellphone, please!"

Tommy was at the cabin, all fished out and anxious to solve the mystery when his phone vibrated.

"Damn, Stan, this is taking forever. Tell me you've got some answers to our problem!"

"Well yes and no. Tommy, the prints and inter-pupillary distance tests confirm there's another intelligence agency involved. The sculpture is our last hope, and we've got 500 people to check out. Do you think Dr. Becker might help with the list of names we have? Maybe he would recognize a name. Perhaps he'd have a hunch or just anything that could help! That's all I'm looking for right now. That's all we have to work with!"

"Stan, I'll try. He's not real pleased with me right now. His wife is even more adamant that I get the hell out of Rob's life. I'll get back to you, but I can't guarantee anything."

Tommy sat down and with a deep sigh, pulled up a phone number from his contacts list. Punching the ten digits into the dial pad, he said aloud to no one in particular, "Lord, please let him answer this call. Don't let it go to voicemail."

I answered with my usual, "Hello?"

"Don't hang up; this is Tommy!"

I didn't say a word for about fifteen seconds, before finally replying, "This better be really important."

"It is, and I'm sorry for ruining your day. I'm in Costa Rica and Juan is here or should I say, was. We're chasing ghosts right now. However, we may have a solution to that mystery we talked about but need to act quickly. If I send you a list of names, would you review it? Then if you recognize any name, please text me immediately."

It took me even longer before responding back. "Okay, Tommy, send me the list, but this is the last time for anything! Do you understand?"

I should've known the answer.

"Can't promise that, Rob. You should know that by now!"

I pressed the issue for at least thirty seconds before I realized there was no one on the other end of the phone. Tommy had hung up. Two minutes later, an email with the list appeared on my phone. I began scrolling through the names, pausing to look at each one, taxing my memory for any link to that name in my past or present life. The list was alphabetized and it took a while to get to the names that began with "S." Scrolling through the names, I suddenly stopped in shock. In fact, for a few seconds, it felt like I couldn't breathe.

"Mark Shaw" was on the list, as clear as day.

"Nah, it can't be the same Mark Shaw who's my friend! There's no way it's the Four Horsemen's silent partner," I said to myself, with a foreboding uncertainty. I continued going through the list to the last name, still in total denial of the name I'd seen. Too quickly, I was at the end of the list, then went backwards, hoping the name had magically disappeared. It hadn't. Conspiracy thoughts racked my brain. Knowing there was no choice, I texted Tommy the name, then went and grabbed a cold beer. Finally sitting down in the chair, I waited for the inevitable call. It came almost instantly.

"Who's Mark Shaw?" were the first words out of Tommy's mouth. It took a while, but I told him everything – from our early years together in college to the formation of our group and everything from that point to the race. I explained how Mark was technically a silent partner of the group and that he was a genetics expert. I also told Tommy that Mark's business did a lot of secretive work with the government. I ended with the fact that I hadn't seen or heard from Mark since before that fateful stakes race in April.

"Where does he live, Rob?"

I told him. There was dead silence while Tommy was looking at the addresses connected to each name on the list. I later found out my list didn't include those addresses. Tommy didn't give any hint that the connection had been confirmed, but I could sense that from his next comment.

"You know we've got to find him, and it may not be pretty after we do. How strong-willed is he?"

"I'm not sure. We were young college students – we were invincible, if you know what I mean." I begged Tommy to not hurt Mark.

"I'll do what I can, but you've got to understand … he's involved with some individuals who are not only powerful but extremely ruthless. I just can't guarantee anything. And one last thing … do you want me to let you know what happens? I owe you that much if you want it."

Again, I paused before eventually answering "Yes." I needed closure – now!

HAPTER 8

Once Nidalas arrived home in the Middle East after the failed attempt on his life earlier in 2016, the horse was entrusted to Halim's care. It was his responsibility to make sure the magnificent equine creature survived. After all, this was one of God's animals and Halim fervently believed that no one person or country should benefit in any way from the thoroughbred.

It was now several months later. Halim left the Saudi horse farm after conducting his daily examination of Nidalas – as always, paying special attention to the thoroughbred's chest sounds. The horse's lungs were clear, with no sounds indicating the presence of pneumonia. Things were looking good, Halim thought.

Halim's thoughts drifted back in time to his sophomore year at The Ohio State University College of Veterinary Medicine – and the horrific events of 9/11 that same year. All too clearly, he remembered the shame and embarrassment he felt for the Middle Eastern country of his birth. Every Arab knew that the denial by the Saudi government of a link between them and Osama Bin Laden was a farce.

He also clearly remembered how his involvement with the US Central Intelligence Agency began – that day, one year post 9/11 when he attended a campus job fair at OSU with a friend. The federal government had a services booth at the event, ostensibly looking for soon-to-be graduates to hire for positions with different US agencies. Halim easily recalled the conversation he had with the person manning the booth, a man also of Middle Eastern descent whom he would eventually come to know as a CIA agent.

Totally unaware on that day that he was speaking to an asset of the United States, Halim talked about his veterinary studies at the university and the country of his birth, making no effort to conceal his disdain for what his homeland now stood for. The asset knew a good prospect when he saw one but felt it wise to not press the issue farther that day. But he would reel Halim in quickly – and in fact he did within a matter of weeks. Now Halim was responsible for sending daily updates on Nidalas' health to his fellow assets in the US.

His attention was suddenly drawn away from those memories and thoughts about Nidalas' continued recovery by a text notification on his encrypted phone. As very few people had his phone number, Halim knew the message was important. He pulled off to the side of the road to unlock the phone and open the message.

Halim quickly read the message: a series of question marks, a picture, the words "Mark Shaw" and another series of question marks. Shaking his head to chase away the random thoughts racing through it – memories of the past and the realities of now – he realized he knew the man in the picture. It was the American he'd been working closely with over the past several months. The man who'd saved Nidalas' life. A man he knew only as Mark.

Responding to the text, Halim wrote: "The man in the picture is American and the same person who has been responsible for treating Nidalas. From the first day when Nidalas arrived home gravely ill until now, Mark has directed his recovery. Since Nidalas is now doing so well, I know that Mark is planning to return to the states. He may have already left."

Stan immediately responded in all caps to stress the urgency: IF MARK IS STILL PRESENT, CAN YOU FIND OUT WHEN HE'S LEAVING AND WHAT CITY HE'S FLYING TO IN THE US?

Halim answered with equal emphasis: I WILL TRY!

Turning the car around, he headed back to the veterinary hospital and the men's locker room to check out Mark's locker. The lock was still in place. That didn't guarantee Mark was still present, but the presence of the lock could mean he hadn't yet left. Grabbing a sheet of paper, Halim wrote a quick note thanking Mark for being a wonderful teacher and mentor. As he was about to slip the note into a narrow opening on the front of the locker, he heard his name called.

"Halim, what's up?"

Halim turned toward the voice. "Mark, I wasn't sure if you were still here but just in case you were, I wanted to thank you for all that you've done for my career. So when are you out of here, and where are you flying to?"

"My fiancée and I leave tomorrow. We're flying into Miami, Florida, and taking a few days off for a mini vacation. I don't think I've ever told you, but I live in northern Kentucky. If you ever get to America, I really hope you'll call me. But I would much rather that you come and visit. It's been my pleasure to get to know you and have the chance to be a mentor to you."

Mark took out a business card, writing his home and mobile numbers on the back of it before handing the card to Halim. The two men embraced before Mark opened the locker to gather his belongings.

"Mark, I have one last question, if you don't mind! Was Nidalas' recovery a miracle? I mean, there's no way he should have survived the ricin attack, and I think you have the answer as to why he did!"

"Halim, it's all about genetics. That's all I can tell you," Mark answered.

For the second time that day, Halim left the facility and headed for his car. Two minutes down the road, he again pulled off onto the berm to text his asset, whom he assumed was based somewhere in North America. It took just a few seconds for the information to show up on Stan's phone screen. A minute later, the same information was transferred to Tommy's cellphone. The information loop was almost complete!

Stan fired off a new text to Tommy and Danny, telling them their target was on the move and heading back to the States. Stan was convinced that the link between Donnie and Mark Shaw was now revealed. It's obvious that Juan's death has something to do with either Mark or Donnie – perhaps even both men, he thought.

He wanted Tommy and Danny to gather their prey and take them to the safe house where both individuals would be interrogated – and answers given, whatever it took. Stan sent another text to Tommy and Danny. "E-tickets will be sent for your trip to Miami. We've confirmed Shaw is not traveling alone. Make sure his partner is included in the trip as part of the package! We don't need any loose ends." Stan ended the message with a final admonition. "Guys, this case is beyond frustrating. It's time to close this chapter ... unless somehow this is just the tip of the iceberg!"

 **CHAPTER 9**

Tommy and Danny were exhausted but pumped up. Their flight would arrive in Miami well ahead of the arrival of Mark and his unknown companion.

"Look, I don't know how you feel, but someone seems to be a step ahead of us. First, Juan's death, and now this guy Mark is in the picture. It's obvious that he's been in Saudi Arabia for over a year. Suddenly he decides to leave and head home. C'mon, Danny, gimme a break! This has all the makings of DIA involvement. The Department of Defense has their bloodhounds hard at work protecting this Mark Shaw for some reason. He's obviously a valuable asset safeguarding something important."

Danny nodded. "That means we've got to make the grab as quick as we can. From what we were told, Shaw indicated that he planned to stay in Miami for a few days. There's no way that happens. There are a lot of possibilities." Danny started to point them out to Tommy. "DIA operators could have plans to meet him at the airport. Or he could rent a car or taxi for the drive to a hotel in Miami where someone would be waiting with new instructions. He could spend one night there and fly out the next morning – and I bet it would be to Washington, DC and not Kentucky."

"You're forgetting that the DIA has several facilities surrounding DC," Tommy responded.

"Damn, you're right. I forgot about that. That hurts us, since we don't know what DIA sector Shaw's operating within. So, let me cut to the chase … what's your plan?" Danny asked.

"I'm assuming the worst and hoping for the best. I'm certain that DIA operatives will be at the airport. Before Shaw even exits past the TSA security checkpoint, you and I, along with a couple of CIA assets, will be there to grab him. If we have to, we'll ignore the person traveling with him. How much pocket change do we have?"

"I'm carrying twenty. What do you have?" Danny asked.

"I've got twelve, I think," Tommy answered.

"Okay, that's $32,000 between us. That should be enough money to help folks turn their heads for a minute. That's all the time we'll need," Tommy explained.

"How does this sound?" he continued. "We flash our credentials at the TSA agents and find out where their first aid facility is situated. We go to it and then start spreading the wealth among the medics," Tommy stated.

"Huh?" Danny asked with a blank stare.

"Danny, they've got drugs that we can use to quiet Mark Shaw. They've also got uniforms and wheelchairs, probably even a gurney. That's all stuff that would help us transport the 'ailing' Mark out of the terminal. Doing it without the DIA even aware of what's happening right in front of their faces would be a big plus for us!"

A huge smile crept across Danny's face.

Both men boarded their flight, traveling as strangers, as they had during their flights to Costa Rica.

It was time to get some rest before the next conflict began.

 **HAPTER 10**

By the time the plane's wheels touched ground in Miami, some aspects of Tommy's original plan were no longer viable. What was still intact, though, was that the airport medics and drugs were going to be part of the plan.

Although prohibited to other passengers on the flight, Tommy used his cell phone in the plane's bathroom to call the Miami CIA office. He directed them to have local agents available at the airport, telling them to bring pre-loaded syringes of the synthetic opioid etorphine and the opioid reversal drug, naloxone. He also advised that they needed to be prepared to help as needed.

Finding the right dosage of etorphine that would subdue but not kill a human being, as opposed to tranquilizing an elephant, wasn't an easy task. It took the agents a little while to find the appropriate level of opioid and the corresponding dosage of neutralizing naloxone – enough to sufficiently subdue two people for a short while. It wasn't in the plan that the twosome would die.

The revised plan was for the agents to be in airline attendant attire while waiting for Mark and his companion at the arrival gate. One would hold a sign that read "Mark" and the other would drive the courtesy cart transporting the two toward the baggage claim area. If the two refused to get into the cart, the agents were directed to immediately inject both with the synthetic opioid. If on the other hand they cooperated, then the injection would be given as the cart proceeded through the airport—by Tommy and Danny. The plan was for the agents, who both would be in EMT uniforms, to jump onto the cart somewhere along the way and inject Mark and his companion. When that was accomplished, the two local agents would leave the cart, with Danny and Tommy driving through the concourse on an apparent medical emergency. Hopefully any ruckus would appear minimal to nearby passengers and airport staff, and not cause any alarm.

Tommy gave his cell phone to Danny, pointing to the plan outlined in print on the screen and hoping for Danny's approval.

Again, the shit-eating grin spread across Danny's face. The plan was in place.

The plane Tommy and Danny were on finally arrived at the gate and they deplaned. At the end of the walkway, the two agent/airline attendants waited with the courtesy cart, one holding a sign with the name Tommy on it. The agent who was driving the cart nodded to the approaching men. A nod back and the verbal direction, "Gate 55," was all that was needed to get the ball rolling. It was a half hour until "go time."

After a short ride, Tommy and Danny were dropped off at the first aid facility. The two agent attendants continued on to the gate where Mark Shaw's Miami-bound flight was due to arrive at any moment.

Tommy introduced himself to the airport paramedics. Holding his Homeland Security badge in the palm of his right hand, he explained what was needed. The EMT in charge, his eyes as wide as saucers after the briefing, extended his hand and glancing down, saw that a large amount of money had just been placed in it. He quickly realized that he was looking at $100 bills and there were more than one.

Tommy pulled the EMT aside.

"I'm going to need one of your ambulances out front, running and waiting for us. You need to tell the EMTs aboard to be patient. Tell them to keep their running lights on and that they'll be making a non-emergency transport of two VIP government officials. Let them know they'll be taken care of in the same manner that you have been. Are we clear?"

The EMT nodded in the affirmative.

Tommy and Danny followed the medic into another room, where they were outfitted with airport EMT uniforms and given official-issue EMT satchels, complete with the full complement of instruments and medicine. Tommy placed two additional etorphine syringes on top of the existing drugs in the bag. They were ready.

Then again, maybe not. Tommy wavered, wondering if they should reverse roles with the local agents but finally determining he had to trust that the assets who were waiting at Gate 55 were competent. However, an outside prayer didn't hurt.

As Mark's plane pulled up to the gate, he and his companion were roused from their sleep by the flight attendant in the first-class cabin. The multiple cocktails they'd downed during the flight had achieved the desired effect. Both were hungover and struggling to regain their faculties. They remained seated and were the last passengers to deplane.

The greeting party was beginning to get anxious and then finally, the targets emerged from the jetway. Mark spied the sign with his name and assumed his government connection had new plans for him. He led his companion, Carole, to the cart, half holding her up as she stumbled twice. They both climbed into the cart without hesitation or question and were off. The second agent immediately texted Tommy.

"Cargo is on board. However, both items are compromised," with an emoji of a bottle of beer attached to the end of the message.

"Damn," Tommy mumbled, catching Danny's attention. Tommy made a drinking motion and a face mimicking someone who was inebriated. Depending on how intoxicated the two were, there could be enhanced effects from the drugs about to be injected. The chances of Mark and his companion going into respiratory distress from the dose they would receive had increased. Grabbing both syringes, Tommy emptied at least half the contents from each cylinder. The drunken state of the two also meant they'd have to administer the naloxone sooner. That could be a problem during the transport phase of the plan.

Screw it, Tommy thought. We'll just have to deal with it. He looked down the concourse and saw the courtesy vehicle approaching.

Tommy started running toward the right side of the cart with the medical satchel in hand. Taking his cue, Danny began sprinting to the left side of the oncoming cart. In an instant both men were aboard and ready to act. Tommy shouted "Syringes," and like a torch relay race, the hand-off was flawless. There was enough pause given for Tommy to grab one syringe and Danny another, each injecting the person in front of them. Within a split second, the tranquilizer was coursing through the bloodstream of the hostages as their heads fell limp.

Not one person in the concourse seemed to notice the turmoil occurring around them.

In less than three minutes from the time they'd kidnapped their prey, Tommy and Danny had made their way past the TSA security checkpoint and were outside at the ambulance. Before loading Mark and Carole into the medical unit, Tommy administered the naloxone. Once inside the van, restraints were placed on the two captives. Duct tape was placed over their lips and a hood covered each of their heads. Neither would ever know their whereabouts. Tommy shook hands with the EMTs and another $10,000 in taxpayer dollars exchanged hands.

The ambulance was on its way to an address that the driver had been given earlier. Twenty minutes later, it pulled into the parking lot of a large shopping center. Running lights and sirens were now off as the EMT driver pulled the van to the rear of the building housing the stores. Tommy and Danny unloaded their hostages and placed them on the floor in the back of a windowless mid-sized delivery truck. Tommy again thanked the EMTs, handing them a note accompanied by another wad of taxpayer dollars.

The note read: "Give us a 30-minute start before you call your dispatcher."

Meanwhile in the baggage claim area at MIA International, four unclaimed bags were all that remained linking Mark and his companion to the flight that had recently arrived from Saudi Arabia. Two men were watching the bags circle on carousel number 2. One of the men was engaged in an extended conversation on his phone. When the conversation ended, the man nodded to his partner, and each grabbed two bags from the carousel before heading to the exit.

Tommy and Danny had been on the road driving the delivery truck for twenty minutes. Danny was fast asleep, and Tommy was downing a second energy drink.

"Shit!" Tommy shouted out.

Crossing three busy lanes of expressway, he exited I-95, searching for a quiet and out-of-the-way place to stop. Danny, now fully awake with his head looking in every direction and his .38 automatic half out of its holster, blurted out, "What the hell is going on?"

"I forgot to bag both of them," Tommy answered.

"Shit, that's my fault. I had them out and totally forgot!" Danny yelled back in frustration.

Tommy found an old gas station that looked like it had been shut down for years. There were no gas pumps, and grass and weeds were growing wild any place there was a crack in the concrete. He pulled in behind the building and turned off the engine.

"They're going to put up a fight, so we'll do the woman first, and then we'll bag Mark," Tommy said. The men climbed into the back of the truck, and as expected, both hostages began squirming around. Danny held Carole's legs at the knees while Tommy slipped the fabric bag over her lower torso. Then Danny sat her up and pulled her arms backwards, stretching every chest muscle taut. Her breasts were thrust forward and Danny couldn't help but be impressed. "Knock it off, you sick puppy," Tommy demanded. Attaching the flap over the top of her head completed the job. She was hermetically sealed.

Tommy turned his attention to Mark. Not in any mood to battle, Tommy put Mark in a sleeper hold and in a few seconds Mark's body was pliant. It took only a couple of minutes to wrap Mark's body.

There was a reason for the bagging. The copper fiber cocoons were made of a material similar to the fabric in newer wallets and purses. Electronic signals couldn't penetrate or escape the cocoon that now encased each hostage. If either of them was GPS-RFID chipped, the signals were now a moot point. Once they arrived at their final destination, Tommy would determine if either of them was broadcasting their location.

They had been.

Now only five minutes behind the delivery truck and continuing to close in fast, one of the DIA operative's eyes suddenly widened, and he screamed, "They're gone!"

The driver screamed back, "What!"

"I'm no longer getting a signal! Dammit, pull off at the next exit," he demanded.

As the driver edged the black Taurus off the I-95 exit ramp, Tommy was driving his truck onto the entrance ramp, in direct sight of the DIA agents in the Taurus. Neither party would ever know how close they had come to a confrontation.

The only things the DIA possessed from their debacle were future garage sale items and egg on their faces.

In just two days, the interrogations would begin. In the meantime, Tommy remained convinced that there was one more guest who needed to join the party.

CHAPTER 11

After driving the last few hundred miles, Danny finally pulled into the driveway of the safe house. Both men were totally exhausted. The detention room occupied by Geraldo days earlier was now vacant and waiting for their new guests. Geraldo had been moved for safekeeping to a place farther south, just outside of Knoxville, Tennessee.

Mark was now conscious and trying to figure out the structure of the fabric wrap. Rapidly rubbing his shackled hands against his shirt, he gingerly touched them to the cocoon. The static charge from the contact traveled throughout his wrap enclosure and he felt the electric shock on his forehead almost instantly. He'd correctly assumed he was encased in copper.

So much for tracking me through the chip in my wrist. It didn't make a difference either that it's hidden by a tattoo and covered by my watch, he thought to himself. No one can find me with this wrap on anyhow. Well, at least they didn't kill us. That means we're going to be questioned by someone. Who it is will determine their interrogation methods. It could be any of several American intelligence agencies, Mark mused.

"You ready to tuck them into their quarters?" Tommy asked as he walked from the vehicle.

"If you insist," Danny answered. Walking into their current home away from home, Tommy quickly came back out pushing a wheelchair. With help from Danny, they rolled their female hostage to the threshold of the truck's back door, sat her up, and managed to get her into the wheelchair.

"Okay, young lady, we're home. Please don't start squirming, because I'm not going to catch you if you fall. Do you understand?" She nodded yes. Tommy wheeled Carole into the house and took her to an unlit room. It was more like a jail cell than a room, containing a stainless-steel toilet and a twin bed with a one-inch-thick foam pad mattress. The bed was chained to the wall.

"This room has metal-lined walls, floor, and ceiling so if you're GPS-chipped, you can forget about anyone locating you and coming to your rescue." Loosening the Velcro that kept her contained within the bag, Tommy removed the metal bag and loosened the hand restraints. The hostage was told to remove her clothing and trade them for a prison-style pajama top and bottom, and a pair of non-slip hospital-type socks.

"Do I get a blanket and pillow?" she asked. Tommy turned and began laughing.

"Welcome to hell," he answered.

He closed the door and engaged the electronic locking mechanism.

They repeated the same process on Mark, with warnings to not expect any rescue. Before undoing his metal fiber cloth wrap, though, Tommy forcibly pushed Mark down onto the thin foam mattress.

"My guess is that you're working with the DIA, doing some kind of covert shit. Well, you're going to have to settle in for a long stay! We are going to get the information we want." Tommy removed the copper bag from Mark, graciously allowing him to change out of his civilian outfit and into prison garb.

Watching the door shut and hearing the electric tumblers grind to a locked position, Mark mumbled to himself, "CIA, it has to be."

Finally, both sides knew where they stood.

"Danny, I'm going outside to give Stan a call. Then I'm going to call Rob Becker. I'll be back in a few. Take care of our guests," he said with a laugh.

∩ ∩ ∩

"Any problems with travel?" Stan asked. Tommy answered in the negative.

"What's your next move, Tommy?"

"I've got one more hostage to round up. Donnie, the trainer of Towers Above, has been working with Mark Shaw. I can sense it. Rob Becker filled me in about Shaw. I can't believe what a disaster Costa Rica was. We were always one step behind, and I've got to believe that Donnie was communicating with Shaw. After I'm done gathering our triple threat threesome, I'll start the Q&A with Donnie. When we break him down, the woman will be next, and Shaw will be the finale."

"Did you check them for chipping?"

"Jesus, Stan, we just drove over a thousand miles and we're tired!"

"Do it, Tommy! End this call and go do it. There's a ton of chatter in DC that we didn't have a few days ago. Someone's talking and looking for your contraband. Text me when you finish! That's an order!"

"Damn it, all I want is a little sleep," Tommy grumbled to himself.

Tommy walked back inside, gesturing for Danny to follow

him. "Stan wants us to check them for chips. Now." They went to Carole's room and unlocked the door. Both men entered and Tommy, while scratching his head in an attempt to appear confused, said, "You know, my boss wants me to find out if you're GPS-chipped. Now we've got this antique scan machine here, but the last person we used it on got too much radiation and he ended up dying on us! Actually, it was a pretty disgusting sight. I'll pat you down first instead."

"You racist, xenophobic misogynist," she screamed.

"Damn progressives, constantly wanting a redo of the 2016 election," Tommy mumbled under his breath.

"Okay, Danny, let's put her on the scanner table. We'll find out where the chips are."

As Danny strong-armed their hostage to prevent her from fighting, she stopped arguing and stammered, "Stop. I'll show you where they are." She pointed to where both chips had been inserted under the skin.

Pressing on the webbing of the skin between the base of her right-hand index and middle fingers, Danny easily located the first chip. The second one was in the lower crease behind her left ear, also easy to find. That job done, Danny escorted her back to the cell. He then pulled Mark from his enclosure.

This time, Tommy varied the approach, leading Mark to the radiology room and strapping him onto the scan table.

"Do you remember how many kVps we gave the last guy?" Tommy asked.

Danny responded, "You mean the guy who got that radiation sickness?"

"Yeah, that guy," Tommy replied. "I don't want to give Mark too much radiation. Jesus, what a miserable way to die. Oh well, let's make it 500 kVps and see how the scan turns out! We can always repeat it a second or third time if need be, until we find the chips."

Mark's eyes grew wide. He knew about the effects of radiation and quickly spoke up. "Wait, I only have one and it's under my tattoo! Here, look, you can feel it!"

Tommy removed Mark's watch and palpated the skin. He immediately felt the encased chip rolling around. "Nice UK tattoo! Wildcat fan, huh?" Tommy said laughing.

Danny took Mark back to his room while Tommy went outside to text Stan about the chips the two prisoners had. A reply came in just thirty seconds.

"Get them removed tomorrow. Have the veterinarian that we always use do it and give him a little extra cash this time."

Tommy texted Stan an acknowledgement.

∩ ∩ ∩

It was nearly 11 p.m. and I was watching the local evening news when Tommy called.

"Rob, please don't hang up. This is Tommy."

"Damn Tommy, another late-night phone call. So how was your trip, and what about Juan?"

"That's why I'm calling. Juan was murdered."

"What! How?" I asked.

"It was a professional hit, and that's all I can tell you, Rob. Donnie is also involved in all of this. I know you want to question my judgment, but you're going to have to trust me. This is what I do for a living. It's my profession. You're a dentist and you can diagnose a problem with just a few key words from a patient. I can do the same in my line of work."

Tommy paused a few seconds before sharing his suspicions and intent with me. "The bottom line, Donnie needs to be interrogated. What's Donnie's routine in the morning? How early does he start his chores and when does the farm's guard detail do its shift change?"

"Hell, I'm not sure, but I think it's just before daylight. Why?"

"Well, you might want to be there to take his place in the morning. Someone is going to have to get the farm up and running, because Donnie is going to be indisposed. I need to begin the interrogations at our safe house and depending on how much or how little he cooperates, he might be away for a while."

There was a long pause while I poised myself for one last request.

"Tommy, I need to know, and I don't want just your word. I need to see proof. Is there a way you can videotape his confession? I don't want to see how you or any others conduct the interrogation. I just want the confession so I can have closure on my end. These are two guys who I considered like brothers to me. I trusted both of them. For them to turn--" I was too shaken to finish my thoughts.

"Rob, I totally understand your feelings. I promise you, I'll record the moment. You'll get closure. One last favor; could you give me the code to the farm's security gate? The last time we were there it was a cluster, if you get my drift."

I gave Tommy the code. He thanked me and hung up.

Sitting down with my head in my hands, I began moaning in agony. "He's doing it again. It's like a black hole. Tommy is slowly sucking me in and there's nothing I can do to stop it. Please Lord, make him stop ... please, I'm begging!"

# HAPTER 12

It was nearly midnight when Frank and Jackson pulled into the driveway of the safe house. They were greeted by Tommy, who quickly briefed the newcomers on the hostages they'd be babysitting. He also provided them with a list of tasks to handle during their absence.

"A veterinarian, who will identify himself as Alan, will come by in the morning. Confirm his identity by saying, 'We have no animals here.' He should respond to that with, 'Well, what about the animals from Miami?' If he gives that answer, then let him in," Tommy said.

Tommy explained that Alan was there to do surgery and that Jackson, who had some EMS training, would need to assist the doctor. "We believe both hostages have GPS/RFID chips implanted in them and Alan is going to remove all of them. Jackson, there's no fancy medical equipment here, just the basics, but it will get the job done safely. Oh, there's an envelope on the desk in the office. Give it to Alan. Do you have any questions?" Neither man did.

Tommy and Danny left at 12:30 a.m., heading for Donnie's farm some 100 miles away.

They arrived at the farm at 2:00 in the morning. Tommy entered the code he'd been given on the keypad, and the gates swung open. Turning the headlights off and proceeding slowly down the drive, Tommy stopped the car about 500 yards short of the farmhouse. The two men exited and slowly crept toward the back of the house that overlooked the stables. Reaching their destination, both assumed a position at the base of the stairs leading from the porch. They settled in to wait for the first signs of daylight and the dawn of a new and hopefully productive day.

The porch lights turned on at 5:30 a.m. As the son of a farmer, Danny assumed the back porch door would open at any moment. After all, the animals were a priority and needed to be fed first thing every morning.

He had assumed correctly.

The door opened and Donnie walked across the planks of the porch, starting down the steps. When he heard Donnie reach the last step, Danny let out a moan. As Donnie turned toward the sound, Tommy sprang to action and was on top of Donnie in less than three seconds. The sounds and smell of electricity on flesh pierced the morning air. When the wire probes hit his neck, Donnie fell to the ground, flopping back and forth like a fish just landed. Donnie had been Tasered.

Tommy couldn't help but laugh. He found it funny any time he had to use a Taser, just watching the involuntary spasmodic responses caused from the electricity. "You know you're a sick SOB, don't you?" Danny asked Tommy, who was still laughing.

Working in tandem, Danny ripped open the baggie with a number of 6x6-inch gauze pads soaked with chloroform. He held the bulky pads firmly on Donnie's mouth and nose until he felt Donnie go limp. Donnie was also restrained and cocoon-wrapped as Mark and Carole had been. Danny and Tommy took turns heaving the limp body over their shoulders and carrying him the remaining 500 yards before putting him in the van for the ride home.

"Flip you for dibs on the passenger seat," Tommy, who was still exhausted from events of the last two days, said.

"Two outta three?" Danny replied.

Tommy lost. In reality, both men lost because Tommy kept nodding off and driving over the rumble cuts on the shoulder that are designed to alert a straying driver. Danny finally gave up after the third incident, shouting for Tommy to pull over so he could drive.

"Damn asshole," Danny grumbled, settling in behind the wheel and noting that his partner was already asleep.

By 10:00 a.m., both men were back at home and ready for bed to get that much-needed sleep. First, though, there was business to take care of. They prepared Donnie as they did their other two "guests," and checked on Mark and Carole. All was as it should be, and what the men needed now was a solid five hours of rest.

In the meantime, the police had been called about the now-missing Donnie and were halfway through their interrogation of Valerie, his wife. I was finishing up Donnie's chores. I called Marty to tell her what had happened and that I'd be bunking at Donnie's house. I fully anticipated another half hour of questions from Marty, while praying that Tommy would finish what he needed to do with Donnie in short order.

That never happened, as Marty didn't answer the phone.

On the plus side, it had been a long time since Towers Above and I had quality time together.

Throughout the morning, I was able to lead visitors interested in the thoroughbreds and possible breeding around the stables and let them photograph TA. I played sales clerk and cashier when they purchased their Towers Above souvenirs and other memorabilia. After, I turned our horse out to pasture, watching and laughing as he rolled around in the sand pit like a kid. It felt good watching him play. At the end of the day, I gave him a bath and a good grooming in preparation for the next day's breeding sessions. There were appointments scheduled with owners who had no concerns about the month that their thoroughbreds would be foaled. The two mares were scheduled for 10:00 and 11:00 breeding sessions the next morning.

I went inside to say goodbye to Valerie, and to try and comfort her. "I've got to get home, Val. Marty's not answering the phone and I didn't get a chance to tell her I was coming here."

"Oh, I called her first thing this morning, Rob! It was almost like she knew Donnie had disappeared. For what it's worth, she said to me, "That's the last straw" and then hung up.

Leaving the farm to go find my wife, I thought, How did she know? Was she eavesdropping on my conversation with Tommy? Great, just great! The sound of that black hole sucking me in just gets louder and louder by the minute. I screamed into the night air.

Danny looked through the peep hole before unlocking the cell door – this woman had a temper. He slid a food tray across the floor for her; she thanked him with a barrage of expletives. Mark and Donnie were his next stops, before sitting down with Tommy to strategize.

Each man had earlier prepared a list of interrogation questions and methods – with a supporting rationale for the why and how. Danny spoke first.

"I think we should interrogate Mark first. Based on his entanglements in the Middle East, I'm sure he's had Survival-Evasion-Resistance-Escape (SERE) military training. Donnie should be next because of the long relationship he and Mark have. We need to figure out what their working relationship is, though, especially since Mark was initially supposed to be a full partner in the Four Horsemen's Farm business plan. The woman goes last. Other than Mark being her boy-toy, I don't know what her relationship with either man is. She's a throw-away. So what's your plan?"

Danny waited as Tommy gathered his thoughts.

Tommy's thoughts were definitely causing him internal conflict. *I shouldn't have done it this way. I should've just said, "This is how we're going to conduct the interrogations and been done with it." No matter what I say, it's going to piss Danny off. How did we get to this place where someone has to be King of the Hill?*

This seems to be the tone of our country since the 2016 election and I'm tired of it!

Tommy shuddered. Danny was as close to a brother as anyone he'd known in his life. A dark thought had just escaped from the furthest depths of his brain, breaking through into his conscious world.

Tommy had no clue just how spot-on those fleeting aberrant thoughts were to what would come next. He had no idea how they would play into the interrogation and the Q&A that would start momentarily.

"Tell you what, Danny; we're not that far apart in our ideas, but I've got a strong hunch that Donnie should go first. I think he's going to be easier to break – and that would make interrogating Mark that much easier." Danny nodded approval, not even questioning Tommy's "King of the Hill" directive.

∩ ∩ ∩

The first thing Donnie saw was a surfboard-type apparatus – and it definitely wasn't for riding the waves. It was built with a headrest and restraint straps.

Then Donnie saw the garden hose. He began to struggle fiercely against the handcuffs and ankle bindings he was constrained by.

"Ahh … I see you're familiar with waterboarding. That's good! I won't have to give you pre-boarding instructions," Tommy said. As he secured Donnie to the board, head down and lowered, Tommy could tell that Donnie's heart was pounding rapidly, as if it was going to burst from his chest. Danny, with a hand covering his mouth to conceal his laughter, realized Tommy had it right. Damn, Tommy read this guy like a book. I bet it only takes one flushing of his sinuses and throat before he starts talking, Danny thought.

Donnie coughed and sputtered water for thirty seconds after the first douse from the garden hose before blurting out, "Sit me up! Now! What do you want to know?"

"You mess with me and I swear you'll get another thirty minutes of water!" Tommy promised the captive.

"Okay, okay, I understand!"

"Where did Juan get the money for the sports car and Ferrari?"

"It was his gambling winnings. He'd been betting on Towers Above from the get-go."

"Were you his cash cow?" Tommy asked.

"Somewhat," Donnie responded.

"Don't give me that bullshit answer," Tommy yelled.

"Not in the beginning! Mark was the seed moneyman – for both of us!"

"And what did Mark get in exchange for the money?" Tommy asked.

"He got access to Towers Above to give him some kind of medicine. Mark was giving TA shots of something, starting the day of his foaling and every month after. He did it for six months."

"Did Rob Becker or the other partner, Mike, know about these shots?" Tommy asked.

"No, the only people who knew were the three of us! I swear!"

"So, when Rob started asking questions about Juan, what did you do?"

"I texted Mark and told him."

"Who does Mark work for?" There was total silence. "Did you not hear me?" Tommy repeated the question a second time, in a tone that left no doubt of the consequences should Donnie not respond.

Tommy signaled Danny, who shut down the recording camera behind the two-way mirror.

"Look, whoever he works for, I wouldn't mess with them. I don't know which government agency Mark is with. He's a scientific genetics guy and the Feds are probably using him for his skill in that particular area. When we formed our corporation, we all knew he had government connections. I'm telling you – that's all I know! Can I please go back to my farm? I'm begging you … please!"

Tommy was hyped up and ready to play. The intelligence game was on! He hated whiney, wimpy individuals, and Donnie was being a wimp. Donnie wasn't going anywhere. He would be staying put.

"Put this wimp back in his cell. We're not done with him yet. Bring out our next prisoner and let's get on with it," Tommy directed Danny.

∩ ∩ ∩

It was Mark's turn. Danny strapped him into the apparatus and Tommy sat, positioning himself so he and Mark were eye-to-eye. "I know you've gone through Survival-Evasion-Resistance-Escape training. You should know I could give a shit about that SERE training. Thanks to Donnie, we know you've been messing genetically with Towers Above, and that you were doing the same crap with Nidalas in Saudi Arabia. I also know that nobody works freelance with the Saudis without our country's knowledge.

"That means you're working with one of our government agencies – and that makes knowing the name of the agency and the project you're working on my priorities. That's really all I need to know. You answer those two questions and we won't have to go through any of this interrogation stuff. If you don't give me that information, well, we'll start with water boarding and sleep deprivation, and then I get to improvise. I'm sure you're assuming that I won't let you die. You would be partly right!

"If you die, it won't be on purpose. It's pretty basic here when it comes to medical care. We don't have the usual equipment to monitor your vitals. I don't even have an AED in case your heart stops. We rednecks aren't that high on the pecking list when it comes to those types of supplies."

Tommy was watching Mark's eyes for any reaction. The idea of dying accidentally from the enhanced interrogation caused Mark's eyes to widen.

Tommy looked directly at Mark as he spoke. "Well, that's it for now. I'm sorry, but no lunch or dinner today. Oh, one more thing, we're out of toilet paper. I'll try to go shopping tomorrow. So settle in and get ready for what's to come. We've got some heavy metal music to pipe into your room as you rest – and we'll start the boarding tomorrow. Any questions?"

There were none.

Tommy continued to stare at Mark, whose facial muscles said it all. The clenching and release of the lower jaw against the upper jaw was an easy tell. He could see that the gears were turning in Mark's mind.

If only I could read your thoughts, Mark Shaw, if only .... Tommy said to himself.

"I can beat these guys. They're not going to let me die. Fuck them!" Mark said under his breath.

# CHAPTER 14

After sleeping on it, Tommy decided they would interrogate their female guest next, and give Mark another day to think about what was to come.

"Danny, you get to question the woman," Tommy said.

Tommy was tired. The theatrics and mental gymnastics of the interrogation had worn him down. He thought he had Mark's attention, then realized he'd guessed wrong. Mark wasn't going to roll over just yet.

Danny was bothered and felt like he was playing second fiddle. He was proud of his interrogation skills and training. He'd majored in psychology – he even held a bachelor's and master's degree in the science. Now it seemed Tommy was tossing him a bone by allowing him to question the woman.

Danny led Carole into the room. She looked at the modified surfboard and said, "You kinky SOB! You're going to rape me on that board! You fascist, racist, redneck fuck!"

Danny glanced at Tommy, who had turned away quickly to cover his smile, but was now nearly doubled over with laughter. Danny was able to keep his laughter at bay since by now, he was used to her diatribe. It was the next words out of her mouth that made Danny snap!

"You're nothing but a Nazi."

Danny's face turned beet red. This woman knew nothing of his heritage. From the time he was a young boy, Danny's father had told him about the Holocaust and his family's Jewish heritage. Danny's great-great grandparents had survived the Holocaust. While they had passed away long before his birth, Danny felt he knew them from the stories his father told and the family pictures – pictures that clearly showed the tattooed identification numbers on their forearms from the concentration camp.

"So you think I'm the scourge of humanity? That I'm the most evil of all human beings? Well, I guess I better live up to that reputation!" Danny promised Carole.

He strapped her to the board … extra tight! As he cinched the strap tighter across her head, the veins on her forehead began to protrude. He dropped the board down, shoving a cloth into her mouth. Rather than thirty seconds of water pouring over her face, he gave her a full minute.

She sputtered, coughed, and retched for over a minute after the board was finally raised. Danny easily saw the fear in her face and could tell she wanted to talk, but he was in no mood to have a discussion. He dropped the board down a second time, repeating the torture. When he finally brought her back up for air, she retched for over two minutes, bringing up the remains of breakfast.

He lowered the board again, about to begin the third round, when Tommy yelled, "Hold on, stop!"

"So I'm a Nazi, huh? Tommy, dammit, don't you dare interfere!" Danny yelled back, looking straight at Tommy.

He dropped her one last time, knowing that Tommy wouldn't allow a fourth event in such short order. He also knew Tommy was aware of his family's history and was giving him a pass. After raising her up for the last time, Danny walked away from the board.

Tommy walked over and waited for her to compose herself. It was time to play "good cop" with Carole.

"Lady, I suggest that you not call him a Nazi ever again. Now I've got some questions I need answers to. The minute you don't answer or I think your answer is bogus, I'm turning you back over to him – and we both know he's still not calmed down. Do you understand? Blink if you agree."

She blinked more than once!

"What's your name, where are you from, and how old are you?"

"My name is Carole. I live in Washington, DC and I'm twenty-eight."

"Who do you work for? Is it Mark?"

"I work for the DIA in Washington."

Bingo, Tommy thought and shot a glance at Danny.

"Which project are you working on?"

Carole hesitated thirty seconds too long. Tommy gave Danny a nod. As Danny got up and started walking toward her, she shouted out, "No! Please no! I'll answer!"

"Go ahead, I'm waiting," Danny said.

But she didn't give up the information, and the board went down for the fourth time. Danny gave her another session to remember him by, with a boarding that lasted at least two minutes. This time, it took her fifteen minutes to recover. Finally, in between rough bouts of coughing and vomiting, she said, "Project Withers."

Tommy kicked back in his chair, realizing that he had most of the answers he needed for the moment. Obviously, Mark was working on the same project, and both the US and Saudi governments were involved. All that remained to find out now were the details of Project Withers.

I'll start on Mark tomorrow to find out more, but I need to share this with Stan now, Tommy thought. Signaling to Danny that he was heading outside, Tommy pulled out his cellphone and called Stan.

"Stan, do you know anything about Project Withers?"

There was a long silence before Stan answered, "Yes and no. When all the intelligence agency directors met with our former president that April, he asked about the project. Hell, now that I think about it, he even said something about a guy named Mark."

Stan let that sink in before continuing.

"At that point, many of us were summarily dismissed from the meeting. Only the Pentagon brass was allowed to stay. Obviously, they're running an operation we're not supposed to know about. I want you and Danny to keep digging. I'll work on it from my end. Thanks, Tommy; it's all starting to come together."

Tommy went back inside, taking a seat on a stool next to Carole, who was still strapped to the board.

"I know a little about the term 'withers.' It's a part of a horse's anatomy. So this project has something to do with horses, right?"

Again Carole paused, but only briefly. She didn't want Danny unleashed on her again. "Yes, you're correct."

"So … what the hell is your job with the DIA and what's your connection with Mark? You obviously haven't had SERE training. Frankly, and understand I mean this as a compliment, you're just too damn beautiful and naive to work in intelligence."

Up to that point, Carole had pretty much avoided eye contact with both Danny and Tommy. Only then did she turn directly toward Tommy and stare for a good thirty seconds. She stared like the devil, burning a hole through both of Tommy's retinas.

"It was my job to kill Mark before he gave up any information or details about Project Withers. I would have offed him, except you two assholes got in my way."

It was enough of a bizarre statement that Tommy believed her. "Well, I'll be damned," he muttered. "She's an assassin." He turned and walked over to Danny.

"Give Jackson a call. We need him and Frank here first thing in the morning. I've got to visit Rob Becker, and we need Frank here to watch over Donnie and Mark. Oh ... and tell Jackson that he'll be transporting the woman to Virginia. She's the viper of this group!"

"By the way, Danny, great effort today. It was worthy of an Academy Award!"

Danny forced a smile in obvious acceptance of the compliment, but in his mind, said instead, I wasn't acting.

 **HAPTER 15**

I was tired from the long day at the farm, and just five minutes from home when my cell phone rang, indicating an unknown caller. I was pretty sure who the caller was. I couldn't help myself and answered.

"Hello," I said.

"Rob, this is Tommy. You got a minute to talk?"

"Yeah, Tommy, I'm almost back home after spending hours at the farm. And yes, Donnie was gone, something I'm sure you know nothing about! So please give me some good news," I said while pulling into the garage.

"Well I was wondering if I could stop by in the morning. I've got video of Donnie to show you and--"

Tommy didn't get to finish his sentence as I cut him off.

"Oh no! God please no! Tommy, she's gone! Marty is gone! She left a note on the kitchen counter. She left me!"

Tommy could hear the distress in my voice and knew he was the cause of this pain. Silently, Tommy waited for me to return to the line.

"Ah Jesus, Tommy she's gone. Marty left me. She went to her sister's place out in Portland, Oregon," I said, not realizing I was repeating myself. "She must have overheard our conversation. Oh God, Tommy, what am I going to …."

"Rob, did you say Portland? Goddamn it!" I instantly heard the fear in Tommy's voice. After the events of April, I'd learned to easily interpret his emotions. "What is it? Why is Portland a problem?"

"I'm on my way to your place," Tommy replied.

"Dammit, Tommy, don't you hang up on me! I swear I'll--"

"No you won't, Rob. Go make a pot of coffee. I'll be there as quick as I can." I heard the click. Tommy had hung up.

Frustrated because I knew there was "a rest of the story" scenario taking hold in Tommy's brain, but it gave me pause to summon up the nerve to make the call to Portland. My sister-in-law, Lauren, answered. "It's about time you called! What do you want?"

I had no quarrel with Lauren ... until now.

"Lauren, you know what I want. Let me talk to my wife, please."

"She doesn't want to talk with you!"

"Lauren, you really don't want to piss me off. Do you want to test me, knowing the connections I have, connections that I'm sure Marty has shared with you?" For a short while, there was just silence and background noise. Then I heard Marty's voice.

"Rob, I really don't want to argue. Until you end this relationship with Tommy, I'm not coming home. I still love you – but you have to make a choice!" Marty said. She was the second person to hang up on me in just ten minutes.

I tried calling back, but each time I dialed, all I got was a busy signal. I even called the operator to check on the connection and was told there was a glitch in phone service.

I headed to the pantry to grab the bottle of Woodford Reserve bourbon. I poured myself a stiff one, straight up. Turning on Fox News, I waited for my albatross to arrive. Two additional bourbons later, Tommy walked through the open door.

∩ ∩ ∩

I was waiting for Tommy as he came into the kitchen. I was ready to take out my frustration on him, but my right hook whizzed by his jaw. Tommy knew my state of mind and was prepared for me. Before I realized it, I was on the floor with my arm tucked behind my back. It felt like my arm was going to pop out of its socket as he forced my forearm up toward the back of my head.

"Rob, I totally understand. Someday you can have a free shot at me. Lord knows I deserve it," Tommy said, loosening his grip on me. I began to sob but slowly pulled myself together. I turned back to face Tommy, who had found the Woodford and was pouring himself a strong one.

"Why did you panic when I mentioned Portland?" I asked, wanting an explanation but not expecting a long discourse on socialism and anarchy.

"Do you remember the post-election events in 2016? I'm talking about protests and riots after the favorite candidate was declared the loser. Well, for the socialist-anarchist progressives, Portland is one of their prime bases of activity. I look at Portland as their main hub on the West Coast. They have many groups, often referred to as Antifa, that have a well-established presence at protests throughout the city. The American public has no idea what's going on, but our counter-intelligence agencies do!"

Tommy stopped to take a long swig of his bourbon.

"There have been over a dozen kidnappings since November 2016. All of the hostages were millionaires and multi-millionaires, and a ransom was demanded for their return. Each time, the hostage's family paid the ransom. No one ever called the FBI to report the kidnapping, the family simply pays. I'm sure you're wondering how we would know about all of this."

"Well, the NSA Stingray systems that are positioned strategically around the city are able to intercept conversations between the kidnappers and the hostage's families. We stake out their supposed drop sites, but each time the exchange of money never happens where we expect it to. Somehow, though, information is still exchanged and the ransom still ends up in the hands of the bad guys. On occasion, we have been able to snatch some of the individuals involved. They're detained but held only for a short period of time because no one talks, which means no charges are filed against them. The individuals involved simply lawyer up and eventually just walk away. It's believed that over 200 million dollars have been paid to the kidnappers so far."

Pausing for me to take it all in, Tommy refilled his glass before continuing with a different, but no less frightening scenario.

"I'm sure you're also aware that gun sales across the country skyrocketed during the last administration's two terms. The states along the Pacific Coast report their gun sales have quadrupled in comparison to the rest of the United States. Yet, these are states supposedly populated with anti-gun citizens. The addresses of those purchasing the weapons check out at the time of sale, but when we investigate later and talk to the people who live at those given addresses, they swear they never purchased any guns. Finally, the most alarming event not publicly reported was the takeover and large-scale theft at a munitions factory."

"Are you serious?" I said.

"Damn serious," Tommy replied with a worried look on his face.

"The Department of Defense is quite certain that a radical

faction of American citizens is preparing for a civil war against their fellow citizens. The bottom line is that our country's citizens appear to be very close to witnessing the start of a revolution," Tommy stated, symbolically holding up the thumb and index finger of his right hand, a quarter inch apart.

Taking an even longer swill of his bourbon, Tommy stood directly in front of me.

"So Dr. Rob Becker, you asked why I reacted as I did at the mention of Portland. Your very wealthy wife is now in a region of the country where active extremists have unofficially declared war on their fellow citizens. Their intelligence apparatus is quite sophisticated, and in the near future they could use it to easily identify your wife, Marty, as a valuable target. When that happens, you'll get a telephone call demanding a truly significant dollar amount. Her safe release will be contingent on you paying the high ransom they demand! When and if you cooperate, she's a free woman – and you will be less wealthy.

"The way I see it, Rob, you have two choices. You can wait for the kidnapping to happen or get your ass on a plane to Portland and protect her. Get your 9mm automatic and ammo, and get going, Marshal Dillon."

I hated when Tommy called me that name.

On the plus side, I'll be out of the picture and Marty will be ecstatic."

∩ ∩ ∩

"Now I need a few more minutes of your attention – and I have something you wanted to see. This is the video of Donnie's confession. You wanted proof about your good friend. Well, you've got it!"

Tommy played the video from the day before. He told me later that my skin went ashen. I was angry, humiliated, and embarrassed, even thinking about using my automatic on Donnie.

"Tommy, I swear, it was only supposed to be about the historical genetic ancestry of the 'X' factor and never about synthetic-engineering of Towers Above's DNA. Never. I'm calling the Jockey Club in the morning to fill them in. The Triple Crown races will surely be forfeited, as will the Challenge Cup title. For that matter, so will any other races at which TA finished in the money. There'll be huge fines and my dream will have ended not just in failure, but in disgrace!"

"Dammit Rob, shut up already! No more negative thoughts," Tommy shouted at me. "First off, you're forgetting that this is now an international issue. Mark was obviously working with the Saudi horsemen, and they're going to use this science going forward in their breeding operations. If you want to shut down the entire worldwide thoroughbred industry, be my guest.

"Second, we still don't know what Project Withers is, and until I get a chance to break Mark and find out what the DIA is working on, not one word of this becomes public! I suggest that you make your plane reservation. Then call Val at the farm, and tell her you're not going to be around for a while.

"Go pack your bag for the trip to Portland and get some sleep. I'll head back in the morning to let Donnie free, but not before I make sure he never breathes a single word about the interrogation and his time at the safe house to anyone. I know we're both exhausted and need some sleep. If you don't mind, I'll sleep on your couch, just give me a pillow. No more talk now. Good night!"

Tommy was asleep in no time.

I wasn't.

 **HAPTER 16**

It was 6:00 when I woke up the next morning. I quickly realized that Tommy hadn't been kidding about just taking a nap. From the looks of things, he maybe slept a couple of hours. Papers were scattered everywhere on the kitchen countertops and table – and I knew he was in the midst of some detailed planning.

"Morning, Rob. What time is your flight?"

"Got to get going right now. I drive to Lexington, fly to Atlanta, and then from there go directly to Portland."

"You got your Conceal and Carry license?"

"Yep, it's packed," I replied.

"Rob, that stuff we talked about last night, it's for your information only. You can share it with Marty, but no one else. Not even a sniff of this to anyone else. Do you understand?" Tommy asked, with a dead-serious look in his eyes.

"I understand, Tommy. Thanks for sharing that intel with me. I know Marty doesn't understand the bond we have – and she doesn't get why I can't just walk away from you. Even though there are times when you piss me off, you've never lied to me – and you always have my back! You're like a member of my family. I've got to go – but stay as long as you need. The code for the security alarm is 1946. Would you set it when you leave? Bye!"

I learned later that Tommy had called Danny while I was still sleeping, directing him to blindfold Donnie and drop him at the nearest rental car company. He also told Danny to stress that

Donnie not tell anyone, not even his wife, about the kidnapping and what had taken place at the safe house. If he did, Donnie could be assured that there would be an immediate leak to the media that Towers Above's genetic make-up had been artificially altered, and horse-racing fans would learn that Towers Above was a fraud, "according to rumors!"

Mark was now the lone hostage at the safe house, and he needed to be broken. Tommy didn't have the time – and he especially didn't have the patience – to continue the waterboarding. And he was done wracking his brain, trying to figure out why a US intelligence agency had anything to do with horses.

It was time for Tommy to get back to the house and get answers from Mark. It was time for Plan B, which could be risky. Plan B could bring immediate answers, but if the interrogee was stubborn, it could result in death before Tommy would learn anything more.

ᛜ ᛜ ᛜ

"Welcome home," Danny said. "It appears that our guest doesn't enjoy heavy metal," Danny told Tommy as he walked through the door.

"Too bad – and by the way, there's a change in plans. I don't have the time or energy to board him, Danny. I think it's time to play Tommy Roulette. If Mark's willing to die for Project Withers, then so be it," Tommy told his partner. "Bring him out and cuff him to the chair. I'll set up my target board in the corner there. Can you get it from the closet? I'll be back with my revolver, ammo, and other gear in a few minutes."

Going to the safe, he punched in the code, pulling out his five-shot .38-caliber revolver and two boxes of bullets. He also

grabbed his safety gear. There were two distinct differences between the boxes of bullets. One box contained standard issue
blanks and the other, specially marked live .38 bullets. The other
difference was that the base of the live ammo had been painted
with a luminous paint, visible only to the shooter when wearing
special glasses.

By the time Tommy returned to the interrogation room, Mark
was handcuffed to a chair opposite from where Tommy would sit.

"Hey, Mark … good to see you again! How about that music
we provided? I bet you've been jamming in your cell!"

"Go fuck yourself," Mark replied. Tommy had expected nothing less than that suggestion from their guest.

"Well, since that's physically impossible, I'm not going to try.
I know you're SERE-trained and that you'll waste my time trying
to sell me a bunch of bullshit. Let me be clear with you; we don't
have time to sort out what's fact or fiction," Tommy warned.

You've got that right, asshole, Mark thought.

"So instead of waterboarding, we're going to play Russian
Roulette, Tommy-style! Okay? Here's my .38."

Tommy placed his gun on the table and pulled the box of
blanks from his pocket. He loaded the revolver with one blank
and closed the cylinder. Just to add a little more emphasis, Tommy
opened the gun and twirled the cylinder before closing it again.
Now pointing the gun at Mark's head, he pulled the trigger and
the cylinder advanced. Mark's eyes remained emotionless. The
gun exploded in a cloud of noise and the smell of gunpowder.
Now he had Mark's attention.

"Well, I'll be damned. What luck – that was the blank bullet.
If this was Vegas, you'd be a winner!" Tommy laughed.

"Okay, now I'm going to show you the real stuff." Tommy

reached into his other pocket and pulled out the box of live ammunition, laying some bullets on the table. He loaded a live round and spun the cylinder.

"The target is there to your right. I'm a pretty good shot, but I'm tired from driving all night, so I might be a little off today." He pointed at the bullseye and pulled the trigger.

"Click" and nothing! Then another "Click" and nothing!

"Oh sweet Jesus, I forgot my muffs." Tommy put on his protective hardware.

"Click – boom!" The bullet pierced the target two rings to the left of the bullseye.

"Okay, it's time to have fun. You gambled on Towers Above, and I bet you made a lot of money. How about we make a wager for each time I pull the trigger? We'll bet on whether the gun will fire live ammo or a blank round. Or maybe it just goes 'click.' Only this time, I'm going to aim for a spot between your eyes!"

Tommy stared at Mark and let his intention sink in. He hoped Mark's eyes would be filled with fear, but they weren't. It was almost as if Mark was hypnotized.

"Okay, so be it. You want to test me, huh? Well, here we go!" Tommy slowly placed the gun in between Mark's eyes and pulled the trigger.

"Click" and nothing! Again, "Click" and nothing!

Tommy could see that the next bullet was a blank round. "Oh hell, if you don't care, I'll put the gun against your temple."

"Boom!"

The shot echoed throughout the room! Mark's body lifted a good two inches off the chair. "Good, I finally got a reaction," Tommy mumbled to himself. He took off his muffs and began to reload.

"You know, if you're so willing to die, why don't you open your eyes and watch the bullet that kills you?" Tommy calmly asked. He was playing the ultimate mind game, hoping the second session would break Mark. Putting his muffs back on, Tommy said, "Ready for round two!" After spinning the cylinder, Tommy saw that the live bullet was chambered and would fire when the trigger was pulled.

"How about another spin for luck?" Tommy gave the cylinder of fortune another couple of revolutions. He pulled the trigger.

"Click." Nothing! "Click." Nothing!

Tommy eyed the cylinder and again saw that the next bullet was live. It was judgment time. He pulled the trigger.

"Boom!" The sound reverberated throughout the room. The smell of the bullet piercing flesh was strong.

"Jesus, my ear! You shot my ear!" Mark screamed. Now jerking violently, he knocked himself backwards and fell to the floor, pulling the chair he was cuffed to down with him. Danny left him there for thirty seconds, letting Mark process what just happened. Tommy could see that Mark now finally understood that this was the day he might die. Danny lifted Mark up and positioned the chair once again so he was directly facing Tommy.

"I had a feeling that was going to happen. That was the last time I intend to be nice! How about we talk?" Tommy was yelling, certain that Mark couldn't hear him, at least from one of his ears. Tommy started to reload while watching Mark for a reaction. The man was physically shaking but giving no indication that he was ready to concede.

"Okay! Here we go, round three."

"Click." Nothing! "Click." Nothing! Then "Boom!" The blank round had discharged! Tommy didn't hesitate, knowing the next pull of the trigger would produce nothing.

"Click." Nothing!

Mark realized the next pull of the trigger could be his last moment on earth. He'd lost track of the count and just couldn't chance it anymore. Tommy pulled the trigger halfway when Mark screamed, "Stop!"

"Yes, I'm working for the government – with the DIA! Please, no more!"

Tommy Roulette was a bitch to play. Someday, Tommy thought, maybe I'll have a chance to tell Mark that the last chamber was empty!

# CHAPTER 17

"I'll be right back. I'm going to get some gauze for that ear," Tommy said.

"God, Tommy, you shot half his ear off!" Danny said, looking at his friend in amazement.

"No, I didn't. Give me a break! I had no choice. He was pushing me to the limits. Let me see the video. We need some negotiating chips in our bank," Tommy told Danny.

After bandaging the ear, Tommy told Mark to start talking, beginning with his first encounter with the DIA. It turned out that Mark started doing work for the government after 9/11. The initial intent was to successfully enhance the human clotting efficiency using a new gene-altering technology.

Mark began to explain. "We were successful with the initial trial programs. Then the government came back with a request for more studies, studies that would focus on the equine species. That was the beginning of what they called Project Withers. I told them it would be virtually impossible to conduct such research, as there was no likelihood that the large number of equines needed for the study would be readily available in just one location.

"Their response to me was, 'We've got a lot of acreage and an entire cavalry unit tucked away on government land in Nowhere, Wyoming.' Since I was blindfolded each time they took me to their facility, I had no clue where the installation was located. But I told the DIA about Rob's idea and they suggested that I include

Towers Above as one of the test subjects. They also wanted a control subject identical to Towers, and the agency made the decision to bring the Saudis into the picture. As I had already conducted thoroughbred lineage homework on Towers Above, I was able to easily identify which thoroughbreds in the Saudi kingdom, when bred, would produce a horse with the same X factor as our horse."

Mark paused briefly, rubbing the area above his injured ear.

"I told those in charge that one horse should get gene-altering injections and the other horse should get placebo shots. I also told them that they'd have to kill me before I altered Tower's genetics. The DIA agreed with my recommendation about the injections and provided incentive seed money that helped convince Donnie to participate. The shots I gave TA were a series of vitamin serums.

"You should also know that even before Towers Above was conceived – and it was natural – my equine-based genetic alterations were already being incorporated into the breeding stock in Wyoming. Hell, I bet some of the horses there have DNA that is nearly identical to that of TA. By now, there's probably at least a dozen other Towers Above progeny grazing somewhere out on the Western prairie.

"Anyway, I'm sure a lot of the intelligence agents were betting on Towers Above and Nidalas during their racing careers, but I have no proof," Mark added.

"I was at Woodlands in April and twenty feet from Rob Becker when he was shot. I was at the rail when Nidalas took the syringe-tipped umbrella in his chest. I witnessed the security guy pick up the umbrella. After that, I called my DIA contact and waited for them to tell me what to do next. It seemed like forever, but they eventually arranged for me to meet up with the Saudis to help escort Nidalas home. I figured he'd been poisoned and told the Saudis to implement the transfusion protocol I'd formulated. Just so you know, I set up the same program with Donnie in case something like that happened to Towers. So now you have the whole story!"

Breathing a sigh of relief, Tommy made a mental note to thank the agency's plastic surgeon when he was back in the D.C. area. Mark hadn't recognized him as the guy who'd picked up the umbrella.

Tommy had some more questions for Mark.

"Was there ever a time in Wyoming when you had occasion to connect with individuals other than those who were part of your staff?" Tommy asked.

"There was just one time," Mark replied. "I had a raging toothache and needed to see a dentist. They blindfolded me and took me to a field clinic. It was pretty basic, a tent with electricity and four dental chairs. So the dentist numbs me and leaves me alone with his assistant for a few minutes. I start making small talk and asked when he and the rest of the cavalry division would head overseas. The guy just laughed and said, 'These units aren't deploying anywhere except maybe to the Smokies, Adirondacks, or the Rockies, if you get my drift.' At that point, the dentist returned and took care of my abscessed gum. I was given antibiotics and pain medication, then blindfolded and escorted back to the facility."

"Did you bet on Towers Above and Nidalas?" Tommy asked.

There was a long pause and Mark lowered his head in shame. "You've got to understand, I wasn't allowed to be associated with my friends. It was selfish on my part, but yes, I did bet! I didn't need the money, but it was too damn tempting to not be a part of the action."

"So when Donnie texted you about the business with Juan and the video on social media, did you call your DIA contacts?" Tommy asked.

"What text, and who's Juan?" Mark answered.

"When you went to the farm to give the horse his shots, who did you see? Donnie, or a farm worker?"

"Sometimes Donnie met me, and other times there was a farm employee. I always gave that guy a generous tip. I figured it couldn't hurt. I'm guessing that was Juan, huh?" Tommy nodded his head.

"So you never got a text or call about a problem with Juan?" Tommy asked again.

"For the most part, my fiancée Carole opened my texts or handled my phone messages when I was in Saudi Arabia. Maybe she took the call and forgot to relay the message."

Tommy's eyes widened and he debated whether or not to break the news to Mark. He decided, What the hell, I might as well do it. She's never going to see him again. It's better to let him down hard now than to let him dangle in the wind.

"Your fiancée, Carole is her name … right?" There was an affirmative nod. "Well, you're damn lucky to be talking with me right now. She's not only also a DIA agent, but she's an assassin for the agency. She was supposed to kill you, but luckily, we snatched the two of you before that happened. "

Tommy didn't say a word. If ever there were a time for a pregnant pause, it was now.

A tear formed slowly in Mark's right eye, quickly followed by the same in his other eye. Tommy thought to himself, Damn, she was good. This poor sap really was fooled. I'm certain she was great in the sack, but I can't believe he thought she loved him.

Tommy shuddered, understanding again why he'd never been able to fully commit to a second relationship with a woman. One sorry marriage had been enough for him.

"Just one more question. How the hell did Nidalas survive that dose of ricin? The thoroughbred should have died!"

Mark answered with pride in his voice. "You're right, he should've died. I gave Nidalas the genetic altering shots. Every time a capillary, arteriole, or vein broke down and bleeding started, the bleed would stop, and the transfusions flushed away any clumped circulatory debris!"

"Danny, take the cuffs off of Mark and give him a stiff drink. I don't think he's going anywhere. I've got to call Stan and talk about where we go from here."

∩ ∩ ∩

Stan answered the phone. "Tommy, what's happening? Give me some good news!"

"I think it's time to have a sit-down with the folks at the DIA. They're operating a huge ranch somewhere in Wyoming and have set up a cavalry unit, division size or larger. Our source here just implied that the Wyoming assets won't be used abroad but will be utilized here in the States. I also have a video you need to see. It's got some info we can run through the computers that may give us a clearer idea of what the DIA is doing."

"Jesus, Tommy, you and Danny get back here and bring the asset with you. We might convince the DIA to share what's going on with us! See you in a few hours."

It was time for another road trip.

Tommy was tired of spending long hours behind a steering wheel.

 **HAPTER 18**

Tommy was road-weary and wished they were flying, not driving, to Washington, DC. Danny drove the first leg, with Tommy in the passenger's seat. Mark was in the back of the van, shackled and silenced.

"What are you thinking, Danny?" Tommy asked.

"You mean about the cavalry unit and their lack of deployment?

"Yep!"

"You're going to laugh at me!"

"No, I won't," Tommy said, starting to laugh.

"I can't remember when I last watched the movie Red Dawn, but that's the first thing I thought of when Mark mentioned all those American mountain ranges. Those are places where horses might hang out, right?"

"Bingo! That's exactly what I thought," Tommy replied, laughing even harder. "The only thing missing in Mark's statement was any reference to Charlie Sheen. And--"

"And what?" Danny questioned.

"Is that all? What else did you think?" Tommy reversed course and pressed Danny to share his thoughts.

"Tommy, I'd be guessing. But someone in DC knows, and frankly, it's above my pay grade to care," he responded. Tommy laughed again, nodding in agreement. He was tired of thinking.

∩ ∩ ∩

Tommy timed their arrival at the Agency for after sunset. Mark, along with Carole, who'd arrived earlier, were processed into CIA custody, disappearing into an area of the facility Tommy and Danny had never seen. The two headed to Stan's office, where he was waiting impatiently for them. Manly bear hug greetings were exchanged before Stan got right to the point.

"Let me see the interrogation video!" Stan watched it three times … wanting to be certain that nothing was missed.

"Well, guys, I'm going to tell you what happened with POTUS at the April meeting, but nothing I say leaves this room – and neither does anything you tell me. This discussion is not recorded and remains confidential. I simply want a free exchange of information – so no holding back, understood?" Tommy and Danny nodded. Stan began by sharing what he knew about the exchange that took place during the spring meeting when POTUS blew up and demanded to know, 'Who's Mark, and what is Project Withers?'

"That was the point when I and many others were excused from the meeting. I was on my way out of the room when I heard the Director of National Intelligence start a briefing about Project Withers. I haven't a clue about the program, but I suspected it was a dark op. So, which of you wants to speak first?"

Never the shy one, and also as the alpha dog of the two, Tommy went first.

"Danny and I have at least one thought in common. The reference to mountains and the cavalry unit reminded us about the movie Red Dawn and guerrilla warfare. 'Always seek the high ground so one can see your adversaries advancing.'

"My next thoughts are too frightening to even consider, but we have to. I think this cavalry unit is intended for battle inside our borders. Our country is preparing for war against its own citizens. The adversaries will be state militias. Stan, we're dinosaurs – so are you, for that matter! Our country is irretrievably divided politically and philosophically!"

Tommy was on a roll.

"Today's college students, most of whom are in their late teens and early twenties, are being taught by left-leaning socialist progressives. Hell, even K-12 students are brainwashed with the same crap. They're being indoctrinated with biased information. The educational systems we learned from during the '50s, '60s, and '70s, as well as how our parents' generation was taught, no longer exist. Our parents' generation earned the moniker of the Greatest Generation, no doubt due in part to the way they were educated.

"History has demonstrated that every dominant society—call them empires if you prefer—is a living, breathing entity. Their existence mirrors the bell curve model. Right now, our society is on the downside of that curve! Ultimately our democracy will cease to exist and after a period of turmoil, we'll end up with a socialistic dictatorship! Our last chief executive wanted to be president for a third term and no doubt would have been re-elected. Term limits prevented him from seeking yet another nomination. Mark my words, there'll be attempts to return to the Golden Days and perhaps those efforts will be successful – for a brief period."

Tommy paused for a moment, giving time for Stan to pick his jaw up from the floor and for Danny to push his eyes back in their sockets.

"Our country has lost its sense of being unique. You know, that feeling of being special. The selective service system still exists, but the mandatory draft into military service ended during the Vietnam era. For me, serving our country was something I took pride in. If you were to ask a young person today if they would serve their country for two years, the majority would look at you and say, 'Why, what's in it for me?' Our country has fought meaningless wars and each time we collectively state 'Never again!' And yet we coddle each new generation even more than the previous one!

"Meanwhile, our country's porous borders remain open to individuals from all over the world, most of whom could not care less about a total commitment to our values and laws. The thought of giving 100 percent to become an American citizen is an anomaly for most illegal immigrants. Instead we have dual-country allegiances that rip at the fabric of our Constitution. This type of attitude is destructive. When the last of the Boomers dies, our country will be stuck with the Me Generations – X and Y, along with Millennials and their me-first mantra.

"That's when the days of a collective 'we' society will be gone, perhaps forever! And don't think for one minute that our country's militias are an exclusive domain for conservative-thinking individuals. Since November's election, the progressives have also been arming themselves and preparing for a revolution. I'm sorry to unload on you this way, boss! Sorry to you too, Danny. I love this country and pray that our government has no intention of allowing a rebellion to occur."

Stan looked at Danny, hoping to not have another diatribe, and asked, "What say you?" Danny found himself wanting to turn around and see if anyone had quietly come into the office.

"Tommy pretty much summed things up for me Stan, although I do have something to add. I may not be the sharpest arrow in the quiver, but there's one bit of technology that demonstrates, at least to me, just how angry and divided citizens of our country have become. It's exhibited every day on social media platforms. People simply don't care that their comments are mean-spirited and cruel. Very rarely do I see any sense of compromise or tolerance in the majority of comments about issues facing all of us in our country. If I was Rip Van Winkle and awakened to the negative discourse shared on social media today, I'd swear the citizens were at war with each other."

There was total silence for at least thirty seconds.

"Well, gentlemen, I appreciate what you just shared. I believe it's time for Bud Ellis, who heads the Defense Intelligence Agency, to take a walk around the Reflecting Pool with me. Nothing like a little exercise and some verbal sparring to shed a few pounds.

"For now, I don't want either of you to leave town. I assume the two of you will start familiarizing yourself with Project Withers first-hand. Oh, and for security purposes, we're going to be on satellite phones from this point forward." Stan reached into his desk drawer and retrieved two fully charged phones and their accessories, handing one to each of them.

"And, guys, good work! Oh, I almost forgot, I have something for you, Tommy!" Stan walked around his desk and handed Tommy a sealed envelope. On the front of the envelope, it said:

CONFIDENTIAL: OPEN ONLY UPON
DEPLOYMENT TO PROJECT WITHERS

Tommy and Danny left the office, closing the door behind them. Stan slumped low in his chair, burying his head in his hands. While he hadn't expected Tommy's rant, he nonetheless understood.

It was well-known to those in the US intelligence field that in-country assets, and for that matter agents worldwide, are trained to be apolitical. It helps preserve their jobs during presidential or regime changes. Stan managed to survive as head of the CIA for almost thirty years because he knew how to maintain that impartiality and because he did a damn good job. The reality remained that all one has to do, he thought, is to pick up a good history book and familiarize oneself with the past. "History always repeats itself. That is a fact," Stan said aloud.

Stan also believed that planet Earth was the Lord's grand experiment and that the human beings who inhabited it were entrusted with its preservation until the end of time – or until man annihilated himself. He opened the center desk drawer and replayed the conversation that had just taken place, listening intently to what Tommy was saying. Stan found himself agreeing with most everything that had been said.

There was no hesitation when Stan punched the delete button on the recording machine.

 **HAPTER 19**

It was nearly 5 p.m. Friday evening and sunset was nearing – prime time to dump cybertrash anywhere in Washington, DC.

The email to the DIA read:

"Hey, Bud, I've got a guy here with a video, and I know you're missing an asset! I think we need to stretch the muscles in our 'withers' and do some furlongs around the Reflecting Pool. How about Monday at noon? Thanks!"

The protocol established from events that occurred during the Obama era was that now, all electronic messaging was done only through government servers. Federal employees finally got the message that any work-related emails running through their personal networks and servers, no matter how secure, were only going to lead to major headaches and hacking.

∩ ∩ ∩

The IT department had narrowed down an area in Wyoming where the acreage required to station a cavalry-sized unit might be. Thanks to Google Earth, it took just half the time initially expected to find the site. Google Earth easily filtered out any classified government location simply by blocking with hash marks, said location, when zooming in on it. A satellite fly-over confirmed the Google findings shown on the screen.

After contacting staff at the Denver office to arrange for the rental of a plane, there were pictures of the base in less than a day, and with a minimum of hassle. Even though two Apache helicopters eventually convinced the pilot of the single-engine plane that he was flying in forbidden territory, enough pictures had been taken of the base. By late Sunday, Stan had everything he needed for Monday's clandestine meeting with Bud.

It was raining that Monday morning when Stan arrived. He was fifteen minutes early. Walking slowly along the path, he looked back often to see if anyone had appeared. Exactly one minute before noon, his earpiece sprang to life.

"You've got company," Stan heard, turning slightly to see a man holding an umbrella about 200 yards behind and quickly closing the gap. Stan last saw Bud in April during the Woodlands Park terrorist threat but couldn't yet identify the approaching man because of the umbrella. The man's pace was fast and he was now alongside Stan.

"This better be good, because I hate rainy walks!" he said.

Recognizing the voice, Stan turned as Bud raised his umbrella just enough for Stan to recognize his face. "Hey Bud, how are Julie and the family?"

"They're well. How about Barbara and the girls?"

"Doing good, thanks."

It took a few seconds before Bud spoke. "So, Stan, you were finally filled in on Project Withers, huh?"

"Why don't we have a seat up ahead, Bud?" Stan replied.

Both men sat. Holding his cell phone, Stan hit the play button on the edited version of Mark Shaw's interrogation video, a version that didn't contain the Tommy Roulette game. This version definitely made Mark look pathetic and weak. Bud quickly realized this wasn't the Mark he knew. Clearly agitated, he asked, "What is it that you want from me, Stan?"

"I want in. I want two of my men attached to your cavalry unit. And they get total access to every bit of information and communication – and without censorship."

"Can't do it, Stan!" Bud stood and started to walk away before Stan brought him to an immediate halt, forcing him to sit back down.

"You walk away, and the leaks start tomorrow. WikiLeaks isn't the only place this information will end up. I'm certain Drudge would run with it!"

Bud looked as if he'd been nailed to the bench, staring straight ahead with a dazed look on his face. It was a good minute before he could speak again.

"Ya know, Stan, you're a damn prick." Stan caught himself nodding in the affirmative. "You're gonna give me those two guys that were in Costa Rica, aren't you?"

"They won't get in your way, and eventually you'll come to see that they're a useful addition to your group of rough riders."

"Are we done?" Bud growled.

"Almost, but I have one more favor to ask. I'm assuming you won't need Mark Shaw in Wyoming unless it's a dire emergency. He knows my guys, and I don't want their cover blown. And the woman assassin, you don't get her back. Do we have an understanding?"

Bud was beyond pissed. It had been a long time since he'd been checkmated. Turning to face Stan, he said, "Understood, but your boys better be able to handle a horse, 'cause they're going to be riding their asses off." Bud turned and walked away.

Stan remained on the bench. Outwardly he appeared calm and collected, but inside he was ready to explode with excitement. He'd won! It was advantage CIA! Stan pulled out his encrypted phone, punching Tommy's number on the dial pad.

"Hey boss, what's up?"

"You and Danny are going to Wyoming. You're now a part of Project Withers. There's a catch, though. If you and Danny don't know how to ride a horse, you better find a place to learn and take a crash course in Riding 101. I really pissed off the head of the DIA and have no doubt they'll put each of you on their toughest steeds. Now get back home and train. Soon as I get instructions from the DIA, I'll text them to you and have e-tickets sent for the flight. By the way, I negotiated a free pass on communication-sharing, so I expect daily reports from you! Good hunting to both of you – and have fun!"

As soon as Stan ended the call, Tommy was on the phone with Ted.

"Ted, this is Tommy. Do you have a minute?"

"Well, how are you, stranger? Are you ready to come in from the cold?" Ted asked.

"I wish I was, Ted. I'm heading west to Wyoming. And don't laugh! Danny and I are going to be riding horses out there! Can you hook us up for some quick lessons at the track? It has to be rigorous training, because I think we're going to end up in mountainous territory."

All Tommy heard in the background was laughter.

"Ted, Ted! Stop laughing! This is serious stuff, dammit!"

"I'm on it right now, Tommy. The horses and trainers are here waiting for you and Danny to arrive. On your way, though, stop by a pharmacy and pick up some pain patches – you're going to need them for your thighs, back, and buttocks!" Tommy heard more laughter before Ted hung up.

"When I see him, I owe him a 'yippee kay yay, mother fucker,' so help me God," Tommy mumbled to himself.

# CHAPTER 20

It was a week since my last contact with Tommy. I had to admit, the separation between us was a blessing. Marty's anxiety had lessened, but unfortunately, she was still determined to stay in the Portland area with her sister indefinitely. I hadn't shared Tommy's intel warning with her, and I was determined to not leave her side – and I would be armed when necessary.

My birthday was in a couple of days and I prayed that my gift from her would be two one-way tickets on Southwest, back to the Commonwealth, and then home!

I walked into the kitchen expecting to join Marty for breakfast. Lauren was standing at the stove making french toast and gave me a glancing smile.

"Where's Marty, Lauren?"

"She went shopping for your birthday, Rob," Lauren replied.

I felt my heart begin to beat faster. "Jesus, she's alone! Where'd she go? How long ago? What car did she take?" These were all questions that needed immediate answers. Yet in the back of my mind, I kept telling myself, "This is no time to piss off Lauren."

"She took your rental about twenty minutes ago," Lauren answered and then turned to face my now empty chair. I hustled upstairs to finish dressing and armed myself. In less than three minutes, I was back in the kitchen.

"Give me your car keys, Lauren!"

"Leave Marty alone, Rob, and you're not taking my car," was

her response.

"Goddamn it, Lauren, Marty could be in danger! I don't have time to explain; just give me the damn keys, now!"

I must have scared Lauren enough, because in forty-five seconds, I was backing out of the driveway. I had a pretty good hunch as to where Marty would have gone. In the early '70s, when I was assigned to the naval station in Newport, Rhode Island my favorite retailer was the original LL Bean store in Freeport, Maine. In 1976, at midnight no less, I was there shopping until 1:00 in the morning. Now I was in Portland, Oregon where my new favorite clothier was the original Columbia Sportswear store in the downtown district. Half of my closet was filled with Columbia clothing – and Marty knew me well.

"She has to be there," I prayed.

With the help of Google Maps, I was downtown in forty-five minutes, looking for a parking spot. I found one and ran toward Columbia's entrance. Upon entering the store, a store assistant asked if I needed any help. I pulled out my wallet and showed her a picture of Marty. "Has this woman been shopping here this morning?"

Oh God, let her say yes, I thought.

The young lady nodded in the affirmative. "I waited on her. She only bought one item for herself and at least a dozen men's items. Is there a problem?"

"How long ago did she leave?"

"Well, I want to say fifteen minutes ago, but someone recognized her and wanted an autograph and a selfie with her."

"What?" I said.

"The person said something about Towers Above and some kind of ownership. It was all foreign to me. Then some other people in the store started gathering around and asking her for autographs too. Who is she, sir?"

"Damn, I'm sorry! She's my wife. Is there a store parking lot?"

"Yes. Go out the door and turn left. Our parking lot is just half a block down the street," she told me. As I opened the door, I heard the lady yell, "Good luck!"

Running as quickly as a guy who is nearly seventy years old can, I reached the parking lot and looked around for my wife.

"Damn – nothing!"

I began walking up and down the aisles of the parking lot when I suddenly saw a car that looked like my rental, sticking halfway out of the parking space. I began running again and reached the car in seconds.

"Oh Jesus, it's my car, and no Marty!" I dropped to my knees and began praying.

"Hey mister … mister." I felt a tap on my shoulder. "Are you looking for the woman?"

I turned and came face-to-face with a teenage boy. "Yes, son, yes I am! Can you help me? Please!"

"I saw it, saw it all. She was backing out when a man jumped behind her car. He did it on purpose. He's one of those demonstrators we have here in Portland. So, he's lying on the ground and she stops the car and gets out to help. That's when a van pulled up. The door was opened from inside and the guy quickly jumps up from the ground and pushes her into the van. The door closes and the van takes off fast. The guy then went to the car she was driving, turned it off and tossed the keys in that direction." The teen pointed to the east.

"And they didn't see you?"

"Nah, I was slumped down listening to my tunes, waiting for

my mom to get back from shopping. Nobody must have seen me. You want me to call 911, sir?"

"No, I will, thank you! But please do me a favor. Describe the guy who faked being hit by the car."

"Well, he was a thin white guy with a black hoodie, black bandana, and red Nike shoes. That's about all I remember."

"Young man, thank you so much. Let's keep this information between ourselves, but give me your name, address, and phone number in case the authorities need to talk with you."

I took his information and put it in my cell phone. I shook the young man's hand and thanked him again, before searching for the car keys. It took me about twenty minutes, but I found them and pulled the car back into the parking spot. I returned to the Columbia store and asked the woman who had helped me earlier to find someone who could show me the security video from the morning. In about five minutes, the store manager appeared.

"Sir, are you a law enforcement officer?"

"No, I'm not, but my wife was here this morning and she was just kidnapped a few minutes ago from your lot down the street. There's no guard in the lot, and if anything happens to her, I will hold your company accountable. All I want to see is the store video. There's a possibility that one or more of the people involved in the kidnapping may have been in the store at the same time as my wife!"

I had to take a chance she would show me the security video. Hopefully she'd accept that my story wasn't a hoax.

"Follow me, please," she finally said.

The video began at 9 a.m. At 10:15, my wife entered the store and shopped for twenty minutes. A woman approached Marty and the two of them began a discussion and then – there he was!

The man wearing a black hoodie and red Nike shoes was now standing next to Marty, obviously listening to the discussion. Five minutes later, he left the store.

I told the store manager to please save the tape, because I was going to file a missing person report with the police. I left the store for a final time. As I headed to the parking lot and my rental car, the Beach Boys song "God Only Knows", began playing from my jacket pocket. I answered the phone, knowing it was going to be the first of many calls from people who shouldn't have any way of knowing that I was in Portland.

"Dr. Becker, she's ours now! No police or she dies instantly! I will call again in two hours!"

Click! There was just silence.

CHAPTER 21

I sat in Lauren's car for thirty minutes, blaming myself for everything and wondering how much physical abuse Marty had endured. She wouldn't have given up my cell number unless someone roughed her up. Marty could take a lot and dish it out verbally as well, but physical intimidation was another story.

There was only one person I could trust for advice in handling this situation. I placed the call.

"Rob, what's up?"

But I froze — and literally couldn't speak. Whether it was guilt, embarrassment or shame, I sat there in a stupor, comatose for a time.

"Rob, I know you're there! Dammit, what is it? Rob, I can't help unless you tell me everything. Spit it out, man!"

If there is such a thing as conscious dreaming, that's what I was doing. I was reliving the day we said "I do." Our lovemaking. The birth of our three daughters, followed by their marriages and then by the birth of each of our five grandchildren. All those moments were flashing through my mind in high-def video — each moment, each memory — as vivid as it could be. My mind was everywhere I wanted it to be, living in the past. Except the reality was that I needed to be living in the now moment, and I wasn't ready to return to that world.

Tommy had experienced similar occurrences in the past with others — the silent sound of the pain he knew I was experiencing.

He knew I was experiencing a type of mental trauma, not unlike the symptoms of those who experience post-traumatic stress. The biggest mistake would be to hang up.

It was up to Tommy to find the right word or words that would unlock the mental tumblers in my mind. It was like the old Groucho Marx's television game show, You Bet Your Life. A fake duck was holding the magic word which would drop from the studio rafters, over the contestant, when that word was spoken. But Tommy's dictionary of magic words was empty.

It took me a good five minutes to compose myself and then finally, the duck dropped.

"Rob. It's Marty, isn't it? She's not just gone from your home in Kentucky – she's disappeared, hasn't she?"

"You know that you're clairvoyant, don't you? You predicted this! Marty's been kidnapped and it's my fault," I said. I explained what happened, sobbing, and starting to break down again. Tommy's brain was swirling.

"Rob, none of the kidnappers saw you, correct?"

"No, I was at least twenty minutes behind Marty."

"Good, that should buy us some time. They have your phone number and they know it's not an Oregon area code. Whatever they demand, whatever the request is, you've got at least a day or two of extra time and that should help. Tell them you're in Kentucky and that it will take you a couple days to drive out there.

"I've already been assigned to Project Wither,s and I'll have Stan move up my deployment. Rob, I'm betting more than even money that Project Withers is somehow related to the recent turmoil and the surge of hostage-taking in the western States. I want you to stall the kidnappers at every opportunity. This will help assure that Marty remains alive."

I began sobbing again.

"Rob, I want you to create chaos for these bastards. Make sure that nothing related to this kidnapping comes easy for them. Each time they contact you, demand to talk with Marty. Come up with questions that have answers only the two of you know. Whatever monetary demands they make, haggle with them.

"Tell them the deal will never be consummated without an even exchange. Demand that Marty be present at the exchange and that she must be released before any money changes hands. Do your damnedest to delay negotiations until I give you the go-ahead message!

"You know me, Rob! We'll get her back, I promise!" Tommy emphatically stated, pausing briefly to let me digest everything he'd just said.

Continuing, Tommy told me, "Listen, Rob, I've got calls to make. I'll bring my partner, Danny, up to speed on this and get the okay from Stan to head out west now. I'm certain the NSA has their Stingray towers on a 24/7 listening mode. I'm also pretty sure they have some idea about the general whereabouts of the kidnappers. Now toughen up! Anyone who can survive a sniper attack can certainly get through this. And we both know Marty! The last thing she'd expect is for you to give up and feel sorry for yourself. Now go fight for what's yours. Stan gave me a new satellite phone and I'll text you the number! Call or text any time. I have to go—love you, brother!"

The cheerleading was over.

"Tommy, wait! I need something right now – and it's urgent! My sister-in-law will raise a major stink when I tell her Marty is missing. Hell, she'll think I'm responsible – that's how much she dislikes me. She'll accuse me of foul play and make sure I'm arrested! Can you help by arranging somehow for her to not be a problem until we get Marty back? She'll only interfere, and we can't have that."

"Consider it done. Text me her name and address, and give me a little time. Talk to you soon. Bye."

CHAPTER 22

Stan was calling it a day when Jan's voice came across the speaker phone in his office. "Tommy's on line 1, should I tell him you're gone?"

"Thanks, Jan, I'll take it."

"How's the horse-riding and training going, Tommy?" Stan asked with laughter in his voice.

"Fine, just fine."

Stan sat straight up in the desk chair, putting his elbows squarely on the desk. During their years together, Stan had come to learn that when Tommy answered that curtly, there was a problem – and it would soon end squarely on his desk.

"Stan, I need some favors."

"Okay, shoot," Stan said, waiting for the other shoe to drop.

"Can you get the deployment orders moved up for me and Danny? We're more than ready, which leads to the second part of this. I just got off the phone with Dr. Rob Becker. His wife has gone missing – she left her husband and has been staying with her sister in Portland, Oregon! Rob followed her there to convince her to return home. If it's foul play, like I suspect, I need some of our assets in Portland to remove Dr. Becker's sister-in-law from her home until this matter is taken care of; otherwise she'll compromise any rescue plans."

Stan leaned back in his chair and dissected what he'd been asked for in what seemed like an eternity to Tommy.

"So, Rob Becker's wife has been kidnapped. Tommy wants to get to his duty station in Wyoming to make connections while organizing and directing her rescue. From Wyoming, no less!" Stan speculated to himself.

"Tommy, I can grant the request for your immediate deployment. That's not a problem. What I can't do is have our regional assets running around grabbing citizens off the streets and taking them out of circulation. Not unless that particular individual's situation is connected to a declared crisis that threatens our country. When you can give me verifiable and factual evidence that her disappearance would be of national priority, you know damn well I'll give the approval."

Tommy sat there in silence, as Stan had after his request for agents to grab Marty's sister, Lauren. Tommy knew it was a violation of agency policy – but he had to ask.

Before Tommy could even push the matter farther, Stan told the agent, "I know what you're thinking! I tell you, if you go rogue, consequences of that action are going to be entirely on you and Danny. I hope you carefully consider that. Having another plastic surgery procedure so soon after your recent cosmetic surgery is not going to work out well, and the Ringling Brothers Circus has gone out of business!"

Tommy wasn't amused by Stan's comments, but nonetheless understood where his boss was coming from. He had been called out and also knew that his conversation was being recorded. Stan had covered his ass, while Tommy's was now bare-naked. Tommy also knew that Stan fully expected that, barring anyone catching him in the act, Tommy was going to do whatever was necessary to not compromise Marty's chances for a safe return.

"Thanks, boss. I appreciate your help!"

"Don't mention it, Tommy, and good luck in Wyoming or wherever. Call if you need anything that involves Project Withers." Stan believed that this last cover-your-ass admonition was necessary, given Tommy's sarcastic reply just seconds ago.

Tommy returned to the training track, in no mood for more riding.

"What's going on?" Danny asked.

"I'm not going to lie to you, Danny. I'm boxed in and don't have clue as to what I can do about it! Do you remember Dr. Rob Becker? He was at the Challenge Cup dinner." Danny nodded yes. "Well, he's out in Portland, Oregon – his wife went missing this morning. We're pretty sure she was the latest in a series of recent kidnappings in that area. Dr. Becker called me for help and I said I'd be there for him. I just asked Stan for help from the Portland office and was turned down. If there's any good news, it's that we're headed to Wyoming earlier than planned."

"You said Portland?"

"Yeah, why?" Tommy mumbled, distracted and not paying much attention to his partner's response.

"My older brother retired from the Army Intelligence & Security Command a couple of years ago. Those INSCOM guys are tight and continue to network with each other, even after retiring. I've heard rumors that when asked, they'll go operational, even rogue if needed. My brother's name is Charles – you don't ever want to call him Charlie," Danny said, laughing.

"What did you just say?" Tommy was now attentive and alert to what Danny was saying.

"You remember. It's the group that was known as the US Army Security Agency during the Viet Nam war era. It was later reorganized and renamed. Charles is one of their veterans. Maybe he could help you directly or hook you up with someone who can," Danny suggested.

This was incredible news to Tommy. "Can you give him a call and introduce me, please?" Tommy begged. He wondered if Charles was a former Army Ranger like the operative that Agent Tibbits worked with in Kansas. Tommy recalled how effective that Ranger was during the April terror attacks on Ohio State University and the Woodlands Park Racetrack.

Danny immediately made the call, making small talk about family with Charles for about five minutes before getting to the reason for his call. He briefed Charles about Tommy and then Marty's kidnapping. Quickly and with a positive nod, he handed his phone to Tommy.

"Charles, I'll cut right to the chase. I've made promises I can't keep right now because my hands are tied by powers above my pay grade. But I'm certain a life hangs in the balance. I know how much your fraternity of brothers network with each other. I'm also guessing your intelligence is almost as thorough as our real-time information is. Marty Becker, the woman who has been kidnapped, is most likely a victim of the radical Antifa group that's been active in the Northwest over the past year. Her husband is Dr. Rob Becker, one of the owners of the thoroughbred Towers Above. I have Rob's cell number – and if you're willing and able, please give him a hand in managing this situation. I'll let him know to expect your call and will catch up with both of you as quickly as I can."

Tommy relayed the info and handed the phone back to Danny, who spoke with his brother for a few more minutes before ending the call.

"He's in!" Danny said, fist-pumping Tommy.

Tommy's scowl turned into a broad smile and he immediately placed another call. If Charles was anywhere near the caliber of the man utilized by Agent Tibbits—well, Tommy's fears would soon be assuaged.

# CHAPTER 23

I remained in the driver seat, stunned and frightened for my wife, and waiting for the kidnapper's next phone call or text. It was a long two hours before my phone again began to play "God Only Knows." After a couple of seconds, I answered.

"Here's what we want you to do ...."

I interrupted the man speaking, telling him, "Whoever you are, I can't do anything right now because I'm in southern Kentucky. Text me your demands or call me back later today, because I have to make travel arrangements. And the next time you call, I want to talk to my wife and hear her voice. If you don't comply, you get nothing!"

I ended the call, my heartbeat accelerating tenfold. I prayed to God that my words hadn't just killed Marty. As Tommy advised me to, I tried to set the ground rules that hopefully would put me in control of the situation. I waited anxiously for another thirty minutes, listening for the ping that would tell me a new text had arrived. "Ping!"

The text read:

"We want $1 million. NOT CASH! Gold Coins—American Eagles! Do not fly – Drive!"

I texted back: "You get nothing until I talk to my wife!!"

My phone rang ten minutes later, with the caller ID showing "Unknown." I answered and heard the shaky voice of a woman – a voice I desperately wanted to be that of my wife. "Marty, if this is you, which one of our daughters had a Donald Duck doll when she was a child? Answer, daughter one – two – or three?"

"Rob, it was two! Rob please, come get me ...!" The call abruptly ended, followed by another text.

"We will text you twice a day. You have three days to get here. If not, your wife dies! The clock starts at 6 a.m. tomorrow!"

"Oh God, Marty's phone! If they're tech-savvy, they'll see that Marty has the Find Friends app, which can pinpoint exactly where I am," I remembered in a panic. Then I realized they weren't using Marty's cellphone! I quickly scrolled through my settings and sure enough, Marty had set up the same application on my mobile phone.

I had to give the kidnapers credit. If bullion was the usual type of ransom demanded for the release of a hostage, it was a brilliant payoff. There are no serial numbers on the gold coins – the coins are all the same, with no identifiers – and the value of an ounce of gold fluctuates on a daily basis. The number of potential buyers is endless.

My phone pinged again, and I could feel the tension rising within me. Nervously, I looked down and saw that the text was from Tommy. I breathed in a sigh of relief – but that was short-lived. Tommy was handing me off to another operative. I slammed my fist against the steering wheel and screamed, "Nooooooo!" at the top of my voice. The despair was crushing me.

Lifting my eyes toward the heavens, I prayed. I'd always firmly believed in a higher power and had asked God for help many times in my life. Not every request I prayed for was granted, but my philosophy had always been and would continue to be, "If a question isn't asked, then one never gets an answer."

In this prayer, I asked that whoever Tommy was turning me

over to – someone named Charles – would be every bit as wise
and brave as Tommy. I needed my Marty back – and I wanted her
back alive!

I started the car and the phone rang once again. I didn't recognize the caller's number, but sensed it wasn't a marketing call.

"Hello!" I answered in what I hoped was an authoritative
voice.

"Dr. Becker, this is Charles. I assume that by now Tommy has
contacted you." Again, there was silence. The situation seemed so
surreal, like we were reading scripts in a play or movie! "Yes, he
did, Charles," I answered.

"Where are you right now?" he asked, and I told him.

"Stay there – I'll be there soon and will find you. I'm wearing
a silver Columbia parka."

Charles hung up and all I could think was, Of course you're
wearing a Columbia parka, and silver no less! After all, it's Portland!

 **HAPTER 24**

For some reason, I was quickly turning my head back and forth, as if sensing that someone was watching me. Over that half hour, the headache I'd had earlier in the day had worsened. My neck was tight, the muscles unaccustomed to this owl-like activity.

Suddenly there was a tapping on the back window on the driver's side of my car. One last head spin revealed a man in a puffy silver Columbia coat. I assumed it was Charles. I unlocked the car doors and waved him to the passenger's side of the car. Opening the passenger's door, he quickly slid onto the seat and extended his right hand. We shook hands. I am always amazed at what a handshake can convey. Charles's handshake was firm and implied skill and confidence. Most individuals will make an instant judgment when meeting someone new – and this handshake left me feeling positive and hopeful about the man.

"Dr. Becker, I don't know if you remember Tommy's partner and friend, Danny. He was at the Fall Challenge Cup dinner in 2016." I nodded. "Well, I'm his brother and have a great deal of experience working in intelligence. So, tell me what you know and what information you have."

I ran through the entire chain of events from the early morning to now and showed him the text messages I'd received. Then I gave him the bad news about the app on Marty's phone. Charles didn't hesitate.

"Give me your phone, please." I watched him open the same app that Marty had on her phone and he turned off my Enable Location icon.

"Okay Rob, that app on her phone can't find you anymore. Now the big question is, did she enable it on her phone so we can see where she is, and if so, when do we go rescue her? If you believe in miracles, start praying that it's enabled."

"It's on!" Charles exclaimed and he turned toward me in an instant, holding his hand up in the air and waiting for me to return a high five.

I silently mouthed, "Thank you, Lord!"

Charles paused briefly, seeing the emotions crossing my face. "I know what you're thinking, and I totally understand. You want to get there right now and rescue your wife, but I'm telling you from experience that we can't. Not yet!

"Do you remember how the term Junior Varsity has been played out in the news these past few years? Well, the people holding Marty are synonymous with that connotation of JV. If these individuals were the top leaders of this group of Antifa radicals, they would not have allowed the location application on your wife's phone to remain active. They also should have realized that you're already here in Portland! I'm also betting they're moving her from location to location. Look, I have a network of associates who are going to join us soon. They're all patriots willing to work behind the scenes to uphold our country's constitutional principles. We need to set up surveillance at the location!"

Charles pointed at a pulsating blue dot on the screen of my phone. "We need to determine if both she and her cell phone are at the same location we see now. When she spoke with you, I doubt that she was talking from her phone. That's going to be the next demand you make."

As if on cue, my phone pinged with a message. It was Lauren, wanting to know if I'd found Marty. I'd totally forgotten about my sister-in-law.

"Geez, Charles, it's my fault. She's a pain and will be a problem if I don't reply." Charles glanced at my text. "So, she's not an asset?"

"No, not at all," I answered, but not wanting to be the one to throw her under the bus.

"Well, we don't need the police involved, so it's time for her to take a vacation. Do you think you can get her out of the house?"

"I'd say there's a 50/50 chance."

Charles took out his cell phone and scrolled through his contacts. "Write this address down. 1251 SW Morrison Street. It's the address of an Italian restaurant, Santelli's. Tell your sister in-law to call Uber to take her there. Include in the text that Marty has decided to go back home to Kentucky with you, and that this is a celebratory dinner for the three of you. Explain that after dinner, Marty plans to ride with you to the airport where you're both catching the red-eye flight home tonight. If that doesn't get her out of the house, then we'll just have to go to her place and grab her. I'd prefer the restaurant. It's a lot cleaner. A disappearance is better than a full-blown kidnapping."

"What's the difference?" I inquired.

"One of my friends owns the restaurant. He'll have a table reserved for the three of you in an elegant private room with a single table. I'm confident that she won't even get a chance to sit down. It will be like she was never even there," Charles stated with a grin appearing at the corners of his mouth.

"Who are you, or should I say, what are you?"

"Dr. Becker, there are seventeen known intelligence agencies in this country. There's no way those agencies can shadow every threat in this country, foreign or domestic. Each agency has sub agencies. In dentistry, you're all general dentists after you graduate, and if you decide to specialize, you essentially become a sub agency of the profession. You still work in the same field, but your job is significantly different.

"It's no different in intelligence work. We have specialties also. After we retire, when asked, we'll supplement intelligence work in other areas that may be deficient in manpower. One thing I ask is that you refrain from asking me which intelligence agency I worked for during my active years. I won't answer that question."

I wrote the text and showed it to Charles, who nodded approval. I hit send, waiting tensely for a text back from Lauren. Five minutes later, there was a response.

"Sorry for the delay. Have to say I'm surprised. I'm on my way. See both of you in 30 min."

I showed the text to Charles, who smiled. He took my phone and scrolled to the locator application and told me to start driving. As I drove, he provided directions to the location currently showing where Marty's cell phone was.

"Aren't we going to the restaurant?" I asked with concern in my voice.

"Dr. Becker, Lauren will be okay. What's important now is to do a drive by of the location that your wife's phone is showing us. We'll find a safe spot where we can observe the location until the rest of my group are in position. Once they arrive, we talk and strategize. Is that okay?"

I reluctantly gave my approval but doubted somehow that pep talk would save me from doing time for kidnapping – in any court of law!

# CHAPTER 25

Early the next morning, Tommy and Danny, both dressed in army fatigues, arrived at the Louisville International Airport. The uniforms were courtesy of Bud and the DIA. Even though Bud had been one-upped by Stan, he still respected his fellow compatriot. Each man had survived several changes of the political guard during transition years – and both were the true epitome of the word patriot.

Nonetheless, Bud had his payback, tagging Tommy and Danny with the rank of Private First Class. The duo boarded a Frontier Airlines jet for the one-way trip to Denver – this time seated together.

As Tommy and Danny walked down the aisle to their seats, several passengers reached out to Tommy and Danny, offering a handshake or a high five and thanking each man for their service. They were in Kentucky, a Red State, where duty to one's country was still respected, for the most part.

The men were soaking up the adulation, grinning from ear to ear. Tommy turned to Danny and whispered, "If they only knew …." Danny just kept smiling.

Placing their carry-on baggage in the bins above the seats, a young man seated in the row opposite, said, "Oh great, I have to sit near these fascist pigs for over two hours! I'm beginning to smell the odor of murder and rancid pork!"

Danny turned and just smiled while his left arm was securely stretched across Tommy's chest, restraining Tommy from doing something he'd later regret. A flight attendant saw and heard what had just occurred and responded immediately.

"Young man, one more comment like that and I'll have you removed from this flight! Please have respect for your fellow travelers!"

"Fuck them! They're killers and rapists. They represent our fascist government and our new fascist president. I am not going to shut up! It's my job to resist!"

With that statement, the flight attendant flashed a hand signal and with a snap of two fingers, pointed at the man in the seat. In less than five minutes, a Louisville police officer was at the plane's doorway and making his way toward the rows in which Tommy, Danny, and the verbally abusive passenger were seated.

It took only ten seconds for the officer to remove the radical from his seat, place him face-down on the floor and with help from another passenger, put the protesting man's hands behind his back and cuffed him. Metro's finest then lifted the man up from the floor, alternately pushing and dragging him off the plane. This was accompanied by a cascading chorus of clapping, and chants of "USA, USA."

"Thanks Danny, I almost lost it! I'm in no mood for that resistance bullshit." Danny knew better than to respond instantly. He knew Tommy was preoccupied with the situation in Portland and that he felt a sense of helplessness. Finally, Danny spoke. "Tommy, you're going to have to trust that my brother has Dr. Becker's back. Have faith ... please!"

The ruckus was over, and it was business as usual for Tommy, who had his yellow legal pad and pen out. He was ready to plan and waiting for the plane to get airborne so he could lower the tray and start putting his thoughts to paper and share them with Danny. These thoughts pretty much centered on the group of people they were traveling west to infiltrate.

Once Tommy started writing, his entries were concise and to the point:

- I expect some kind of greeting party will be there when we deplane to escort us.
- Once we get our gear loaded into the vehicle and we're out in the boonies, I also expect that our heads will be covered in some way so we don't see the route we're traveling along. I intend to tell them that we already know the location of their base, but I doubt it will do any good – you know how orders go!
- I doubt that our greeting party has a clue as to who we really are.
- They may try to test us with trick questions. I would if I were in their situation.
- We are going to look out of place age-wise and with the rank we've been given – this is going to raise questions.

WHAT SAY YOU? – he finished, handing the pad over to Danny and turned to stare out the window.

Danny read the list over and over again, to the point where he'd memorized what Tommy had written. He didn't really disagree with Tommy's take on the situation, but he didn't quite buy into it either. For some reason, Danny felt sure that everything Tommy had written would turn out differently. Danny figured that during their travel time with their "guards," there would be ample time for the other agents to brief the two on the activities of Project Withers and any upcoming events in the works. Danny wrote his thoughts down and passed the legal pad back to Tommy.

Tommy read and re-read what Danny had written and resumed staring out the window. After about fifteen minutes, he turned back toward the almost-asleep Danny – who suddenly felt the piercing gaze of his friend. Tommy was grinning as he handed the pad back to Danny. What Danny had written now had triple check marks in the margin.

It took less than fifteen minutes for both men to fall fast asleep.

ᑎ ᑎ ᑎ

The plane's final approach was typical for flying into the Denver International Airport. Varying layers of thermals coming off the mountains caused the plane to sway back and forth over the plains, seemingly steering the plane due east and parallel with Colorado's Rocky Mountains. Both men had experienced this type of landing before, but touching down with the plane almost positioned sideways to the runway wasn't meant as an experience for the first-time traveler. The pilot slammed the right wing down hard after the left wheels touched pavement. Some passengers began applauding when they finally sensed all was well.

As Tommy and Danny headed up the escalator to baggage claim, Tommy spied two army enlisted men – one was holding a sign that read Tommy Withers. Tommy noted, though, that the two men had more stripes on their uniform than he or Danny had. They approached their counterparts and saluted.

"Gentlemen, welcome to the West. I hope you're both ready for some horseback riding." Tommy and Danny both nodded their agreement. Tommy was curious, however, as he also noted that the older of the two soldiers seemed to be his and Danny's age or perhaps even older. Tommy stopped at the men's room and said, "We need to hit the bathroom before we start traveling."

The older soldier nodded, and he and his partner remained outside to wait.

"Something's off. The one guy is as old as you or me, Danny. Be on your toes!"

Tommy and Danny grabbed their duffel bags and in fifteen minutes were bouncing around in an Army vehicle, heading for I-25 and north to Wyoming. Nearly two hours later, already in Wyoming, the senior enlisted man sitting in the front passenger seat undid his seatbelt and turned directly toward the rear seats. Tommy began slowly reaching for his 38mm weapon in his ankle holster.

"Okay, what are you two bozos really up to?" Tommy didn't relax and replied, "Come again?"

The man began reaching behind him, but Tommy had his weapon pressed against his temple in a split second.

"Excuse me, but who the hell are you and why are you still an enlisted man? You're almost as old as I am. You've got five seconds to start talking, or I'm going to be in your lap!" Tommy shouted.

"Wait, let me get my wallet out and show you my ID."

"Do it damn slow!" Tommy warned, while Danny now had his weapon pointed at the back of the driver's head.

Tommy looked at the military ID – and the photo matched the man in the passenger seat, but not his rank. The man was actually General Glen Matthews, US Army. Tommy wanted to say, "You asshole" but bit his tongue instead.

"Sir, it's a pleasure. My name is Tommy, and my friend who's now holstering his weapon is Danny. We're honored to be of service to you."

"Okay, you two, let's stop this bullshit right now! Our driver is my aide. What's said in this car stays in this car, understood?"

"We're all in, no problem," Danny and Tommy said virtually at the same time.

"Good!"

The next hour of conversation was jaw-dropping.

"Danny, I talked with your brother, Charles, last night. He sends his regards and wanted me to tell both of you that everything's under control with Dr. Becker. They haven't found Marty yet, but Charles and his fellow ex-Rangers are confident that things will soon break their way.

"And yes, I'm a Ranger. Your brother and I went through basic training together, and after that, Ranger training. Son, it truly is a small world." Danny turned to Tommy, and sure enough his mouth was also wide open in amazement.

"Do the riots in the Portland area have anything to do with what your unit is preparing for?" Danny asked.

"Son, this is off the record, but yes, they most certainly do!" Tommy finally was able to gather his wits and joined in with a barrage of questions.

"We know about Operation Withers or Project Withers, whatever you choose to call it. Are you saying our government is going to begin a military action against its own citizens in the contiguous forty-eight states?" Tommy questioned of the general.

"Just call it Withers. The program began during the Bush administration. We observed how important a cavalry force was in Afghanistan. The Special Forces unit that was situated there suffered no losses, but the horse fatalities were staggering. The elder Bush oversaw the Star Wars program in the '80s during the Reagan years, while his son, George W. was the one who asked for a program to decrease the morbidity levels on the equine side of the equation. Then all of a sudden, the two of you start sniffing around one of our research operatives who was heavily involved in the program. Unfortunately, you were about to shed light on some very dark special ops," the general explained.

"All the officials at the DIA were expecting our first actions as a unit to take place in the eastern United States. The Pennsylvania militia has 10,000 plus soldiers. If they were to decide to attack DC and our government, they could capture and take over the Capitol in one day without breaking a sweat. The number of right-leaning militias has exploded in this country! There are more than three hundred militias, countrywide. The number has tripled over the past two decades!

"The progressive or left-leaning folks have also formed militias. The leftist militias, with funding help from at least one and maybe more progressive billionaires, have suddenly become very active. It's no secret that the last presidential election emboldened those on the left. Their organization's tentacles have spread up and down the Pacific coast, and into Arizona and New Mexico. Not only are they rioting in urban streets, they crossed the line when they raided one of our munitions facilities! Thank God they didn't get their hands on some surface-to-air missiles! But what they stole is still considered a helluva lot of munitions! And yes, we believe they're responsible for the disappearance of Dr. Becker's wife. She has become another in a long list of wealthy individuals who have been kidnapped.

"The same day she went missing, one of our operatives, a Ranger, also went missing. We had three of our men embedded in the Portland Antifa militia – and he was one of them. We pulled our other two guys out of the fray after he disappeared. I'm guessing we're getting too close to their inner circle of leaders. So far, their top echelon can't be penetrated, and it's frustrating that we've been unable to accomplish that task."

When I heard the two of you were being assigned to our unit, I said to myself, if anyone can extract the information from their underlings, it would be you two CIA guys. So, I ask the both of you – are you up to the task? I need to know, because we begin deploying tonight."

This time it wasn't Tommy who answered.

"You bet your ass, General; we're more than ready!" Danny stated.

Tommy was deep in thought, concerned about Marty, and said a silent prayer to the Lord. His was a simple request, asking that she be allowed to live.

Charles drove a circuitous route as the Find Friends app on my phone directed us closer and closer to Marty's phone. I prayed that she would also be there alive!

"Looks like this small warehouse is where your wife's iPhone is. Doc, I don't want to raise your hopes. Her phone is inside, but I'm almost 100 percent convinced no one's home." We sat in the car for what seemed an eternity. My patience quotient was quickly approaching zero.

"Come on Charles, let's go check the doors! I've got to do something. I can't just sit here any longer!"

"Doc, see that guy standing by the doorway? He's a friendly. Right now he's scanning rooftops for enemies. There's another one of our guys on the other side of the building doing the same thing. They're looking for the least conspicuous method of entry and egress, while at the same time checking for a security system. If there is a security system, hopefully it will be connected to a regular phone landline instead of to a wireless system. If it is a landline, our guys will interrupt the phone connection, but we'll still have electricity once inside. If not, they'll disable the power to the building, and we'll have our access that way."

None of what Charles had just said calmed my nerves very much.

"Doc, do you happen to have any spare Valium in your pocket that you can take? I totally understand your angst, but you have to let us do our work! From this point forward, the word of the day is—TRUST!"

I took several deep breaths, silently willing myself to relax. I looked at Charles and could have sworn he was praying; for what, only God knew. I later found out that he was indeed praying – for an old- fashioned alarm system with a landline connection. Charles pointed out to me that the older landlines are more difficult to booby-trap – and safer for all of us.

All of a sudden, the Ranger directly in our sight held up his arm, pointing with one finger toward the sky.

"Alright, alright, alright!" Charles stated exuberantly. I couldn't help myself. I snickered under my breath, telling Charles "That sounded like a great Matthew McConaughey imitation. So, your guy just signaled some good news to you?" I asked.

"You betcha! Their alarm system is really antique. They must be cheap-ass anarchists, skimping on their security." In another five minutes, Charles turned to me and said, "Let's go."

The next thing I knew, we were running full speed across the street, and within a few seconds were inside the building. There were five ex-Rangers; I rounded the group up to six. Charles and I huddled in the entranceway while the other Rangers spread out, military style, throughout the first floor. Every communication between the men was by hand signal, because there was still another floor yet to be surveilled, and silence was necessary. Waiting was extremely difficult for me – and my impatience was palpable. Charles could tell and took tight hold of my wrist. I couldn't have broken free even if I wanted to. His vise-like grip was turning my fingers purple. Finally, a shout resonated from the second floor.

"CLEAR!"

I remained frozen in place, not even aware that I was holding my breath. Questions were swirling through my mind. What did clear mean? Did it mean that there were no bad guys? Was Marty in the building, injured, or even worse ... dead? Had they found her phone?

Charles finally let go of my wrist and in a no-nonsense voice told me to "Stay." Like my golden retrievers always do when commanded in a similar manner and tone, I slumped to the ground. Finally, Charles called down to me from the second floor. "Dr. Becker, come on upstairs." I could tell from his voice that everything was okay but not perfect.

When I arrived on the second floor and neared Charles, I could see he was holding Marty's phone. Next to him though, on the floor, were her clothes. I began seething inside. If those bastards raped my wife, I'll kill every last one of them, so help me God!

Charles interrupted my thoughts. "Doc, she's good, real good! I'm assuming they had her tied up, but somehow she managed to wedge her cellphone down deep between the cushions of the couch. I mean, it was buried! Give me your wife's passcode so I can unlock the phone."

After checking the phone for nearly a minute he handed it to me, asking if I recognized any of the numbers shown in her recent calls. The only one I recognized was mine, and that call was over a day ago. No other calls had been made.

Charles tapped on the photos icon, scrolling through them and began forwarding pictures Marty had taken since her arrival in Portland to someone. I watched Charles's men, who were harvesting fingerprints and collecting items that could be analyzed for DNA signatures, which hopefully would match a set of fingerprints on file. Suddenly it hit me. I was standing in the middle of a real life NCIS investigation conducted by former Army Rangers.

Every item that had been fingerprinted was cleaned up and put back in its place. I was impressed by how fastidiously the Rangers had marked every location and what had been in that particular spot. No detail was left to chance. One of the Rangers had taken digital photographs with his phone to make sure that every coffee cup and glass would be put back in the right position. I went to pick up Marty's cellphone, quickly realizing there was a charging pack attached to it.

"Put it down, Doc. I'll take the quick-charge pack off her phone in a few more minutes," Charles advised me.

What the hell are they doing? I said to myself. I just wanted to hold Marty's phone. It was like Charles knew I was questioning his motives, as out of the blue, he answered my unspoken question.

"Doc, we're about ready to get out of here. We've left everything the way it was when we entered. That includes Marty's belongings. I know you're wondering why, but we've been here long enough. Just hang tough—I'll explain it to you in a few minutes."

Turning to his team, Charles urged them to hurry. "Come on, guys, it's time to close up shop! Thanks for your hard work—as always, you did a great job—and you all know what to do with our harvest! So if nothing else urgent comes up in the next 24 hours, we'll meet tomorrow at 20:00 hours and zero minutes and go over our findings."

We left the same way we had come in, once again running at a fast pace to the car. When I finally sat down in the passenger's seat, I was winded and totally out of breath. Silently, I reminded myself that I was too old for this shit!

Charles turned directly to me. "Doc, the next call you get from the kidnappers, I'm sure they'll ask where you are in your traveling. I want you to hang up on them. Don't worry, they'll call back. Remember—TRUST! When they call back, you demand to talk with Marty personally...just like before. But this time you will stress the demand to speak to your wife on her cellphone, or the deal is off!"

The light bulb in my brain turned from dim to bright. Who are these guys? I wondered.. They aren't the FBI, but they sure act like it The day had been grueling but was coming to an end. I was exhausted. I'll ask that question again tomorrow and try to figure out the answer, I promised myself.

 HAPTER 27

We arrived back to where my rental car was parked. I turned to Charles, asking, "Your car or mine?"

"Yours," he said.

"I take it that you're bunking with me tonight?" was my next question, as we headed back to Lauren's house, which was now minus Lauren.

"Until Marty is free, consider me your shadow," Charles responded.

Torn from the emotions of the day and from what I had learned over the past few days about the "revolt" in Portland, I blurted out to Charles, "I know it's an understatement to say our country is divided!" I wanted some form of comfort and reassurance but was flashing back to an earlier conversation with Tommy. I didn't want to accept his conclusions about the anarchists – I wanted what I had believed in all my life – the American Way. To me, this meant hope and positivity. My brain was clamoring to find the words to say all that.

"Doc, don't beat yourself up. I understand what you're trying to say. This state of affairs didn't happen overnight. Almost a decade ago, our army began to plan for urban warfare. The Department of Defense produced a video derived from what our military learned during the Iraq War. The video was designed to preview future battles, chaos, and yes, warfare, in our megacities."

Charles paused to let me think about this.

"The army has already built urban facilities—fake cities, if you will—where urban warfare is practiced on a daily basis. They're preparing American soldiers to do battle against their fellow Americans in some of the largest cities in the country. Doc, all of us Rangers and other members of the Special Forces are constantly wrestling with these concepts. We don't have any doubts about what is right. We've been trained to preserve this country and to uphold the Constitution. We are disciplined to never doubt what our mission is as Rangers. We are truly blessed to live in a country that gives its citizens the freedoms we have. Unfortunately, there are those less-than-patriotic individuals who are trying to destroy what our forefathers constructed. They must not be allowed to succeed. They must be defeated."

"So who is it that our country is about to go to war with? Who's creating the turmoil and the revolutionary momentum?" I asked.

"Doc, I'm not certain I can answer your question 100 percent. But I'm going to throw out some different analogies for you – that might help you get a better grasp of what's happening.

"First, you've got the worker bees. I'll call this group the anarchists. They're tools – and they're society's losers. The leaders tell them to go protest here or there, set some fires, break some windows ... you get my drift. Perhaps they'll do some looting and everyone's happy. They're paid good money for a few moments of chaos, and if they're lucky, they can boost their resume with another overnight stay in jail. The best of them have criminal records and have spent jail time in all fifty states. Wherever there's turmoil and dissent, it's a fair assumption that somewhere in the scheme of things, they're going to be there."

Charles continued to the next layer. "Now, the drone workers have more responsibility. These are the folks who maintain the infrastructure of the organization. They implement the doctrine, the plan that keeps the group focused on the end goal. And that is to overthrow capitalistic entities like Wall Street and corporate America, which they consider to be aligned with the 'dark side.' In their mind, these long-time symbols of America have to be repudiated and replaced. The drones are the middle managers and they make sure the anarchists bring home the nectar from the fruits of their labor."

It was time for Charles to explain the top layer of the anarchy structure. "And of course, overseeing the entire group is the Queen Bee, or in this instance, what is considered the Troika. This Troika is similar to the Castro brothers and Che Guevara in Cuba. We Rangers—hell, for that matter, all those soldiers attached to Special Forces intelligence—have insider sources on the Left Coast and a couple other heavily populated Latino states. Those in the Troika are directing the group-think and their so-called Revolutionary Movement. And Doc, trust me, I'm not trying to treat your question as inconsequential."

"But you haven't answered it, either!" I replied in frustration. A sideways glance told me that frustration was also surfacing within Charles. But I wasn't a Millennial and wasn't about to drink the Kool-Aid; I wanted answers.

"So much for my analogies," Charles said somewhat sardonically. "They're not Asian or Blacks. For the most part, those two ethnic groups are sitting this one out. This group of revolutionaries is made up predominantly of Caucasians and Hispanics.

"Doc, have you ever heard of the group known as MS-13? This is a group of El Salvadorans who began immigrating to the US in the latter part of the 20th century. They were migrating here slowly at first, and then multiplying exponentially during the past seventeen years thanks to our open borders. They're a big part of this new revolutionary front. These folks can operate in any social environment. They make money selling addictive drugs to our citizens and have no sense of remorse. The inner cities on the East and West Coasts are their primary havens – but don't let that fool you. They're in every state. Furthermore, they compete against organized Black gangs, mainly the Bloods and Crips."

"And for God's sake, don't be confused by the Black Bloc protestors. These folks are not to be mistaken for the Black Lives Matter group. The Black Bloc members dress in all black and wear black ski masks to hide their identities. The mainstream media calls them Antifa, short for anti-fascist. The group here in Portland is named Rose City Antifa and dates back to 2007. They're nothing more than the antithesis of far-right wing entities. Take a look at their webpage sometime. Hell, maybe you'll agree with some of their doctrines. Besides, you can get a cool hoodie from their online store. Make no mistake, Doc – they're anarchists and they're socialists. It's fascinating that they're so well financed. We're not talking just black Levi's jeans and jackets. These people dress GQ!"

Charles wasn't yet done with the dissertation.

"And finally, ask yourself this one relevant question, because it relates to everything we human beings rely on and that's money. How, where, and most importantly what, is the direction for the flow of money with these revolutionaries? It's quite obvious there's one billionaire or perhaps more, who are linked to this multi-state revolutionary cause. The overarching agenda is open borders with a socialistic Utopian one-world philosophy!

"Our intelligence has fallen short of being able to identify their upper-echelon leaders. There's no doubt that these folks are philosophically socialists/communists. They're a hodgepodge of Hispanics who came to the states from many Latin American countries and Caucasians from many of the fifty states. We do know they're primarily Millennials.

"So there you have it, Doc; the group's structure is a mixture of brains and brawn, and ethnicities. It's the same lethal combination of the Third Reich that dominated the first half of the 20th century. These are the same folks who have the gall to call our country's leader, as well as people like myself, Nazis and fascists!"

"Any more questions, or have I scared the shit out of you?"

Just then my cell phone rang, causing me to jump in my seat.

# CHAPTER 28

Late in 2008, the CEO of Trinity Industries, Inc. and the president of its subsidiary, Trinity Rail Products, were visited by a general from the Department of Defense. The general, dressed in civvies, had a morning appointment with both men at Trinity's home office in Dallas. The folder placed on the CEO's desk was clearly stamped "Top Secret – Property of the US Government." For two hours, the three men discussed the design and manufacture of rail cars that could carry quarter horses and donkeys. The last time the rail industry transported large quantities of livestock in America was in the mid-20th century. In the past, horses transported in rail cars were loosely lined up, head to tail. For the DOD's needs, though, that was no longer acceptable.

The DOD wanted approximately 200 new livestock freight cars built, each able to transport eight to twelve horses or donkeys. The new cars were to be equipped with padded stalls that had a divided feed and water trough for each animal – and they were required to have climate control. There also had to be room in each car for every horse's rider and valet that would accompany their respective steed. There would be no skimping – period.

The Pentagon's bottom line was that if these animals and the men or women accompanying them in the rail cars were possibly going to make the ultimate sacrifice for their country, then no expense would be spared for their comfort.

∩ ∩ ∩

Both Tommy and Danny got some well-earned shut-eye during the last hour of their ride to the base before hearing, "We're home, gentlemen."

Tommy glanced at his GPS locator and silently said to himself, "Thermopolis, Wyoming?"

"Guys, your horses haven't been loaded on the freight car yet, so I suggest you go familiarize yourself with them. I'm sure they'd like to get to know who they're going to throw off sometime or somewhere along the trail!" The general couldn't help laughing at the thought.

"Here are some mints to help the two of you win them over. You each have your own valet, and they are already at the corral waiting for you. I suggest mounting up and riding a few circles to get used to their gait. Make sure the saddles are comfortable, and please don't forget to adjust the stirrups to the right length for you. These next few days are going to be long, and the last thing I need is having someone with leg cramps because the stirrups are too short. I also need you both to give me your height and weight measurements, along with pant waist size and length so we can get clothing and other gear selected and loaded into the rail car."

It took a couple of minutes for the walk to the corral. Once there, Tommy pulled up short and stared.

"What's wrong?" Danny asked quizzically.

"Danny, you're not going to believe this, but these two horses, even though they're quarter horses, are nearly identical in every way to the thoroughbreds that raced in April! These horses look just like Nidalas and Towers Above, only smaller!"

"That's crazy, Tommy," Danny replied.

"Is it, Danny? You never had a chance to see Nidalas up close, so hear me out. A few seconds ago, I would have agreed with you, until I remembered what Mark told us. Remember, Mark was the one screwing around with genetic engineering and in fact told us that Nidalas had been genetically altered. Towers Above was the control animal in his work!"

The two finally entered the corral to meet and ride their horses, as the valets steadied the animals so they could be mounted.

Tommy turned and asked the valet, "What is this beautiful animal's name?"

Jeff answered, "His name is Calypso, and the other horse is Chief. They're truly our best quarter horses, but I have to admit, I'm biased. Calypso is barely a three-year-old, while Chief is two and a half."

Tommy liked that. Without prompting, Jeff had anticipated his next question. He wondered if Jeff was more than a valet and also more than a private in rank. There might be more than meets the eye with Jeff, Tommy mused.

Danny had already made three trips around the perimeter of the corral on Chief and seemed quite at ease in the saddle. "Damn, you look like a veteran cowboy," Tommy shouted. With a slight kick to Calypso's sides, Tommy and his horse were quickly off—heading straight toward the corral fence line. Tommy knew what was going to happen next and was in no mood to do his best Superman imitation. He pulled hard on the reins, but to no avail. Finally, just two yards short of the black fence, Calypso took a hard left turn, changing pace to a slow canter around the corral.

"Dammit, Jeff, you put me on a juvenile delinquent!"

Tommy stood, again pulling hard on the reins. It was time that he and Calypso had a heart-to-heart talk. The horse stopped and Tommy dismounted with both reins still in his hands, heading to the front of the horse. Calypso and Tommy were now face to face. Tommy tightened the reins even more.

"You aren't the boss, and you never will be! The sooner you understand that, the better off we'll both be! You have a choice, damn it! Starting right now! DO YOU UNDERSTAND ME?" he shouted, while giving the reins a sharp tug downward.

Danny, Chief, Jeff, and the other valet, Pete, all stood frozen in place. A silence had descended on the corral. It was as if there was only one conversation taking place throughout the entire world. Everyone was waiting for Calypso's answer.

It took about fifteen seconds. "Harrumph," Calypso snorted through his nostrils. Tommy saw that the animal understood. He reached into his pocket and pulled out the mints, holding them in his hand for Calypso.

From that point, horse and rider performed as a team.

CHAPTER 29

The first of three freight trains were almost fully loaded and ready for travel. Each train had three 6,000 horsepower GM diesel-electric locomotives in the lead. The two remaining trains sat on side spurs, awaiting the loading of their livestock and passengers.

"Get down to the corral and fetch our guests; their train is about to load and they need time to settle in. Bring them here first, though. I have some papers for them," General Matthews requested of his aide.

Tommy and Danny had already dismounted their steeds and were deep in conversation.

"I'm betting our two valets are DIA operatives! You saw how my guy offered up information without my even having to ask. I'm also betting they're here to keep an eye on us and report back to Washington, just like we're doing," Tommy said to Danny.

"I don't disagree with you. So how long do we let the charade go on before we clear the air?" Danny asked. "Let's wait until we board, get the horses buttoned down, and the train is underway," Tommy answered.

"There's no way my eyes are closing until we know who these guys really are. I'll signal you when to move."

"It looks like the general is ready for us – his aide is waiting for us at the gate," Tommy said.

The general's office was in a one-story ranch house converted into a military residence. When Tommy and Danny entered, General Matthews was in the kitchen making coffee.

"Coffee?" he offered. Both men nodded, saying at the same time, "Black please."

The general began to speak. "Our Special Forces have trained for years, knowing the likelihood that this type of battle was inevitable. In my hand are papers that contain the most current information about the who, where, and how of the operation we're about to embark on. The what is still the unknown factor. Our intelligence is sparse concerning the number of enemy fighters and their specific locations. We assume some of their armament is contraband, stolen during the break-in and skirmish at the munitions factory. We've inventoried what they didn't steal and know exactly what is in their possession from that heist. It's assumed they have additional weapons, but we don't know what kind. With today's technology, I should already have all this information, but I don't. It also means our foes have excellent technological capabilities.

"This will most likely be my final military assignment. I'm the top dog and leading my men into battle against fellow Americans. Like the B-29's most famous World War II pilot, Paul Tibbets, who was responsible for unleashing the first A-Bomb, and Neil Armstrong, the first man to walk on the moon, I'll be hounded unmercifully by the media in the future years.

"These papers are not only for you to understand what's about to take place; they're also for posterity. Considering how our country's various intelligence agencies operate, these documents are all about the truth – and it's up to the two of you to make certain that the real story gets told. If there is still a United States of America left after this battle is complete, I want to preserve the honor of my men. This despicable act will forever bear my name, in shame, just like General Custer's fiasco. It's a sad day indeed when America has to declare war on fellow Americans!"

The general was hedging his bets. There was a long pause as he appeared to stare into nowhere, before he suddenly focused again.

"Your gear is already loaded onto the freight car. Good hunting, gentlemen. It has been an honor to work with you, even if our time together has been short!" The general reversed rank, snapping to attention and saluting Tommy and Danny. The two also snapped to attention, returning a demonstration of their respect back to the general.

As they left the office, Tommy said, "Danny, if there ever was a true patriot in your life, it is now!" Both men were led to the freight car where they joined their valets, horses, and six donkeys – creatures that at first glance, physically looked to Tommy like zebras without stripes. "Jesus, Danny, those donkeys have been taking too much testosterone." Both men began laughing when Tommy suddenly remembered that the donkeys had also been genetically messed with. His laughter stopped.

Tommy and Danny found a quiet corner in the freight car where Tommy began reading the papers from the general, before passing each page on for Danny to read.

There was a letter too.

∩ ∩ ∩

Gentlemen,

I too have connections in Washington! Tommy, your exploits in April of 2016, at the racetrack in southeastern

Kentucky, were exemplary. And Danny, the same goes for you and the work you did in ensuring the downing of that plane before it reached the "Shoe" on Ohio State's campus. I also know your brother, Charles, and have worked with him on some interesting projects. Tommy, I was watching your eyes when we arrived in Thermopolis. You need to bring Langley up to speed as to our base's GPS location. Yes, there is another ranch in Wyoming with significant acreage that mirrors our location here. Sorry for the fake-out! It's too important to keep our location top-secret. The citizens of Thermopolis constantly speculate if we're "Government," but none of the troops are ever in uniform, even in town! Citizens believe we're just one huge working quarter-horse farm. We also have a cattle operation that you didn't see.

All the trains will head south on the Burlington Northern Santa Fe track. When the trains reach Cheyenne, they'll switch engines. There, the trains will commence travel on Union Pacific track, with Union Pacific diesel engines for the duration of the trip. The engineers are not railroad employees. They're Rangers who've been trained by corporate railroad folks. From Cheyenne, all three trains will head west. You'll be passing through these urban areas in the order below:

1. Ogden, Utah
2. Pocatello, Idaho
3. Hinkle, Oregon

Once past Hinkle, you're almost at the drop-off point. Forty miles east of Portland is Bonneville, Oregon. The only thing there worth talking about is a huge dam built in the 1930s under the auspices of Roosevelt's Works Progress Administration. Everyone disembarks there. All Special Forces will take a chow break and let the horses get their land legs back. From there, you'll head into the Mt. Hood Wilderness. You can't miss Mt. Hood – it stands 11,239 feet high. Southwest of the summit's peak is Government Camp on Highway 26. It's also north and slightly east of Tom, Dick, and Harry Mountains. Stop laughing and YES, I'm serious! This will be the entire unit's home base camp. The bad guys are somewhere in this wilderness, dug in very deep!

The writing continued:

Intelligence folks think the enemy has been digging tunnels and building hideouts in different locations over the past several years. The park rangers finally found their archived photos from the past five years. However, they can't find the previous five years of pictures. The photographs show supposed park-ranger work crews entering the wilderness with tunneling tools and treated lumber that appeared to be structural in nature. However, there were no orders for the materials or any projects requiring this type of lumber to be used for trail maintenance through the Parks Department. Our best guess is that the lumber was utilized to reinforce tunnels. The fake workers appeared to know where the trail cameras were positioned, and each time, successfully shielded their faces from any chance of identification. Night time photos were useless because the Parks Department photography equipment is so antiquated.

I've enclosed topography maps of the Mt. Hood wilderness as well as its hiking and horse trails. The weather conditions are currently fall-like, but weather there can change in a heartbeat. The Air Force has been flying infrared and photo surveillance drones for a month. Other than verified Parks workers and wildlife, nothing has shown up though. The Army Corps of Engineers even set up additional sophisticated earthquake sensors throughout the park. So far, nothing major has registered on their sensors. However, there have been several mini quakes, detectable only by seismic equipment.

Intel also believes that the enemy—I'll call them revolutionary moles—are hunkered down and hibernating for the winter. They must have plentiful supplies and are living comfortably in a 55-degree Fahrenheit environment! There has been NO direct link between Portland's rash of kidnappings and the moles, but that doesn't mean one doesn't exist! And yes, Tommy, I'm aware of the current situation with your friend's wife who is missing and presumed to be the latest kidnapping victim.

Command communications will be via the Blackphone II. Intel is convinced the enemy is equipped with advanced electronic technology with capabilities that necessitates usage of the black phones. You each have one of these packed in your duffel bag, along with a user handbook. Familiarize yourselves with their apps and features. Finally, communicate with me only in an emergency!

Again, good hunting, Tommy and Danny!

With this letter, the general's bet was laid down!

# CHAPTER 30

Slumped against the wall of the freight car, Tommy let his mind begin to wander. The general is right! Eventually, somewhere in Mt. Hood's forest, there's going to be a historical marker embedded in the ground.

Maybe it'll say, "The first shot of the Second American Revolution was fired on …" and give the date. Maybe it'll be erected in a year, possibly in a decade … or perhaps never. It depends on the duration and outcome of this conflagration, Tommy thought.

Historians are going to tear General Matthews to shreds, along with the troops that obeyed his orders. History is going to lump me and Danny in with the Special Forces Cavalry Unit. No matter how hard our friends and family members fight to uphold our reputations and integrity, we'll always be an evil footnote in American history! All of these thoughts raced randomly through Tommy's mind.

To his sudden dismay, Tommy realized a tear had fallen from his right eye and was rolling down his cheek. Danny also saw the drop on Tommy's cheek, traveling along the creases in his face created by stress, many battles, and his recent plastic surgery. "Something in your eye?" Danny asked.

"Yeah. Must be an eyelash – it's been bothering me all day," Tommy replied, quickly rubbing away other tears threatening to spill forth.

"Penny for your thoughts," Danny said, knowing full well that if Tommy even answered, it would be bullshit.

Tommy knew that every option short of battle had been exhausted, but he wasn't about to share his thoughts aloud. That didn't stop him from thinking, though. When the enemy ... whoever they are, attacked a National Guard Armory and killed a dozen reservists, a fail-safe line was crossed. No weapons of mass destruction were stolen, but the shear nerve and violation of law demanded a government action, he thought.

What Tommy hadn't been told by the general was that the total amount of explosives stolen was equal to that of a MOAB or "Mother of All Bombs." At least eleven tons of TNT was probably now hidden somewhere in the Portland/Mt. Hood wilderness – hopefully nowhere near a ground fault in the dormant volcano, which had last erupted in 1790.

Danny knew all about Tommy's dark moments. He had his share of such experiences with Tommy during their active-duty Ranger years. Pulling out his pen, Danny wrote a message on the back side of one of the general's notes before handing all of them back to Tommy. Danny pointed at what he'd just written. "How soon do we get rid of our 'garbage'? I need to get in position," it read.

Tommy had been so engrossed in his self-pity that he'd totally forgotten the valets were on board, too. Tommy retrieved his mobile phone and tapped the screen, looking for and finding the phone's GPS app.

"We're almost due north of Shoshoni, Wyoming, not that it makes any difference. We're traveling through prairie country, Danny. There's nothing out there but antelope, coyotes, and rattlesnakes, and luckily for them, the snakes are in hibernation. I have a plan – but we need to distract both guys enough so that they can't put up any resistance when we go on the attack. Above all, we need their weapons and phones. Don't let yourself get between me and them. I don't need you to become a hostage," Tommy said with a touch of worry in his voice.

"They're standing over there by the loading door, and Calypso is the horse closest to them. I'm gonna grab some alfalfa from the feed bin and put it in his trough. I'll ask Jeff to come over and look at Calypso's shoe on the left back hoof. Hopefully Pete stays put. I'll take care of Jeff and you can draw down on Pete. Whatever you do, Danny, don't get between them and me!"

Tommy made his way to the opposite side of the freight car and eased alongside Calypso's enclosure. He reached into his pocket and pulled out a mint, unwrapped it, and watched Calypso's ears rise to attention. "Yep, you smelled it, didn't you? Okay, hang on while I get you some feed," Tommy said, hoping that what he was doing with the feed would physically separate Jeff and Pete. It succeeded.

"sir, I'll get the feed, that's my job. Let me help," Jeff said.

Tommy stepped back, allowing just enough room for Jeff to slip by him and grab some alfalfa. Tommy made his move and as Jeff turned back to Calypso's trough, he found himself looking down the barrel of Tommy's revolver. In the meantime, Danny had slowly made his way to the other side of the railroad car and as Tommy corralled Jeff, Danny surprised Pete, who, at that moment, was reaching inside his coat.

"Gentlemen, we sort of have ourselves a stand-off, huh?" Tommy said pointedly. "I'm betting both of you are armed, so we're going to move real slow now." Danny had seen this routine before and fake-coughed a couple times to squelch his laughter.

"It's time for someone to get naked!" Danny mumbled silently, turning his head slightly.

"I want both of you to take all your clothes off – every stitch – but you're going to do it one at a time. Jeff, you go first, and it better be slow." It took close to five minutes for both men to get butt-naked. "Danny, would you take a photo of these fine men standing together in their birthday suits with their ankle holsters and guns still attached to their legs."

"Yeeh-haw! Don't they look stunning?" Danny asked with a drawl as he snapped a photo with his mobile phone. "Okay, now get down on your stomachs and extend your arms straight forward. I swear to God if you make any funny move, any twitch, I'll shoot your asses right now," Tommy promised. Danny disarmed the prisoners and gathered their clothes, one set of clothing at a time.

"Danny, I expected more weapons than these two pea shooters, didn't you? Go through their clothes, and check for more guns." Quickly, an additional two automatics fell to the wood floor. The guns had been hidden in rear waistband pouches of both men's trousers. That clinched it for Tommy.

"Danny, I don't believe these trousers are standard government issue. This is some fancy custom tailoring. Oh hell, I'll ask anyway. Are both of you working for the DIA?" The only sound piercing the air was the train wheels clacking along the steel tracks. Danny inventoried the booty and put it in a pile. Going to the loading door, Danny unlatched and opened it. The early winter air permeated the train's interior. The horses began to snort their displeasure, followed immediately with objections from the donkeys, which also didn't care for the suddenly cold temperature.

"Gentlemen, it's almost time to jump. I know you're aware

there's a third train following ours. Hopefully they'll stop for you – but honestly, I doubt it. These trains and their cargo are 'dark ops'! They don't exist and neither does the cargo they carry. Think about it. Do you really believe a train is going to stop for two naked cowboys running alongside the track, arms waving frantically? The good news is we're not totally cold-hearted. Your clothing will be tossed out a few seconds after you both jump – and oh, by the way, the temperature outside is 48°F. I suggest you both haul ass."

Danny carefully stepped away from the door, keeping a safe distance between him and the soon-to -be-exiting hostages. Tommy was now in charge, obviously relishing the impending moment when the two would-be assassins would make their exit from his and Danny's lives.

Tommy motioned them to the door. Jeff was the first jumper and he didn't hesitate. Now that's a true warrior, Tommy thought. Pete was another breed. "How about we talk? What do you want to know?" he asked as he approached the doorway.

Danny started to shake his head in amazement when suddenly, Pete too, was gone into the night. "God, Tommy sure does hate whiners," Danny muttered to himself. "Tommy, really? Did you have to have them strip and …?" Danny never got to finish the question.

Tommy whirled around and glared at Danny. "Partner, those two guys would have slit our throats if we didn't get to them first! The way I figure, one of them now has a broken leg and the other has a broken ego." Tommy reached into his pocket and pulled out his handkerchief, throwing it in Danny's direction. "If you want to shed a tear for them, be my guest. I'm not!"

Seven hundred yards ahead, a cluster of pronghorn antelope

were getting ready to bed down for the night when two duffel bags crashed into their space, each kicking up clouds of prairie dust. The antelope had no clue that in a few minutes there'd be two new animals in their midst to disrupt the night.

CHAPTER 31

Danté didn't usually involve himself with trivialities like the ongoing negotiations that his fellow revolutionaries performed during this latest kidnapping. Most of his time was spent underground, running other operations and keeping clear of any possible detection by law enforcement. However, this latest abduction had sucked him in for a very simple reason – thoroughbred racing was one of his favorite pastimes. He'd followed Towers Above's journey as a three-year-old and wished he could have attended all three of the horse's Triple Crown races. When word reached him that Marty Becker had been snatched, it was a no-brainer to get involved – and because of who her husband was, Danté ordered the ransom to be reduced to a mere $1 million in gold bullion.

He was a big dreamer and had no intention of allowing Marty to be released. What he wanted was for Dr. Becker to take the bait … and then join his wife as a hostage. In reality, Danté was upping the ante because he had a bigger pay-off in mind – he wanted Towers Above for himself and would settle for nothing less.

Portland's Antifa members, along with other groups in the brotherhood situated along the West Coast, were ready to advance their agenda. They were primed to move on to the next level, and eager to have events in place that would soon trigger the start of the final conflagration—and America's second revolutionary war.

The Great Recession in America and other countries around the world in 2008 and 2009 convinced Danté that Americans, especially the Millennials, were ripe for change. He felt sure that they were now more receptive to the ideology of socialism and would be willing to embrace it.

∩ ∩ ∩

Danté Perez and his best friend, Javier Morales, spent their entire lives training for this moment. Both men were revolutionaries in the most basic sense. Even though they were Cuban-born and educated, each man knew that the revolution in their country had morphed like an aged vintage wine. Outwardly, it might still look good to Cuban revolutionaries, but its taste had soured and was bitter.

With the relaxed border and immigration laws that were in place during the previous administrations, both men easily crossed into America in early 2010, and headed to the Northwest. They had considered California, but opted instead for Portland, Oregon because it was an area with a long socialist history.

Both men immediately embroiled themselves with fellow dissenters – like-minded brothers and sisters who regularly participated in local revolutionary activities. Danté began writing socialist propaganda and was an active participant in local anti-capitalist protests. As he was skilled in writing software code and in computer illustration, he redesigned several webpages for the group. He constantly badgered Portland's newspaper, The Oregonian, with letters to the editor promoting the group's socialistic agenda.

Javier was equally skilled, but the propaganda/philosophical side of socialism didn't interest him much. He was more hands-on and believed that every anti-capitalist revolution needed an enforcement factor when converting doubters into disciples. ISIS was the modern-day embodiment of physical and mental intimidation, and it was readily displayed in the Middle East. Javier knew that similar Sharia-type tactics would have to be employed by Antifa to convert reluctant American citizens over to socialism. And if that didn't work—well then, they would just have to die.

He knew inherently that at least two-thirds of the Baby Boomers would resist conversion. "How ironic would that be?" he wondered aloud. "Our motto is to RESIST, but the resistance to our socialist agenda will most likely come from a large percentage of the senior population because they're enamored of capitalistic principles. And they're the ones who are armed to the teeth!" Javier had gone so far as to pick out several remote sites in the state between Portland and Salem that would be perfect for mass graves for these Boomers.

Thinking back to the past few years, Javier recalled how he and Danté had each advanced higher in the hierarchy of Oregon's socialist organizations. Those individuals who had objected to their advancement were mysteriously eliminated by Javier.

Danté hadn't shared his plans for Marty Becker with Javier – he wanted to see that through to completion before Operation Lex-Con started. What he didn't realize, though, was that by delaying the beginning of hostilities, he was giving the government—and more specifically, the "cavalry" unit—a much needed advantage.

It had been a couple of months since Danté's men had raided the army munitions facility. Everything that had been stolen was now safe and secure in storage, and it appeared that the government's search of the acres and acres of wilderness lands around

Mt. Hood was finally over. Since the end of autumn was nearing, he knew winter wasn't the time to start a revolution, Danté had no hesitation in devoting another week for his quest to get Towers Above. Once he had the champion steed, he'd let Javier tidy up any loose ends.

The Lexington-Concord American Revolutionary battle of the late 1700s would soon have an addendum in the history books. Now 250 years later, the Battle of Portland, Oregon was going to begin.

# HAPTER 32

Danté had a makeshift residence and office at the bottom of an old abandoned minerals mine. As he leaned back in the desk chair, Danté suddenly felt the chair begin to fall and quickly planted his right hand against the wall of the mineshaft to steady himself. An unexpected sensation of heat registered in his mind when his hand hit the wall.

"Damn, that's warmer than usual," he thought. After fully regaining his balance, he began to explore and touch the wall in different spots. He reached as high and wide as possible, wishing he had a tool handy to measure the temperature of the wall. He climbed up the rope ladder to the next level, continuing his exploration of the wall. The walls on the second level were still quite warm, but not as hot as the level below.

The warmth of the walls worried him as that had never happened before – and he knew Mt. Hood was a dormant volcano. It especially concerned him because over the past year, there had been a number of earthquake swarms in the Mt. Hood wilderness region that extended all the way west to Portland. In fact, the quaking traveled 50 miles in every direction.

Some of the explosive materials from the munitions factory raid were still stored on the floor he occupied, as well as on the level above him. Glancing at the temperature reading on the weather station, Danté saw it read 58°F – and that was a little high. The normal ambient temperature in the mine was generally around 55°F. Considering that the mine was almost 7,000 feet above sea level at its deepest point, and the outside temperature at this time of year dipped into the 30s, there was cause for alarm.

Danté was more than just slightly panicked. He sent one of the workmen to go fetch Javier, who was standing watch somewhere outside the entrance of the mine. Five minutes later, Javier had made his way down the ladder to Danté's office.

"Hey D, what's up, and why are you feeling up that wall?" Javier asked, unsuccessfully holding back a laugh. "Come here and feel this! I don't remember the wall ever being this warm. This isn't normal," Danté said, with obvious worry in his voice.

Javier walked over and began the same type of wall massage as Danté had thirty minutes earlier.

"This is not good, D, not good at all! It's going to be tough to move all this shit to our secondary site and still launch our assault in two weeks. Especially since people are starting to gather at their assigned rally points. If I was a betting man, I'd say this mountain is going to erupt, even though I'm not a geologist or seismologist. I'm not sure we even have one of those folks on our team, but let me put out the word. What's the weather forecast for the next ten days?"

"The last forecast I saw indicated a 50% chance of a significant early winter storm in about ten days. That could work for us, but first I need to be involved in the final negotiations with the Becker abduction."

Javier shot a look of astonishment at Danté. "Did I just hear you say abduction? What the hell is going on? C'mon, Danté, why are you so tapped into this particular kidnapping? You've always stayed at arm's length from this phase of our operations." Javier patiently waited for an honest answer.

"Here's the scoop. We have a good chance for a huge windfall with the Beckers. My end game is snatching the champion thoroughbred Towers Above. That horse will bring at least $50 million in ransom, and that amount of money will get us even more weapons. Look, we can't rely on the government being sloppy anymore when it comes to protecting their assets. All our attack did was to motivate them to increase the number of guards on duty, or even worse, move their munitions to more centralized bases. And I doubt our progressive billionaire benefactors are going to up how much they give to those channels that funnel funds to us so we can buy more weapons."

Javier mulled over what Danté said and couldn't disagree, especially since a good chunk of that $50 million would end up in his bank account.

"I'm down with that, but you better close the deal no later than four days from now! Our men have enough weapons and munitions for the first phase of battle – but we've got to get all the ordnance stored here out—right now! I want to start the move tomorrow night, and that includes everything in this old mine," Javier said emphatically.

"I hear you," Danté replied. "I'm going to head to town, and you can start the evacuation. I'll hook up with you when I'm done with the Beckers. Remember, all cellphones should be off— and make sure they're all metal barrier-bagged. You know there's going to be that one person with an open app and its location tracker working," Danté reminded Javier.

It was time to pack his laptop and the tactical papers relating to Antifa-Portland and their New Day revolution. As he sorted the important documents from those not so important, Danté couldn't help but reflect on his time in this mountain home.

∩ ∩ ∩

Danté could've taken credit for discovering the old mine, but it was Randy who actually led him on a hike to the mine area. It was late spring of 2011 when he and Randy took down the Do Not Enter and Danger signs placed at the entrance to the mine by park officials to protect people. He remembered Randy saying that he played in the mine when he was a youngster and it served as a refuge during his rebellious teen years. Unfortunately for his parents, Randy couldn't shake the anger and rage he felt when told, "Randy, You can't do that."

At eighteen years of age, Randy left home to begin his life's work as an anarchist. The pay wasn't great, but it put food on the table and a roof over his head. If ever there was someone who lived one day at a time, it was Randy. He was truly a psychotic individual and well-suited for the coming revolution. Unfortunately, he was currently serving time in the state prison for destruction of property during Portland's 2016 post-election Antifa riot.

∩ ∩ ∩

The original mine shaft extended some 50 feet down and had lateral tunnels of differing heights nearly every ten feet. It was a perfect hiding place. After exploring the mine in 2011, Danté and his fellow revolutionaries immediately began shoring up the roof of the mine along with the aging wall supports on the main floor. Over several months, their repair work extended deeper into the mine shaft. Each level had its own gas generator, which supplied electricity for lighting and other electronics on each floor. A hand-cranked elevator was fashioned to move supplies, weapons, and munitions from floor to floor. Cots were purchased and eventually the mine accommodated over 200 workers at any given time. Whatever was brought in or out was packed and carried, including bodily waste. It was primitive but functional.

Floor fans constantly circulated fresh air throughout the mine and the carbon monoxide by-products from burning fossil fuel were trapped and efficiently vented to the surface. It would be difficult for anyone to pick up a heat signature from any activity in the mine, and besides, volcanos are known to have natural steam venting from them.

The thing Danté was most proud of was the camouflaged opening at the entrance of the mine. A structure that looked like a huge boulder had been designed and fabricated by several revolutionaries in the group. These individuals had graphic and industrial design skills and experience. If anyone touched the boulder, it felt like volcanic rock, which wasn't too far off base. The boulder was manufactured from slurry of fine volcanic crushed rock and Sakrete cement. Volcanic-colored stain was then added to the slurry to replicate the color of the rocks indigenous to that mountain region. A series of pulleys, heavy rope, and cranks opened and closed the boulder door.

It was time to head to town. Now at the entrance of the abandoned mine, Danté gave the command to open the boulder to the outside. Lookouts gave the all-clear signal as the boulder slowly slid sideways just enough for Danté to pass through. He was on his way.

 **HAPTER 33**

Hardly anyone noticed the news story in the March 1 issue of The Oregonian.

The article reported on the construction of four new fire towers by the US Forest Service in the Mt. Hood wilderness. It was the type of story usually written by a neophyte journalist just out of college – the type of story used to fill space on the last page of the daily tabloid. Fire towers from the early 1900s up to the 1950s were normal fixtures within the forests of almost all national parks in America.

These particular towers were designed for a dual purpose. Installing the latest in seismic detection equipment in the towers was indeed factual and necessary. Scientists wanted to more closely study the correlation between quake storms and any possible link to the thinning of the magma dome, as well as any relationship leading to a volcanic event. And Mt. Hood was most certainly overdue for such a happening.

From the mid-20th century forward, the Forest Service's philosophy toward forest fires had been one of managing the fire, rather than aggressive control, negating the need for additional towers.

Until now.

Perhaps the Forest Service had never considered a possible duplicitous need for a fire tower/cell tower combination, but the Department of Defense sure had. These four new towers strategically placed on the grounds surrounding Mt. Hood would be manned with DOD agents dressed as park rangers. Their role was to protect the third-generation Stingray tracking units, also strategically situated atop the towers. The towers were set up in a broad square formation in hopes of picking up any electronic communications from the dissidents currently residing some-where in the forest. DOD intelligence knew they were out there but couldn't locate them.

∩ ∩ ∩

Danté traveled only in the deep of night when coming and going in the Mt. Hood wilderness, and always with two modes of communication. Being in the forest tonight with no cell service meant he'd have to use his satellite phone to talk with others.

Mateo answered the call but didn't speak. "Mateo, Danté here. I'm on my way to see you. We need to speed up transfer of the bullion. I'm moving up the time schedule on everything. Give Dr. Becker a call and tell him he's got less than 24 hours to get out here or he'll never see his wife again."

"Okay chief, but he's not cooperating … at all," Mateo replied.

Danté wasn't in the mood for excuses. He could sense that time was running out. "If we have to cash out on this one, then so be it," Danté replied in a huff, unwilling to compromise with Mateo. Again, there was silence. Mateo had been doing all the heavy lifting and if anyone had to do time for the kidnappings, he knew it'd be him and not Danté. The Becker ransom and what he intended to skim off the top would be his payoff – a well-deserved bonus for all his previous trouble and efforts.

Danté took the phone from his ear and looked at it quizzi-cally. Yep, he was still connected to Mateo. "Dammit, Mateo, do you understand me?"

Mateo understood and hit the end key on his phone.

It was a good thing he did because if there had been another verbal outburst from Danté – suffice it to say that the revolution would've been over before it had begun.

At the sound of hooves, Danté dropped to the ground and folded himself up into a tight ball of what he hoped was nothingness. He had unconsciously made himself into a giant mushroom on the pine needle carpet of the wilderness.

The procession of horsemen took about twenty minutes to pass by – with nobody noticing the rolled- up human being on the ground just a few feet away. Danté's legs were cramping, but he somehow maintained his stiff composure. The pain was intense, and after seeing the last rider go around the bend, he stood – immediately falling back to the ground as his legs buckled.

"Did you see that?" Tommy asked Danny, who was abreast of him on the mountain trail.

"See what? We're in the woods and it's dark," Danny responded laughingly.

"I'm serious! I saw something move, smartass," Tommy barked in response.

The men reined in their horses and both riders were now completely still on the path. Tommy pulled out a utility flashlight, slowly scanning the woods for any sign of movement. Danté kept his head down, knowing that if the light reflected off his eyes, his presence would be quickly revealed.

"It was probably a mountain lion or bobcat. C'mon, we're falling way behind the others!" Danny exclaimed. "Danny, it was a person! The hair on the back of my neck is tingling and you know what that means," Tommy quickly replied. "Mark the spot on your GPS app and we'll come back in the morning and do an extensive search with more men," Danny shot back.

Tommy opened the app on his phone and marked the location.

He realized, though, that Danny was right – now was not the time to explore, but his sense of danger was keener than ever. Tomorrow might be too late. Why they had deployed without night-vision goggles was a nagging question that would remain unanswered. Tommy tugged on the reins to get Calypso turned back to the forward position, nudging him onward.

Danté remained in position for another ten minutes, making sure no one else was on the trail. Now able to stand, he saw the satellite phone was still turned on, but Mateo was no longer on the other end. Continuing to exit the wilderness, he was determined to seriously dress down Mateo for his insubordination.

The northwestern fire tower registered the electronic signal almost simultaneously with the southwestern tower.

At NSA headquarters, the on-duty tech assigned to monitor the Oregon towers suddenly bolted to attention. Something was going on with phone signals. He began plotting the signal's direct location by tracing the vectors of each tower to the spot where both crossed each other. The tech pushed a button on his console to listen to the live broadcast of what sounded like garbled noise. He instantly recognized that the call was from a satellite phone and that it was encoded. The tech recorded the entire conversation as well as the minutes during transmission when there was no connection to a second party. This harvested information was immediately sent to the DOD and the CIA, in that order.

At home in Virginia, Stan heard his pager sounding and called into Langley for the secure message. A furrow deepened on his forehead and after checking the time, Stan typed an encoded message that Tommy would get in just a few seconds. The message was short:

23:20 GMT

Been following your exploits.
The general's money was on U-2.
Thought you should know this also:
A BOGEY PINGED this P.M.
Sending coordinates to GEN. Matthews
Don't want you to catch a cold...
Stay safe ... MOM

Tommy and Danny nudged their horses to pick up the pace, finally catching up with the rest of their group. In another thirty minutes, the troops were settling in at camp as the valets watered the animals and set up a temporary corral for them.

The troops bedded down for the night, while Tommy headed for the general's tent.

Approaching the command tent, he saluted the soldier standing guard and requested permission to speak with the general. The guard checked Tommy's name badge and entered the tent. A few seconds passed before the entrance to the tent opened for Tommy. He entered and stood at attention.

"At ease, soldier," General Matthews said quietly. "Why the hell did you have to throw those valets off the train? And don't answer!"

Tommy had no response, as the general had begun laughing out loud in apparent amusement. "Fucking naked flying cowboys!" he said, still laughing. Tommy couldn't hold back his smile while still standing at ease.

"You know, I told your boss to put down a Benjamin for me on you guys. The valets didn't look all that experienced, and they were real twitchy. I was guessing they were FBI, but hell, what do I know about that kinda stuff? Get over here and sit down."

Tommy walked the few paces to the general's table and took a seat across from him. The general grabbed his satellite phone, which displayed a large topographical map of Mt. Hood and the surrounding wilderness. Rising to stand next to Tommy, the general read off the longitude and latitude numbers captured by the NSA agent a few minutes earlier. At first, Tommy wanted to say "Huh," but fatigue was setting in and Tommy asked the general to repeat himself twice. Suddenly the general's intentions became clear. Tommy manipulated two straight edges to a perpendicular point on the map which he perceived equaled the proper coordinates, while glancing at the general with a look that was begging confirmation. The general spent another three minutes adjusting straight edges and came within a sixteenth of an inch of where Tommy's mark was on the map. Tommy then remembered the GPS app from his sat phone and retrieved the data from earlier in the evening. His mind was now in high gear, taking only thirty seconds for him to realize that his intuition had been right. They had been only a few feet from the enemy.

"I knew it," Tommy blurted out, slamming both fists on the table.

The general placed his hand firmly on top of Tommy's trembling fingers.

"Tomorrow at sunrise, you, Danny, and another half dozen or so of my men go back to that spot and then head toward the mountain. Take your time. They've been in this forest for years. I doubt you'll find anything, but give it your best shot. Now go get some rest."

Tommy did.

# CHAPTER 34

The next morning, Danny woke before Tommy, having set his phone's alarm for an hour before sunrise. He knew that the hunt for the ghost in the forest from the previous evening would begin at dawn. He gave Tommy a slight poke, waited thirty seconds, and poked harder. The last time they'd been "roughing it" in the field like this, it had taken six or seven jabs to complete the job.

"You do that one more time, and I'll poke you back—hard," Tommy growled before Danny could jab him again.

"Touchy this morning, huh?" was Danny's quick reply. Tommy rolled over but didn't answer, as he was checking his phone for any new messages from Stan. If the general knew what was going on, it was because of Stan, who was feeding him the information. Tommy also wanted to call and find out the latest with Marty, but there was a communication blackout and he wouldn't be able to make that call yet.

"C'mon, Danny, get the lead out. It's time to hit the trail."

Tommy finished taking a leak, grabbed a granola bar, and downed a cup of coffee, all in five minutes' time. The troops were standing at the ready beside their steeds when Tommy and Danny arrived at the corral. A valet approached Tommy with Calypso in tow.

"They've had some feed this morning, but whenever you can, take a few minutes and let them graze and rest a bit ... please!"

Tommy nodded. All eyes were on Tommy. Guess I'm in charge, he thought, before ordering the troops to "Mount up, and proceed single file!"

It was time to cowboy.

Since it was daylight, it took less time to reach the spot that Tommy had marked on his GPS. "This looks like the spot, don't you think, Danny?" Tommy asked.

"Think so," Danny agreed. Tommy dismounted and tied Calypso to a small sapling. He wandered about for half a minute or so, before pointing at one of the soldiers that he'd eyed earlier back in camp.

"Soldier ... what's your name?"

The young man looked over his shoulder to see if there was another rider behind him and seeing none, he responded. "Steven, sir!"

"Do you have any hunting experience, young man?" Tommy replied.

"Some," said Steven.

"Ever track a wounded animal?"

If Steven wasn't awake before, he was now. According to his family lineage, he was one-third Sioux and proud of his Native American heritage. He wanted to respond a little sarcastically, but remembering who he was talking to, Steven reconsidered. He also knew that Tommy was profiling him. "Yes sir, I have," he finally responded.

"Men, Steven is your boss now. He'll be in the lead." Tommy motioned for Steven to dismount and walk with him a few yards deeper into the woods.

"Son, no disrespect, you could have said 'No' and I would have been fine with it. Yes, I profiled you back in camp. I had to ask the question because I know nothing about tracking animals. Not one thing! Last night there was a man right here."

Tommy then waved his arm in a broad gesture indicating an area about 100 yards distant. "You may or may not be proud of your Native American heritage, and frankly in this politically correct society we're living in, I couldn't give a shit! But you can't hide your genetic make-up. You have an opportunity to break this hunt for the enemy wide open, and the sooner we do that, the less chance these sons of a bitches have of irreparably destroying this country. I want you to lead us, but take your time, because this is not the time for speed. Head in that direction toward the mountain, because that's where the guy was coming from."

Tommy put his arm around Steven and gave him a reassuring hug, the kind that a father and son would have been proud of. Steven turned and half smiled at Tommy. The hunt was on!

"Take my horse, sir. Most of this, if not all, is going to be done on foot," Steven stated.

"Men, dismount!" Tommy bellowed. "Danny, Steven and I will proceed ahead. Give us a wide berth and catch up every 200 yards or so," Tommy shouted.

And they were off, very slowly. It took an hour to advance a half mile. Tommy gave Steven space to do his sleuthing. It was well past mid-morning when Steven waved Tommy over. "Sir, it took me awhile to unravel the pattern, but I think I've figured it out."

"Huh?" Tommy asked with uncertainty.

"I'm sorry, sir; I'm getting ahead of myself. There are cairns marking the trail about every 300 yards or so!" Steven said.

"Huh?" Tommy said a second time.

"You know, sir, a pile of rocks that are man-made. They might as well have paved their path, sir!"

Steven could tell Tommy was still confused and led him to the final arrangement of rocks that he'd discovered. Tommy quickly remembered something that made sense. "I'll be damned," he said in amazement.

"That's not all, sir! Take a look at these tiny rocks. They look normal, but they're not from this region. In fact, they're fake rocks, not volcanic but probably resin. Now watch this!" Steven had collected a half dozen of the artificial pebbles and cupped them in his closed hands where they began to glow. Tommy just shook his head. He'd seen advertisements for luminescent landscaping rocks, but never in action. "Great work Steven, and please, no more 'sir.' Just call me Tommy! That's an order," Tommy said.

The next four-plus miles went somewhat quicker, as Steven stayed afoot, as did Tommy with both horses in tow.

Tommy felt that he and the rest of the group, including the horses, needed a break. They'd been climbing and gaining altitude. He gave Steven the time-out signal and tied up both horses. The other troops quickly arrived at the small clearing. Danny shouted an order to dismount, gave his horse to another soldier, and joined Tommy and Steven near the trail that led farther up the volcano. A large boulder and rock wall stood in their way, forcing hikers and climbers to go left and up to the summit, or right to continue circling Mt. Hood. The only thing they had to show so far for their day's efforts were a few glowing resin rocks and a trail of cairns.

Sitting down, Tommy propped himself against the huge boulder and broke out another granola bar, this time chewing slowly. He was no longer in a hurry. Danny was sitting a few feet from Tommy, observing his friend's body language. He could tell that

Tommy was falling into a funk. The signs were all there, indicating intentional human traffic on the barely used trail they'd just traveled, but there were no answers or leads. There just wasn't enough evidence to warrant additional investigation, and most likely, Tommy's sighting the previous night would officially become a figment of his imagination. Tommy looked like he was in a trance, just staring off into nowhere.

Danny saw Tommy break off the tops of some blades of grass, toss them into the air, and watch as they fell harmlessly to the ground. He repeated the same a second and third time, with equal results. In what seemed to be one motion, Tommy jumped to his feet, letting out one utterance.

"Shit!"

Danny was by Tommy's side in seconds. "What? What is it?" Danny asked.

"Watch this!" Tommy grabbed a handful of grass. "Do you feel any wind?"

"No," Danny replied. Tommy dropped the clippings from above his head and watched as they dropped straight to the ground.

Tommy then pointed to a lone wildflower growing at the base of the boulder a short distance from where they'd been sitting. He broke off some more clippings and walked over to the flower, stood above it, pausing for effect. From above, an observer couldn't see, but the stem of the flower curved out and away from the boulder as it grew from the ground, with a "C" type growth pattern, before then growing straight up.

Tommy had another bunch of grass in his hand and was letting the blades fall next to where the flower was growing. Then suddenly a gust of wind blew the grass blades at a 90^0 angle at the same height as the top of the C curve of the flower stem. He performed the experiment a couple more times and moving sideways along the path, did it twice again. Everybody was watching wide-eyed.

It was almost as if one could see the wheels turning in Tommy's mind.

Going a few feet into the brush, Tommy pulled out his utility knife and cut a long, thin branch from a shrub, stripping away its leaves. Returning to the spot with the disfigured flower, he turned to the troops with his finger to his lips. Everyone remained hushed as he turned and began poking the stick at the base of the boulder until all four feet of the branch had disappeared.

They had found the Antifa wilderness hideout!

Pulling out his sat phone, Tommy opened the GPS app to mark their location and texted Stan the following message: "If I call you in five minutes, can you have NSA intercept my coordinates and pinpoint where I AM LOCATED ... EXACTLY?"

Stan, at his desk working, read the text immediately and placed a call to Jamie, an agent with the NSA. In less than two minutes, he had an answer and texted back to Tommy.

"Yes, but stay on the line for three minutes, with no interruption of signal!"

Thirty seconds later, Stan's mobile phone began to ring, and he answered. There was no talking, just the connection. Tommy and Stan had a non-discussion for four minutes before the connection abruptly ended. In just five minutes, a satellite was moved to a different position in orbit, where it began beaming video of the Mt. Hood environs. A half hour later, Stan was watching Tommy and his troops live in his office. He sent another text, which read:

SMILE – I SEE YOU!

Love, Mother

Tommy read the message, showed it to Danny, and then shook Steven's hand. Shaking his head in wonder, he recognized that there are times when something happens and there's no earthly explanation for it. He glanced at the lone flower before looking heavenward to give a silent thanks.

Tommy took a deep breath of relief and barked out, "Riders up." The troops headed away from what they expected to be a future site of conflict and back to base camp.

 **HAPTER 35**

Thoughts were whirling through my brain at 90 miles an hour. Memories of events and occurrences in our lives – both wonderful and sad – would come and go, parading as clear as day in front of my eyes. Even when I closed them. Not a decade of our life together was overlooked. Every vision ended with the time that I first laid eyes on Marty.

I was sprawled out on one couch; Charles was doing the same on another couch, but unlike me, he was fast asleep. The hours rolled by, 1:00, 2:00, 3:00 – I saw the clock hands pass by each hour with no possibility of sleeping.

The hour hand on the clock had just passed five when the sound of Carl Wilson and the Beach Boys startled me.

"What the hell?" Charles exclaimed as he bolted up, wide awake.

"It's my phone! It's them," I whispered in a low voice, as if the kidnappers could actually hear me. "Answer it," Charles told me.

"This is Rob ...."

"Listen carefully. We've changed your arrival time. You have 24 hours to get to Portland or your wife dies! We'll call you in 24 hours for ..."

"No!" I yelled at the kidnappers. "I want to talk to my wife on her cell phone. I don't believe you have her! No deal until she calls me! Those are my terms." I hung up and prayed.

Mateo turned to Danté with a questioning look. "Call him

back and give me the phone," Danté said.

My phone began playing the same song a second time. I quickly answered. Danté spoke first. "Listen up, you don't dictate to us! Follow our--" This time, the call was ended by Charles, when he grabbed the phone from my hand.

"Damn it, Charles, my wife's life is on the line!" I shouted. He gave the phone back to me without comment.

Danté just stared at the phone. One look from him was all Mateo needed, saying, "I told you!"

"Okay, where's her stuff?" Danté shot back. Mateo walked into another room and returned with Marty's purse, dumping its contents out on the table, gesturing as if to say "So now what?"

"Damn it, Mateo, where's her phone?"

"How the hell do I know? I wasn't at the warehouse. It's probably somewhere there!" Mateo yelled, heading back into the other room to look for the phone.

Charles and I just sat, neither of us saying a word. I wanted the kidnappers to call back immediately so I could talk with my wife. I needed to talk with her more than anything at that moment. Charles was hoping for the opposite. No call-back meant that someone was heading to the warehouse to look for Marty's cellphone.

I glanced at Charles, who was staring intently at his watch. Five long minutes passed before he grabbed his phone and made a call. "Heads up. You're about to have some company. Make sure the cameras are on, and alert the other teams to get ready for a tracking relay."

"What? What's going on? What did you just tell your men to do?" I screamed at Charles.

"Rob, shut it right now," Charles said tersely. "I told my men to get ready for someone to return to the warehouse to get your wife's phone. When we were there before, my men installed cameras that will video anyone who enters the building. When that person leaves, several teams already in place will take turns following them by car. They'll hand off the surveillance to each other in intervals, traveling in different cars so they won't be detected."

"Rob, this is it – if we lose this opportunity to find Marty, there won't be a second chance. When the kidnapper finally finds her phone and heads back to where she's being held, well, then you'll know the phone is in Marty's hands. You're going to have to stand firm when they call and insist she talks with you only from her cellphone.

"First thing they'll do before they call you, though, is disable all the location-finder apps on her phone. As long as they don't open the phone and find our chameleon GPS chip that we planted, I can guarantee you, we'll find her," he told me.

"What if they find that chip? Marty is as good as dead!" Once again I was screaming at Charles.

"Jesus, Rob. Stop already. Just stop. Unless they have an Apple engineer in their midst, they won't find it. It's undetectable because it's a perfect replication of the data chip that Apple uses in their iPhones."

Charles collapsed on the couch in apparent exhaustion from my theatrics. I sat there with my head buried in my hands. I was emotionally shut down, mentally incapable of logic or even the comprehension to analyze the situation.

And so, we waited.

Tommy and Danny were leading the men toward the main trail and camp when Tommy dropped back to join with Steven, who appeared morose and deep in thought. Taking the cue, Danny nudged his horse into a canter, which the other horses matched. Tommy, though, pulled back even more on Calypso's reins, slowing him to a walk and indicating that Steven should do the same.

"Steven, you seem troubled by what's going down." After a short pause and no response from Steven, Tommy continued. "I'm guessing you're probably the youngest Ranger assigned to this detail. So how many years has it been?" Tommy asked.

"This is my first combat duty and frankly, sir, I'd rather be over in the Mideast fighting against ISIL than here fighting my fellow citizens!"

Tommy lowered his head in thought, knowing he had to give the right response. Nothing like cutting to the chase. I'd best be careful with this young man. He may be ready for battle, but is he ready to kill? Especially since he most likely would have to kill some fellow Millennials, individuals who in some way might as well be his kin. Nothing like walking through the minefield blindfolded, he mused.

What Tommy was up against was no different than what any parent with young children faces when justifying, to them, the consequences of American laws and the rules that have guided our society since its founding.

"Steven, I'm going to call you son, because first of all, I'm old enough to be your father and second, because you keep calling me sir. Thank you for the respect you've shown me. Now that we've got that out of the way, I want you to know what I'm about to say isn't up for debate. I am your senior, not only in rank, but in age and experience.

"The last time I checked, our style of government is still considered a republic, which in real basic terms means the majority rules. In elections, there is a winner and there is a loser – there are no what-ifs or maybes. But if someone thinks the outcome was manipulated as a result of individuals circumventing the system, well, our government has a mechanism in place for correcting any wrongs that may have been committed."

Pausing briefly to let Steven digest what he was saying, Tommy pointed at Steven before continuing.

"I'm well aware there is a generation – your generation – that believes folks like myself have had our time in the sun. We should harness our convictions and silence our opinions because we as the Boomer generation have outlasted our usefulness," Tommy said while pointing at himself.

By this time, both men had pulled their horses to a full stop on the trail, with Tommy hunched farther over the saddle as he continued his sermon.

"This last presidential election showed me one thing. There are still some of us old farts, plus enough others who enjoy sipping the same old Kool-Aid. We have been and remain in the majority.

"Son, these revolutionaries that we're about to fight, those who call themselves Antifa, well, I really doubt they're much into

American history or even world history. I can't tell you how many of them there are, but a lot of them are your age, Steven, and you especially need to heed my next words, because they're relevant.

"Every person needs to understand the past in order to accomplish what's right for now and for the future! History always repeats itself – and I don't care what form of government people choose. Sorry, check that last statement. I do care! Again, in any election, there are going to be winners and losers – and there will be leaders and followers. Some individuals will be rich and some will be poor. Some will be physically strong and some will be weak. Whether in an election or an athletic event – or even the game of life – you can hand out all the participation trophies you want to, but I guarantee you that each and every person that participated knows deep down which side won and which side lost."

Tommy paused once more, not so much for Steven to think about what he was hearing, but to find the right words to continue on and provide some reassurance to Steven.

"Now, when you add weapons to the equation, the winners will always be those who are strong and smart – and who have the biggest and best weapons. It's easy to underestimate Antifa's warriors because they come into battle with sticks. At least that's what our media is leading us to believe. Well, Steven, what happens when you sharpen one end of the stick to a point that can pierce flesh? What happens when you place that sharpened stick in a long cylinder with gunpowder at the base and light the explosive while pointing the cylinder directly at a person?

"Son, these people have crossed an invisible line in the sand. You're standing on the other side of that line – the side of good – and you're in their way. Their goal is to be King of the Hill, and they will attack you because they hate what you stand for. You represent the status quo, the old guard, the group that just 'keeps on keeping on.' They will not hesitate to kill you!"

Tommy was exhausted from the mental jousting. He'd used every analogy and metaphor he could think of in an attempt to assuage the mind of his Millennial partner. But he wasn't done talking yet – Steven had to make a decision.

"My job is to bring you home safely. Whether you honor the commitment you made to your country is on you. You need to search deep down inside and decide if you can pull the trigger against an enemy who believes he or she has a better answer for governing America. This enemy strongly feels they have a better solution than all of the past generations—those folks who accepted our founding fathers' and subsequent leaders' laws and amendments, for the past two and a half centuries.

"The young in each new generation always think they have a better way, but as they mature in life and begin to really understand the past, most realize and accept that things don't need changing." Tommy paused one last time, staring at Steven as if looking deep into his soul.

"If you can't commit to what America stands for--if you can't look your brothers in arms square in the eyes, knowing they expect you to have their backs on the battlefield—then you need to tell the general you're out. And do it no later than this evening, so we can move forward without you."

Tommy turned Calypso around and let him take his lead. Horse and rider were galloping in short order.

Steven remained fixed like a statue on the trail, pondering his allegiance.

# CHAPTER 37

It was just after sunset when Tommy arrived back at camp. He immediately proceeded to the general's command tent, pacing back and forth outside until finally he was accompanied into the tent by one of the general's aides.

"Thanks for updating Stan with the latest details, Tommy. The Pentagon is already surveilling the area you indicated. By the way, you weren't alone today. There were at least two teams observing your movements on the mountain today."

Tommy didn't answer, but thought, Why am I not surprised?

"General, we need to get back there, right now! I'll take Danny and your man Steven with me. Let me grab some sniper rifles, ammo, and a valet to tend the horses, and we can be on the trail in a half hour."

The general didn't respond immediately. He really wanted his two novice Rangers to stay close. But he also knew Tommy was right in wanting to head back quickly.

"Tommy, you've got less than two days, at best. We'll attack no later than 48 hours from now. I'm waiting for some heavy equipment to arrive that we'll use to break through the entrance you found to the old mine. I've gone over different scenarios in my head many times and each time, I end up with the same conclusion. We've got to act strongly – and there will be no mercy for these revolutionaries.

"If we treat this rebellion in the wrong way, our hesitation will only encourage future rebellions. I won't be responsible for the demise of this great country of ours – and I'll be damned if that happens on my watch!" General Matthews slammed his right fist atop the table covered by topographical maps with neatly drawn arrows and markings. Papers flew in all directions.

Tommy's mind was in overdrive, but his tongue was tied. He knew that warfare in the 21st century, especially when fought in one's own backyard, would be anything but conventional. All he could see were the future historians referring to the conflict as the Facebook Revolution.

All the rules of battle would be tested, and each individual skirmish would play out on social media.

Hell, I bet participants will live stream the conflict, and that'll make the rules of engagement that much more difficult, Tommy thought.

"General, I fully understand your concerns. Perhaps we can short-circuit this revolution so our worst fears don't come true. But before I leave, I need to ask you to be completely honest with me. What specifically does the enemy have in the way of armaments – and is there anything at all that you're not telling me?"

General Matthews shook his head. "Off the top of my head, I don't think there's much we haven't touched upon. The reason we're waiting for the heavy equipment is because of the earthquake swarms that have been happening in the area. The army's seismologist believes Mt. Hood might be working itself up to a venting event and that the mountain is going to literally depressurize. He doesn't believe there's going to be a full-scale eruption, but he did caution against any actions that could produce a major explosion of any kind in close proximity to the mountain."

The general continued, "Now, if you can define what major

means, then you're better than me. I asked our earthquake expert, and all he kept saying was major. That's why I told you about the tonnage of munitions that was stolen, and how that might roughly equal the output of a mother of all bombs. So I'm guessing that an explosion equal to a MOAB or something of greater tonnage would be considered major and not wise."

Tommy lowered his head, thinking, Jesus, General. It's one thing to stomp out a revolution and another to rein in a potential geological catastrophe! That wasn't a shoe you just dropped in front of me, it was a size-16 boot! And I distinctly remember you said armaments, not munitions. I haven't time for semantics.

"General, what exactly was stolen from the military facility in Oregon?" Tommy demanded of him.

"They stole C-4, Tommy—plastic explosives."

"Is that all? You're telling me they stole enough plastic explosives to equal the effects of a MOAB?" Tommy asked incredulously. "Christ, General, give me the short version as to how that happened!"

"Up north along the border is an old Army facility, the Umatilla Chemical Depot. The US made chemical weapons there after World War II. Then after the Cold War drew to a close, they built another facility to destroy them. The public is being led to believe that all the chemical weapons have been disposed of, but the truth is that the army now uses that facility to manufacture C-4.

Tommy, the manufacturing program is a well-guarded military secret," the general warned him.

"I can't give you the exact number of pallets of C-4 that were stolen. I'm not privy to that information. It was a soldier, an Antifa convert, who allowed the attackers on base. He's currently being shuttled from country to country and from interrogation site to interrogation site. The CIA's not been able to break him yet. But he's a typical anarchist, and C-4 has always been a favorite weapon of terror for anarchists. If not plastic explosives, then they'll use Molotov cocktails or ammonium nitrate. Homeland Security is monitoring the sales of ammonium nitrate, but they can't stop revolutionaries from home- brewing the stuff."

"So you're saying intel now thinks the old mine we discovered today might be housing the stolen C-4?" Tommy said in a tone that was more a declaration than question.

The general nodded in the affirmative.

"You might want to check with your boss about the status of the soldier being shuttled around. Maybe there's new information that could help. Good hunting, and I expect regular updates," the general said. Turning his back to Tommy was an indication that the discussion was over.

Tommy left, heading to the corral to meet up with Danny and the valet.

"No Steven, huh, Danny?" Tommy asked.

"Not yet, Tommy. What the hell happened to you guys?" Danny asked.

"Later ...we gotta go," Tommy said, noting that Danny was looking in the direction of the fading daylight on the horizon.

Steven had finally arrived, oblivious to what was taking place.

Tommy approached Steven and the horse, putting his hand to the halter to bring the steed to a stop. Not a word was spoken. Steven dismounted and an animated discussion commenced, well out of earshot of anyone.

"And your answer is?" Tommy challenged Steven.

"Leave me alone," was his lamentable reply.

"Well you see, that's a problem! I'd venture that all of your fellow soldiers' parents are counting on you to do your job. They don't want a government vehicle pulling up in front of their homes and a soldier striding up their walkway, knocking on their door, with an American flag in his or her hands. I'm not going to let that happen. You'll continue to ride with Danny and me! Our parents are dead."

In the meantime, the valet walked over, relieved Tommy's grasp, and took Steven's horse to the corral, exchanging it for a fresh mount already geared for battle.

If a photographer had been present when the valet returned with a fresh quarter horse, the assumption would have been that everyone there had traveled back in time to medieval times.

The new horse was adorned with a chamfron, protective gear designed to protect the horse's head. This device was made of a lightweight composite material wrapped in several layers of Kevlar. The horse was also wearing chest-plate armor constructed of the same material, along with armor protecting two-thirds of its body and rump. The Kevlar had a camouflage design and coloring. This protection, combined with Mark's genetic altering technology, had made the quarter horses used by the military almost invincible. Only a perfect shot to the leg or a head shot could bring a steed down instantly. Thankfully, the enemy had no way of knowing that. Seeing several horses adorned with 21st-century armor, reminiscent of Knights of the Round Table, should give pause to the enemy.

Tommy was in mid-sentence when Steven glanced over his head, his eyes expanding into large circles and his mouth fully agape. Tommy whirled around, his face morphing into the same position. The three men spent about fifteen seconds in stunned silence, looking at the horses, before Tommy began laughing uncontrollably.

"Holy shit, man! Where the hell is Sir Lancelot?" Tommy said, trying to stifle his laughter.

The valet was not amused and handed the reins to Steven. He turned, heading to the corral as Tommy pleaded for him to come back. He did in short order, returning with Calypso who was now adorned in the same manner as Steven's horse. Next, Danny's horse was brought up from the corral, also similarly attired. The three knights were now ready to ride.

Finally, the valet returned with his horse and two donkeys in tow, used to carry weapons, ammunition, and backpacks filled with accessories. The valet paused, giving Danny and Steven a large badge to place between the eyes of each horse.

"I figured this would be appropriate for Calypso, sir," he said, giving a replica of the Punisher Skull badge adopted and worn by Chris Kyle while serving in Iraq. Tommy held it briefly before passing it back to the valet to affix to Calypso's chamfron.

Looking at Steven and Danny, the valet said, "You both also have the same coat of arms as Mr. Tommy. I thought it only fitting that your horses wear this badge when going into battle," he said proudly.

It was at that moment when the reality of what would lie ahead hit Tommy full force – and he, Danny, and Steven weren't adorned in protective armor like their horses were!

# CHAPTER 38

Danny took perfect aim, snapping a photo of the three horses regaled in their finest armor and texted it to his brother Charles – but with no words of explanation. Within seconds, the group had mounted their horses, heading out on the same trail they'd traveled just a bit earlier.

A few miles away, Charles looked at the photo from Danny and bolted to attention. The light bulb had turned on – the horses were in battle garb! "The cavalry has obviously found their target," he said to himself, mulling over the implications the picture had created in his mind.

He texted back to Danny, "Need location and details. Imperative!"

Danny texted back, "In a few minutes."

This photo, in addition to numerous other photos he'd received from Danny, created a story board for Charles of where Danny and Tommy were traveling. It effectively created a timeline of the ongoing events and helped Charles in planning his next moves. Charles had no doubt that Marty's kidnapping was linked to the same group of individuals that were about to start a revolution.

∩ ∩ ∩

'Time to go, Doc. Things are about to happen," Charles said. I stared at him in confusion. What the hell has changed? I thought. One minute we're lying around, and all of a sudden he says it's time to go.

I summoned up the nerve to ask. "So Charles, where is it we're going, and why all of a sudden?"

"We're heading to my friend's military supply store and then back to the warehouse," Charles said, way too casually in my opinion.

It was early morning and the sun was just beginning to brighten the eastern sky. We arrived at our destination in less than thirty minutes, but I had no idea where we were. We entered the store through a door off a side alley. I was introduced to Bruce, who in less than fifteen minutes took me on a whirlwind shopping extravaganza. I was given item after item to put on and when Bruce was finally done, you would have thought I was the poster boy for Cabela's wilderness attire.

After putting my own clothing back on and collecting my new wardrobe, Charles and I left the store. Presumably we were on our way to rendezvous with the rest of Charles's team.

"I'm guessing that we're sleeping outside tonight?" I asked, laughing. It was the first time in days I'd laughed or smiled.

"Yeah, we are – and give me that gun you're concealing."

"Huh?" I asked, trying to act ignorant.

"I know about your exploits on the racetrack, Marshal Dillon. If you're in a position where you have to shoot somebody, you need a gun with a silencer.

Now, I have no clue how good you are with a weapon, but there's a Glock 19 with a Ti-RANT 9 suppressor in the glove compartment. There are also four boxes of sub-sonic 9mm-147 grain ammo there. By your reaction, I'm fairly certain you've never fired a weapon with a silencer, but where we're going, silence is critical. Now, give me your gun!" Charles demanded. I reluctantly gave in, handing him my gun.

"Thank you," Charles said.

"Okay, time out!" I shouted. "How the hell do you know so much about me? You haven't received any calls, and I certainly haven't been communicating with anyone other than the kidnappers. I know your brother is CIA – I met him that night when we celebrated Towers Above and his victory at the Challenge Cup dinner. C'mon, man, trust needs to be on both sides – at least that's what I'm used to!"

Charles didn't take his eyes off the road. He reached between his legs, grabbing his mobile phone and extending it to me. I grabbed it and he said, "9-1-1-0-0-1."

"What? Come again?" I asked.

"Those numbers unlock my phone. You're not the only person affected by what happened in New York that beautiful Tuesday morning in September," Charles replied, as he stiffly repeated the numbers.

"Okay, your phone is unlocked—so now what?"

"Go to Snapchat. There should still be a picture on the screen. That's a photograph of Danny's and Tommy's horses. They've been prepped for battle. That means the army knows where the enemy is hiding and that hostilities are going to begin at any time! The picture will literally disappear in about an hour – that's the beauty of Snapchat. Danny trusts me enough to share the picture and he knows there will soon be no trace of that photo and that he won't be compromised. At least not by me."

Charles stared intently at my face.

"Ever since Danny asked me to help, I've been learning about you, Doc. It's not that I don't trust you, but I need to know if you have any other bizarre quirks. I've already learned that you have a short fuse. So I'm giving you fair warning. I'm guessing you've figured out that we're going to meet up with my men. Our hope is that whoever shows up at the warehouse looking for Marty's phone also knows where your wife is being kept. We figure the earlier flunkies with her at the warehouse screwed up by allowing her to leave a clue. So now they're sending in the big guns. I'm also pretty sure that you're thinking about breaking away from me at the warehouse and going solo because you're not convinced we'll save your wife. Doc, if it comes to that and you go rogue on me, I promise that I or one of my men will take you down. We'll take you down the same way you were taken out at the racetrack, a few months ago."

I was totally disarmed, realizing I'd been unmasked by an expert. After all my years in dentistry working with people, I thought I'd become extraordinary at reading their thoughts and gauging their personalities. Charles flat-out had me pegged.

"You promise me you'll get her back?" I stammered.

"Dr. Becker," he started, but stopped with what seemed to be an endless pause … "You can count on it," Charles said in a comforting tone.

I felt a calming peace surround me as I relaxed in the passenger's seat.

Not so with Charles, who suddenly felt every muscle in his body, as well as his gut, begin to cramp. It wasn't that he'd lied, he just hadn't told the whole truth.

There was always a chance that Marty would return to me … dead!

# CHAPTER 39

M ateo had Eduardo circle the warehouse before telling him to stop the car, two blocks from the entrance. After waiting fifteen minutes, Mateo opened the passenger's door, got out, and headed to the building.

He unlocked the warehouse door, climbed a few steps, and unlocked a second door which opened into a spacious abode. He was unaware, however, that his movements had activated the three cameras installed by the agents the previous day. He was also unaware that these cameras were recording his movements from all angles. The camera system immediately alerted the team that the building had been breached and that someone had entered the kidnapper's lair.

Video was streaming live to the entire team, including Charles, who was conducting surveillance from his car. He held his phone in front of me so I could watch the action.

"Can you make the video larger?" I asked.

Charles immediately sent a text, and within just a few seconds, the video was enlarged. We both watched the video from our surveillance location. Even though I was mentally exhausted, the memory of the video from the Columbia retail store, when Marty was talking with the suspected kidnapper, was fresh in my mind.

"That's him! That's the kidnapper!"

I grabbed the handle of the door and opened it. One leg was

already out when I heard the chambering of a bullet.

"No you don't, Rob! I totally understand, but get back in the car, now!" Charles ordered. I knew he wouldn't hesitate to shoot me.

I climbed back into the car and closed the door, trembling with hate, anger, frustration, and many other unhealthy emotions.

Charles continued watching Mateo, who was now tossing the contents of the room and focusing on an area in front of the wet bar. Couch cushions were flying in all directions, when suddenly Mateo stopped to crouch down and pick up what appeared to be a cellphone. Mateo began to look around the room – up, down, sideways. If the video had sound, Charles might have heard Mateo say, "That was too damn easy!"

Doing a walk-around of the room, Mateo stopped, apparently now more relaxed. Heading back to the bar, he took a seat on one of the stools. He then reached into his pocket, pulling out what looked like a small plastic baggie containing some type of powder. Mateo carefully poured some of the powder from the baggie onto the bar top, and using a stir stick, began arranging the powder into five neat rows before taking a straw from a cup on the bar.

"I'll be damned," was all Charles could say.

For the next few minutes, we watched as Mateo snorted the five lines of what we could only assume was cocaine.

To Mateo, the cocaine high was a reward for a job well done. He'd found the missing phone and shortly would head back to begin the final process of gathering the ultimate reward, the ransom payoff.

Charles and his men watched as Mateo went to the couch, where he collapsed in a blissful state of mind. His body's dopamine release was now flooding all the synapses of his brain's pleasure neurons and the high was quickly accelerating. Mateo knew he was violating one of MS-13's cardinal rules but could not care less.

The rule was:

Drugs are sold or used to ply the weak-minded and are not to be used personally by the leaders of the group. Our members of the brotherhood must be strong, while the users, the lower echelon, would become their slaves. They were worthless pawns to be manipulated. Alcohol, marijuana, meth, and cocaine would be used to create craving and dependency among Danté's Antifa followers. Danté was also known to provide opioids, and the ultimate drug, heroin, when it suited his purpose. Each of his enslaved Millennials could become chemically entrapped, if Danté chose. He enjoyed owning their brains.

Mateo continued tripping for another fifteen minutes when his phone rang, interrupting the high. He grabbed his phone to answer.

"Are you there?" Danté asked.

"Yeah, I'm here, why?" Mateo answered.

"I just got word from The Hood. They had company yesterday. There were several riders out there who looked like law enforcement of some kind. They seemed to be snooping around in the wilderness and then everyone took a break, right at the base of the mine's entrance. Kelly was in one of the sniper bunkers up on the mountainside and he's worried. I want you to forget the kidnapped woman. Let her go. Blindfold her and get her out of the mine. I've got a bad feeling!"

Charles couldn't hear the conversation, but watched as the streaming video showed the lounging druggie drop his phone to his side and then began banging his fist up and down on a chair cushion.

"Mateo, did you hear what I said? Hello?" Danté looked at the phone to confirm he still had a connection.

Mateo raised the phone back to his ear and defiantly told Danté, "I'm not letting her go, Danté! I'll take her to my place if I have to, but I'm not giving up on this payoff! Screw you!"

Charles then watched as Mateo braced himself and slowly rose. He stumbled to the bar and in one swift motion, sent everything within reach flying with his right arm.

Charles quickly texted his men.

"Get ready, group. The target is aroused, drugged, and angry! Marty Becker's cell phone is the key. If he leaves her mobile phone, then it's solely on us. We can't lose sight of him!"

Mateo headed for the door and in an instant Charles realized Mateo still had Marty's phone. The tracking chip was actively following Mateo's travel.

"C'mon, let's go! We're going to lose him," I shouted.

Charles ignored my clamoring. He was texting a copy of the video to his brother Danny and another copy to an ex-Ranger that was a detective working for the Salem Police Department in Oregon. He ended the text with, "Do a facial recognition on this guy. He's a prime player in a kidnapping up here. Hurry with an ID if possible."

He finished texting and must have been watching me out of the corner of his eye; he held up his hand in a halt signal and resumed staring at his cellphone's screen. A good twenty minutes had passed since the kidnapper had left the warehouse. Charles suddenly slammed his fist against the steering wheel and shouted, "We've got you now, you son of a bitch," and he started the car. Before we moved, he sent Danny one more text.

"Marty Becker's kidnapper is heading your way!"

# CHAPTER 40

Steven was in the lead on the trail, with Tommy and Danny six lengths behind. Further back in the rear position was the valet rider with the two donkeys in tow, trailering supplies and two containers with some form of wildlife.

"What is that guy hauling back there, Danny?" Tommy asked.

"I thought you knew," Danny answered.

Tommy shouted for Steven to halt before turning Calypso around and heading back to the valet. He stopped next to the donkeys and dismounted Calypso.

"Soldier, what's in those two containers?"

"Bald eagles, sir!"

Tommy felt liked he'd been punched in the gut – bald eagles? He wanted to laugh but couldn't. The supposed idiocy of the response had taken his breath away.

"What the hell kind of answer is that, young man?" Tommy finally asked.

"Sir, they've been training with our unit for over a year," he responded.

Tommy was stumped. "Pardon me?" was all he could say. By now, Danny and Steven had arrived on the scene and were taking in the conversation.

"Why the hell are we in the business of releasing birds of prey back into the wild?" Tommy asked, his voice reflecting a rising anger.

"Sir, these eagles are drone hunters!"

Tommy was thoroughly confused, knowing it was reflected on his face. Perhaps it was a slight indication of his personal fatigue, but Tommy genuinely had no clue what the soldier was talking about.

"I'm really sorry, sir, maybe you're thinking too big. Think small, real small!"

Tommy lowered his head, not wanting to appear any more embarrassed than he already was. And then it hit him like a two by four smacking right between his eyes. Oh my God, he's talking about quad-copters, those recreational drones, Tommy thought.

"Sir, maybe it's been a while since you've attended a War College, but mini drones have and are being used by ISIS in the Middle East. The general and his superiors assume Antifa might also be using this technology in some deadly manner. For certain, they're using them for surveillance. They don't have the sophisticated drones our government uses, nor do they have satellite surveillance. This is their next-best choice."

Tommy turned to look at Danny and Steven – both of whom immediately lowered their heads, just staring at the ground. That moment of stupidity was squarely on Tommy's shoulders, and he knew it.

"Can I look at the eagles?" Tommy asked sheepishly.

"You all come here, c'mon. Gather around," the valet said.

Each container was large enough to allow the eagles to fully extend their wings. The enclosures were covered with a camouflage canvas on all four sides and on the top. The valet unlatched the top cover and three heads immediately were drawn downward, eyes gazing on the majestic bird of prey.

"Gentlemen, I present to you Icarus. That name may ring a bell, but I assure you he is not trained to fly as high as the sun!"

Icarus quickly turned his head to observe the three strangers fixated on him. The bird instantly recognized they were not drones, just humans, and lowered its head.

"Icarus' soulmate is in the other crate. Her name is Naucrate. When y'all get a chance, search the annals of Greek mythology to learn about her name and history," the valet suggested.

Tommy suddenly remembered his manners, and extending his right hand, said, "I'm Tommy, and your name is…?"

"Sorry, sir, my name is Jerry. I'm pleased to meet you."

The rest of the group exchanged similar pleasantries; Jerry was now a member in the exclusive fraternity.

"So, Jerry, you're not army, are you?" Tommy asked.

The stunned look on Steven's face was instant. Danny, however, knew the question was coming. He and Tommy were simpatico.

Jerry didn't flinch. He looked Tommy square in the eyes and said, "I'm as much army as you are, sir."

"Touché," Danny wanted to say. Steven's eyes were ready to burst out of his head.

"It's that obvious, huh?" Tommy replied with a smile on his face.

"Sir, you and Danny have been the talk of the group ever since you arrived in camp back in Wyoming. Everyone's trying to guess which of the seventeen government intelligence agencies you two are attached to!"

Tommy just grinned and answered, "You know that old saying, if I tell you, I'll have to kill you! So what's your story, Jerry? C'mon … spit it out."

"Like I said, I've been training with the unit for over a year. It's my job to protect the soldiers from injury from drone attacks."

"Okay, so you're saying those two eagles are our drone

defense?" Tommy questioned.

"Just on this mission, sir. There's a whole bunch more that my company brings to warfare—way more than just raptors."

Tommy knew it was checkmate, and that made him uncomfortable. He was used to being the aggressor and winning. "Are you at liberty to share information about the military contractor you work for, with us?"

"If I were to tell you, sir, I'd have to kill you!" Jerry calmly replied.

Danny covered his mouth and faked a cough to mask his laughter. Steven's lower jaw was hanging slack and his eyes, now safely tucked back in their sockets, had that look of WTF?

Tommy couldn't stop the smile that began creeping across his face.

"We'll continue this later. We've got to get in position before the moon comes up." He mounted his horse, returning to the front of the group. Steven again took the lead, as Danny sidled up next to Tommy.

"You think it's time to check in with Stan?" Danny asked Tommy in a lowered voice. Barely an instant had passed before he felt his phone vibrate in his pocket, leaving no time to press the matter with Tommy. Retrieving his phone, Danny read the text message from Charles. "My brother just texted. We're about to get company out here in the woods!"

Tommy appeared deep in thought for a moment before saying, "Yes." Giving Calypso a slight nudge in the side quickened their pace. In mere seconds, Tommy caught up with Steven and issued a few orders. The group was now double-timing it on their way to setting up an ambush.

The start of America's second revolution was edging closer.

CHAPTER 41

It was time for Tommy to give directions to Steven and for the men to find shelter.

"I need you to find an area with a huge canopy. Since most of the leaves have dropped from the trees, Douglas firs are our best hope for cover. If we're going to deal with drone surveillance or an attack, I want the enemy to have no choice but to bring their UAVs in at a low speed and low altitude. That should give the eagles the advantage of swooping in from above undetected. I have no idea what size or range their drones have. I'm pretty sure, though, that we traveled at least eight miles or more each way earlier today. Don't go more than a mile or two off the main trail – and don't scare the crap out of us when we catch up with you!"

They continued at a canter for a couple of minutes before Steven and his steed pulled away, quickly disappearing from sight. For the next half hour or so, Tommy and Danny cantered along the trail, with Jerry bringing up the rear at a slower pace. He couldn't go any faster because of the eagles they were transporting. Checking the GPS to gauge their location, Tommy realized they were just a half mile from the point where they'd branch off and head east toward Mt. Hood to rendezvous with Steven.

Tommy reined in Calypso as Danny did the same with his horse, both slowing to a walk. Tommy pulled out his satellite phone to make a call.

"Are you calling Stan?" Danny asked, with concern in his voice.

Tommy nodded yes.

"Hang up, dammit," Danny said, his voice raised.

Tommy ended the call, scowling at Danny. "Let me call my brother first and find out what's going on!" Danny begged, already hitting speed dial to reach Charles.

Charles answered immediately, giving Danny a concise summary of what was taking place.

"We've identified Marty Becker's kidnapper, and he's headed in your direction. I'm not telling you what to do, but this guy must have the answers to some pretty important questions. Me and the team intend to join up with your group later. I'll be in the lead and for Christ's sake, don't shoot me! Right now, the kidnapper is just short of entering the wilderness on foot. Text me your coordinates so I can relay back to you exactly where he is. By the way, we're tracking him by GPS, and he has no clue that he's tagged. Oh, and Rob Becker is with me, and he's also armed."

Charles ended the call. Danny updated Tommy with what he'd learned before telling him, "Okay, now make that call to Stan."

Memories surfaced in Tommy's mind of that spring day at the Kentucky racetrack when Dr. Becker had pulled his weapon and was immediately brought down by their sniper. Not again, please Lord, not again, Tommy silently prayed.

Tommy shook the thoughts from his head and again dialed Stan – this time the call went through, ringing several times before Stan, in a sleepy stupor, managed a scratchy-throated "Hello?"

"I'm busting my ass out here in the mountainous forest and all I get is a stinking hello? Wake your sorry ass up! Get some coffee or something!" Tommy covered the phone with his hand and laughed. It felt good to laugh. Danny was listening intently, enjoying the live entertainment.

Stan was now wide awake and fully alert as he walked into the anteroom just off of the bedroom. "Talk to me," he said.

"Sorry for the late-evening news brief. Do you have any idea of what's about to go down out here?" Tommy asked in an agitated voice.

"Yes! I do. The president's chief of staff called a meeting this afternoon. Bud from the DIA was there. We met before everyone gathered at the White House, and he gave me a preview of the agenda.

"The president is furious, and I can't say that I blame him. He believes the situation is another example of the intelligence community blindsiding him. He asked a lot of questions about why Homeland Security, and specifically the FBI, weren't able to disrupt Antifa's earlier activities. He asked why and how this happened, how they allowed a rebellion to fester and grow, one that is now resulting in open hostilities. Thankfully, he'd been briefed about the break-in at the munitions factory – but not one intelligence agent bothered to inform him of the possible link to revolutionaries. Between you and me, Washington, DC may not be a swamp, but it's one helluva bog."

Stan wasn't done talking.

"Since his inauguration, he's given the Pentagon free rein with American conflicts throughout the world. Today, he gave the generals his go-ahead to smash the revolt – and to smash it hard! It's clear there will be no mercy. Honestly, I'm convinced that the president could not care less if he has a second term. The last thing he said to us was, 'Those assholes may think it's time for a change, but I'll be damned if this country's governing laws and Constitution will be forsaken!'"

Tommy wasn't surprised at what Stan had just said, but the words nonetheless gave him pause. There never is enough time for analysis, he thought to himself. If only there was the opportunity to sit down with respected and apolitical historians for advice, before any military action. Instead, we'll be learning from our mistakes afterwards. Maybe then America's actions, or perhaps its inactions, would become clearer. God only knows how many lives would be saved.

"You still there, Tommy?"

"Sorry, boss, just daydreaming," Tommy said, returning his attention to the call.

"Stan, Danny and I are pretty much winging it right now. We're blind as far as the battle plans are concerned. We had a short primer in quadcopter warfare and counter measures a bit ago. Can you tell us anything at all about what the Pentagon thinks the bad guys are going to throw at us?"

Stan began to speak again. "That matter was heavily discussed at the White House today. Antifa doesn't have the same sophisticated weapons that our government has, and the generals are convinced that UAVs will be their primary weapon. Our folks admitted that they couldn't discount the very real likelihood that Antifa is in possession of the stolen C-4. If they weaponize the C-4, that could be a problem. If multiple drones are dropping C-4, we all know that could drastically change the length of the conflict, along with the number of casualties."

"The air force has already dispatched a half dozen A-10s, you know, those Warthog planes for air cover. You'll also have drone coverage with infrared capabilities and live video feed. And you already know about the existing satellite look-down assets. Don't be surprised if some new technology also shows up on the battle-field. It's my understanding that ISIS and their UAVs was a chal-lenge for our military. Our ability to detect and destroy UAVs is some hot, top-secret shit that currently is being tested in the field. The National Guard has been called up and the media is going nuts trying to sniff out some info, but so far there have been no leaks." Stan paused again briefly to let Tommy take it all in.

"We've entered every possible scenario into our computer – so has the NSA and probably every other intelligence agency in the country. The collective consensus is that there will be at least two or three phases to Antifa's attack. What's going on at Mt. Hood presently isn't considered an attack ploy – that's simply one of Antifa's safe bases. Some major infrastructure is probably going to be one area of attack. Hell, there's a dam where you got off the train – we figure an attack is going to be along those lines. Targeting wealthy or influential individuals is most likely going to be another measure they'll employ. Rob Becker's wife is no doubt an Antifa victim.

"Tommy, we've moved our captured military conspirator from the C-4 manufacturing plant to different interrogation sites around the world and so far, have gotten nothing out of him. We're sorely lacking intelligence. Instead of being proactive like your group was in sniffing out Antifa's Mt. Hood hide-out, General Matthews's detachment is just going to have to be reac-tive and mobile.

"If you can capture just one high-level revolutionary who will roll over, the carnage that is expected will be half of what is cur-rently estimated," Stan finished, bringing the conversation to a close.

Tommy wanted to respond but decided not to. "The target presently moving toward me could be that breakthrough we need, but I can't count on it, he thought instead. "Stan, thanks for the info, and say a prayer for us. I'll touch base with you in about twelve hours."

Tommy signed off.

By now, Jerry, with the mules and eagles in tow, had reconnoitered with Tommy and Danny. As a group, the three headed for their rendezvous with Steven.

It was forty minutes later and farther along the trail, when Tommy straightened in his saddle, suddenly seeing a small red dot lighting upon Calypso's right ear. Tommy pulled on the reins, halting his horse, the others following suit. He watched as the red dot moved slowly away from the horse, finally settling on Tommy's chest, where it remained for what seemed like an eternity.

It was the effect Steven had hoped for. He slowly made his way toward the team.

"How's your heart now, Tommy?" Steven was no longer calling him "sir," and Tommy took note. He tried staring Steven down but the fact that he was a civilian and Steven a soldier made a difference. Danny couldn't help it; his laughter pierced the night air, followed by bellows of additional laughter from Tommy and Jerry.

A grinning Steven said, "Follow me please, men."

Fully aware that he was the sole active military member of the group, Steven was technically in charge. The group followed their "leader" about 600 yards due north before he held up a hand to halt them and dismount. Tommy glanced up at the sky, noting that the brightness of the night was dimmed significantly above their interim camp.

"Great location, Steven," Tommy said.

Danny searched 150 yards farther north and set up a mini corral for the quarter horses and donkeys. Jerry quickly threw down some hay and filled watering buckets for the animals.

Pulling Danny aside, Tommy quietly asked him to make contact with Charles.

"Hey bro, I was about to text you. Are you settled?" Charles asked.

"Yes," Danny answered.

"What's the GPS showing as your coordinates?"

"Hang on a second." Danny walked over to Tommy to get the exact latitude and longitude and repeated the numbers to his brother.

"Okay, your target is only a mile and a half away from you. We're pacing two miles behind him. We'll go ahead another half mile and then stop until you message me that you've got a capture. I'm going silent. Good hunting! I'm out!"

Danny quickly relayed the information to Tommy who gestured Steven to join with them. "Danny, you and Jerry go muzzle and hood the horses and donkeys. The last thing we need is for them to be carrying on. Steven, come with me."

Tommy led Steven to a bend in the path where two stout fir trees straddled the trail.

"We're going to string this thin piano wire across the trail. Take the slack from it until it's lying slightly loose on the ground. I'll be behind the other tree. When you feel me tug slightly on the wire, immediately pull it taut about a foot off the ground. Let's go practice a couple times."

The two men positioned themselves behind their respective fir trees, going through several practice sessions before Tommy spoke. "Steven, we only get one chance at this. This guy's probably armed to the hilt, and we need him alive. Once he's down, we have to pounce and hold him down until Danny gets here."

Jerry felt like a fifth wheel, wandering among the other men. "Can I help in any way?" he asked. "Thanks, Jerry, but no. We've got this. You're too important to get physically involved in this shit!" Tommy replied.

"Danny, I think you should find a good spot to hide yourself back a bit on the trail. When the guy goes down, run here to us and help keep him down while we get control. Do you agree?" Tommy asked.

Danny nodded his agreement.

"Okay, let's get us an Antifa!" Tommy stated. Everyone took positions, except Jerry, who had melted somewhere into the surroundings of the forest.

The only thing Tommy heard was the usual noise of a forest. Branches rubbing against branches, the occasional hoot of an owl, and a scampering rabbit or ground squirrel foraging in the now waning moonlit evening were the only sounds of the night.

Until the sound of branches crunching underfoot, exploded into the night air.

Jesus, I don't remember us making that kind of noise on the trail, Tommy quickly thought. He carefully peeked down the trail and saw nothing. Then out of the corner of his eye, he saw a man literally leaping from spot to spot, nowhere near the path that he and Steven had set their trap on. Damn, we're screwed! Tommy thought. Get on the fucking trail, man. C'mon!

Tommy removed his 9mm and attached the silencer. He hoped Steven was doing the same but didn't dare rise from his crouched position to make sure.

More branches cracked, and suddenly their prey was in front of Tommy … but beyond the trap waiting to be sprung.

Tommy was slowly rising with Steven doing the same when suddenly, they both froze.

Their prey, Mateo, was flailing with both arms at a sleek stealth drone, its propulsion mechanism barely making a sound. The drone was like a huge horsefly, darting first at Mateo's face, then backing away before faking an attack on his legs. The drone had begun to circle Mateo's head in a dizzying fashion when Tommy and Steven simultaneously jumped him, bringing the man to the ground with a rib crushing thud. Danny quickly jumped into the fray, binding Mateo with duct tape before dragging him toward the corral.

"Jerry, you son of a … way to go!" Tommy shouted with exuberance into the night air.

Jerry emerged from behind a third fir tree, wearing virtual reality goggles – and a huge grin on his face as he gently maneuvered his drone back safely to the ground.

CHAPTER 42

"**D**amn, Jerry, besides saying thanks, where did ... how ...?" Tommy stammered.

"I'm a 'what if' kind of guy and I thought I'd be prepared, just in case," was Jerry's humble reply. Tommy extended his hand to Jerry in a gesture of gratitude.

Steven secured Mateo behind the corral, covering him with a camouflage tarp before rejoining the group.

∩ ∩ ∩

"Charles, we got him. You have our location ... come now!" Danny's text read.

Until he saw that message on his phone, Charles's mind had been racing with possible scenarios, but didn't move on any of them because he and his team still held the trump card: Marty's phone.

I was standing about 20 feet from Charles when he yelled "Yes!" into the night air. My feet couldn't move quickly enough, yet still allowed Charles to intercept my geriatric sprint. He issued a command to his men.

"Okay, guys, time to hustle. My brother's team took down the bad guy. Let's move!"

And that was a problem.

I figured we were going to travel on foot now, and I was at least twice the age of Charles and his fellow soldiers. There was no way I could jog even a short distance. "Charles, I'm not going to be able to keep up with you guys. You go ahead – somehow I'll catch up," I said, realizing, however, that I had no chance in hell of knowing the terrain or finding the final destination on my own.

"Rob! Dr. Becker! Damn, hold on! My brother's on horse-back. Did you really believe I'd leave you hanging – or for that matter, that the rest of my guys would be on foot? In about five minutes, a trailer will pull up here and offload some horses. Now go change into that gear we bought this morning. By the way, I don't want to hear that you don't know how to ride. Anyone who is part owner of a horse like Towers Above has to be a horseman," Charles pointed out, smiling. I was totally embarrassed.

I retrieved my outerwear and layered up. The Ariat boots weren't totally Western – they were more a hybrid for hiking and riding – but they felt good. The challenge was reattaching my weapon – I wanted to be able to retrieve it quickly if I had to, but that was going to be impossible with the coat. I holstered it back on my hip and under the coat.

The trailer pulled up and in fifteen minutes, Charles and his men were matched up with their respective quarter horses. Charles waved me over and introduced me to my horse, Spike.

"Rob, this horse rides like a Lincoln Town car; I've ridden him before. He moves in one fluid motion – smooth! You'll be amazed how easily he glides along the trail – and it makes no difference if it's a trot, canter, or gallop. The only thing he lacks is stamina. That means he needs longer breaks to regain his energy. So you're not going to be leading the pack, even though he'll want to be out front. Just be ready to rein him in – and keep us in sight."

Charles gave me a hand up and I eased into the saddle. My

stirrups were adjusted, and I was as ready as could be. There were also three pack mules with the group, and I could only guess what they were carrying on their backs.

Charles mounted his horse, and we were on our way.

∩ ∩ ∩

"You want me to go start the interrogation?" Danny asked in a matter-of-fact tone.

"Let's wait till your brother gets here," Tommy answered.

Danny knew a blow-off response from the get-go. Time was growing critically short and now they had an asset that could hopefully give them the answers they needed. "Why are we sitting on our thumbs?" he mumbled to himself.

"Jerry, talk with us a few minutes, okay?" Tommy found a small boulder to sit on and motioned for Danny and Jerry to join him. They each sat, Danny doing so reluctantly. Steven remained standing, halfway between the three men and their captive. He was close enough to hear their discussion, and also keep an eye on the prisoner in case he tried to pull a Houdini.

"You men and the other team coming are my responsibility. I've put them in harm's way and Jerry, I desperately need your help. Forget about security clearances and top-secret information for now. I know about unmanned aerial vehicles – you probably call them systems. I was given the controls of one some time ago, but I quickly handed it back. I didn't want to crash what I considered was a toy. I'm guessing I was wrong about what these UAVs can do. So, start educating us. I need to level the battlefield as much as possible."

"How much time do I have?" Jerry asked.

"Until the guys from town get here," Tommy answered.

"Okay, I'll break it down for you. It all begins with the operators. The person working the controls has most likely been a gamer for years. His or her experience came from playing with products made by companies like Nintendo and Xbox. Tommy, I consider people your age as 'Tweeners.' You were born too late for Atari and Intellivision – and you were too occupied climbing the corporate ladder when the Game Boy was invented.

"Today's operators are younger and have been gaming since before they started kindergarten. It's as if they're chemically enslaved by the dopamine release in their brains, the neurotransmitter emitted in the brain's pleasure centers. This happens from reaching the particular game's next level or scoring more points than an opponent. Need I remind you that our government also actively recruits this type of individual to remotely control and pilot UAVs – for instance the Predator drone? These people have been operating weaponized UAVs for years."

Jerry paused to take a quick break before continuing.

"For the controllers, the battlefield is their video screen. They truly are detached from the reality of the moment. When the UAV drops its killer payload, the target becomes a reward to be collected. Destroy the target, and you earn points and experience ecstasy from the thrill of capture.

"Those handling the controls are pampered pawns, always craving the next contest. They've been rewarded all their lives and truly believe they are owed this type of lifestyle. They probably are also paid very well and rank high on Antifa's food chain."

Danny appeared agitated. Whether he was seriously interested or wanted to bring the discussion to a close was anyone's guess. Tommy's facial expression gave away his sense of skepticism.

"And the Pentagon's reaction to the idea of weaponized mini

drones is a flock of trained eagles?" Danny remarked with a touch of sarcasm.

"Yes, that's one aspect of our defense," Jerry explained. "General Matthews took over about a year ago. He was in Iraq when ISIS began to successfully use drones as weapons carriers. He's determined to have the Pentagon, along with Homeland Security, fund the development of anti-drone technology. He's a visionary!

"The general was one of several people who recognized that the miniaturization of delivery systems and their payloads would be an integral part of future battlefield experiences. He'd read about folks in Europe training golden eagles to attack consumer drones and was determined to incorporate that concept as a defensive weapon for the US Army. He knew that other types of defense weaponry would be developed, but raptors were already proven to be successful.

"He also felt sure that this type of mission, like the one we're on now, was a distinct possibility – and he didn't have to search very far to get me on board. In my opinion, this guy is a true military genius! I can guarantee when the entire unit shows up for battle in a few hours, you'll see the entire package of defensive weaponry firsthand."

Sensing Danny's continued agitation, Jerry tried to end the discussion on that note, but Tommy pressed the issue. "Do we presently have a definitive response to the threat we're about to encounter, or for that matter, a homeland terrorist drone threat?"

"No!" Jerry emphatically stated.

"However, there are multiple defensive models currently in testing, and with varying results. An article was recently published about a well-known defense company and its use of a modified dune buggy, an all-terrain vehicle if you will, with a mounted laser weapon. The company implied that their weapon was the answer to successfully combating a consumer drone threat. But I was there when that system was tested in the field. It failed during a comparison test to another system.

"Also, tracking consumer-type drones is done manually. Right now, our government doesn't have an automatic radar tracking capability for this type of offensive weapon. The platform that performed the best in field-testing used the Stryker armored personnel carrier. The Stryker is manufactured by General Dynamics – and now they've added a Boeing laser weapon to it. During a live armed drone simulated attack, the Boeing product with a mobile high energy laser (MEHEL) did the best."

Tommy had lowered his head while Jerry talked. Not only was he totally out of his element, but he was now being told that America's military forces were essentially no better off. Meanwhile, Danny had finally realized that this discussion and what he was hearing had precedence over torturing their prisoner at that moment.

"What else?" Tommy asked, with resignation in his voice.

"Well, there's the Drone Defender. It's a weapon that jams the signals sent to the drone by air from whoever is controlling the drone. The weapon looks like something out of Star Wars or Ghostbusters, minus the backpack."

"Let me explain. When consumer drones operate, commands are received via a specific radio frequency. The FCC regulates the varying levels of radio frequency and their utilization. Your cell phone, microwave oven—and yes, drones—are generally factory-set to operate on a 2.4 GHz radio frequency. Perhaps you've heard of Battelle? It's a research, technology and science facility, located in Columbus, Ohio. They invented the Jammer Gun. Well, the Jammer Gun, which is a line-of-sight weapon, operates on that same frequency. The gun's radio waves flood and overwhelm the drone's communications, thereby neutralizing the drone. The drone simply hovers in place before it's destroyed by a conventional weapon of choice.

"Easy-peasy, right? Or maybe not. I hate to say this, but the bad guys, if they're worth their salt, just change the frequency the drones are operating on, effectively negating the jamming. Since there's no dial a frequency option on the Battelle Jammer, it becomes a moot point on the battlefield. And then there's the Anti-UAV Defense System, which has …."

Danny finally reached critical mass. He exploded.

"Jesus Christ, enough with the bad news! We've got a guy back there who probably has enough information to tell. We can lay waste to this Antifa operation. We're wasting precious time!"

Tommy began to respond but was stopped by a shrill whistle from Steven. Hand signals indicated that someone was approaching – it took only thirty seconds for the group to become invisible in the dark wilderness.

A minute passed before Danny's cellphone vibrated.

The text read, "I'm close and now approaching your location. Don't shoot, for God's sake!" Danny emerged from hiding, heading back along the path to find Charles. Some 300 yards later, his brother came out of the darkness, reins in his right hand and his left hand raised high. Danny rushed to him.

After a strong embrace, the brothers separated. Danny quietly but emphatically said, "Thank you for being there for me. I love you."

"How many others are with you?" Danny asked.

"There's a half dozen of us, including Dr. Becker," Charles replied.

"I only see five," Danny said, as four other military veterans came out of the night darkness.

"Shit!"

"Shit what?" Danny asked.

"He was right behind us! He knows you've got one of the kidnappers – and he's armed!" Charles shouted anxiously.

If there'd been a starter's gun, the casual observer would have said that both brothers broke away in a dead heat at the beginning of the race.

Jerry stayed put on the boulder during the commotion. He took in a deep breath and let out a sigh of relief. He didn't have to reveal the ultimate drop-dead defensive weapon in the military's arsenal. Or how all hell would break loose if it was used!

# CHAPTER 43

I dismounted and tied Spike's reins to a sturdy branch of a near-by tree. "Thanks for a smooth ride, Spike. I'll be back in a bit," I said, as if the horse understood.

I had no idea what I was going to do to the dude. I just want-ed to know where Marty was – and he had the answer. I was never fast afoot, but I made up for the lack of swiftness with a good sense of stealth. Circling the encampment, I suddenly recalled a junior high school beat-down from a bully. He'd hit me and then he'd run, over and over again. I called upon every ounce of energy and adrenaline my body could give – but I had been whipped, outwitted, and humiliated.

Not this time, I promised. The enemy was out there, some-where in front of me – and he wouldn't be able to escape my fury. I intended to pummel the hell out of him. Somehow the present situation would become payback for what happened to me so many years ago.

I tightened my circle of search and finally came upon the makeshift corral. I spied what I assumed to be one of Tommy's men, crouching next to a lump on the ground. He silently threw what appeared to be a blanket over the mounded object and walked away. It made clear sense for me to go examine what lie underneath the cover.

I crawled the last 20 feet to the target on my hands and knees, finally reaching slowly to uncover the hidden treasure. What my eyes saw rewarded the rest of my consciousness. In an instant my right arm cocked and quickly smashed into the left cheekbone of Marty's kidnapper. I was preparing for a second attack when a loud boom echoed through the night air and a bullet swooshed by, just missing my right ear.

"Don't do it, Rob. Stand up slowly with your hands up in the air. Do it now, Rob!"

I was mulling my chance of getting in one more solid punch when a second gunshot kicked up a chunk of mountain soil and dried lava to my immediate left.

"Jesus, Tommy, I heard you! Give me a chance to get up."

I stood and in no time, had my weapon confiscated, wrists zip-tied behind my back, and ankles bound. Next thing I knew, I was dragged and propped up against a pine tree. Tommy approached me and knelt down. "I'll set you free if you promise no more interruptions or funny stuff!"

I nodded yes, knowing that Tommy only half believed me. The real punishment was in losing my weapon.

Tommy stood and walked away, leaving me still restrained. I started to object but stopped as a full-on argument was taking place no more than 15 feet in front of me.

"Can we get on with it now?" I heard an angry voice say.

I looked up and quickly remembered the face. It was Danny, an operative from one of the seventeen federal intelligence agencies that had helped Tommy during the 2016 spring attacks in Ohio and Kentucky.

"What do you expect us to use? We don't have any interrogation equipment with us. Let's take him back and let the army do it," Tommy replied.

"Then I'll make do with what we've got," Danny said.

"Great, just great, what are you going to do? Oh I know, you're going to use a pocket knife and remove a few finger and toenails from the guy, huh?"

"C'mon, Tommy, by the time we get back to camp it will be too late. We know Rob's wife is in that mine. He was bringing her cell phone to the Mt. Hood hideout. You know they've got to have at least one back door into the mine. Where is it? How many revolutionaries are in there? What about the sites they're going to attack?" Danny wasn't finished with the tirade. His mind hit the refresh button as he paused to reload his next salvo of questions.

"Dammit, Danny, he's a drug addict, according to your brother. He's nothing but a messenger boy. Hell, Steven searched him. What did he have stashed on himself, Steven?" Tommy asked.

"He had a little coke, some 'H,' and an allergy syringe. Oh, we can't forget the Bic lighter, a spoon, and two cell phones," Steven added.

Sensing the win, Tommy tried to settle the escalating argument.

"Besides, you and I aren't allowed to interrogate him on American soil. Stan was emphatic about the CIA's involvement in a domestic crime. I'm sorry, but Marty's kidnapping doesn't involve a foreign threat. Hell, none of this does, unless you can definitively say that the kidnapper is an illegal and part of a plot by a foreign government. Danny, I'm walking away right now if you pursue this interrogation idea any farther. Think about this, too – your brother and his team are inactive reservists in the Army, and I don't think they want any part of what you're proposing!"

"I'll do it," I said.

"Rob, shut up!" There was a short pause and Tommy stammered, "What the hell did you say?"

"I said, I'll do it. I'll get him to talk," I repeated.

"What are you going to do? Are you going to say open wide?" Tommy said half laughing.

"Yeah, I'll get him to open and then he'll stay open! And I'll stick him! I'll stick him with that allergy syringe needle. Oh, he'll tell us what we want. You guys have done this before and know a lie when you hear one. I'm sure he won't give up anything at first, but I can do this!"

The expression on Tommy's face revealed everything he wanted to say. He motioned for Danny and Charles to join him—the three men walking deeper into the woods and out of my earshot.

"Well?" Tommy said.

Neither man answered.

"C'mon guys, speak!"

Charles spoke first. "Why not? Write the questions down and let the doc do his thing. When the dude gives an answer, we'll give Doctor Rob a thumbs up or down to show Rob if we believe the information, or we do it by messaging with our phones. Either way, we're not directly involved in the process. It's all about plausible deniability."

"Danny, what say you?" Tommy asked in a pleading voice.

Danny was looking for a reason to say no but realized it might work. "Let's do this!" he said, clapping his hands together once, as if the three men had just broken a huddle on the one-yard line.

Tommy slipped out of the darkness into the moonlit night, heading straight toward me. He cut my restraints and helped me up from the cold ground.

"Let the asshole know right off the bat that you're Marty's husband. He's got to know that you have skin in the game. We can't be anywhere in sight, but we'll communicate by texting from our phones. Another civilian, his name is Jerry, will be your backup.

If you want, let him handle the communications between us. And don't allow too much time in between the needle sticks. There's a fine line between recovering from an adverse stimulus compared to nervous anticipation and creating fear over when the next cycle of pain starts. Good luck, Rob, but before I go, I've got to ask … where are you going to stick him?"

I looked Tommy square in the eyes. "In the roof of his mouth," was my immediate answer.

Tommy shuddered twice and quickly turned, hoping Rob hadn't seen his reaction. Pulling out the satellite phone, Tommy stared at a new message from Stan for a few seconds before walking away.

The message read:

DON'T KNOW WHAT YOU'RE DOING!!! BUT DRONE INFRARED SHOWS THAT THE COCKROACHES ARE SCRAMBLING FROM MT. HOOD.
GEN. MATHEWS IS AWARE!
MIGHT WANT TO CONTACT HIM FOR UPDATE!

Damn, it had to be the sound of the shots, Tommy thought. It was 3:00 in the morning and it was going to be another all-nighter.

# CHAPTER 44

Steven handed me the allergy syringe. "Could you give me a hand, please?" I asked.

"Do I have to?" he asked with apparent uncertainty.

"Look, you don't have to watch. I just need you to hold his head steady while I get his mouth propped open, if that's not too much trouble," I said while glaring at him. I left Steven with our "guest" briefly, heading into the woods to find a couple of rocks that could be used to keep the prisoner's mouth open and keep him from biting me. Returning with rocks in hand, I asked Steven for his help – and he could tell I was in no mood to be pleasant. "I hate to trouble you, but sit him up so I can talk to him," I demanded.

Steven sat the prisoner up as I knelt down opposite him. "Como se llama?" I asked.

"Eres una puta!" he responded—at the same time dragging his throat and aiming a bolus of sputum directly at my head.

"You're in no position to be insulting me with a gay slur!" I said angrily, after successfully dodging the wad of spit he'd lobbed at me.

"Your friends in the mine have my wife! You're the one that kidnapped my wife – I saw you on the store's video. You're going to answer my questions, or I will hurt you! And I know you understand me and can speak English."

"Oh, tu esposa era una gran cogida!"

"Really? Really, you raped my wife!"

The rage was building inside me. Marty wasn't a teenager anymore, and menopause was a long-ago memory. This low life had to have ripped her insides to shreds.

"Jerry, I see you've got some heavy gloves on your waistband. Do you have any lighter-weight thin gloves?"

"Sorry, Doc, I don't," he answered.

"Well, I'll just have to give it a try," I mumbled to myself. "Give me the right-hand glove, okay?" I asked. Jerry immediately gave it to me.

I moved over to Steven and whispered in his ear, "I'm going to approach this guy quickly and will stick my finger in his mouth. When his mouth opens, I'm going to jam a rock on one side of it and will need you to hold his head steady. We can't have him thrashing around. Nod if you understand."

Steven nodded, and knelt on the ground behind the "patient," using both hands to keep his head steady.

I bent down toward the man, with the rock positioned in my left hand. It was time to make my move. I pounced, using the index finger on my gloved right hand to force his lips open while sliding my finger along tightly clenched teeth until I found the spot I was aiming for. It was the area by the last tooth adjacent to the upper and lower jaws where my finger was able to slip inside the gap. As a dentist, this was a piece of cake for me. My finger pushed into the fleshy part of the muscles attached to his jaw – and within a split second, the lower jaw popped open. In another swift motion, my left hand had also maneuvered its way into his mouth, easily wedging the rock between the upper and lower first molars. He struggled, opening even wider so he could breathe, which let me push the rock back even farther between his teeth. It was now resting between the second molars, top and bottom. And as much as he wanted too, he couldn't open or close his mouth – nor could he spit at me again, no matter how hard he tried. All he could do was make a strange gurgling sound.

I quickly shoved the second rock into the opposite side of his mouth, and his lower jaw was now irretrievably forced open until I determined otherwise.

I hope that hurt as much as you hurt my wife, I silently said to myself.

I spent almost all of my working life building a reputation as a painless dentist. But tragically now, that was going to come to a shameful end. I'd never experienced this level of hatred in my life.

I'm going to hurt you for what you did to Marty, I silently promised.

Jerry handed me the list of questions I was supposed to ask, but my first focus was causing as much pain with the first jab as I possibly could.

"Listen up, punk. I know you think you're tough, but I doubt it. So this is your last chance. Nod your head if you want to answer my questions."

From the depths of his throat came his first words in English.

"…u..c..K…uhh," was his rock-propped response.

"Wrong answer, asshole!" I shouted

I motioned Steven to move away, taking his place on the ground and kneeling behind the prisoner. I stuck the index and middle fingers of my left hand in his nostrils and pulled his head backwards. For the first time, a look of fear flashed across his face, but my deep hatred wasn't going to be denied. I was focused on one specific spot – a smooth, tiny rounded hump of tissue just behind his two upper front teeth, on the roof of his mouth, known as the incisive papilla—that was about to be punctured.

"Jerry, please sit on his midsection. He's going to buck like a stallion when I do this."

Jerry did as I asked, but the cringe on his face told me he wasn't going to watch the action and turned his head away. I waved the allergy needle in front of the punk's eye's before plunging the needle into the tissue. I quickly pulled it out and struck a second and then a third time in rapid succession. His body arched – and Jerry nearly became airborne from all of his thrashing.

Charles told me later that the sound of our prisoner's scream echoed through the wilderness, giving them all goosebumps.

I checked his carotid artery for his heart rate. It was only elevated to 125 beats a minute. Jerry glanced at the man, quickly turning his head away a second time.

"He's bleeding, Doc. Can he swallow?"

"He's okay," I answered.

It was time to strike again and I looked for the second site to inject. A site I knew would also bring significant pain. On the lower jaw, near the inside front of the cheek and between the roots of two teeth, is the main nerve that runs through the lower jaw. This area has a small opening, like a tunnel, that's called a foramen. Nerve tissue is accessible in this area, but it's not as easy to locate as the upper jaw's incisive papilla. It didn't matter – I was determined to find the foramen, and I did!

For another twenty minutes, I alternated between the papilla and mental foramen – and the prisoner's heart rate steadily increased.

"Damn, Jerry, this needle is starting to get dull. Oh well," I stated sarcastically. I showed the prisoner the needle once more and was about to begin anew on the upper jaw, when his head began to shake violently from side to side. I stopped myself from doing the nostril hold – and looked him squarely in the eyes. The man seemed ready to yield. He rolled his head to the right, while blood-tinged saliva rolled from his mouth to the ground. Beads of perspiration covered his forehead, and his nose and face were flushed. Reluctantly I took out the mouth rock props.

"Como se llama?" I asked, as we started over again.

"It's Mateo. Water, please?" he asked in a pleading voice.

Jerry fetched a glass of water. I knelt in front of Mateo, slowly and carefully pouring water into his mouth. It was a chance for him to spit at me again, but instead his eyes stared into mine. It was a stare of submission.

"She's in the mine. She's okay. And that other thing that I said I did, well, I didn't!" He was in pain and defeated, and so was I.

I changed position and knelt behind him again. I began massaging the closing muscles on both sides of his jaw to ease his pain as much as possible. Tears of remorse were rolling down my cheeks. I had violated the most important tenant of a healthcare professional: "Doctor, do no harm."

And I had violated my covenant with my Lord, because I had promised him I'd never intentionally hurt another human.

I vowed at that moment to never touch another patient for the rest of my life.

# CHAPTER 45

Tommy needed to brief Charles on the events that had taken place, but first he had to respond to a text from Stan. Dialing Stan, Tommy said, "You're up early. Fill me in, sir, if you can now."

"I've been up all night, dammit. I'm on an Air Force plane, heading to your neck of the woods. I received a flash message earlier that two groups of people have left the mountain hideout. One group is currently circling around you and seems to be headed in the direction of Portland. The other group is heading north toward the river, at about the same spot where you guys got off the transport train. Does that mean anything to you?" Stan asked.

"Can't say that it does, but we're interrogating a prisoner – maybe your information and his will match."

"Damn, Tommy, I told you not to get involved in that kinda shit!" Stan screamed into the phone.

Tommy held the phone about three inches away from his ear and smiled. "Stan! Stan! Listen up! Danny and I are not involved! You're not going to believe this, but Doc Becker is inflicting some serious whoop-ass on the dude! All I did was give Doc the questions that we need answers to," Tommy replied.

"Oh God!" was Stan's retort.

"Stan, is anyone going to intercept these folks?" Tommy asked, changing the subject while at the same time trying to ignore the ongoing stream of tortured screams echoing through the forest.

"The FBI is on it, and we're streaming their locations to the agents even as we speak. We're giving the revolutionaries their space until they clear your locale."

"Stan, that's fine, but I need real-time information. Is there any way you can hook me up with these sources so I can have live eyes on the target too, same as the folks at the Pentagon?" Tommy begged.

"General Matthews is linked up, but I don't think I can connect you. I'll give it a try, but don't hold your breath. Hey, I gotta go, Tommy, but keep your phone handy. I'll update you every few minutes about the hunt." Stan was gone.

Tommy headed to the corral, where he caught a glimpse of a distressed Rob, who was hurrying away from the prisoner.

Arriving there, he saw that Jerry and Steven were finishing the interrogation. Moving closer to the prisoner, Tommy immediately recognized that this was a beaten man. He saw no outward signs of physical abuse, knowing it was well-hidden. Who'd have thought that Rob Becker could've pulled this off? Tommy wondered quietly to himself.

Steven motioned for Tommy's attention.

"Well, someone talk to me!" Tommy demanded, standing next to Mateo.

Steven stood, grabbing Tommy by the arm and leading him away from the site of the bloodletting. "He's not an all-star. He kidnapped Dr. Becker's wife and was heading to the mine to take her cell phone there. Apparently they screwed up when they snatched her. All we got from him are a couple of names to check out. That's it."

"Damn," Tommy replied. He wheeled around quickly, and within a matter of seconds, had the barrel of his gun placed against Mateo's right temple.

"Do it, man, get it over with," Mateo begged.

Tommy had done enough interrogations to know the captive was finished. He removed his gun from Mateo's head. Taking the piece of paper from Steven with the answers to their questions, Tommy walked away and called Stan for the second time in just thirty minutes.

"What now?" Stan asked.

"I've got two names for you to run down. One is D as in dog, A, N, T as in Tom, E as in evil. Last name is P as in Paul, E, R, E, Z as in zebra. The second name is J as in Jack, A, V as in victory, I, E, R as in Robert. Last name M as in more, O, R, A, L, E, S as in Sam."

Stan repeated the names back to Tommy, who corrected him a couple of times.

"Anything new with the actives under surveillance? Are they still on the move?" Tommy asked.

"One group, the northern group, has disappeared. The other is almost past you but is in an extended single-file position. That means the northern hostiles have tunnels," Stan declared. The call ended abruptly.

Tommy looked skyward and cursed.

Why are these two groups roaming around in the early-morning hours? They know we're here. Are they begging us to engage? Tommy thought in the pre-dawn hours.

Jerry was facing the sunrise when the eagles began to make a commotion. Breaking into a run, he headed to their cages. Within just a few minutes, the majestic birds were in flight, soaring up into the early morning sky, and streaking due east.

"Jerry, what's going on?" Tommy yelled.

Jerry didn't respond. Instead, he swiftly motioned with his right hand, as if pushing air down to the ground, in quick repeated succession. This indicated it was time to take cover.

Everyone obeyed.

I observed as Jerry removed the canvas covers from the raptor's enclosures and followed him to a clearing as we watched them soar higher into the sky. Suddenly, I noticed what at first appeared to be a small speck in the sky. It was definitely out of place and was quickly becoming larger as it moved in our direction.

From behind a fir tree, I identified the object as a copter – but a miniature version. This was my first real quadcopter experience. As it came closer and closer, I realized that it wasn't very large. It stopped and hovered about 30 yards from our position. The mini-chopper was only about 20 feet above the mountain floor.

Glancing 30 degrees farther to the north, I saw another speck heading in our direction. In an instant, I realized that the light-colored object was one of Jerry's eagles. It was quickly streaking toward us when suddenly, it did a low dive and disappeared from sight. Then, wham! The eagle pulled the quad from where it was hovering and was now heading toward Jerry's position. In less than a minute, Jerry had the eagle mounted on one arm, and the drone quad tightly clutched in his hand.

Icarus had downed his first wartime enemy aircraft on American soil!

If Jerry could have, he would have recorded the moment's victory by painting the image of his prey on the bird's side feathers, just like World War II air jockeys did on the metal skin of the side of their aircraft.

Icarus enjoyed breakfast, a double portion of mice, in reward for a job well done.

Naucrate was still airborne, patrolling the skies.

Jerry was dissecting the quad, carefully removing its camera. He next removed the rotors, and carefully gathered the remainder of the body and other parts.

The morning sky was now bright and well-lit, and as I glanced straight up, I watched Icarus's mate circling above us. Every few seconds, the unmistakable shrill squawks of a hunting raptor pierced the air.

Jerry, who was scanning the sky from the east with his high-powered binoculars, suddenly shouted. "Here comes another one!"

We all took our hiding spots again, when almost on cue, Naucrate began her attack dive. Talons were extended as she eye-balled a strut attached to two rotors on top of the sports drone. Wham! A second quad was now out of commission. She had jarred it off its flight path, driving it laterally at a speed of about ten knots.

She was hauling the disabled prey with her talons back to camp, when suddenly a huge fireball lit the sky, followed by a shockwave that literally bent all of us slightly backwards. Jerry sprinted toward the area of the flash, followed by Tommy and Steven.

They reached the debris zone. All that remained were feathers and bits of metal and plastic. Jerry's eagle was dead.

Jerry began sobbing. Icarus, sensing his mate was gone, began a series of mournful screeches.

It was 0730. The sun was shrouded in a post explosive haze. We had experienced our first casualty.

 **HAPTER 46**

Tommy waited a few minutes to see if there would be more drones probing our position.

"Well, that's a question we can knock off our list," Tommy said, turning to Jerry and touching his shoulder. It was obvious that Jerry's emotions were going back and forth between grief and anger from the loss of one of the eagles. "Jerry, I'm really sorry. Go tend to Icarus; his heart is broken far more than ours." This was the Tommy I'd almost forgotten, the compassionate guy who visited me in my hospital room the evening after I'd been shot at the racetrack.

I glanced at Mateo, still prone and restrained on the ground. There was no demonstrable emotion on his face – the cavalry wasn't coming to his rescue, and he knew it.

For the third time in less than an hour, Tommy tapped his phone. Stan was expecting the call. "What the hell was that?" he exclaimed.

"You saw it, huh?" Tommy replied.

"I think we both knew they'd weaponize the C-4. The only question is, how much have they removed from the mine and how much is still inside?"

"I've got two electronic feeds running concurrently, and hopefully we'll get some more answers. One is coming from the satellite, and the other from a Boeing drone above you right now. You may think that having both technologies is redundant, but they each serve multiple different functions. We had the quadcopters on radar, you know!" Stan said in a matter-of-fact voice.

Tommy mouthed a snide remark while actually mumbling, "Thanks for the heads up! By the way, what's the status of the rogue Antifa groups?" he asked his superior.

"There is still no visual on the northern group. The group that headed toward town broke off into two smaller groups, which is strange. One group is really lagging behind and--" Stan said, leaving the thought unfinished.

"And you want me to intercept them because my group is the closest to them?" Tommy finished Stan's sentence.

Tommy heard laughter.

"Ya know, Stan, sometimes you really piss me off! We'll move out in twenty minutes, if--and only if--you get me real-time GPS on these stragglers."

The location of the two hostile groups appeared almost instantly on Tommy's phone screen.

"Damn show-off," he said.

∩ ∩ ∩

Javier couldn't stop pacing.

Dante had been talking with Javier over the satellite phone. He told Javier that Mateo was on his way to the mountain hideout with their hostage's cell phone, but that he should have arrived there hours ago.

Back and forth, the conversation went on between the men for at least thirty minutes, with each successive discussion heightening their angst. Something was wrong.

It was nearly daybreak when Dante knew he'd have to make a tough decision. Javier gave no opinion, as he already sensed he was under surveillance. He knew he had no options.

What Danté hadn't told Javier was that he was leaning toward capitulation and was convinced it was time now to abandon the mountain enclave. Most of the drone teams had vacated the mine a couple of weeks earlier … they had their assignments and were ready for the assault to begin.

"Javier, we've still got three drone teams remaining on site. I want you to have two of them move out right now. Draw straws if you have to, but send them back to town. They know where to go. I also want you to have Magdalono bring the woman here to me. She's an asset we can't afford to lose!"

"Done," Javier replied. He wasn't fooled in the least. He wasn't going to surrender his mountain home without a fight. If it came to that, his life would end in a mine shaft.

Javier decided earlier that day that it was time to see where his potential adversaries were and what they were up to. The sound of gunshots resounding through the mountain air in the early morning hours had alerted the Antifa rebels to an unknown weaponized human presence in the area. Whether the gunshots were responsible for Mateo's absence was still unclear, but the decision had been made to send out some drones to look around. "This just might be resolved with some high-tech surveillance," Javier told himself.

The group's aircraft leader was told to stagger the flights of the two quadcopter drones. The controller and his assistant donned their virtual goggles in preparation. Quad 1 was to be used solely for eyes on. They counted on the rising sun to slow the detection of Quad 1, as it skimmed along the terrain. Dodging in and out of the fir trees, then resuming flight at 10 feet above the ground, the drone traveled about two miles before the control pilot toggled back on its speed. Now the copter could proceed in 30-yard spurts, hover for a few seconds, and then perform a panoramic scan. Quad II followed the same path as the first copter, but its start was delayed by three minutes.

Fifteen minutes passed and the first drone was three miles from the mine, as the crow flies, when some unknown force took control of its flight direction. Whatever had control of the drone was preventing the camera from rotating at a 360^0 angle, but the camera lens somehow managed to still rotate. That's when the quadcopter control assistant caught sight of the curved beak of what she assumed was a bald eagle, because of the coloring of its head.

"It's a bald eagle," she shrieked.

The pilot pushed a button on his controls, sending a signal to the drone's lithium battery pack. An electric pulse should have traveled through the defensive wire circuitry on the skin of Quad 1, shocking the eagle, but nothing happened. The electric shock had failed.

The drone was being controlled by the raptor. The control pilot and assistant standing outside the entrance to the mine were helpless. Then, unexpectedly, the control screen came to life – with the camera lens revealing what was taking place on the ground. They saw a man with a gloved arm outstretched, seemingly drawing the bald eagle in for a landing and ultimately using a forearm for a perch. The man then reached over and removed the drone from the grip of the bird's talons, but not before the camera had zoomed in on the encampment and a group of men in all-weather gear with rifles strapped over their shoulders. The camera had also captured a man lying on the ground – and there was no mistaking his identity.

"They've captured Mateo," he blurted out to his assistant.

Javier wasn't visually linked with his drone team but was linked by audio – and he heard what they said. "Damn! When that son of a bitch starts to reach out for Quad II, I want you to blow him up! Do you copy?"

The copter team simultaneously answered yes, but the lead pilot manning the controls wasn't about to commit murder. All of a sudden, the reality of committing a terrorist act and killing another person became inconceivable to him.

The control pilot observed Quad II traveling the same terrain as the previous drone. He knew the distance was closing quickly and that the drone was nearly at the encampment. Slowly toggling the altitude switch, he climbed the quadcopter to 35 feet. Instead of pushing the payload release button, he pushed a different button, one that triggered an impressive fireball above the mountain floor of the Mt. Hood wilderness. What he didn't see, though, was the bald eagle latching on to the radio-controlled drone.

Months later, a jury would return a verdict of "guilty of murder by terrorism."

Just like bomb-sniffing dogs, the bald eagles were deputized property of the US government and considered by law to be federal law enforcement agents.

∩ ∩ ∩

Javier still had a couple of weapons remaining in his arsenal. The first was the Millennial equivalent of a nuclear bomb.

Somewhere in the outskirts of Portland, a computer set up in an unoccupied apartment was awaiting an order to broadcast a message on a social media site. Javier dialed the number attached to the computer, and it awoke on the first ring. The computer sprang to life, with a message that had been crafted months earlier, and sent it speeding over the world's number one line of communication ... the internet!

The message was an SOS intended for leftists all across America – and it was blasting on real, as well as fake, social media sites. It read:

"Right now, the United States government forces are physically attacking one of our fellow environmentalists in the wilderness that surrounds Mt. Hood! Our brother is wounded, please help!"

Turning what was initially a rumor meant to incite anger into a real fact, Javier added a photo of Mateo in restraints, looking whipped and haggard, to the message. And while the written message itself was untrue, the posting nonetheless became a rallying cry, engineered to create an anti-establishment frenzy among Antifa supporters from coast to coast.

It worked.

The supercomputers of every social media entity have multiple algorithms. These social media conglomerates are no different from a local drug pusher – they know how to stimulate the brains of those who regularly use their social media platforms. Millions of people have no clue how they've become addicted and so dependent – except they're getting a high from a social media blast instead of a drug.

Javier could visualize in his mind what was happening on the West Coast and even perhaps across the country. It was going to be exactly like the atom bomb experiment that he and so many others performed in the pre-teen school years. One hundred mousetraps are set up side-by-side and end-to-end. The spring on each trap is under tension and armed. Sitting on top of each trap, where bait would normally be placed, is a ping-pong ball. The teacher then drops a separate ping-pong ball somewhere along the grid of the pre-set mousetraps.

Pop - pop - pop! pop -pop - pop - pop! pop - pop - pop - pop - pop - pop! Ping-pong balls instantly began flying everywhere.

Javier watched his social media feed, gratified and thrilled as hundreds and then thousands of Antifa sympathizers responded and shared the social media post in a matter of minutes. Like the old childhood game known as Telephone, something invariably was lost in translation from one text or comment to the next. The latest messages bore no resemblance to Javier's original blast.

And the posted comments were vile, hateful, and threatening!

The always vigilant Cyber Division of the FBI tried to keep pace with forensics of the developing crisis. Their supercomputers were diligently working to identify the source of the initial online threat and had narrowed the origin of the post to Portland, Oregon. But the activity levels with this post across the country were making it difficult to narrow the exact source down any farther at that moment. The Cyber Division had different threat levels, similar to the Pentagon – and this problem had reached critical mass.

Alarms throughout the country's intelligence agencies were triggered.

Then, suddenly, it appeared as if Antifa communications went silent. In actuality, Antifa had developed its own form of online communication, which was now in place. It was a code developed among their followers which allowed them to organize protests and hold rallies. They could do so at a moment's notice, not only on the West Coast but in and around other urban areas of the US. These urban areas had been determined long ago and most of them would be active within 24 hours.

The FBI sent a flash message to every law enforcement agency across the country, alerting law officials to be on the lookout for dissidents blocking roads, flash riots, and other acts of civil disobedience.

The message was a huge understatement!

There was one more task Javier needed to finish.

At the end of the main tunnel in the mine was a huge crevice. Both he and Danté wondered what caused it, but since neither man was a geologist, they never figured it out.

And that was a shame!

What he planned to do would most certainly anger his left-of-center supporters and anyone who had respect for Mother Nature.

"Danny, we gotta go!" Tommy shouted.

"Huh! What?" Danny replied.

"Jerry, you surprised us once. What other high-tech gizmos do you have in your bag of tricks?"

Jerry's eyes lit up. He'd been called upon for help and he wasn't about to disappoint. "Hang on, I'll be back in a minute," he replied. He was gone about five.

For the first time that morning, the forest was still. Tommy could hear the mountain birds in song, foraging for their food. I imagined they were more than happy that there were no farther weapons of war at the moment.

A stellar jay chose that moment to land on a tree branch above my head. He stared at me for a good 30 seconds before flying off toward Danny and Tommy. I was fascinated by how close it was to Tommy. The beautiful blue bird showed absolutely no fear of humans.

Marty and I had watched stellar jays for years when we visited our friends Dennis and Linda at their mountain retreat in Estes Park, Colorado. The memories of the Dude Ranch, Long's Peak Inn, and our kids' first horseback rides in that area flashed from the depths of my brain. These memories from long ago brought back some of the fondest moments of my life with Marty.

The jay hopped from branch to branch, moving even closer to Tommy. It was about two feet from his head and squawking loudly. It had Tommy's attention.

Tommy was almost nose to beak with the jay when it rolled itself upside down, hanging from the branch seemingly in what appeared to be the throes of death. Tommy jumped back at least two feet.

Jerry suddenly reappeared from the depths of the forest, reminiscent of the movie Field of Dreams, and laughing uncontrollably. Tommy, myself, Danny—hell, everybody—we were all frozen in place, looking at Jerry and the control box in his hands. We were wondering what the hell was so funny when virtually at the same time, we each turned toward the jaybird as it spun itself around again – this time, 180 degrees into an upright position.

Again, the forest was filled with the sound of laughter. Every human eye was transfixed on a robotic stellar jay.

After all, DreamWorks doesn't have exclusive rights to every technological innovation.

Jerry actually took a bow, to more laughter and applause.

"Ask and I shall receive, huh? Jerry, you're good, very, very good," Tommy said, returning the bow as his satellite phone began to vibrate. "Hello," he answered.

"Are you moving yet?" Stan asked in a distressed voice.

"Almost! What's going on?" Tommy questioned.

"Antifa put out the word on social media that they're getting their asses kicked in the wilderness, as you call it, and now a bunch of them are showing up at different park entrances. They're headed into the forest to help their brothers in arms. Park rangers are trying to hold back the masses, but some are slipping through the blockades and appear to be headed toward the previous targets we've identified. We can't let them meet up! Everything I'm seeing is in real time, and you should be receiving the same intel by now.

I suggest you get a move on!" Stan hung up.

Tommy summoned Jerry, Danny, Steven, and me and quickly briefed us on the imminent new mission. Why I was included in this mission, I had no idea. He must know there's no way I'm going to repeat that syringe-torturing routine I just administered, I told myself.

We headed to the corral to saddle our rides. Jerry hooked the caged Icarus to a donkey. He grabbed the long lead rope and attached that to his horse's saddle. It was time to move.

I assumed that at a certain point on the trail, we would halt, and Jerry would deploy the stellar jay drone. I had no idea who we intended to intercept, and frankly, I didn't give a damn. All I knew was that the last opportunity for recovering Marty had turned out to be a big nothing.

Tommy took a final look at the location of the smaller target group from the screen of his phone. He plotted the approximate speed on horseback and the miles we had to go, coming up with a guesstimated arrival time. The larger target group was nearing an exit point out of the wilderness and in near proximity with the group of Antifa supporters who had come from Portland.

Tommy had no idea why the group we were targeting had almost come to a stop. The last thing he wanted was a confrontation, or more drones armed with C-4 bombing our position. He circled back and handed me my automatic handgun with the silencer.

As he gave up the weapon he said, "Please, Rob, I'm begging you. If you fire that gun, it had better be righteous." I deserved that warning.

Tommy, Danny, and Jerry headed out at a fast pace. All I could think was, If Jerry's going to deploy the drones and raptor,

Tommy's going to have to stay with him. There's no way Jerry can handle it otherwise.

Steven and I were the rear guard. It wasn't hard for me to figure out that he was my chaperone in case I misbehaved.

I could tell that Spike was fired up. Whether it was the cool morning air or the overcast skies, this horse was ready to run. I loosened the reins and he was off. I passed Jerry and pulled up alongside Tommy before Spike slowed to a gallop. I hadn't tugged on the reins or otherwise done anything to slow the animal down. I figured it was simply one of those moments when the horse didn't want to eat dust or breathe in trail dirt from another horse. I shrugged my shoulders at Tommy and kept moving ahead. After thirty-odd minutes, Tommy slowed, holding up his hand and bringing us to a stop. Jerry quickly caught up, followed by Steven.

Tommy talked briefly with Jerry, who quickly dismounted and headed to the donkey. Pulling on his raptor glove, he opened the cage door, through which Icarus emerged and began to stretch its wings. Jerry held Icarus on his right wrist and with his left hand, carefully placed the stellar jay drone on the ground.

Icarus began screeching.

"Damn, they've worked together in the past! Does Icarus think this blue bird drone is real?" I wondered.

In an instant, Icarus was up and away as Jerry quickly slipped on his virtual goggles. He then picked up the robotic controls and the jay drone was soon airborne too. Icarus assumed a patrolling position, circling about 600 feet above the ground. The stellar jay also climbed above tree level.

Jerry answered the unasked question by handing Tommy a set of goggles. Tommy was now Jerry's navigator. Jerry explained the directional intricacies and after a couple short-distance dry runs, the raptor and his drone buddy were on their way.

I wondered how Tommy would coordinate where the jay drone would go, not yet realizing that the fake bird had a transponder. It was sending signals to Tommy's phone with the flight path superimposed over the forest geography, while also tracking the target group. Occasionally, Tommy would nudge Jerry and with hand motions, directing him to turn the jay slightly left or right by directionally using the control handset.

Every few seconds Tommy was alternating between looking through the goggles and looking at his phone screen, doing both in order to refine the stellar jay's direction.

It wasn't long before Tommy poked Jerry, who lifted the goggles up to see Tommy tracing circles in the air. This indicated that their target was somewhere below the jay drone's present position. Jerry began bringing the stellar jay lower beneath the canopy of trees. Almost immediately, the drone's camera locked onto the targets.

A single male was dragging a woman across the ground. The woman did not appear to be resisting and was definitely not clothed appropriately for cold weather. Upon closer examination, it was obvious that the woman was unconscious.

Jerry turned and told Tommy that one of the targets was an older woman. Tommy dropped to his knees. He felt queasy. Some call it intuition. He didn't need the virtual goggles. He knew it was Marty!

Jerry lifted his goggles while the drone settled on a tree branch. Jerry put his hand on Tommy's right shoulder in a comforting fashion as Tommy looked up with moisture welling up in his eyes.

"That's Dr. Becker's wife," he whispered. His head drooped

down, and he was turning it side to side as if to say, "What else can go wrong?"

∩ ∩ ∩

I remained on my horse as Tommy and Jerry monitored the drone and the Antifa group headed our way. Spike was grazing on grass that hadn't yet been stunted by a hard freeze. My mind was wandering, and I never noticed that Danny and Steven had also disappeared. Their horses were tethered to trees nearby, but the men weren't in sight. At this point, I wouldn't have cared.

"They're about 1,000 yards away," Tommy said, pointing in the direction of Marty and her captor. "I want this guy alive, if at all possible. The other person with him is Marty Becker." He paused to let that sink in. "On camera, she doesn't appear conscious, so subdue her captor quickly. We've got to get her Medevaced out of here as soon as possible. Jerry and I will be watching on camera. Godspeed, guys." Steven and Danny were off.

One man headed west and the other went east, and both were in position in just a few minutes. Danny pointed to Steven to bring the dissident down. There was no way Danny was in good enough shape to slither on the ground and get close enough, to within a short striking distance. Steven's muscles easily rippled underneath his outer clothing—quite an accomplishment unto itself. Danny had no idea Steven had won Tough Mudder competitions the past three years in a row.

As he controlled the jay drone and camera, Jerry finally spotted both men in their respective hidden positions. Marty was still limp and the man pulling her was hunched over trying to catch his breath. Jerry throttled the jay drone into flight, sending it buzzing at the man's face, and circling tighter and tighter. The "jay" was then sent into a kamikaze dive to attack Marty's captor, not once but three times.

On that third approach, Steven quickly got to his feet, sprinting a short distance to the target, and then taking him down with a roll block maneuver to the man's rear side. Steven sprang back up and pounced, knocking him out with one punch. Danny arrived in quick fashion, placing restraints on their newest hostage.

Tommy had already texted Stan their position, requesting an immediate Medevac helicopter.

Now came the tough part.

It was time for someone to tell me that Marty was free and no longer held hostage by the Antifa radical terrorists. However, if she was going to live, at a minimum she would still be a hostage of her own mind.

By default, the responsibility rested on Tommy's shoulders. The only question that still needed an answer was, "Just how alive was she?"

# CHAPTER 48

I heard the distinct sound of a helicopter and could tell it was coming from the west. It was becoming louder by the minute and obviously was very close. Suddenly it appeared above me, hovering before slowly moving toward where Tommy and Jerry had been, just a few minutes earlier.

I could only assume Tommy had summoned help for some reason. I too began to move in the direction of the descending chopper. In the last few yards, I saw it start to descend below the treetops, coming in to land.

Jerry suddenly appeared around the corner of the makeshift trail and came to a brief stop. He was looking at me, but in an odd way. It seemed like his gaze went right through me, as if I wasn't really there. He said nothing as he rode past me with the donkey and trailer in tow.

Then Danny was coming up the trail, not far behind Jerry. He too rode past me like I didn't exist. "Danny! Danny! What's happening, man?" I shouted after him, but got no response. A sense of unease began to shake my being to the core.

That left Steven and Tommy, and everyone knew how close Tommy and I were, except when something bad would occur. I gave Spike a thump to his flank, and our speed quickened.

Just a few more yards to go, I thought as I could hear the blades of the copter doing their slow rotation as I broke through into the clearing.

I'll never forget what I saw.

A medic was on her knees next to Tommy, who was cradling the head of someone with long hair. Standing slightly behind Tommy was Steven. My heart began beating faster as the distinctive coloring of the long hair became more familiar and recognizable.

The last words I remember saying were "Oh no, no, no. Please God, no! Not Marty--"

I dismounted the horse even as it was still moving, falling face-down on the ground. I got up and began sprinting toward my wife.

A tree root on the path brought me down a second time.

Shouts of "Rob down!" echoed through my mind, taking me back to the '80s and '90s when I regularly took tumbles down several of the Rocky Mountain National Park's hiking trails.

Just like back then, I was up and stumbling forward again. My heart felt like it was trying to escape my chest. Two hundred yards became a hundred yards, and I was calling Marty's name.

I could see Tommy stand and head toward me. "Get out of my way," I screamed. The next thing I knew, Tommy had wrestled me to my knees and wasn't letting go until he had my attention.

"Rob, listen to me!" he screamed. I wanted to be free and continued to struggle. I had to reach my wife. "Rob, dammit, listen to me! Look me in the eyes, please!" Tommy begged.

There's only so much adrenaline the body can handle before its production shuts down. I'd reached that point. Trembling uncontrollably, I managed to turn my eyes toward Tommy. In times like this, Tommy had a gift very few humans possessed. His words were always calming.

"Rob, she's alive, but unconscious! Go to her; maybe your voice or touch will bring her out of it!"

I literally crawled the last few feet to my wife's side.

I held her head in my arms and began unconsciously stroking her hair. Maybe it was because I had done it so many countless times during our nearly fifty years of marriage.

My heart was slowing and the sad reality of what was happening totally sank in. My tears flowed heavily with multiple pleadings to the Lord to spare my wife's life.

As I held her head in my arms, it was as if we were each wrapped in our own separate bubble. I hadn't even noticed that the attending medic had inserted an IV and was placing leads that would soon be attached to the heart monitor in the Medevac.

I didn't hear the medic say, "It's time to go"

The next thing I knew, Tommy had pulled me away from Marty, as Steven and the medic placed her on a stretcher, which they were now carrying to the helicopter.

Tommy gave me a solid hug, assuring me, "Everything's going to be fine." I believed him, as if he had a direct connection to the Lord. "Get your ass moving," he said, shoving me toward the helicopter. As we lifted off, I saw Tommy standing next to Steven with his right arm draped over his shoulder. I remember thinking to myself, That's strange, as we became fully airborne.

I was free from the frying pan that Tommy and I always seemed to be in.

Nobody bothered to warn me, though, that I was headed for the fire.

# CHAPTER 49

The drone pilot and his assistant dropped their equipment. The controls and virtual goggles were abandoned, left on the ground. Both young men headed to town and back to their parents' abodes. They were done with the revolution.

The stark realities of battle and the possibility of death and destruction are consequences revealed in every war.

A post-Civil War novel, The Red Badge of Courage, by author Stephen Crane, had been a mainstay in educational curricula across the United States, not just in the late 19th century, but throughout most of the 20th century. No doubt the reason was because of the book's descriptive content on the realities of war. It resonated deeply with young, impressionable minds.

It was always my opinion that war can be hell for anyone involved, and that too, was a primary message of the novel. But Millennials wouldn't know anything about that because too many had lived pampered lives. No longer is this iconic book required reading for many of the school systems in the country.

In addition, the fact that a teen's earliest sense of responsibility seems commonly focused around Nintendo and Microsoft making drone warfare training easy to do. The concept of abandonment came just as easily. The Millennial generation's motto seems to more often be one of "We won't" and "We can't." Then, when all else fail, it becomes "We quit!"

∩ ∩ ∩

Javier anticipated that whoever was destroying his drones knew about their Antifa hideout. They'll be coming in force, but not today. They'll attack tomorrow, after the sun is high in the midday sky. So tonight my men will take their positions and wait, he thought.

He reviewed the domain of each sniper on the mountainside. They would be positioned facing west toward Portland. He knew these men were true Antifa loyalists. They'd trained with him for over five years and all were excellent marksmen. At least half of them were Latino. More important, all of them had been vigilant anarchists for years. They weren't quitters, and there was not an ounce of cowardice in any of them.

Their mountain positions were shielded with camouflaged Mylar drapes glued to plexiglass igloo-style enclosures. The igloos were topped with a layer of lava rock. The snipers would be clothed in absorbent black fabric to minimize the escape of heat and avoid infrared detection. Any body heat that did escape would be minimal. This was a moot point, he felt, since the snipers were embedded on the side of a volcano and the temperature gradients varied very little from one location to another.

Infrared thermal detection would be fleeting. Their only exposure would be detection by a government drone or satellite during the few minutes it took to sprint from the mine to their respective positions.

Javier had a solution for that problem, too.

Across the face of the mountain, a daisy chain of flares had been set in place. They were hooked together and electronically configured to ignite almost simultaneously. When the flares were set off, they would initiate a blinding infrared blast of thermal imagery that would make it nearly impossible to definitively track anyone's movements.

Javier had one more major task to finish, but first he had to call Danté. Making his way to the back door of the mine, he ascended the ladder and raised the rock-covered hatch door to the outside, ever so slightly. This gave just enough exposure to the elements to allow a strong connection for the satellite phone. He called Danté one last time, knowing the conversation would be difficult.

"Why? Why did you do it, bro? Now they know for certain. Any element of surprise is gone, dammit!"

Danté was calling Javier out for exposing the group's prime weapon of terror. He, and most likely a good percentage of other Antifa dissidents on the West Coast, had seen the Facebook picture of Mateo lying shackled on the ground. Danté knew their primary targets were no longer viable. No doubt the feds were preparing to deploy the government's drone defense systems in every megacity in the country known to have an Antifa presence. It was time to shift to Plan B.

After another minute of an angry expletive-filled tirade from Danté, Javier was finally able to get a word in. He knew Danté was right and made no attempt at excuses. Instead he asked, "Did Magdalano make it out with the woman?" he asked.

"No, dammit!" Javier responded.

"Well, brother, I guess there's a good chance this will be our last conversation. As soon as it's pitch dark outside, I'm sending out the snipers and will wait for the assault on the fortress to begin. I'm truly sorry that I let you down," he said. "We'll take down as many of the fascist troops as we can. I only wish I could be there when our brothers and sisters bring the government stooges to their knees. I love you, brother. What a great adventure this has been!" Javier ended the conversation with a heavy heart.

He closed the door and clambered back down the ladder to begin that last task. It was time to fill the crevice.

Javier couldn't see to the bottom of the crevice, not even when directing the beam of light from his tactical LED flashlight downwards. He began to methodically drop bricks of C-4 into the endless pit – and none had igniters attached. After about five minutes, he started throwing items into the pit that could incriminate thousands of radicals. Computer hard drives, reams of paper documents and photographs disappeared into the abyss. Back and forth for an hour, he rotated between tossing down C-4 and additional incriminating documents and other materials.

The increased compaction of explosives would intensify the effects of the impending explosion. With help from some of the snipers, Javier finally topped off his landfill with a couple of Generac gasoline generators and some residual C-4.

The last few C-4 bricks were equipped with an igniting timer that Javier had pre-set. He intended to ignite the dump fifteen minutes after the flare light show started. He wanted that window of time to allow his marksmen to get in their positions.

Javier did a final walk through of every nook and cranny in the old minerals mine. The snipers were huddled on the upper floor of the mine, quietly thinking about their mission and patiently awaiting the go signal.

ᴖ ᴖ ᴖ

The wilderness was unexpectedly alive with noise a few minutes before sunset. Birds that normally would be quieting down after their daily activity suddenly began emitting screeches of distress, signaling the imminent intrusion of a huge movement of troops.

Steven was the first to realize that there were others approaching. Tommy was checking his phone for messages, and Jerry was too busy feeding Icarus to notice. And Charles, his brother Danny, and the other Rangers were positioned away from the encampment in a half-mile radius, ready to protect against ambush.

A rising cloud of dust in the distance should have told the rest of the group that General Matthews and the remainder of the cavalry unit was near, but no one had eyes in the sky at that moment. The general and his men suddenly emerged from the shelter of the trees and into the clearing of the tiny encampment. The group had now quadrupled in size. Smiling slightly, Tommy wondered to himself, Where's a good stellar jay when you need one?

Tommy stepped forward to grab the steed's halter and hold the horse steady as the general dismounted. "Damn, these horses sure look weird with all this camo Kevlar!" Tommy said to nobody in particular. "Welcome, General. Everything has been quiet since our scrimmage earlier today."

"How's Dr. Becker's wife doing?"

"There's been no communication yet, sir. I don't know."

"Thanks for your excellent work, Tommy. It's much appreciated," the general said as he offered his hand for a congratulatory handshake.

"General, it wasn't anything I did," Tommy answered. "You put together a helluva' strong group, and Jerry was the one responsible for the successes that we had."

Before the general could respond, an armored apparatus of

sorts came crashing into the clearing, belching out diesel fumes. Tommy had no clue what the machine was or what it did. He did realize that it was some new device and that other than field testing had probably been kept under wraps as a secret weapon. While Tommy walked around the behemoth machine, the general went a few feet away with some of his staff.

Tommy continued to watch as other high-tech machines and equipment appeared. These have to be some of the other new weapons that Jerry talked about earlier, he thought.

As the rest of the general's unit settled in and took up positions, Tommy decided to get some sleep before the conflict started the next day. He was soon awakened by the sight and sound of a pair of A-10 Warthogs streaking low across the canopy of the forest toward Mt. Hood. They apparently were letting the revolutionaries know it wasn't too late to abandon their foolish plans.

General Matthews was documenting everything. He would make sure that future historians had his version of this developing story.

He wrote:

There's a fleet of small trucks equipped with satellite dishes already in the area. They're setting up in the main parking lot near the Mt. Hood wilderness entrance. Representatives from CNN, Fox News, Sky News, and the three major networks, ABC, CBS, and NBC, are all here and waiting for their respective news anchors to arrive.

I remember the days of Chet Huntley and David Brinkley, John Chancellor and Walter Cronkite and the ethical journalism they subscribed to. These giants have been long gone for decades and so has reporting of the truth.

Reporting news is no longer about the "who, what, when, where and how" of a story. In the realm of news reporting in the 21st century, opinion has become an integral ingredient of the story. Whether it's the reporter's personal bias or a general reflection of the network's owners—news has become as subtle as the slant of the reporter's words. Or perhaps an inflection is introduced in the telling of the story.

And then there is outright lying and fabricated news, which my current commander-in-chief regularly refers to as fake news.

Every news media outlet has established a specific philosophic style which naturally results in attracting viewers who share those same beliefs. No longer are news shows a twice-daily event. The media has turned news into a 24/7 event – and it comes with a price tag. The larger the viewing audience, the more advertising revenue is garnered.

News reporting is closely aligned with the adage "Follow the money!"

News has always been under a corporate direction, but most Americans don't understand that. And now the presentation of news has become a polarizing force that is contributing to the division of the people of our country and is feeding the seeds of revolution.

The general put the pen down, putting his writings away in a pouch of personal papers.

∩ ∩ ∩

Unknown to each other, Javier and the general had something in common, even though they were adversaries. Javier's motive behind his social media blast a few hours earlier mirrored the thoughts the general had just put to paper.

The consequences of social media postings that were currently dominating American's consciousness were continuously being fed by several million likes, hateful emojis, and shares on social media. Words and pictures were now pushing people toward conflict!

Albert Einstein, the pre-eminent physicist who established the authenticity of $E=mc^2$, had a brilliant mind. Javier did not. He was right in wanting to destroy the physical evidence, but he was no physicist. Each of the C-4 bricks, when exploded, would generate a certain amount of TNT, an explosive by the chemical name of Trinitrotoluene. More importantly, TNT is the measuring stick for how explosive a substance is. He had no idea how many tons this TNT explosion would generate. While the mass of all the bricks of C-4 explosive he'd tossed into the crevice could have been measured, that wasn't Javier's focus. The only thing he cared about was creating a big destructive boom!

If Javier had been able to actually see the shape of the crevice at the bottom, he would have realized the crevice was widest at the top — it was a fault in the shape of an ice cream cone with a narrow taper at the bottom. Tamping down the C-4 with intermittent layers of extraneous debris created an imbalance. The vectors of the explosion would be directed downward at the volcano's magma dome, which had already been sending signals to geologists that it was in the process of thinning out.

The old saying, "Don't mess with Mother Nature," was about to come true.

∩ ∩ ∩

General Matthews was in direct contact with the White House. For once, POTUS had no sharp-tongued tweet about the imminent conflict.

The orders the general received were short and to the point: "Under no circumstances are any of your troops to fire the FIRST SHOT against the revolutionaries."

General Matthews knew POTUS had been tagged by detractors with almost every word in the dictionary that ended in "ity." The most popular descriptors revolved around his "mental capacity" or lack thereof. Surely he has to be guilty of insanity, the general told himself, while laughing heartily. Nonetheless, those who are so quick in these judgments should know that he didn't arrive at this point in life by luck or good fortune. POTUS is no Forrest Gump.

The general continued his pensive thoughts. No doubt historians will someday agree that the 2016 election presented American citizens with a choice of two of the most flawed candidates ever, in the history of presidential elections. POTUS' saving grace is the military and business experts that surround him. I know he and his cronies will be damned if they let this crisis destroy his presidential legacy.

∩ ∩ ∩

Military experience told General Matthews that the enemy was either still inside the old mine or scattered outside on the mountain. Nonetheless, the overhead drone and satellites were unable to detect any infrared signatures of human life form, inside or out. The A-10s were continuously refueling and flying ground-hugging passes over the wilderness surrounding Mt. Hood, looking for any indication of life.

The evening was coming to a close and the new day was ready to begin when the mountainside came alive with a pyrotechnic light show. If it hadn't been late fall, observers might have thought it was a July 4th celebration.

The Air Force drone with its thermal imaging camera did its best to filter out and identify heat radiating from a person versus the explosive's thermal temperature readings. Streaming video began to record the rapid movements of soldiers across the mountainside, when all of a sudden, their images mysteriously disappeared.

Military analysts across the country and on the ground were left scratching their collective heads. The live feed at the White House showed expressions of exasperation.

Ten minutes passed before a single thermal image registered on the drone's screen. A person was exiting the mountain enclave on a path that quickly led to a trail heading away from Mt. Hood and toward Portland.

And then ... a huge boom emanated from Mt. Hood that was heard for miles. The mountain was the epicenter. The noise was immediately followed by an earthly rolling rhythmic sine wave, or curve. It was like a huge ocean wave coming ashore, retreating and then coming ashore again – and repeating the same process over and over. The upheaval and subsequent retreat of the rocky ground could mean only one thing. The earth was quaking!

Several hundred miles away from the epicenter of the earthquake, extending in concentric circles outward, people on the West Coast wondered if this was finally the big one!

Operators of the government drones had no problem staying focused. Their drone was airborne, and they watched the image of the single person near the mountain, who now appeared to have been knocked to the ground and was having difficulty getting back up.

Suddenly, a second drone operator shouted, "Jesus, look at all the IR heat images that just appeared on the mountainside!"

What the intelligence folks didn't realize was that at least half or more of the camouflaged infrared- absorbing igloo structures had loosened from the ground moorings. The structures were no longer protecting Antifa's elite sniper corps from detection. Intelligence agencies on the East Coast were feeding coordinates of every live person image appearing on the screens into their computers. This information was also instantly directed to the Ranger Command Center at the Mt. Hood battleground.

A few Antifa snipers were trying in vain to salvage their igloos, while others simply gave up their futile corrective attempts. Precious time was being wasted. Frustrated, the snipers who hadn't lost their protective cover began seeking out targets and were soon rejoined by those who were now fully exposed.

General Matthews had no idea what had just happened, but in his mind, it couldn't have been more timely.

"Baker Team, commence your attack! Commence your run, Wart One."

Baker Team had been on a march that started shortly after Tommy and his group left the base camp hours earlier. They were on horseback, circling Mt. Hood from the southeast, climbing as high as they could before splitting up to travel the rest of the way on foot. Half the forces continued to head in the same direction, while the rest were now coming in from the northwest. Tactically, they would control the high ground and launch their attack downward onto the enemy.

"Boar Man" was the call sign of the lieutenant colonel who

was piloting the lead A-10 Warthog fighter wing. The planes were flying from west to east, ready to start bombing the side of the mountain with hundreds of M-84 stun grenades.

The government's pyrotechnic show commenced.

General Matthews was quite sure their adversaries had not gone through flash-bang grenade training. The explosive blinding light can cause havoc on any person in close proximity to the device. Visual disorientation can last for a few seconds, but the concussive effects on a human's inner ear are far more devastating. Stumbling and lack of coordination were just a couple of side effects occurring among those targeted by the stun grenades.

The general knew this battle would be one of attrition, with their opponents quickly losing ground and capability.

The A-10s were gone. Baker Team took the advantage and moved in quickly, easily neutralizing five Antifa sniper teams with no casualties.

A new wave of A-10s came in low, this time dropping canisters of tear gas and pepper spray. But not every sniper had a gas mask on. Another disorienting maneuver had again thrown Antifa off their game. Some snipers began wildly firing at the A-10s in desperation – but the muzzle flashes gave away their positions. Another half dozen sniper teams were soon neutralized – again with no fatalities.

There was a slight lull in hostilities as Pentagon analysts coordinated with the general's lieutenants and homed in on the remaining GPS identified positions of the enemy.

Baker Team was given new orders to resume the flash-bang assault on the most peripheral sniper positions. It was a pincher action designed to grind down the opposition. With the grenades coming in from above, the rebels knew they were outflanked.

Their next move was tactically correct and totally expected. The rebels abandoned their mini fortresses and moved to lower ground, where the cavalry was silently waiting.

Waging war is not child's play, and Antifa knew that. But actual conflict is something that's learned from live training. That means live fire. Warfare is a game as sophisticated as chess, and not simple like checkers. Computer simulation is learned in a classroom and taught by experienced battle-hardened soldiers. And real war is not a computer game named "Call to Action" or any other war-simulation software used by gamers.

War is about Einsteinium numbers, technology, and experience. And none of the Antifa troops had attended war college!

 HAPTER 51

I was strapped into a seat on the helicopter, transfixed by the onboard monitor that was continuously updating Marty's vitals. I'd seen this routine too many times in my life. Marty's blood pressure was wavering between 85-95/55-65. Her pulse was 50-55 beats/minute.

"Can you please tell me if she's running a fever?" I asked the paramedic, who was adjusting the flow of the IV drip.

"Doc, does she run a 98.6F normal temperature usually?" the tech asked.

"No," I replied. "She doesn't, as a matter of fact. Her normal is usually a degree below that reading." That was my first indication that Marty was in good medical hands. "She's asking me for a baseline temperature, which is good doctoring," I thought.

"She's reading just a bit below 97°F. That's not bad, considering how she was dressed and what the outside temperatures were today."

"Are you a physician?" I asked, trying to reposition my body and read her name badge.

"Yes, I've got the Life Flight duty this week. My name's Ellie. It's a pleasure to meet you, Dr. Becker."

"Have we met before?" I asked.

Ellie smiled. "I'm from Lexington, Kentucky, Dr. Becker. You know how we horse folk keep up on our thoroughbreds." Her smile broadened.

As if she could read my mind, Ellie started talking to me in a soothing voice. "Doc, don't go there. She's going to make it. Right now, I don't have all the answers, but your wife is going to be okay."

Her voice was almost angelic, and I felt a calming sensation wash over me. I settled back in my seat as the chopper slowed to descend to the hospital heliport. For some reason, Dr. Ellie reminded me of my middle daughter, Kathy.

I made a mental note to seek her out at the hospital before the day was finished.

In an instant, the copter was down, its door opened, and Marty was whisked away for emergency care. I was right behind her and had no idea which hospital we were at. I was walking fast, trying to keep up with the medics transporting my wife's gurney. We moved through two sets of double doors before I was grabbed by a hospital employee and led away to a waiting room. I could see Marty going farther from me in another direction. I'd also been through this routine too many times in my life. Before I could speak, the escort told me, "Someone will come to take you back to your wife in a few minutes." And then that person was gone.

"I hate hospitals!" I wanted to scream.

I headed to a table in the corner where I picked up a hospital brochure. I learned we were at the Oregon Health and Science University. Hmm, the name is not that different from OSU, a university that I was more than familiar with. Maybe this hospital is affiliated with Oregon State University, I thought.

I was reading the brochure, learning that this particular hospital was ranked highly by the U.S. News and World Report vs. other hospitals in the country, when another staff member appeared. This time, I was led through different double doors, finally coming face to face with a man in scrubs. I rightly assumed he was Marty's attending physician.

"Dr. Becker, I'm Dr. Gentry. We're prepping your wife for emergency surgery. She has a bowel obstruction, possibly a perforation. We've not yet identified why she is unconscious, though. We need you to give us signed permission for the surgery."

The question "What choice do I have?" immediately came to mind. During the seven seconds of this quick conversation, I had to form a trust with this person that was asking me to make an immediate decision. Marty's life was in his hands. "Please, Doctor, don't let her die; she's all I have left in this life," I begged. And then I signed the form.

Sitting in the surgical unit's visitors' waiting room, I began to question my decision to trust the surgeon. I wept a bit, prayed a bit, and felt sorry for myself a lot. Was this normal behavior, given the circumstances? I wondered. Then in seconds, I was fast asleep.

 **HAPTER 52**

General Matthews' command center was jam-packed. There was a continuous humming sound of gas generators that were providing power. Several large computer screens served as the primary source of lighting. Screens displayed the tactical layout of government troops and their positions. Some also showed the known and theorized positions of the enemy. Troop movements were detected and visible, thanks to satellite and drone infrared surveillance. A separate computer screen was dedicated to the airborne assets.

There were two Air Wings, with one of the units continuously circling the battlefield. Even though air-to-ground communications had recorded several incoming shots from Antifa snipers, the A-10 was an airworthy attack plane. It had survived many hits from bullets when flying in Iraqi conflicts.

Tommy and the rest of his group were thankful for the break in action. But he couldn't help himself – every couple of minutes, Tommy sidled over to the general's position to observe the battle underway. He too had seen the image of that lone person leaving the mine on the west side of the volcano just before the earthquake. As quickly as that image first appeared, it disappeared.

Tommy tapped Steven and Danny on their shoulders to wake them up. Both men were in the first stages of REM sleep but shuddered and quickly pulled themselves out of that state of sleep. "C'mon, guys, get your gear. We gotta go," was Tommy's only statement.

Jerry, along with Charles and his men, were standing down and would not be part of this new mission.

Tommy proceeded to the temporary corral and was on his satellite phone when Danny and Steven got there. Tommy gave a time-out hand gesture, as he was deeply immersed in the phone conversation. Both men assumed it was Stan on the other end. Danny was curious – and good at leaning in closer to eavesdrop. He'd done it a couple of times already during this particular trip.

"We're on our way. I'm telling you, yes, I saw the image too – but whoever that was is no longer being picked up by the scan. Listen, Stan, I understand. If someone's out there, we'll find him! Just make sure you tell the general that we're the good guys and to keep those A-10s off us!"

Tommy ended the call, giving Danny the "I know what you were doing" stare before saying, "Guys, the thermal scan detected a person who left the mine right before the earthquake but after the fireworks display. That person has since disappeared. Right now, we have zero information about Antifa's intentions. This part of the battle is going to be finished by daylight. I doubt that any of the captured revolutionaries are going to know any more than our previous captives. I also don't believe this is the end of hostilities. Do you?"

Tommy looked at both men, and neither one could honestly answer yes.

"I figure the person who left the mine somehow went dark, just like the others, once the earthquake happened. I have that individual's last known coordinates. We'll flank the location and slowly work our way out of the forest toward the first set of service roads. This time around, though, we don't have Jerry and his robotics. We have to assume our target is armed."

Tommy turned and walked a short distance to Calypso, placing his left foot in the stirrup and pulled himself onto the saddle. Danny and Steven followed in short order. The three were on their way, night vision goggles in place, as Tommy took the lead.

They were about a mile from the target's last known GPS location when Tommy brought the group to a halt. He and Steven split off from Danny as planned, with the two groups maneuvering in a circle to the expected site. Steven was the first to reach the coordinates, where he immediately saw a discarded Mylar pup tent. "The guy hid out here for a bit," he mused.

Tommy and Danny arrived soon after. "So, we've got an infrared-savvy opponent. Okay, Steven, you'll be at the tip of the spear. I'll take the far right, and Danny, you take the left. Spread out about a quarter mile each and we'll head due west."

Tommy checked his phone for messages and there were none.

Tommy had long ago stopped counting the number of search and detain missions he'd been on. But he could still count on one hand the number of times he'd had a brush with death during any of those events. And each time that happened, he remembered the sense of foreboding and trepidation he'd had at the start of the mission. That dark feeling was back, and no matter how hard Tommy tried to quash that feeling, it surrounded him in a smothering manner.

A mile in front of Tommy, Javier was preparing his ambush.

The park service road that had been excavated years earlier suddenly veered sharply north with a small bluff at the bend. Fir trees had established themselves along with the usual indigenous ferns. Green moss covered almost everything. This is a good place to see and not be seen, Javier thought.

He took a position at the top of the slight incline and calmly waited. Javier knew there was no reason to rejoin his comrades in town and that he'd screwed things up royally. The demolition was meant to cover everyone's tracks. But he'd done more than that. "An earthquake? Are you kidding me?" Javier said aloud to himself. He was shaking his head in denial that the explosion he caused had generated a catastrophic event. Javier unsheathed his assault rifle and attached the suppressor, placing all the loaded magazine clips down by his side. He practiced loading and re-loading the clips half a dozen times.

The only unknown in his mind was who the adversary would be. Through the years, Danté had successfully ferreted out any pretenders and spies that had infiltrated Antifa's elite forces. That led Javier to believe the intruders who had discovered their hide-out had to be federal officers. From descriptions given him by his lookouts on the previous day, he figured they were FBI agents or US Marshals who were pursuing him. As he waited on the bluff, Javier relished the idea of killing a few of America's finest patriots.

Tommy had Calypso on a tight rein, and he knew that the horse despised it. The steed obviously preferred a full charge-ahead stride to stepping his way daintily through the brush. Calypso was coming to a bend on the trail, waiting for a signal on which direction to go. His ears shifted to full forward, with Tommy missing the ear-turning signal by no more than a half second. It was too late!

Javier aimed. The first round thumped into Calypso's chest and became buried in the Kevlar armor. Another round tore through Tommy's left bicep and a section of his triceps. The bullets passed through his arm, barely missing his humerus bone. Thankfully, other rounds in Javier's first clip missed both horse and human flesh.

Javier rolled slightly left, quickly changed clips, and thumped the cartridge in place.

It took Tommy a couple of seconds to realize he'd been shot. It wasn't pain that told him. It was more that the force of the bullet had moved his arm in a direction he hadn't willed it to go. Instinctively, Tommy tucked and rolled to his right. The shift in weight on the saddle caused a tug on the reins, which Calypso interpreted as a "move right" signal. The horse started the abrupt turn. It would be his last.

The fifth bullet from the burst of five muffled shots penetrated Calypso's left eye and instantly brought the magnificent quarter horse to a halt, toppling him to the ground. Calypso's brain stopped functioning even before his hindquarters slammed onto the ground. A final exhalation of breath exploded from both nostrils.

Tommy had been thrown clear and was instinctively reaching with his right hand to check his left upper arm, which was now throbbing with pain. He never saw Calypso's killer rise from his hiding place and begin walking to where Tommy lay.

Javier's arrogance got the best of him. He had to know who had discovered Antifa's secret mountain hideout after all these years.

He stopped five feet from Tommy, with the muzzle of his AR-15 pointed at his head. "Who are you? Are you FBI? Answer me, man!" he demanded.

It was quickly apparent that Tommy wasn't going to answer. Javier's index finger prepared to pull the trigger and finish the kill.

Suddenly, a bullet was launched at rocketlike speed from the end of the rifle's suppressor, past a fir tree! It traveled 300 yards before falling to the ground. It missed. A second bullet followed, and it didn't – as nearly half of Javier's head landed on the ground less than a foot from Tommy's arm. The rest of Javier fell to the ground at the base of Tommy's feet.

From the forest came the sound of rustling and breaking branches, with Steven and his horse bursting onto the service road. The horse came to an immediate stop and within seconds of taking the shot that saved Tommy's life, Steven was cradling Tommy in his arms.

"Jesus, Dad, thank God you're still alive!"

Tommy reached out with his good arm, wrapping his arm around Steven in a gentle embrace that was long overdue.

CHAPTER 53

The little sleep I got was interrupted again and again by a voice on the hospital intercom calling for first responders to go to a certain room and help someone who was coding.

The flat-screen TV was on, but its remote control was nowhere to be found. CNN was the channel of choice for the latest news. This wasn't a surprise, considering where I was and what was going on currently in Oregon. The news anchor was reporting on the crowd gathered at one of the entrances to the Mt. Hood National Forest. It was obvious that Antifa followers were actively protesting. People in the crowds were dressed in black clothing with bandanas and hoodies, and carrying protest signs Many were wearing sunglasses, even though it was nighttime. The reporter never once referred to the individuals as members of Antifa. For me, POTUS was correct—CNN was the distributor of "fake news."

The reporter went on to say that a young hiker had been physically attacked by a group of armed horsemen, adding that the assailants were most likely part of a white nationalist paramilitary group. At least they're somewhat right about that, I thought.

For most Portlanders, paramilitary means a right-wing militia group. The fact that the Air Force's A-10 fighters were flying overhead was apparently inconsequential, with no concrete connection to the supposed incident in the forest that surrounded an inactive volcano. I had no inkling that was about to change in an instant.

Things began to move.

It was as if someone had lifted the entire hospital building and set it down on a huge slab of Jell-O, before giving the building a shove. I instantly recognized what was happening and hit the deck. This is worse than the North Lake Tahoe earthquake in 1998, I told myself.

The building began a rhythmic swaying. Furniture in the waiting room was pulled away from the walls. The mounting bracket holding the television to the wall began to pull from the drywall. In thirty seconds, it made no difference what I was watching.

Because of my previous experience with a 5.0 earthquake experienced on the 11th floor of a Hyatt hotel, I knew to lie still and accept whatever was coming my way. Only this time it was much worse! The swaying was more violent and intense. The "glass half empty" part of my mind took over, and I figured I would see Marty on the "other side."

After about a minute, the swaying stopped. I sprang to my feet and headed to the restroom. Sure enough, all the water that had been in the toilet was now on the bathroom floor. "Damn, just like Tahoe; the quake sloshed it all out!" I mumbled.

Staff began quickly moving throughout the hospital to evaluate the damage. Emergency generators kicked on, restoring electrical service. Staff went room to room checking oxygen lines and listening for alarms going off in patient rooms that had oxygen in use.

Marty was already in Intensive Care, recovering from surgery but still unconscious, when the earthquake started. She was one of many patients who, before the quake, had been receiving oxygen post-surgically.

For some inexplicable reason, Marty's eyes had opened half-way through the shaking and quaking. She too also felt like she was experiencing 1998 all over again. But this time, there was a tube down her throat and into her airway.

A nurse came to the still-standing but slightly damaged waiting room, giving me the good news that Marty was now conscious and I could see her. I was thrilled, but at the same time, nervous because I knew at some point, we would have to talk about what she'd gone through. Questions would be asked to learn as much as possible about the kidnappers.

I stopped at the doorway of her room. Marty turned her head in the direction of the door, anticipating my arrival. The look on her face told me that she knew who I was. She was smiling. As we embraced, a tsunami of tears began to flow from both of us. For at least that moment, all was right in my tiny slice of the world.

# CHAPTER 54

"My left arm! How bad is it?" Tommy asked.

Steven quickly but gently rolled his father onto his right side, and then gently rolled him back.

"It's a clean wound, but we need to put some pressure on it!"

Going to his horse, Steven grabbed the first-aid kit from the saddle pack and dropped to his knees to dress his father's wound. A barrage of questions was swirling throughout his brain. "You've known from the get-go, haven't you?" was foremost in his mind at that particular moment.

Tommy had been filled with anxiety, even a bit of fear, upon opening and reading the contents of Stan's letter after his deployment to Wyoming. He wondered how much Steven's mother had shared with their son. Collecting his thoughts, Tommy bundled them into a "what the hell" moment. The catharsis was long overdue.

"My boss at the agency gave me an envelope with instructions to open it when I arrived at your base camp in Wyoming. The note told me that you were one of the Rangers involved in Project Withers and not to be surprised by your presence. Your mom has always been great about writing me. She's kept me abreast on how you've been and was constantly sending pictures of you. I know everything you've accomplished in your life so far." Tommy paused to catch his breath. His heart felt like it was about to jump out of his chest.

"I don't know if you know this, but Steven is my middle name. That's the one thing your mom and I could agree on. That day I called you out – that day when I saw you for the first time, you just don't know how difficult it was! I was bursting with pride in you!"

"Dad, please stop! I've got to tell you something! Just before that shot I took, well ... I almost didn't take it! I hesitated, and then I saw him pointing the rifle at your head. I just--"

Tommy struggled to his feet and collected his wits for a few seconds. Even a clean gunshot wound can be a shock to the body. "Steven, we've got the rest of our lives to catch up on things we've missed together. Things we should have shared. But the one thing you didn't miss was that shot!

"I have a big favor to ask. Danny has no idea that you're my son. My career at the agency is nearly at its end. The only person who knows about you is my boss, and I want it to stay that way. Can you honor that, please?"

Steven bowed his head, turning it slightly to hide the tear that was forming in his eye. He was able to shake the tear away at the same moment when Tommy extended his good hand. Steven grabbed his dad's hand and the distance between each man, a distance that until now had been expansive, closed as father and son embraced in a strong and long hug.

A minute later, Danny arrived at the bend where the partially decapitated body was lying on the ground. He saw Tommy and Steven seated on the small bluff and talking.

"Day late and a dollar short again, huh!" Danny asked sardonically.

"Thanks for the sympathy card, partner!" Tommy said, pointing to his bandaged arm.

"Oh shit, I'm sorry!" Danny said, and he truly was.

"C'mon, Danny, get your butt off that horse and help me with Calypso. And we need to go through that guy's backpack and his pockets. He sure as hell isn't going to tell us anything."

Tommy, Danny, and Steven went to the fallen horse first. They cut away the Kevlar armor and removed the harness. Draping the armor over Calypso's body, Tommy gently closed the animal's eyelids, lowered his head to Calypso's ear, and said a short prayer. For someone who was not a born horseman, he'd gained a solid respect for these animals that for centuries had carried warriors into and out of harm's way on countless battlefields.

Danny covered the part of Javier's skull still attached to his body and proceeded to strip him down. There was nothing in the man's pants, not even a wallet. A cursory check of his jacket and pockets also revealed nothing. All that was in the backpack was Javier's satellite phone.

Danny began a more thorough check of the coat and backpack. Using his utility knife, he began quartering the backpack. By the time he finished, there were eight sections of the backpack shredded and on the ground.

He began to do the same on the jacket and on the third cut, felt something hard sandwiched between layers of fabric. Carefully pulling the material away from the outer layer and inner lining of the front panel of the jacket, he pulled out a plastic card with a picture of Javier imprinted on it. The back of the card was blank. The photo was similar to what you'd see on a driver's license, and diagonal to the picture was a vertical bar code. "Someone forgot to finish this ID card," Danny thought. He finished shredding the rest of Javier's outerwear, but found nothing else. He called out to Tommy who was still trying to regroup.

"You'd better call Stan and have him send a 'copter for this guy's satellite phone. Our hackers will want to try and break it down, for sure. And this card was sewn into his coat. Obviously, it's not a finished product, but maybe it'll match a parking garage code – or maybe it's just an unfinished ID for a business somewhere in the region. Good luck with that, huh?"

"Don't pitch any of his stuff, Danny," Tommy said. "He could have hidden a decal or laminate of some sort to put on that card at a later time. If he went to that much trouble to hide the card, well then, there's got to be another piece of the puzzle nearby. In fact, throw all of his stuff together. Let's not get rid of anything."

Tommy turned away but quickly stopped in his tracks. "The same goes for his body! The agency can get him out of here on a chopper, too. When they have his body in custody, then they can do an orifice check on him. You just never know what might be hidden, huh? Unless of course you want to do it now, Danny!"

Tommy turned away, shooting a look at Steven who was obviously enjoying the verbal exchange between his father and Danny.

Tommy was back in full form. That surge of adrenaline was all he needed. His internal supercomputer was again fully operational, and Tommy was ready to bring this chapter in his life to a close.

Steven had experienced the same internal chemical reaction, but for him, it signaled a new beginning and purpose to his life.

# CHAPTER 55

The three men had each taken a position on the bluff when the sound of twirling rotors suddenly echoed through the forest. The loudness indicated that there was more than one helicopter approaching. The first of the helicopters to land was an MH-47G Chinook.

The second, an OH-6A observation helicopter, touched down a few yards beyond the Chinook.

The crew on the Chinook were out quickly and on the ground, checking out the payload they would be transporting. It took all of them to load Calypso onto an oversize cart and into the aircraft. They then retrieved the decapitated body, leaving strewn parts of the severed skull and brain for the four-legged and winged scavengers.

Tommy walked to the person who was obviously in control of the group. "Make sure a complete autopsy is conducted as soon as possible, and don't forget the cavity search. Tell them not to miss any opening and that his entire digestive tract better be empty when it's done!"

After no more than thirty minutes on the ground, the Chinook was airborne once again.

The transport copter was safely away and on to its final destination when a lone figure emerged from the smaller aircraft, walking toward his two agents.

"Men, good morning."

Tommy and Danny, quite used to the brevity of conversation from their boss, answered, "Good morning, sir."

"Sir, I'd like to introduce Steven. He's the young Ranger who has been a wonderful asset to us during these past few days," Tommy said.

Steven stepped forward and shook Stan's hand.

"Glad to meet you, young man. I must say, you remind me a lot of an operator we have in the field right now."

The statement flew over Danny's head but slammed into both father and son with blunt force. Both men lowered their heads, trying not to smile or laugh.

"Steven, if you don't mind, I'd like a few words with my men. Excuse us, please."

The three operatives walked over to the bluff. Tommy and Danny sat as Stan stood and began to speak.

"We've captured fifty of the revolutionaries and I'm happy to say there were no casualties on either side. The prisoners were taken to Salem for interrogation. As we expected, none of them have yet offered up any useful information. We're running their fingerprints and will try to establish their identities. We need to confirm if they're even citizens. If they're illegals, we'll figure out their country of origin and most likely ship them back. Or perhaps send them to Guantanamo and let them ferment there for a while.

"If they're not American citizens, sending them back to their land of citizenship accomplishes two things politically. It makes our president look good, and it embarrasses their native countries. They might end up doing some prison time back home, but that's doubtful. Another option is if Congress does something stupid and attempts to force a closure of Gitmo, then we'll put them on trial for treason."

Stan paused for a few seconds before continuing.

"I also need to let you know that the general, with the president's approval, has two reporters embedded with the troops. One is from the Wall Street Journal and the other is affiliated with the Christian Science Monitor. POTUS believes these two particular news organizations will offer the most ethical and journalistically sound reporting of this conflict. Their first stories are going to run this morning. Rest assured that they were not allowed to photograph any of our horses in dress uniform!"

Tommy and Danny looked at each other and if lasers could have shot from their eyes, Stan's head would have instantly exploded. Stan instantly recognized their reaction. "Don't interrupt me. You'll get your chance in a minute!

"POTUS and General Matthews agree that this proactive action may end the conflict instantly. Outing the revolutionaries seems to be our best chance of bringing the hostilities to a quick end. The president knows there will still be some pockets of resistance, but no one would ever expect him to respond in a manner that uses the media.

"The other reason for the government's transparency, if you want to call it that, is our intelligence agencies are in agreement that it's the best way to disarm and neutralize the mission of these socialistic Millennials. Our government has been collecting data on American anarchists for years, and it's safe to say we've identified 95 percent of them. When the Feds figure out their specific involvement in this uprising, they will be arrested swiftly.

"And yes, I do know that this course of action feeds Antifa's contention that America's government is not democratic but fascist."

Again Stan paused, but not long enough for the others to get a word in.

"What I'm about to say is my opinion at this point of time. If hostilities can be nipped now, hopefully we can delay a full-blown 'war' for a few years. This would stop, at least temporarily, the budding secessionist movement on the West Coast of our country. In the meantime, we'll let the FBI folks begin to round up the revolutionaries and hopefully send them to the Caribbean for a little hard labor amidst the sunshine. Maybe then these people will understand there are consequences for their actions.

"Finally, I doubt you realize the totality of what happened last night. The earthquake measured 6.8 on the Richter scale. The damage extends more than 100-plus miles in all directions. You guys can't see it, but Mt. Hood is now an active volcano and is smoking up a storm. So is Mt. Saint Helens up north and even farther north, Mt. Rainier. To the south, Mt. Shasta is experiencing earthquake swarms."

Stan, obviously on a roll, stopped to once again catch his breath.

"In the early spring of 2016, this entire northwest region was experiencing earthquake swarms. Every seismologist was wondering which mountain or mountains would go active. All of these volcanoes are geographically on the Cascade fault line and in the so-called Ring of Fire.

"The seismologists are already convinced yesterday's event didn't have to happen, and the intelligence folks agree. They believe there was an explosion first because the damn idiots mishandled the stolen C-4. This resulted in the explosive force which opened an already weakened fissure, which set off the chain of events that created the potential now for an environmental apocalypse along the West Coast! There's going to be a press conference at 9 this morning, and believe me when I say that Antifa will get blamed for this nightmare!

"So the consensus among the intelligence community is that after the rest of the press and the public hears and digests this information, at least two-thirds of Antifa supporters will seriously consider jumping ship. They're pretty much all hard-core environmentalists, and the flames of revolution just might be extinguished. That's it; I'm done now."

Tommy stared at Danny and finally said, "You or me?"

After three shoulder shrugs from Danny, Tommy stood up. His left arm was aching, and he was flashing back to the race track in Kentucky when he'd broken a car window with his bare fist. His current level of pain hadn't quite reached the hurt he felt on that day, but it wasn't far off. And that was putting him in a foul mood. Tommy wanted nothing more than to crawl under a blanket and hide out for a while and catch some sleep ... and then it hit him.

"Jesus, Danny, those guys we saw a couple of days ago ... you know, the ones who looked like they were leaving the old mine and heading north before they disappeared from the drone's monitor. They had to have been wearing that Mylar material to avoid infrared detection. You know, the same kind of cover that our dead guy had. And damn, they just hauled him out of here with Calypso. I totally forgot about those others because they weren't heading to town! So I'm going to hold that thought for a minute!" Tommy turned to face Stan.

"Stan, here's what I think! I've heard this junior varsity shit in the past. I ignored it back then and I'm asking you, Stan, be with me in ignoring it now too. These young people aren't dumb

– actually, they're pretty intelligent. The only thing they lack are the sophisticated tools of war that our government and military has. Just because we shine a light on them as the government is proposing doesn't mean they're going to scurry under the baseboards and disappear like cockroaches. No way! No fucking way!"

The pain in his upper arm gnawed on Tommy a bit more. He took a deep breath to try and control it before continuing.

"I tell you what we've done – we've screwed up their game plan. There's no way we were supposed to get our hands on Rob Becker's wife when she was forcibly being led to another hiding place. And I think we upset their timetable by finding that old mine. I guarantee you, that mine was a hideout and staging platform for them. Their targets are in an urban area somewhere. Whether it's Portland or Salem, the state capitol, I have no clue. That guy who took a chunk of tissue from my arm had some kind of plastic ID card well hidden in his coat. That plastic card wasn't meant for use in an ATM in the woods! Something is going down in a major city somewhere on the West Coast, and I'm betting they still have enough C-4 to do major damage. Don't forget, we've already seen how well they use drone technology. Shit, this damn arm ...." Tommy momentarily paused.

"What the hell is north of this volcano that could be a target? Where the hell were those guys going the other day?" Tommy wondered out loud.

Stan's and Danny's facial expressions deepened into belief and worry as Tommy checked off his shopping list of concerns in a way that only a seasoned agent could express with confidence and conviction.

Danny finally spoke. "I fully agree with Tommy," he emphatically declared. It was clear that Stan was giving serious consideration to what Tommy had said and began shaking his head.

"Damn you, Tommy! I wish what you said didn't make so much sense. I had convinced myself we were over the worst!"

There was a long pause when no one had anything else to add. It was now on Stan to make the next move. He motioned for Steven to join them.

"General Matthews is packing as we speak to head north to the transport cars and back home. There's no way we intended for he and his troops to carry out urban warfare. The less the public knows about Project Withers the better. I'll tell him--"

"Stan, stop for a minute, please," Tommy asked. "Have any of the general's men searched the mountainside for evidence? I mean, with an explosion of that magnitude and with all that shaking and rolling going on, there has to be some form of evidence that could help us going forward!"

Stan shook his head no. After the snipers were neutralized, the general ordered all troops off the mountainside. He'd assumed the old mine was now bulging at the seams with hot lava after the explosion and earthquake. In addition, when smoke started billowing out of the volcano, the government seismologists emphatically told everyone to clear the area immediately.

"Tell you what, Stan; the three of us will go in there again and take a quick look around. There might be some clue on that mountainside that could make a difference."

Stan walked away from Tommy, Danny, and Steven, placing a call from the satellite phone to some government higher-up thousands of miles off to the east. After about five minutes, Stan hung up, and walked back toward the waiting three men.

"The General is sending a half dozen men back up the

mountain with directions to harvest anything that looks like a clue. Tommy and Danny, I am not sending either of you back up there – nor are you returning to Wyoming. The General has agreed to that. He is also in agreement that if you want, Steven, you can extend deployment and continue to work with these two. The General is still at the campsite where they're breaking down tents and packing up. I suggest all three of you head back there now. Once the mountainside has been checked again and the general gives the final order to clear out, then this phase of the operation is over."

Stan changed his course of thought, giving the three men final instructions.

"Determine which horse can carry two of you and once you're back at camp, find out if there's a spare horse you can use. If the general's men return from their scavenger hunt with anything, pack it up and bring that with you. Give me a call when you're ready to be extracted and I'll have the Chinook pick up all of you and your horses."

Tommy didn't bother telling Stan that they already had an extra horse. It only figured that Tommy would end up riding Rob's horse, Spike. Steven had been dragging him around since Rob left with Marty on the helicopter.

Stan shook the men's hands and began walking to his copter. He was carrying the bag with the remnants of clothing stripped from the shooter. Tommy and Steven were thankful that the general had also been informed about what was becoming a not-so-secret relationship.

The number of those in the know was steadily increasing.

# CHAPTER 56

Marty was asleep, and I needed some fresh air. I stepped outside, hoping to catch the sunrise in the eastern sky. Unfortunately, the seasons were changing in the northwestern part of the country and grey was the typical prevailing color.

I took time instead to thank the Lord for sparing Marty's life, as well as mine.

If the sprawling hospital complex had been a living entity, it would have taken a deep breath in anticipation of morning classes, patient admissions, outpatient tests, surgeries, and the coming and going of hundreds of visitors.

I stared at the lighter shade of grey horizon and began to laugh at my misdirected thoughts. There certainly weren't fifty shades of grey today.

Suddenly, the sounds I'd heard a day earlier began to again reverberate in my ears. It was that same buzzing sound that was emanating from the attacking quadcopter slightly more than 24 hours ago. I quickly turned my head right and then left but saw nothing. Even so, I found myself flinching and looking for cover. When I finally spied what I thought was the drone, it was climbing, and darting laterally and then it was gone. My heart rate slowed, and I regained my composure.

"Thank God, no explosion this time," I said to myself.

I retreated into the safety of the hospital lobby. I wanted to talk with somebody but quickly realized I was in civilization and not in the wilderness anymore. "Is this what PTSD is?" I silently wondered.

I forced myself outside once more. It was more of a "pinch me, I'm not dreaming" moment this time. I looked everywhere in the sky and on the horizon and saw nothing. This gave me much-needed reassurance, which helped my psyche.

Returning inside once more, I made my way to Marty's bedside. I had rationalized away my drone moment, telling myself it had to have been a flashback or a hallucination, but it definitely wasn't real.

I realized that I'd slept all of maybe two hours in the past day and desperately needed a full night's rest. My mind and body had to be running on fumes. My thoughts were suddenly interrupted by the vibration of my phone.

∩ ∩ ∩

After Stan's helicopter departed, Tommy looked at Danny and Steven, telling them "C'mon, let's get back up on that mountainside! No offense, Steven, but Danny and I know how to do a search, and if there's something out of the ordinary, we'll find it. Let me give Rob Becker a quick call first and see how things are going, and then we'll head out. Oh, and Danny, give your brother a call and tell him he can join the party if he and his men want to."

Tommy dialed Rob while staring at the grey sky to his east. That's a different shade of grey, he thought, laughing to himself, in the same way Rob had done just a few minutes earlier from the hospital rooftop.

I answered the phone. "Hey Rob, please tell me some good news," I heard a voice say on the other end.

"Oh God, Tommy, she's conscious! She needed emergency surgery, but she's going to be fine, I think."

If Marty had been awake to hear what I just said, she'd have told me, "Stop that glass half-empty stuff, Rob!"

At that moment, I realized how relieved I was now that I was no longer on the mountain with Tommy.

There's got to be another way of solving societal differences without resorting to hostilities and outright warfare, I found myself thinking. I started to tell Tommy about the bizarre events I convinced myself had taken place in my imagination just a few minutes earlier but stopped myself.

I shouldn't have.

"Listen, Rob, we're pretty much finishing things up out here. This revolution is far from over, and I'm certain the media will refer to these events as minor skirmishes. The fact that there were zero fatalities shouldn't mean we can overlook the destructive and treasonous mindset of those revolutionaries. By the way, when I talk to Charles, I'll have him get in touch with the people who are detaining Marty's sister and have them release her.

"Rob, we have no idea where the revolutionaries might strike. I have no doubt the National Guard will protect the usual potential targets. If you see anything suspicious, call me! Gotta go!"

"Tommy, Tommy ..." I called out, but it was too late. I'd hesitated and shouldn't have. I began arguing with myself.

"Damn!"

"Too late!"

"Call him back, dammit!"

"Don't you dare, dammit!"

I ended the argument with my alter ego. "It wasn't real, you idiot!" My brain was spinning out of control and what I needed at that moment was some kind of a controlled substance. I knew a strong Long Island iced tea would help, but also knew the last place I'd find a bar was in the hospital.

I got up and went back to the visitors' waiting room and sat down. Sure enough, CNN News was reporting the events exactly as Tommy had predicted. There was no mention of any possible cause that triggered the pending volcanic venting or even the likelihood of a full-on eruption of Mt. Hood.

Nor was there any mention of any stirrings of the other volcanoes in the northwest region. The National Guard's presence had become a story about a conflict caused by White Nationalist groups that had gathered in response to the Antifa protesters at the entrances to Mt. Hood. Wherever Antifa was, so were their polar opposites.

Only later did I learn that the best source for news was now the Wall Street Journal, which wasn't sold in the hospital gift shop.

My frustration level was escalating, and I felt trapped. I didn't even have the luxury of escaping into the world of dentistry, since I had burned that bridge earlier this week after my torture of another human being.

"God, I miss Kentucky!"

CHAPTER 57

It took Steven an hour to lead the group back down the mountain to the encampment. The last of the tents were coming down, and from the clearing where the general's war tent had been, the men got their first look at Mt. Hood, surrounded by what appeared to be a haze of smoke.

However, it wasn't all smoke. At that moment, clouds of steam produced by lava were forcing their way through the fissure and mixing with the moist cold air surrounding the volcano. The fissure was deeper and wider than before the explosion.

Tommy spotted General Matthews, who along with a couple of his aides were having an animated conversation with a man he'd never seen before. I wonder what that's all about, Tommy thought as he got off his horse and walked closer to listen in on the conversation.

"The lava will escape through the fissure and push its way out, while following the path of least resistance," the man was saying. "This is a classic example of a fissure volcano, and how long the lava flows is anyone's guess. There'll be fires that will break out as the flow progresses. However, there won't be a big blowoff of lava or a significant amount of volcanic ash produced."

Tommy figured the guy was a geologist who was an expert in the area of volcanoes and earthquakes. The discussion was winding down, with the man stressing that everyone should steer clear of the fissure until they could determine which direction the lava flow would take. What once had been a mineral mine was now a cauldron of molten lava that was searching for and seeping toward daylight.

General Matthews saw Tommy out of the corner of his eye and headed toward him when the conversation was over.

"You know, if you were one of my men, you'd be getting a Purple Heart."

Clearly the general had talked to Stan. Tommy took in his remark before both men smiled.

"I know what you're planning to do, and I can't let my man Steven go with you. He's under my command and I haven't lost anyone yet," the general told Tommy, with a wink. "One more thing, Tommy. Your son has been placed on leave for thirty days. Take good care of my soldier. I want him back in one piece, if you don't mind." Tommy was now beaming.

"Thank you, General!" Tommy exclaimed, shaking the general's hand and saying his farewell.

∩ ∩ ∩

Danté tried for a sixth time to connect with Javier. He'd figured out that Mateo had been neutralized and was quickly becoming resigned to the fact that Javier had met the same fate. The warehouse was useless now. Anything and anyone that had been utilized in the past 48 hours was assumed to be a worthless asset.

Next in the line of the Antifa leadership was Ricardo, named after his father, who was a revolutionary from Colombia. Father and son were both avowed communists and experienced anarchists. Danté hadn't moved the younger Ricardo up in the cadre's hierarchy because of his propensity for violence which kept him doing prison time more often than not. But now, Danté thought,

The only answer to the intervention of the US government is violence!

Danté summoned Ricardo to his apartment.

Thirty minutes later, the two anarchists were reviewing their secondary targets. They quickly realized that one of the primary targets was still active, and all indications were that the government hadn't found it yet.

"These are the targets that I want destroyed. Every one of them represents capitalism. When we strike, it will inspire our brothers and sisters and lift their spirits. The entire West Coast will explode in rebellion," Danté said.

Ricardo never argued over instructions. When told to do something, he did it – he was now in charge of Antifa's quadcopter Fighter Wing.

Danté gave a list of drone operatives to work with to Ricardo, adding that he hoped the targets would be attacked no later than 7:00 the next morning. Ricardo left with a huge smile on his face, excited at the thought of blowing up several targets.

∩ ∩ ∩

"Danny, can you see if Charles and his men can join us?" Tommy asked. Within a few minutes, they were all gathered together.

"Men, we have to go back to the site where the mine was. I say 'was' because there's probably nothing left of it now. An explosion in the mine set off the earthquake, and now the volcano is active. I just heard a seismologist say that we'll most likely run into a lava flow near there. Now I've never seen anything like that ...."

Tommy was interrupted by nervous laughter.

"I'm not going to downplay the seriousness of this. There

could be hazards from the volcanic flow and ash. Be prepared to react quickly. Especially if you smell something different or weird in the air, get the hell outta there—fast. There could be toxic gases coming out of the volcano.

"We're looking for evidence and clues. Things you wouldn't normally see in a mineral mine. Normal would be a pick or a shovel or some kind of miner's light. Not normal would be a toy, an iPad, or any other type of electronics, for that matter. Don't assume something is inconsequential. You've got ten minutes to grab your gear before we head up the mountainside. And I can't say thank you enough for what you're willing to do," Tommy told the group assembled in front of him.

Ten minutes later, the men were heading up a trail that by now was quite familiar to Danny and Tommy.

As they neared the vicinity of the old mine, Tommy began to have second thoughts. The air was putrid. Tommy reined in his horse, putting a hand up and signaling the men to stop for a moment. He pulled out a handkerchief and placed it over his nose and mouth. He indicated for the others to do the same.

It was obvious that this search mission would be very short — fifteen minutes tops, Tommy thought. Danny and Tommy went in one direction while Charles and his men went the opposite way.

Danny quickly found remnants of an HP printer with its registration number still attached. "Trace the registration and maybe you get a name," he reasoned.

Tommy was finding nothing and was mentally dealing with the thought that he was leading the men to their deaths.

Meanwhile Ralph, one of Charles's men, had come across a "not-normal" item Tommy had cautioned them to look for.

Wedged among the debris above the mine's entrance was a shattered diver's mask, and not far from that was a regulator gauge normally used on an oxygen tank in scuba diving. Mt. Hood was known for skiing on its glaciers well into the spring months, but it was not known for deep sea diving, Ralph thought.

After twenty minutes of searching, both teams knew they had to give it up. They quickly made their way back to an altitude where the air was pure. Within seconds, they were all coughing and vomiting in an attempt to purge from their bodies the toxins they had breathed in.

It was time to check their booty. Every item the men had collected was put in a pile and sorted through to determine each item's importance. One look at Ralph's mask and gauge told Tommy and Danny they'd hit the jackpot.

"Are you shitting me, Ralph? You did good, young man. Now we need to figure out what would be a good target and also be underwater in this area of the country," Tommy said.

"I'll be back. I have to make a call," Tommy said, heading to a clearing where he could call Stan.

"Talk to me," Stan answered.

"Plug into one of your supercomputers and put in the following target information," Tommy said in an urgent tone. "Let me know when you're ready," he added.

Stan connected to Langley on his laptop.

"Okay, I'm ready. What do you have?"

Tommy gave instructions. "Type this in: Government/infrastructure assets that are located on or near salt/fresh water in Oregon or Washington."

"Are you shitting me?" Stan yelled into the phone.

"Just do it, boss!" Tommy replied.

"Okay, I did! Now explain it to me," Stan demanded.

As he was talking, Tommy returned to the group, signaling them to saddle up and head back to the area where the encampment had been. Along the way, Tommy continued his conversation, telling Stan about what Ralph had found. He also gave Stan coordinates of the former encampment so the group could be picked up.

It was time for their extraction. Hopefully, a couple of black Chinooks will arrive shortly, Tommy thought. He was also hoping for a late lunch, a hot shower, and some sleep.

 HAPTER 58

Tommy and Danny had never been to the CIA's satellite office in Seattle – a short hop from Portland. Stan, however, started his career with the agency in the Northwest. This was a coming-home moment for Stan.

Javier's clothing was carefully and bit by bit under dissection.

Agents in the forensics lab were having a good morning. It helped that they were given a huge clue in the search – the plastic card. For them, it was no different than having a piece of a jigsaw puzzle, except that they needed the other pieces that fit around it. And they found them, sewn between the layers of fabric in the right cuff of Javier's shirt.

Already known was the exact placement of Javier's photo and the bar code. The missing pieces would indicate their own specific placement on the card – once the right position was determined. It was like a Rubik's Cube. Turn a piece here … no, that's not right. Put that there and this one here … that's not right either.

After trying every possible combination, the agents found the placement they felt was right. Each maneuver and positioning had been video recorded, along with the agent's conclusions. Findings were fed into the supercomputer. All they could do now was to wait for the final analysis. Ninety percent of the time, the technician's findings were in sync with their non-human super technological "friend." Of course, there was also the unspoken but very real competitive spirit among those in the lab.

It was man versus machine! And those ten percent instances when man was wrong were not happy occasions.

It took about thirty minutes before results were in. The men in the white coats had nailed it! There was a 99 percent certainty that the card puzzle pieces were put together correctly.

All that remained was to take that data and feed it into another software program that contained archived information on countless ID cards. The archive included the majority of ID cards from businesses and organizations throughout the northwest United States, including Oregon and Washington states, as well as northern California.

The likelihood was strong that the card's barcode would provide a wealth of information. Most ID cards these days were designed with embedded microchips that contained all the user's personal information. The computer would eventually give up the information on the entity that issued the ID card – but the analysis could take some time.

∩ ∩ ∩

I was outside on the hospital grounds with Lauren, explaining everything that had taken place over the past days, when I heard the buzzing sound again. I quickly turned to look, and there it was, a drone quadcopter just hovering in the air about five stories up. It's not an aberration, I told myself. Then suddenly, a payload was released. Some unidentifiable object hit the ground and in a split second, a cloud of debris rose up into the air.

I watched as a man appeared out of nowhere, scrambled to the still unidentifiable object, picked it up and then ran to retrieve the drone which had just landed. The man, whom I assumed was the pilot of the drone, began running away, after first looking toward the area I was watching from.

I yelled for the man to stop, which of course he didn't. I grabbed my phone and dialed.

"Rob, what's up?" Tommy asked.

"Jesus, Tommy, I'm outside at the hospital, talking with my sister-in-law and a few yards away a guy is flying a quadcopter!"

"Rob, that's okay. It's pretty much the rage these days as far as hobbies are concerned," Tommy replied.

"I know that, Tommy, but I've never seen anyone dropping something from them! The damn thing had a payload, Tommy, just like around Mt. Hood earlier."

Tommy paused to digest what I'd just told him. If I was planning to attack something with a brick or two of C-4, I'd want to practice beforehand too, Tommy told himself.

"Hello? Tommy, you there?"

"Sorry, Rob, I was lost in thought. Stay out of this. I got it! Go back to Marty. Promise me you'll do that! Hello? Rob, you there?"

I'd hung up on Tommy. There was no way I was sitting this one out. Not after what they'd done to my wife. I remembered my experiences at the track and my personal dealings with the head of the Human Resources department.

"Lauren, I've got to go, I'm sorry!" I headed inside the hospital and asked the first employee I saw for directions to the hospital administration offices. I was soon face to face with a receptionist whose name was Caroline.

"Caroline, is the HR director here today?"

"Yes he is; do you have an appointment?" Caroline asked.

Oh God, it's the answer a question with a question routine! Please Lord, don't let her shut me out! I thought. "Caroline, if you've been watching the news, you've probably realized that something is happening in this region right now, and it's not good. I was at Mt. Hood in the midst of it. Your hospital may soon also be involved. This isn't a prank! I need to talk with your HR person now!"

"You're not a local, are you?"

"Nope, I'm a Kentuckian."

"Larry, I've got a man from Kentucky out here and he has something to share with you about a security issue. Can I send him back?"

"Sure thing, Caroline."

"Go through that door. It's the third office on the left. His name is Larry Holt ... and Go Big Blue." I shook my head in dismay. Another Kentuckian in Portland, Oregon. Go figure, I said to myself.

I shook Larry's hand and gave him a quick narrative of the events that had transpired around Mt. Hood. When finished, I again called Tommy. "Why the hell did you hang up on me?" he demanded to know. "I'm in the office with the head of HR here at the hospital. Please explain who you are and what's going on with drones in the area."

I gave my phone to Larry, who listened to Tommy for over five minutes. Larry handed my phone back, indicating that Tommy wanted to talk to me.

"Rob, Larry has to check something out. If you get any names and addresses from him, write them down correctly and text them to me. I'll forward the names to Stan and he'll get some guys right on it. And Rob, stay the hell out of this. I know you; don't do it!"

Larry was the consummate human resources official. He made it his business to know everyone else's business. No piece of gossip was ever ignored.

Within minutes, Larry had two names and addresses and even better, the cell phone numbers for each of them. The employees were Luis Sanchez and Enrique Hernandez; both men were bio radiologists. The materials they handled would make a wonderful biological weapon, especially when dropped from a quadcopter.

And the HR director knew it.

Once again, I was proving to be a conundrum for Tommy. He could have abandoned our relationship now that he and his son had finally become a family. Perhaps it was because of Marty that Tommy felt an obligation.

"Charles, would you mind doing me a huge favor?"

"Not at all, Tommy; you name it!"

"Rob Becker has probably stumbled on to the first solid tip and I know he's going to get himself in trouble. The man has no sense of limitations. One of my rooftop snipers had to bring him down during the Stakes race over a year ago, when Towers Above and Nidalas finished in a dead heat.

"The guy means well, and I understand his convictions, but he's going to get himself killed. I need you to head back to Portland. I guarantee Dr. Becker will be somewhere close to the address he just sent me. I'm sending this same information to Stan, and I'm certain operatives will also be there in quick order.

"In the meantime, Danny and I are heading to the rail cars with Steven. Maybe we'll get lucky and come across those missing Antifa revolutionaries who were heading in the same general direction. I suspect they used the Mylar cloaking materials to hide their infrared signature."

Danny and Charles embraced and said their goodbyes. Charles and his men gathered their gear and in twenty minutes were headed back to the horse trailers and eventually town.

"Thanks, I owe you!" Tommy said to Charles. He turned away and called Stan.

"Talk to me," Stan answered.

"I just got a solid tip from Dr. Becker. It seems that he stumbled across a couple of quadcopter hobbyists screwing around on the grounds of the hospital where his wife is recovering. They weren't just sport-flying the quads – they were practicing payload drops. Becker somehow got the executive in charge of the hospital's HR department to release their names and addresses. I'll text that to you when I hang up. Then Danny, Steven and I are heading back to the drop off point to do some reconnaissance.

"I know the Coast Guard and Portland's Metro police are most likely surveilling the city's port facilities. I just can't shake a memory from the other day when we offloaded the horses. There was a dam nearby. I don't know its name, but it would make one helluva target. And if someone's thinking about taking it out, well, that definitely matches up with the pieces of diving equipment we found around the mine!"

"Tommy, stop! Shut up for a minute and let me give you the latest. We've got two Navy SEAL teams protecting the port. They were brought in almost immediately by Pentagon officials. Meanwhile starting at 4:00 tomorrow morning, sheriff deputies, FBI agents, US Marshals and Oregon state troopers will begin to launch coordinated raids at every known address of anarchists and Antifa loyalists. This will happen not just in Portland, but in all the surrounding counties – and authorities already have search warrants for each address. This should put a dent in the number of supporters that Antifa has on the streets. I can cross-check the addresses you send me against the list of targets that will be raided in the morning. Hopefully Dr. Becker's perps will be on the list!"

Tommy wasn't convinced. "Stan, if you think this sweep is going to put a crimp in the number of drone operators, you're mistaken. These operators are Antifa's elite corps. I've seen them in action, and their threat is very real – and so is the potential for significant destruction. Why not try to isolate one of them and get him or her to turn on Antifa and become the new Benedict Arnold? That could end this revolution in a heartbeat."

"Time's running out, Tommy. POTUS can't wait for a miracle turncoat to show up. The National Guard will protect the downtown shops, courthouses, and other government buildings. I know General Matthews said he was pulling out, but that's not quite true. The horses and donkeys are being loaded on the freight cars as we speak, and that's all. The general and his men will return to Portland and also patrol the downtown district. They're sharpshooters and will supplement the army's tactics. Honest to God, Tommy, I don't understand what more you want the military to do."

"Stan, I've always been a reactive type of guy. You punch me, and I hit back harder. Get me the GPS coordinates for that dam and let's put the SEAL teams on notice that I might need their help. Danny's brother is headed back to town with his men, and hopefully he will find Dr. Becker."

"If the drone attack is stopped, this revolution dies!"

∩ ∩ ∩

I was standing at the entrance to the hospital waiting for an Uber ride to town, hoping that my rental car Marty had driven days earlier was still in the parking lot and not impounded. My phone rang and I answered.

"Dr. Becker, it's Charles! Do you need a lift somewhere?"

I shook my head in disbelief.

Charles had called me out. I met his question with silence. I assumed he was still driving Lauren's car, as that was what we used when following Mateo. I could have gone back inside to ask Lauren for her license plate number and report that the car was stolen. Doing that, though, meant I'd have to explain what was going on now, and face a barrage of questions and eventually a confrontation. Charles might as well have said "Checkmate" and been done with it, but he was diplomatic.

"You know what's going on, don't you?" I finally answered.

"Yep," Charles said.

"Promise me you won't interfere!"

"Dr. Becker, you know I can't promise that, but there's no reason we can't work together."

"I'm at the hospital's main entrance. Come ahead," I humbly answered.

# CHAPTER 60

The window of opportunity in which to strike was quickly closing, and Danté knew it.

The National Guard had taken up position at several locations in Portland that had been flash points during the three days of rioting after the presidential election in November 2016. There was no communication from anyone at Mt. Hood, and current news reports were frequently citing articles in the Wall Street Journal and the Christian Science Monitor. These articles clearly discussed Antifa's insurrection and attempt of their followers to create a revolution.

Mt. Hood was still spewing lava. Businesses and families throughout the northwest were not only cleaning up after an earthquake but still very much afraid that every dormant volcano in the region was going to come alive.

In short, Danté was losing the propaganda war. He felt that even if his followers still wanted to believe the messages Antifa was promoting over social media, that wouldn't be enough. It was becoming more and more apparent that the number of individuals willing to join in immediate civil disobedience on the streets of Portland was diminishing.

ᑎ ᑎ ᑎ

The university could always be counted on as a place to hold meetings. It was there that Danté and his elite team of drone operators held their final planning meeting before the early-morning attack the next day.

Luis and Enrique were among the sixty quadcopter pilots and drivers anxiously awaiting their final instructions. Both men proudly wore the mantle of being nerds. The reality was that this duo was one man shy of being modern-day Three Stooges. They arrived at the downtown campus meeting site at different times. As Luis sat down, Enrique glared at him.

"Where's the drone?" he whispered.

Luis shrugged his shoulders. "I thought you were bringing it," he replied.

"You idiot, go get it and get your ass back here, pronto!" Enrique ordered.

If Ricardo or Danté had seen the interchange between the two, they would have stepped in. Danté had lost too many of his fellow insurgents, and his level of paranoia couldn't be any higher.

It was his intention to introduce the group to the Pixhawk Autopilot modules that would be installed on every quadcopter in their possession. Once installed, the module would control the flight of each drone, essentially turning off the pilot's receiver. Simply speaking, the drones would fly without human assistance. Each autopilot module would be pre-programmed with GPS points directing each drone to fly to a specific point. The machines would fly in a consecutive order: GPS point A followed by B, followed by C, and so on until the final GPS point was reached.

Timing was critical. Each drone would have a limited amount of battery power dedicated for flight, plus energy for the release of the payload. And some of the quadcopters would carry more bricks of C-4 than others.

There would be no central launch point. Rather, the initial release of the quadcopters would take place in a ten-block radius. Once released, the drones would converge into one massive flight line. Danté knew that the government's radar was capable of picking up the drone's infrared signature, as well as the standard electronic signature of the incoming bogies. But this flight line would appear on the radar as a single attacker. And just like in the movie Top Gun, at a certain point each drone would peel away from the line and head for an individualized target. The drones would initially climb to a high altitude, position themselves and then drop down. This would effectively shield the drones from attack by any military aircraft. As time would be of the essence, each drone would also be programmed to self-destruct upon launching their respective payloads.

Danté knew his programmers had created the ideal technological weapon, Zombie Drones.

His only unanswered question was "How sophisticated is the US in combating this type of threat?"

Addressing the drone teams, Danté smiled and said, "Ladies and gentlemen, tomorrow morning at dawn, it's game on!"

Opening the passenger's side door, I climbed into Lauren's car, which Charles was still driving. "Charles, thank you! Thanks for everything you've done these past few days!"

"Not a problem, Doc. I should be thanking you for everything. Who'd have guessed hooking up with you would have led to all of this fun! So, where are we going now?"

I hadn't laughed in days and it took a few seconds to compose myself again. I gave Charles a sticky note with the address. "Is it near?" I asked.

"It's downtown in the university area," he told me. "There's a bunch of old homes that have been converted into several individual apartments. It's a big draw for college students and Millennials. We'll be there in about twenty minutes. Do you have any ID on these guys?"

"Yeah, the HR executive at the hospital gave me copies of their work badges. I hope we're not too late to get in on the action. I sent Tommy the same information, and I'm sure he sent that on to his boss."

"Well, maybe we'll get lucky. Other than that, these guys were fooling around with drones. What makes you think they're a threat?" Charles asked.

"I just have a hunch, Charles. I took a peek at their personnel files while the HR guy was printing out their ID information for me. These two dudes handle hazardous materials at the hospital. They're responsible for not only receiving but disposing of the radioactive materials used in diagnostic testing and treatment therapies. I don't think Antifa's only offensive payloads are limited to stolen C-4 explosives. You know as well as I do that the idea of using radioactive weaponry strikes fear in people every time. It's pure terrorism!"

I looked at Charles, who was deep in thought. There was at least three minutes of silence in the car as we headed toward town.

"Doc, what you said a few seconds ago ... well, I have to tell you, a vision of skull and crossbones – the traditional symbol of death – came to mind immediately. And you're absolutely right; anything radioactive used as a weapon is horrific. Obviously we're not talking about a Hiroshima type of nuclear explosion, but the idea of being exposed to an invisible killer like radioactive material will send shudders up anyone's spine. So tell me, if we happen to stumble across one of these misguided youths, what the hell are you going to do? No, wait! I know! You're going to sit down with one or both of them and peace out. I can see all three of you sharing tokes on a joint of marijuana!" The evidence of Charles' sarcasm was betrayed by the sly smile on his face.

"Charles, I'm really not in the mood for a sarcastic attitude at the moment. If given the chance, I'll give them their options. They won't have a clue who I am. But they'll sure as hell listen, especially when I've got a gun pointed at them. They're Millennials, for God's sake. When I tell them they'll face the death penalty for their role in using a weapon of mass destruction, I'm willing to bet they'll crumble like a sand castle."

I paused for effect. I needed Charles to understand how totally serious I was. "I won't use the syringe that's still in my pocket. But if for some reason these two want me to pull a Clint Eastwood 'make my day' moment, I will. I'll shoot each of them in the kneecap. And if they still don't talk, then I'll shoot them in their other kneecap!"

Once again, Charles was at a loss for words. I wasn't the timid, meek person he'd met a few days earlier.

"You understand, don't you, that you might screw everything up by tipping off these guys, and that they'll simply change or postpone their plans? You've taken that into consideration, right?"

"Charles, call it a hunch if you want. I feel strongly that if we can turn one of them, this revolution might end with a whimper."

Charles rounded the corner, parked and turned off the car. He pointed at a two-story brick building that looked like it had been constructed in the '50s and rehabbed in the past decade.

"Now what, Rockford?" he asked.

"Just chill a minute, okay?" I answered somewhat tersely.

It wasn't more than thirty seconds later when Luis came around the corner in a full sprint and entered the apartment building.

"What do you think? We couldn't be this lucky!" Charles blurted out. "Did you notice he wasn't carrying anything?" I replied.

I quickly jumped out of the car, heading to the entrance of the building, much to the chagrin and protestation of Charles. I was close to the entrance when Luis burst through the door, nearly running into me. I saw the quadcopter in a large cloth bag that Luis was now carrying. As he passed by me I turned and said in Spanish, "No daría otro paso!"

No sooner had I uttered those words than Charles was in front of Luis, blocking his path. With Charles' handgun drawn, Luis' choices were limited.

"Spanish, really! Where the hell did that come from?"

"I don't know. When I was waiting for you back at the hospital, I googled it, hoping I'd get a chance to use it."

"Okay, Rocky, you're on!" Charles again spoke sarcastically.

"Luis, I know you speak English, so let's be quick. I also know that you and Enrique are part of Antifa and you're planning to attack several targets with your weaponized drones. But in your case, the weapon is radioactive materials that you and Enrique stole from the hospital. Radioactive isotopes, in case you don't know it, are biological weapons of mass destruction. If you unleash a WMD, you'll seal your fate. You and Enrique will be put to death! Look at me, son!" I screamed. "Is this what you really want to do?"

Luis turned toward me and I saw it in his eyes. After four decades of leaning over and talking with patients, I was never just a dentist. My roles included being a pastor, counselor, a shoulder to cry on, a financial advisor, but above all ... I was a psychologist! Luis was carrying a burden that he wanted to be rid of.

"C'mon, son, time's short! Either you do or you don't, but do the right thing for humanity!"

Luis haltingly spoke. "What do you want me to do?"

I glanced at Charles – it was his eyes that gave him away. The look on his face said it all: "I'll be damned. Becker was right. Oh my God!"

I sat down on the stoop leading to the apartment, motioning Luis to do the same. He began telling us about the radioactive materials that he and Enrique had stolen. Enrique had the payload stored in the trunk of his car in a lead-lined container routinely used to store radioactive materials.

Almost on cue, three sedans and one SUV pulled up in front of the apartment building. Tommy's fraternity brothers had finally arrived. Charles turned and walked over to the group, briefing them on the situation. I helped Luis up and we walked over to the agents – there was no way I was walking away from this situation. They handled Luis with kindness, even as a female agent attached a hidden wire under his clothing, before they departed.

It was time for us to do the same.

"If I've learned one thing in sixty years, it's to never doubt your intuition," I said to Charles as we walked back to the car. "It's like flipping a coin. It's going to be heads or it's going to be tails. As we go through those decades of life experiences, the odds of calling it right can only increase."

# CHAPTER 62

Stan texted the physical coordinates of the dam to Tommy. The information refreshed Tommy's memory from a few days earlier when the cavalry disembarked from the railroad cars, very close to the Bonneville Reservoir that was created by damming of the Columbia River. He entered latitude and longitude data into the GPS app which immediately computed the shortest distance between their current location and the dam. Tommy pulled Steven aside.

"You take the lead again, and we need to move fast. I know what I saw in the general's makeshift office, and I'm convinced something major is going to happen on the river. That dam—and by the way, there's a whole bunch of dams along the Columbia River—is a perfect target. Antifa would love nothing more than to destroy it. This particular dam was built by the US government and named in honor of a late army captain by the name of Benjamin Bonneville. Even though I'm asking you to hustle, I also need you to take time in checking out the surroundings. Just don't be careless … do what you feel is right. Danny and I will be a bit behind you."

Tommy and Steven rejoined Danny on the trail as they all mounted their horses. Steven mounted and gave his steed a solid kick. He was out of sight in about a minute.

"I know it's none of my business, but why did you leave his mother?" Danny asked.

Tommy just stared at Danny. He should've known that Danny would figure it out. Tommy lowered his head slightly as a sad smile crossed his face. "It wasn't my decision. She was carrying our child but couldn't accept my line of work. She refused to move to the DC area and truly hated that I worked for the Agency. I still love her, even to this day, but I gave up on ever reconciling our differences. She never re-married, and the idea of ending the pregnancy wasn't an option for her—or me, for that matter. I've watched him grow through pictures she's sent me, and most of my vacation days were spent on trips back home where I could watch him from a distance. If Steven knew how well my surveillance skills were honed, from watching him over the years, I'm sure he'd be pissed big time. A part of my heart has been ripped out of me for these past few decades. You can't imagine the joy I'm feeling now, Danny!"

Danny steered his horse next to Tommy and extended his right fist toward him for a fist bump that showed a true sign of friendship and brotherly love. Danny was flush with other questions, but now was not the time or place for farther discussion. Both men continued on course, slowly closing the distance to the Columbia River and Bonneville. About two miles short of their destination, Steven was unexpectedly waiting as both men rounded a bend on the trail.

"I came across an encampment about a half mile ahead. The embers in the campfire were still warm. The campers probably had breakfast there this morning. Now get this—there are still three tents set up, and at least a half dozen empty diving tanks inside the tents. There are also three Mylar backpacks and sleeping bags in the tents. I didn't find any C-4, but there's a crate of rifle ammunition that's AK-47 ready!"

Steven looked his father square in the eyes and said, "You were right, and my impression is that they're coming back. There's also way too many signs of activity in that camp for just two or three people. My best guess is that others have joined the main party of revolutionaries. I counted at least four different sets of footprints around the campfire. I'm also pretty certain there are at least six different people in play."

Tommy gave Danny a look that said nothing and yet meant everything. Danny had seen that gaze many times before. Both men tied up their horses, heading to the woods to relieve themselves.

"We need some help, right?" Tommy asked in midstream.

"Damn straight. Make the call right now!" Danny replied.

Tommy walked back to his horse, pulled the satellite phone from the pack, and made the call.

"Stan, we've got a situation here near Bonneville. There are a significant number of hostiles. We've got first-hand intelligence that confirms the dam at Bonneville is the target. Considering the number of empty diving tanks and the amount of time they've had, they're probably almost done placing their explosive devices."

There were fifteen seconds of silence before Stan replied. "Let me get the navy on board and get at least one SEAL unit in the air ASAP! I have no idea how soon they'll arrive, but I suspect they'll immediately deploy. Do you need additional land back-up?"

"If I said no, I'd be bullshitting you, Stan. You know Danny and I can handle us, but my son is here. I've been basically paternalistic with all the situations ever since I arrived out here—Steven has performed flawlessly. But Jesus, Stan, if I lose my son in battle, I just don't ...." Tommy's voice trailed off.

"Tommy, there's no way I can get reinforcements to your position and not tip off the hostiles that y'all are nearby. I'm sorry, but I need you to engage the enemy, so the navy guys can deploy. Place your son in the least vulnerable position of your attack perimeter, and Tommy, Godspeed to all of you!"

"Great, just great! Steven knows exactly where the revolutionaries are, and I'm supposed to make him less vulnerable. He'll be in the lead, for God's sake," Tommy said to himself. He raised his head to the sky, asking for divine protection of what was now the most important thing in his life.

Tommy turned toward Danny and his son. "A SEAL team will soon be joining the fray, but I expect they'll be in the water, so it's up to us to neutralize the enemies that are on land. Steven, you know where their camp is. It's your mission to command now. Get us close enough on horseback, and then we'll spread out on foot and engage them if necessary. We're closing in on sunset, so have your night-vision gear handy. The hairs on my neck are standing on end, guys. I don't expect the hostiles to give up – so here's the plan. Select your first target, and as soon as they fire at us, drop your primary adversary. The next targets will be more elusive."

Tommy looked at Steven.

"You can do this, son!"

Tommy lifted himself astride Spike, and they were off.

# CHAPTER 63

Normally the FBI would be the agency on the listening end of Luis and his wired conversations, but the President's Chief of Staff and the Joint Chiefs favored Langley's finest in this particular instance. There were too many questions left unanswered. Many of these revolved around the Deep State and the FBI's agents that had conflicted allegiances and prejudiced beliefs. It had been established earlier that Danté's roots were firmly based in Cuba. This meant the possibility also existed that a foreign entity was already directly involved in this revolution.

Luis returned to the campus meeting site, taking a seat next to Enrique.

"Took you long enough. Where the hell have you been?" Enrique asked.

"I ran all the way here. When I checked the quad's battery, it wasn't fully charged, and I had to wait until it was topped off! You do remember that Danté said our drone needed a completely charged battery, don't you?" Luis replied. Enrique nodded his head yes, even though he'd forgotten about that.

Danté was almost done with the briefing when he said, "Enrique and Luis, your drone is going to be the last one launched. The same applies to the special payload. Please stay in your seats; we'll talk after I'm finished here."

After asking his loyal audience for questions and hearing none, Danté thrust his right fist in the air in a manner reminiscent of some past communist leaders.

"Comrades, we'll gather here again tomorrow at 5 a.m. We'll arm each quadcopter with the special software and the C-4 payloads. Here's to the beginning of a new America – and true equality and wealth for everyone." After several cheers, the meeting adjourned. Danté made his way to Luis and Enrique.

"I have a change of plans for the two of you. Your payload is not going to be in with the main group of drones in Operation Top Gun. We know some of the military's drone defense capabilities. In fact, they've got a special drone rifle and a defensive mobile radar/laser platform. And then there's the AUDS anti-drone technology. You can find all of this information on the internet, but I wouldn't call it common knowledge.

"It's the government's defensive systems that we're unaware of that we have to worry about. So we're going low-tech with an unmanned aerial vehicle that will be carrying your payload. About an hour before we launch the main attack group, we'll load your material onto the aircraft and then countdown to launch. Get some rest. I'll be back in a few hours."

Luis waited until Danté left before turning to Enrique and peppering him with questions.

"Okay, what did I miss, and what's this Top Gun stuff?" Luis demanded, hoping Enrique didn't catch on that he was fishing for information.

"You didn't miss much. He told us that no one will be piloting the drones – they're all be self-piloting. All we're supposed to do is drive to a specific location and at a set time. All of them will be launched simultaneously. The drones will be programmed to merge into single formation at some pre-established GPS point. That's supposed to cause a radar signature that appears as just one

bogey, like that scene from Top Gun. From there, the drones proceed to another GPS-selected spot where finally, each drone peels
away and heads for its predetermined individual target. It's a total
bummer! I was looking forward to piloting our drone. On the
plus side, everyone will leave after they've finished their launch,
and no one will be apprehended. I assumed it would be the same
with us, but just now, he implied it's going to be different. I guess
we'll just have to wait and see!"

Luis took a deep breath.

"You realize we have the most to lose in this attack, don't you?
If this revolt doesn't succeed, we're going to be caught and ex-
ecuted. The government is going to figure out where the radioactive material came from. I'm thinking as soon as our drone is
launched, we should head for Arizona and the border," Luis said
with a tone of finality.

Enrique sat there with a stunned expression on his face. The
reality of what Luis said had hit home.

∩ ∩ ∩

Stan was linked to the voice feed of Luis's wiretap. Any threats
of war that a few seconds earlier were presumptions had now become reality. Definitive actions could now be incorporated into
planning for the defeat of Antifa.

He'd seen his share of theoretical drone attacks formulated
in war game scenarios during the last few years. The Top Gun
maneuver that Antifa thought was their secret weapon had in fact
taken place in real-time government training the previous year on
a top-secret desert military base.

The government knew the maneuver worked because on that
day of testing, commercial airliners flying in the area at roughly

30,000 feet reported a sudden loss of functioning GPS instrumentation. The LA control tower immediately contacted officials over the military frequency demanding an immediate halt to whatever testing was being conducted in the desert "as the weaponry in use was jeopardizing civilian life."

The government was ready to protect and defend.

There were now four active AUDS mobile systems strategically positioned in the Portland and Mt. Hood region, ready to thwart Antifa's planned attack.

General Matthews's sharpshooters had been issued drone defender point-and-shoot RF series rifles. The general would soon deploy the troops to areas where Antifa had been active during the 2016 riots.

On the outskirts of Portland, a squadron of six Blackhawk helicopter pilots had been notified that Operation Gone Fishing was now live.

Thirty minutes after Luis's first wire transmission, that same squadron of Blackhawks took off for one last training flight south of Portland. Bystanders on the ground wondered if there was an upcoming air show, as the helicopters were flying in synchronized formations. They weren't in a tight pattern like one would see with the Blue Angels, but the coordinated moves were still every bit the aerial ballet that folks expected from an elite corps of fliers.

Charles had already determined which Antifa target would be their priority and was driving with a sense of urgency to that location.

"Hey, where are we're going?" I asked.

"You can ask anything you want, but all I will say now is that we'll be there in a few minutes. I figured you'd want to be at ground zero!" Charles replied with laughter in his voice.

"That's not funny," I mumbled to myself.

Meanwhile an emergency news bulletin was scrolling across televisions from every media television network in the northwestern states. It was also airing on every AM and FM radio stations in the region.

The bulletin read;

"Portland International Airport is closed! Contact your airlines for inbound flight information."

There was no reason given and speculation was wide.

Mt. Hood had become a lava nightlight as another day of anxiety had just ended.

A new day, one that would forever be etched in the minds of adults and children across the country, was just beginning.

CHAPTER 64

Steven had been gone no more than twenty minutes when farther north and close to the Bonneville Dam, a huge fireball suddenly appeared in the sky. It was immediately followed by the sound of an explosion and a stream of black smoke.

Tommy and Danny instantly kicked their horses into high gear, abandoning all semblance of cautious surreptitious travel, dodging trees and boulders along the path. Finally, a thousand yards ahead, Tommy spotted Steven frantically waving them toward his location.

Ted, had he been present, would have been proud of Tommy's horsemanship. He did a running dismount and sprinted toward his son, his heart beating furiously the entire distance. He fell to his knees just short of Steven, quickly realizing an embrace wouldn't be the manly thing to do at that moment.

"I thought you were gone!" was all he could manage. In that moment, Steven understood how much his father loved him. He reached down and pulled Tommy to his feet, wrapping an arm around him. Danny watched and couldn't help feeling a bit envious.

"I returned to their campsite and when I went into the tent where the spent oxygen tanks were, I quickly spotted the C-4 explosives strapped to them. I was outta there! After that explosion, the remains of any evidence can't amount to much. My best guess is that the Antifa's dissidents are down by the interstate waiting for pickup."

"Yeah, and if they hear or see a helicopter dropping off the SEAL team, they'll be pissed!" Tommy thought to himself.

"We've got to head toward the interstate and the shoreline of the reservoir. We need to provide cover for the SEALs when they're dropped off!" Tommy shouted. He pulled out his phone to call Stan.

"What's up?" Stan answered.

"Tell me you can warn the SEAL team about possible hostile fire when they're dropped off," Tommy said with urgency in his voice. He explained the current situation to Stan, who put him on hold. Thirty seconds later, Stan was back on the line. "Done, and by the way, there are two teams of SEALs coming. One unit will be tasked with anti-demolition and the other will back you guys up. Is there anything else?"

Tommy said "No" and "Thanks" before ending the call.

"We've got backup coming, let's get going now!" Tommy said, remounting Spike.

Steven maneuvered his horse next to Spike, while Danny moved his horse to Steven's right flank.

"What's the plan?" Steven asked.

"There are a couple of service roads ahead that we'll cross and then we go across I-84. Once we're past the railroad tracks, we'll set up a perimeter on the shoreline. I'll be on point, while you and Danny will flank me about 100 yards on either side. I figure Antifa will have a lookout on the interstate who will be in communication with a rescue group.

"When they rendezvous, the remainder of the Antifa group will rush to the expressway for pick-up. Then they'll be gone ... if it hasn't already happened! Who knows what's going to happen if they're still around when the SEALs are dropped off? If they're true devotees to the cause, I'm sure they'll head to the shoreline and we'll have ourselves a firefight. We better get our night vision gear ready, because in another twenty minutes, it's going to be totally dark."

∩ ∩ ∩

The best thing about the SEAL team's helicopters is their stealth. You can't hear them until they're right on top of you. Often, an adversary doesn't even realize that the SEALs have been deployed until it's too late.

The first SEAL team chopper swept in from several miles north of the Bonneville Dam. Their approach took them across the state line into Washington's airspace and then south to Oregon. The Blackhawk hovered over the water, dropping the team silently into the dam's reservoir. Following behind the Blackhawk was a Chinook helicopter carrying the watercraft for SEAL Team 10. The SEALs loaded their gear into the boat for the swift trip to the edge of the dam.

Tommy, who was settled in at the apex of the defensive triangle formation, checked his satellite phone for messages.

"You have six hostiles moving in your direction! The second SEAL team is now in hot pursuit. The SEALs are crossing I-84 and will engage with the enemy at any time. Keep in mind, POTUS wants minimal bloodshed! The last thing he wants is to create martyrs for Antifa."

Stan's message had come through five minutes earlier but was still more than timely. It was like hitting the refresh button in Tommy's brain.

"Shit, I forgot about the drone above us. So, that second

SEAL team parachuted in behind both of our positions. I wonder if they'll use...."

Before he could finish the thought, Tommy had his answer. "Flash ... bang, flash ... bang." Blinding white light and loud booms were exploding in the sky from six different sites. Temporarily blinded by the flashes, he quickly flipped up his night vision goggles. Yes, he thought, the SEALs are repeating the same attack that had been employed earlier on the mountainside – and with great success. Tommy would later learn that the enemy had become disoriented and distracted and were firing their AK-47s wildly into the night air. Slowly the SEALs peeled the insurgents one by one from their now useless line of attack. A sequence of flash ... bang, and random shooting and shouting, followed by silence quickly became the order of battle. This was the ultimate defeat of Antifa at the Bonneville Dam.

In the darkness Tommy heard repeated shouts of "clear." It was time to make sure his men were also in the clear.

"Steven, you good?"

Steven's response came from Tommy's right. "Okay here."

"Danny, you good?" There was silence. "Danny?" he asked again in a loud voice.

Tommy quickly stood and shouted even louder, but there was still no response. His heart was again beating hard in his chest as adrenaline was coursing through his body. He was in a full sprint to where Danny had been positioned when suddenly, he spotted the motionless body of his partner and friend. In three seconds he was at Danny's side, falling to his knees. He shook Danny to no avail. He checked for respirations. There were none. As he reached to check for a pulse, Tommy felt the final seeping of warm blood pumping out of Danny's torn left carotid artery.

Tommy refused to accept Heaven's verdict and began chest compressions. Memories of past military engagements were rushing through his mind as he repeatedly screamed "Medic!" Another minute passed when Tommy felt a hand placed on top of his interlocked hands.

"Dad, he's gone. Let it go. Please, Dad, let him rest in peace."

Tommy slowly moved his hands, which were still locked together. He raised his head toward Steven, his eyes filled with tears. But this time there was no sobbing. Of all the skirmishes he and Danny had been through together in their careers, the thought of him dying at the hands of these pampered, spoiled socialist pukes was too much to accept. Steven would later describe Tommy's demeanor as one of fierce questioning and anger.

The SEAL team had finished handcuffing their Antifa prisoners with zip ties when Tommy walked up to the team leader and introduced himself. "Please tell me there's something more I can do for you," Tommy said to the man.

"Well sir, it won't be for us, but it would sure help our brothers out there," pointing toward the dam. "They need to know where these guys placed their charges and how they're set to go off. We're not allowed to interrogate prisoners of war, sir, if you get my drift."

Tommy nodded and asked the commander to have all the captured prisoners seated so he could get a good look at them. He asked for a flashlight and in an instant was armed with the only tool he needed at the moment. Tommy knelt in front of each prisoner and pointed the flashlight at each man, one at a time. Of the six men, four stared directly at the light. Their pupils, dilated from the darkness, immediately shrank. The other two prisoners refused to look into the light, which made Tommy lift their eyelids with his fingertips.

Neither of the men's pupils responded to the blinding light; instead, they were dilated. These two men were on a high from whatever drug or drugs they'd taken before going into battle. Tommy knew the four who weren't on drugs would be tough to break. The two drugged men were the weakest soldiers. Now it became a game of Eeny, Meeny, Miny, Mo! Tommy looked at their hands. One had untrimmed and soiled nails. The other one had neatly trimmed nails. He was the one that Tommy chose to answer his questions. It was a shame this young man wasn't more of a grunge. Tommy definitely had found a mama's boy.

"Commander, this is the man who's going to help us. Can your men move him a few yards out of sight?" Tommy followed the SEALs as they moved the prisoner down to the shoreline. "Thank you, men, you can leave us now."

Once the SEALs were out of sight, Tommy turned his attention to the one person who would unfortunately be on the receiving end of his grief.

"I'm not interested in your name. I want you to know that. You have a pain-free option. Answer my questions, and you won't be hurt. I'll start with your toes first. When I break them, the pain won't be as bad as fracturing your fingers. The problem with the toes is you may never walk right again – and I can promise you that! So tell me, where are the explosive charges placed against the dam, how will they be detonated and what time are they supposed to go off? I'm going to count down from ten, because time is short."

Tommy began the countdown but there was no movement or sound from the prisoner. He undid the man's right shoe and roughly pulled off the sock from his foot—there was still no reaction or response. Using his index finger and thumb, Tommy easily snapped the "wee wee wee all the way home" little piggy ligaments from their boney connections. It took just a nanosecond. What the young man didn't know was that of the five toes, the little toe can produce some of the most intense pain. Now the young man fully understood what this pain felt like.

The howl that shattered the quiet night sent shudders up and down the spine of every SEAL team member still in the region.

"Okay, let's move on to the 'little piggy that had none.' What do you say?" Again Tommy started the countdown and still there was no hint of fear. He counted down to one then stopped, moving to the man's other foot. Again, he undid the shoe and removed the man's sock. "You know, I'm an equal opportunity torturer. I may as well even things up on both feet, huh?" The countdown began again and quickly, the other little toe was broken. The second scream equaled the first.

It was time for a pause. Tommy knew that the pain from the first fracture in combination with the pain from the second fracture would be horrific in a few minutes. "You know, one of your fellow revolutionaries just killed the best friend I ever had in my life. It's payback time!"

"It ... it wasn't me," the prisoner responded in a meek and pained voice.

You're mine now, Tommy said to himself.

"Now how would I know that?" Tommy barked at his prey.

"I didn't have an AK-47. I'm the demolition expert."

"Okay, that's a start. How many more toes is it going to take, because I'm telling you, those two broken toes will be amputated once you get to a hospital. The good news is you'll still be able to walk. You won't even miss them. Now if I have to do ...."

"Stop, please! I'll tell you all of it ... promise me you'll stop!"

Tommy shouted for the SEAL commander, knowing he was nearby. As Tommy left, he paused and said, "This guy's ready to talk. Get to the point quickly with your questions; otherwise he may pass out and go into shock from the pain."

In less than thirty minutes, SEAL Team 10 had recovered and disarmed all of the C-4 satchels that had been placed against the dam's facade. At that point, Bonneville Dam became a footnote in history. In a few years, the grounds around the dam would display another historical marker, placed most likely next to the antique historical marker honoring Captain Bonneville.

Tommy pulled out his phone and called Stan.

"Talk to me, Tommy," Stan said anxiously.

"Danny's dead." There was a long silent and painful pause to the conversation. Finally, Tommy summoned the strength to speak again, telling Stan, "I need an aerial pickup for Steven, myself, three horses, and Danny's body. The dam is now secure. The SEAL teams have already called for their extraction. Stan, if there's any way you can get it approved, I want these three horses to come back with me to Kentucky."

Stan was at a loss for words. One of his best operatives was gone. In the background, he could hear Tommy mourning, but he didn't hang up. Soon, another voice came through the phone.

"Sir, this is Steven! I've got this. I look forward to seeing you at Danny's funeral service. Maybe we can talk then, if that's okay?"

"Son, it would be my honor," Stan replied. "Do me a favor and please coax Tommy to get back on the line with me."

 HAPTER 65

"Do I have your attention, Tommy?" Stan asked.

"Yeah, sure," Tommy answered.

"Damn it, Tommy, I know you're hurting inside, but we've got other assets who are working their asses off. If you want to call it a day, just say the word and you're out! Now put Steven back on the phone."

"You know, Stan, sometimes you can be a real prick!" Tommy said in a hoarse voice. "What the hell is so important that I can't have a minute to grieve for my friend?"

"Well, your other friend, Dr. Becker, just busted this revolution wide open. Somehow he got a member of Antifa to roll over. The turncoat is wearing a wire, and we're getting new intelligence on the attack planned for early tomorrow morning. Charles is with Dr. Becker. I want you and Steven to hook up with them, but first I need to know that you'll be focused. And that includes making the ultimate decision about how and when to tell Charles his brother is dead!"

Tommy had totally forgotten about Charles. So much of the day's operation had centered on Steven, Danny, and himself. Now he was being tasked to be something he wasn't. He had no training in grief counseling.

"Stan, I'll do my best; that's all I can promise you. Now where are they?"

Stan was still skeptical but plowed ahead. "There'll be a car waiting at the airport when the helicopter lands. The driver will take you to them and by the way, we have anti-radioactive hazmat outfits for you, Steven, Charles, and Doc Becker. Antifa got their hands on some biologic radioactive materials and they intend to use it as a weapon, along with the C-4. The radioactive material has a shelf life that could be several days, or it could be years. We're not talking Chernobyl-type radiation, but it's still danger-ous – and there will be mass hysteria if the American people hear about it."

In all of Tommy's years devoted to working for the agency, he'd never been confronted with an invisible threat like this. And just like any normal citizen would be, he was taken aback by the idea of it. "Stan, what the hell are we talking about? What's the radioactive material?"

"I haven't had a chance to research this stuff yet, okay? Here's the list: Cesium-137, Iridium-192, Strontium-89 and Iodine-131. They're all radioactive materials used for treating different cancers and other diseases. Some of these are in liq-uid form, others are tiny wire/needle structures, and some are seed-shaped – possibly like grass seeds. Obviously, the seeds and wires have to be surgically placed, while the liquids are injected. Using our best guesses, we believe that if there's an explosion, the materials will be propelled into the air, and therein lies the problem. We also believe that for someone to be harmed from this stuff, they'd have to be in close proxim-ity to it. Either way, they'll probably be killed from the C-4 explosion. It's really all about the psychological effect this type of weapon poses.

"Anyhow, by the time you land at the airport, I'll have more information for you. If anything changes, I'll send a message to you."

The Chinook arrived and within minutes, the horses and Danny were loaded on board, along with father and son. Tommy put his head in his hands and wept.

# HAPTER 66

"I'm going to ask one more time, Charles. Where are we going?"

"We're heading to the Edith Green-Wendell Wyatt building downtown. It's the federal building and I'm betting it's at the top of Antifa's hit list."

I had no clue how far we'd traveled or how much farther it would be until we arrived. I sat back for the rest of the ride. As we rounded a corner, Charles quickly hit the brakes, slamming the car into the curb! My seatbelt tightened, keeping my body from hitting the dashboard full on. But my head jerked hard in a classic whiplash movement. "What the hell?" I blurted out, staring at Charles in amazement. Did an animal run in front of the car to cause this sudden stop? I sure hadn't seen one. I continued staring at Charles, who was looking to his left in shocked silence.

"Hey man, you okay? Charles!" I shouted.

He continued to look out the driver's side window, and then said something in a strange voice that made my skin crawl. "Something's wrong! My brother's gone!"

My mind went into overdrive. The word gone means dead! Danny is dead? was my immediate thought. Having experienced two afterlife experiences myself in the past, I wondered if Charles had just gone through a similar event.

"Tell me what happened. Describe it. Come on, man, spit it out – it was real! I've been there!" I forcefully demanded him to speak.

He spoke. "Everything suddenly became very bright; it was almost like looking at the sun! I didn't want to crash the car. Then I heard Danny's voice telling me, 'Finish this ... I'll be with you. I promise!'"

Charles slowly turned toward me. I couldn't see his eyes but was pretty sure he was tearing up while also questioning what just took place. "It's your call, Charles," I said to him. "We can end this pursuit right now, but what you experienced is real." I then explained the personal experiences I'd had after the deaths of my mother and my father-in-law. Then, I shut up.

It seemed like an eternity when the dam of silence broke loose from Charles. "You're right; it was real, and Danny and I weren't raised to be quitters! I will finish this mission and be damn proud of it. Doc, if you want your car back, I'll continue on foot. We're only a couple blocks from the federal building now. I'm certain the area around it is swarming with assets and defensive weapon systems that I can join in with."

Looking me squarely in the eyes, Charles continued. "You've acquitted yourself admirably and should be proud." Charles opened the car door to get out.

"Where the hell do you think you're going? Get back in here," I demanded. Charles did a 180, sliding back into the driver's seat and restarting the car. We drove the remaining two blocks, only to be stopped at a military checkpoint that had been set up around the perimeter of the federal building. Charles presented his credentials, to no avail. We were not allowed past the blockade. My phone rang, and for once I eagerly answered Tommy's call.

"Tommy, we're just short of the federal building downtown. But the troops won't let us near the building. It's cordoned off."

"Rob, please give your phone to Charles for a second," Tommy asked. He had the same foreboding tone in his voice that Charles's had minutes earlier. I handed my phone over to Charles, mouthing Tommy's name.

"Yes, Tommy?" Charles uttered.

Tommy paused, lowering the phone and looking at it before raising it back to his ear. "Charles, General Matthews should be somewhere nearby. Find out who the highest-ranking officer is at the checkpoint and insist on talking with that individual. Have them tell the general's aide that I'll be there shortly. Don't hang up – I want to know that you can gain entry." Tommy sensed from the way Charles answered the phone that he somehow knew his brother had died.

Charles's military ID showed a high enough rank to force the guard into action, and in less than three minutes, Charles and I were waved through the barricade.

"Okay, we're in," Charles said to Tommy before giving the phone back to me. As Charles drove the short distance to the entrance of the building, I spoke. "You still there, Tommy? There are more guards," I told him.

"That's alright, they'll direct you to the general. I expect he's already up on the roof. Let him know we'll be joining up with you in a bit."

It was my turn to lower my phone and quizzically stare at it. Tommy said we. Maybe Danny is alive, I thought.

General Matthews greeted us with a stern look and a firm handshake. "Men, thank you for all that you've done. Dr. Becker, if you hadn't flipped that Antifa drone pilot, we'd be operating blind right now. I told POTUS about your service and he wanted me to personally thank you." He then directed us to a seat away from the ongoing action.

I wondered what the president would think of me when he learned I had tortured a prisoner a few hours earlier. I decided that I didn't much care at that moment, but deep inside, I knew those feelings would change.

After about five minutes of inactivity, my eyes began to close. I fought the urge to sleep, but there's only so much stress a body can handle. My mind needed to escape reality, and quickly, I was out. Maybe I slept a half hour and maybe I slept longer when I felt someone touching me.

I should have recognized the hand that was shaking me from my slumber.

"Jesus, Tommy, I'm sorry," I said, even though I had nothing to apologize for. My eyes were wide open and I saw Steven and Charles but no Danny. I bowed my head and said a quick prayer before I again fell fast asleep.

# CHAPTER 67

For me, sleeping in a chair other than a La-Z-Boy never allowed for uninterrupted sleep. Nodding off always caused that sudden snapping back to attention type of movement. After the fifth or sixth jerk of my body, I awoke and spied someone whom I quickly recognized. The man was engaged in a conversation with General Matthews and Charles was standing by his side. What is Jerry doing here? I asked myself. I recalled the anti-drone information he'd shared earlier on the mountain. I found myself wondering what he hadn't shared with us.

I started to rise from the chair but felt an arm plop heavily across my chest. I knew immediately who the person was by the restraining strength of that arm. I couldn't stop the grin that slid across my face. "How long was I asleep?" I asked.

"I have no idea," Tommy answered. "Real quick, I've got to ask—Charles knows that Danny is dead?" I nodded.

"I'm not going to say anything to Charles right now. There's just too much on our plates that we all have to deal with first. When everything is over, we'll take the time to talk and reflect. Now let's see what's going on." With that statement, we both stood and joined the group of men who appeared to be in deep discussion.

We silently merged into the group and listened intently as Jerry finished his briefing.

"I'm 99 percent certain the net will work, and yeah, am I

worried there's a one in a 100 chance it will fail? You bet I am," Jerry said. "I'm never happy unless it's 100 percent perfect!"

General Matthews gave his update. "The Blackhawks will launch right before dawn. Now I need to go watch the video feed as they do one last practice run. Here's to good fishing," the general said as he walked from the mobile command center to another spot on the roof of the building.

Tommy stepped forward and shook Jerry's hand, then did the same with Charles. Charles hesitated before grabbing Tommy's hand tightly. I watched as Tommy grasped Charles's hand with both of his, the two just standing there as if giving each other comfort. There was no need for words, as unspoken messages passed back and forth through the sensory nerves in each man's fingers and palms. That's too easy, I thought. Maybe it's a military thing, I speculated.

"So Jerry, what's this net thing?" Tommy asked.

Jerry looked at his watch before answering. "There are six Blackhawk crews in their copters and they just now went airborne. The copters have extendable pole-like adaptors attached to their platforms which hold a very large metal net fabricated from tungsten and copper. The alloyed metal netting is honeycomb-textured, with thousands of three-inch octagonal shaped patterns woven throughout its matrix. Just like Blue Angel pilots, the six helicopter pilots are every bit as skilled at special maneuvers. But you've got to understand, this isn't precision formation flying. Visualize, if you will, a 30-yard-long hexagonal net dragged through the sky in every direction. The air flows right through it with almost no resistance. These crews have been flying practice runs, without the net, for the past couple of days around Portland. I know, because the fly-arounds have been reported on the news and--"

Tommy suddenly interrupted Jerry with an outburst.

"Shit, Jerry! You're going to net you some drones, aren't you?"

Jerry broke into laughter. "Yeah, Tommy. I can always count on you getting it 100 percent! By the way, if you haven't heard, that guy standing next to you somehow managed to flip an Antifa drone pilot. He's now wearing a hidden wire for the feds. We think we know their attack plans, or I should say, we hope so. If the enemy's drones do what's planned, the Blackhawks will be able to harvest the majority of them. The netting has enough built-in play to cushion all of Antifa's quadcopters that crash into it."

He paused for a few seconds before explaining more about how the netting would perform.

"The two northernmost Blackhawks in the formation will dive slightly to the south, while the southernmost two will climb to the north. The remaining two Blackhawks at each apex of the hexagon will simultaneously increase their speed to finish bundling of the enclosure. Heavy-duty magnets at each end point of the hexagon will engage together and lock the trap. And because of each helicopter's propeller rotation, the entire net is electrified. It becomes one huge Faraday bag. Antifa's drone operators can send all the electronic commands they want to their drones, but those commands won't penetrate the enclosure."

Jerry finished his summary with an explanation of how the net capture would end.

"The four Blackhawks that crisscross each other will unlock and separate from their netting hooks while the two helicopters will drag the package west over the Pacific Ocean. This all has to be done in a timely manner that allows for detonation of every quadcopter's C-4 payload over the ocean. The Blackhawks will detach from the bundle of captured drones, which will drop toward the Pacific Ocean. Once the choppers are clear, two A-10s that have been circling the area will drop down from above and fire on the net of entangled quadcopters. I guarantee there'll be one helluva explosion over the Pacific Ocean!"

Jerry's summation had made a pretty strong impression on us when we were interrupted by the general's aide, who reminded Tommy it was time to suit up in our hazmat gear. As we headed for the elevators to take us to street level, I realized that our plans had already been changed.

**HAPTER 68**

Danté was not alone in the campus meeting room.

"Did they buy it?" the other anarchist asked.

Danté nodded his head in an affirmative manner and mumbled, "I think so."

"Great! Call those two guys with the radioactive materials and get them back here. I need to get going!"

"Randy, are you sure you want to do this? I mean, are you certain that there isn't a chance you can have treatments and survive?" Danté pleaded.

"Danté, this is the last time I'm going to talk about it. It's called HPV. Out of forty or more viruses, I supposedly am infected with HPV number 16 or 18. Hell, for all I know I could have both of those viral types. They caused a cancer which first appeared on my right tonsil. My smoking and drinking habits didn't exactly help the situation. The cancer has spread to my lymph nodes, and now it's everywhere in my body. I know you don't exactly get concierge healthcare in prison, and that they paroled me because I am dying. All of this from oral sex!" Randy stated, while ironically chuckling about his fate because he knew nothing could change it.

Danté didn't fully comprehend what was happening to Randy. A disease that had become the silent assassin among too many Millennials was ravaging his best friend's body. Javier was originally going to pilot the ultralight, a plan obviously scrapped because of his death. And now, Danté knew he could fall back on that original plan and he trusted Randy to carry it out successfully.

With hatred in his voice and fire in his eyes, Randy demanded, "Don't you dare deny me this opportunity to nail these capitalists! I'll be revered and remembered as a great revolutionary!"

Randy gave his friend a strong embrace and both men went over the timing of his attack one last time.

"Exactly thirty minutes before sunrise, you'll launch the ultralight. The first wave of drones will have launched fifteen minutes earlier. A second wave will launch fifteen minutes after you start flying your plane. Some of the other drones will fall in place behind you for a bit, a full hour after sunrise and after you've completed your attack. Hopefully by then, the military will have used up all of their defensive armaments, including any experimental weapons that we don't know about. I am pretty sure they're prepared to defend against our use of quadcopters."

Danté continued, "We have to trust that they'll focus on you and your ultralight, and that will let us pull off surprise attacks elsewhere. It's very important that you keep the device flying at a low altitude in case the government has aircraft in the air. I'm sure there'll be numerous snipers positioned throughout the city trying to pick off the drones—and our people, for that matter. Keep your eyes open, because the Kevlar outfit you wear won't prevent a fatal head shot. Once you have the federal building in sight, flip the toggle switch and the plane will fly itself using its inertial navigation system. There's no computer chips on this plane. This ultralight is truly an antique!"

"No problem! I'll turn the key, start her up and be on my way," Randy said in a cavalier manner.

"No! That's not right. You'll prime the engine and pull the

cord. Once it starts to turn over, you flip the choke switch and pull the cord again until it starts. Once the engine fires, throttle it up for a few seconds to warm it up. It's a Briggs & Stratton engine and it's reliable," Danté responded.

Danté walked a few feet away to call Enrique and check on the payload. Returning, he told Randy that the payload was on its way.

Enrique and Luis arrived and were taken to a different meeting room on campus. Danté walked in shortly after, giving both men an embrace. "There's been a change in plans. Another comrade is going to deliver your material to the target. Go get the container so we can give the radioactive bomb to him for delivery."

Luis' heartbeat quickened and he could feel beads of perspiration seeping from his pores. He was silently praying that Danté wouldn't recognize his sudden nervousness as Enrique returned with the lead-lined radioactive container.

Luis composed himself and blurted out a question. "If we're not piloting the drone that will drop our material, then who is? We've been practicing this drop for days!"

"Well, judging from how nervous you are, you should be happy someone other than you is doing it," Danté fired back at Luis. "Besides, who said it's a drone?" Luis was on the receiving end of Danté's angry stare. He backed away from any farther questions.

∩∩∩

Almost instantly, the question "Who said it's a drone?" streamed across the Heartland from a cell tower to a satellite and onto the two satellite receivers attached to the NSA and CIA supercomputers. Meanwhile, folks at the Pentagon and the White House were waiting impatiently for a preliminary analysis of the expected situation.

Stan knew Antifa's stockpile of C-4 would be the group's primary weapon of destruction. The radioactive material was the big unknown. Luis and Enrique had been sneaking the biological radioactive material out of the hospital, a bit at a time, for months, and he had no idea just how lethal the stolen mix of materials was. Now that a drone might not transport the radioactive weapon, it was anyone's guess how it would be delivered. One thing was becoming obvious to Stan. Danté was playing the game of war as unconventionally as anyone could, and for that reason, he had to tip his hat to him.

If he wasn't a communist, I'd hire this guy! His downfall is going to be the lack of resources available to him, Stan silently reminded himself.

It was then that Stan phoned one of those resources, a local Agency asset in Portland, to confirm the agent was prepared for the morning flights. Call it a hunch, Stan thought. It made no sense for anyone to be going on a sightseeing trip with everything that was occurring in and around Portland.

"Who goes up in a hot-air balloon when it's almost freezing outside?" Stan mused as he punched numbers into the satellite phone.

 **HAPTER 69**

Luke Roberts was the prototypical CIA asset whom Stan phoned.

The agency had provided Luke with the seed money for his hot-air balloon business back in the '90s. "THE BEST HIGH IN PORTLAND" wasn't a business intended to make Luke a millionaire. It was a break-even venture at best. The big attraction was tethered flights that lifted off from Pioneer Courthouse Square in the heart of downtown Portland. When aloft, the 360-degree view from the balloon's basket was breathtaking.

From the start, the agency was very adept at setting up dummy businesses and staffing them with individuals who would spy on locations or citizens that had been deemed anti-American. Whether it was in foreign countries or in the USA, it made no difference. The assets were selected for their abilities to obscurely blend into the communities where their business ventures were established.

Luke grew up in Portland and left home for college at Texas Tech and the University of Texas, studying business and law. He was one of a select few individuals who'd earned dual master's degrees in business and law. It was in Texas that he learned that vexing societal issues didn't only have liberal solutions. It was in that environment that he became a staunch advocate of capitalism and the American way of democracy.

That philosophy soon became a conflict upon Luke's return

to Portland. His law practice floundered. He'd become a round peg trying to squeeze through a square hole in a very progressive city. He had no clue that his education and career had been watched and followed by the agency. When he felt he couldn't sink any lower, he received an offer of employment from the agency. There wasn't much to think about, Luke told himself. He was shunned by his family and community, but nonetheless decided he wouldn't be intimidated into leaving the region that he loved. The agency's opportunity allowed Luke to reinvent himself. Life began to improve in Portland as slowly perceptions flipped and the community accepted him.

Two days previously, Luke got a phone call from a man asking about reserving a hot-air balloon for a sunrise flight that would take place in just a few hours. Taking into account the eruption of Mt. Hood, the myriad news reports of turmoil occurring in and around that mountain, and Antifa's protestations, Luke determined that the timing of this request was too bizarre to ignore. He notified his contact at Langley Headquarters about the phone call. It was late evening the night before the oddly timed balloon trip when his cellphone rang.

"Mr. Roberts, sorry for this late interruption. My name's Stan, and I'm calling from Maine. I want to verify that you placed an order with us, but our online server is down right now. Could you tell me what you ordered?"

Luke was prepared. He'd already retrieved his personal password for the new day and replied, "I ordered a sky-blue chamois long-sleeve shirt, neck size 17-1/2." If Luke had not included the word chamois in his reply, Stan would have hung up.

"Luke, this is Director Stan Long. I'll keep this brief. There will be three gentlemen meeting you at your office in a short bit. One will identify himself as Tommy and the other two are Charles and Steven. And don't be surprised if a slightly older man is tagging along—his name is Rob. Whatever happens, don't let Rob go up in the basket! He's not an operative, but expect him to be armed. These men will be your business associates for the next twelve hours or so. Make sure at least one of the other three operatives goes airborne with you on the flight. I expect the number of guests going on the balloon will be at least two, but there could be more. This flight might be legitimate, but my hunch--which is not shared by anyone else at the moment—that your customers are revolutionaries. And please, whatever you do, follow the orders of my men. Do you have any questions?"

"Sir, can you tell me what's going on?" Luke asked.

"My men will fill you in when they arrive. Is there anything else?" Stan replied.

"No, sir," Luke stammered.

Stan ended the call. Luke went to the gun safe and armed himself before leaving home and heading to his office. There he waited for his new assistants to arrive.

# CHAPTER 70

The four men had just stepped out of the elevator when Tommy's phone began to vibrate. He stopped and answered the call as the others took a much-needed breather. Stan explained the change in plans to Tommy. Steven watched closely as his father took out a pen and notepad, writing down the information Stan was giving him. While writing, Tommy began shedding his hazmat attire. It became obvious there was a change in plans.

Outside, a black SUV was waiting for us near the front entrance. Tommy checked the supplies in the vehicle as I and the rest of the group piled in. Once we were settled, the vehicle headed to Luke's small office close to the Pioneer Courthouse Square. It was late and no one was on the streets, which made our assignment that much more curious. I doubt the citizens would defy the rules of martial law that have been declared by Oregon's governor. After all, they'd be subjecting themselves to immediate arrest, I thought.

The SUV pulled up in front of the office with its bright lights on and shining directly through the windows. Luke unholstered his weapon. He doubted that these men were his morning clients, but caution prevailed. Luke was again password-challenged by Tommy, and once said, we quickly were in the office and were seated on folding chairs around a card table.

Tommy spoke first, describing what Stan believed was going to happen and how they would deal with the situation if it did indeed occur. The plan was that Tommy and Charles would be in the balloon basket with Luke and his "guests" while Steven and I would work the tethers from below. The entire meeting lasted less than thirty minutes, after which we proceeded to the square. Luke was behind our SUV, in a vehicle trailering his balloon and all of the auxiliary paraphernalia. Once at the square, it took another forty minutes to set up the equipment we would use for the morning flight.

Now we waited. There was about an hour until sunrise when a car pulled up in front of where the balloon was in place and waiting. The driver parked and he and the other occupants of the car got out and headed toward our group.

"On your toes, gentlemen. It's show time. Follow my lead. If I draw down on them, be ready for a firefight," Tommy said.

Danté stepped forward and introduced himself. As there was no disguising his Latino heritage, he was going by the name of Gabriel but preferred to be called Gabe. He reached for his wallet as Tommy was prepared to reach for his gun.

Danté's ID card indicated that he was an employee of KGW, the NBC affiliate in Portland. "We'd like to shoot today's sunrise aboard your balloon this morning. And, I'm not going to lie to you, if there's any Antifa activity today here on the square, we'll be filming that, too."

"Well, Gabe, you know we have to check your bags before we take you up," Luke said, extending his hand for an introductory handshake. "I'm Luke and these are my assistants." Tommy, realizing that Luke might not remember our names on such short notice, immediately stepped forward and introduced himself. The rest of us did the same. Gabe also had a couple of assistants, but none spoke at that moment. They just smiled and flashed their credentials. Charles and I recognized Luis immediately and assumed his fellow compatriot was Enrique. We didn't dare say anything, and neither did Luis.

And Tommy was suspicious. He had no reason to prevent Gabe and the other men with him from carrying out their tasks. The two men who still had not spoken quickly passed by Tommy and boarded the basket. After a cursory check of the guests' carry-on bags, Luke started the burner and began filling the balloon with hot air.

It was a half hour until sunrise and the balloon was still filling when Tommy's phone again began to vibrate. He glanced at the phone screen and read the text message.

"First enemy drones have launched! It appears they're again coalescing into the Top Gun formation," it said.

∩ ∩ ∩

"Crank up the generators," General Matthews bellowed to his men from the command center.

The AUDS anti-drone units that were positioned on all four corners of the roof were already operating. Each unit's generator was humming a loud beat. The invisible radio frequencies emanating from the four units were drone assassins!

The general watched the video streaming from the lead Blackhawk as it vectored toward the group of Antifa quadcopters, all of which were morphing into a single radar image. The pilot radioed that the group of drones didn't appear to be carrying payloads, but they were nevertheless proceeding with a round-up. In the next ten minutes of flight, the Blackhawk pilots performed flawlessly. Once the enemy's drones were packaged and the noose tightened, the net was carried out over the Pacific. The two A-10s swept in for the grand finale, and the ten bogies were unceremoniously destroyed.

Antifa's first wave of attack had been a well-executed feint.

∩ ∩ ∩

The hot-air balloon was almost fully inflated and tugging to free itself from the fixed tethers. Steven and I were so focused on keeping the balloon stable that we didn't notice the gradual but increasingly rambunctious crowd of protestors gathering on the square. "So much for martial law," I shouted to Steven who nodded his head in agreement.

The scene was as if someone was directing a theater production. Seemingly out of nowhere, Antifa supporters, dressed in black with bandanas and hoodies covering two-thirds of their faces, had arrived at a set time. Most were carrying printed signs blaming the fascist administration currently occupying the White House for the beating of their friend in the Mt. Hood forest. There was the usual loudly chanted anti-capitalist rhetoric being shouted through bullhorns. The crescendo of the protesters' angry vitriol was rising quickly. Tommy was frustrated, watching the bedlam occurring below him. He knew the action of the assemblage was happening exactly as planned, and there wasn't a damn thing he could do about it. He searched the crowd from his vantage point on high for the group's ringleader, but to no avail. Luke's so-called news professionals were busy videotaping the chaos unfolding below from the basket of the balloon. They were smiling and laughing. Tommy found their actions somewhat strange, considering they were supposed to be impartial in their presentation of the news.

∩ ∩ ∩

An Air Force drone circling above Portland detected a new and unidentified flying object that was quickly verified as an unknown via satellite surveillance. It was moving at such a slow speed that the satellite's electronics had to reboot before getting a final confirmation.

For a few seconds, General Matthews and his men were confounded. They had the same intelligence information as Stan, but this object was moving faster than a hot-air balloon. "I need answers, men!" the general shouted. This time the information came straight from the Pentagon. Quickly the word "ultralight" was dispatched from the Pentagon to the command center in Portland.

"I need eyes on this target," the general said to the teams on the listening end of the transmission. The two A-10s abandoned their Pacific Ocean positions and closed in on the unknown target.

The pilot of the lead A-10 swept in over the unknown aircraft for a close fly-by. Randy casually waved at the plane. He did the same when the second plane cruised past him.

The military pilots did two more passes, with their cameras snapping pictures of Randy in the pilot's seat of the antique ultralight aircraft.

"The unidentified aircraft does not, I repeat, does NOT appear to be armed," the lead pilot reported.

This was a major problem for General Matthews. If the unidentified pilot and plane are out for a joy ride, then it should be ignored, he thought. And of course, Randy had done his best to appear as if he were enjoying a casual jaunt.

The generals at the Pentagon were highly skeptical. They knew the president wanted minimal casualties, as much as possible. But they also knew that the likelihood of a pilot out for a carefree Sunday flight in the skies of Portland on that particular day was pretty slim, especially with everything that had taken place in the region over the past few days. It made no sense. Their advice to POTUS was to shoot down the aircraft. A frenzied debate raged between the White House and the Pentagon generals for over a minute. The generals were convinced the plane was the vehicle carrying the radioactive bomb to an unknown target. The only problem was that the radioactive sniffers in place, around the city, had not yet detected anything radioactive.

The lead A-10 pilot interrupted the quiet dawn air. "I need a decision right now, General! In a few seconds, I'll be over heavily populated areas with homes and businesses. I'll have no chance at taking a shot then!"

General Matthews was ready to make the call, when the voice of the president was heard over the group com-link.

"This is the president! I'm ordering you to take the shot!"

"Roger that, sir," the pilot acknowledged.

Immediately, the plane throttled up, positioning itself for a clean attack. Roaring from the A-10 was the signature sound of it firing a Gatling style cannon.

"Brrrrrrrrrrrrrrrrrrt" ———— "Brrrrrrrrrrrrrt." The Warthog belched. One burp of the cannon was enough while two was extreme! Firing two rounds on the ultralight was overkill. The 30mm shells shredded the ultralight in a less than two seconds.

Randy got his wish. Martyrdom would fit him well.

Everyone in the basket was occupied with the gathering crowd of protestors when Enrique bent down, momentarily shielded by Luis's legs. Reaching into his duffel bag, he lifted the flap of the false bottom which held the hidden vehicle minus its propellers. He had to work fast to avoid detection by any of the crew members and quickly began attaching the props.

Keeping up his masquerade as a member of the news crew, Enrique pulled a different camera lens from the bag and stood up with it in his hand. As he switched out the lens, he casually looked at the others in the balloon, making unexpected eye contact with Charles. Charles appeared to be a casual observer, sitting with arms folded and one leg crossed over the other – but his face had that look of "I'm watching you." "That dude won't take his eyes off me," Enrique mumbled. Sneaking a sideways glance, he saw that Charles was now looking down over the basket's edge.

Luke yelled to Steven and me to release the restraints. One by one, the ropes were loosened and the balloon slowly began to ascend. That left only two other ropes that controlled the speed of the rising sphere for us to handle. We switched over to the two fixed cleats that were anchored in the square and corralled the two altitude ropes. The only things preventing the hot-air balloon from floating away into the sky were my hands and Steven's as we handled these two ropes.

Tommy's satellite phone vibrated again. He turned toward the rail of the basket to read the message out of view of the others.

The text from Stan read simply: "Your passengers are Antifa and the second wave of their drones has launched."

The number of drones in the air was uncertain at that moment. The enemy flight patterns had again condensed, presenting a radar image of one large attacking aircraft. Thirty seconds later, radar now indicated that about twenty quadcopters had split off from one another, each traveling in individual directions. Each drone was also creating its own IR-radar signature on the screens of those watching.

General Matthews knew this group of aircraft wasn't a second feint – it was the real thing. Those at NSA, CIA, and the Pentagon had already identified targets in the city most likely to be attacked. Many were similar to businesses that Antifa had attacked in the post-election riots of 2016.

The general watched the screen and silently prayed that his troops would prevail, while still realizing that some of the enemy drones could reach their targets. It remained his call on when to commit farther specific defensive assets.

As the terrorist's drones zigged and zagged their way toward the hub of the city – downtown Portland – the general gave the go ahead to the ground-based AUDS platforms to start tracking the drones. These 'Anti-UAV Defense System' units, identical to the rooftop fixed equipment, were on mobile vehicles. They emitted multiple radio frequencies designed to neutralize the drones continued advancement. He couldn't chance that Antifa's unmanned aerial vehicles would be autonomous.

It was a wise decision.

It took intelligence analysts just two minutes to figure out that the enemy drones were using Pixhawk Flight Controller software. This meant that the drones were initially launched by the Antifa pilots on the ground – but once in the air, the drones would not be under radio control. It appeared that these drones were flying from GPS waypoint to GPS waypoint until finally reaching a specific pre-programmed target. There was a sense of certainty that if the target site was reached, the payload would detonate, causing destruction and possibly death, while also destroying the drone.

The AUDS units on the roof of the federal building, as well as those dispersed throughout the city, were able to track the enemy unmanned aerial vehicle in a 360° radius. Unfortunately, they could only effectively broadcast their UAV drone-killer radio frequencies only in a 180° direction. To compensate for that deficiency, the rooftop units were set up in a formation that allowed overlapping coverage. The general hoped that the electronic radio frequencies wouldn't miss any of the drones, but he knew the downtown landscape of tall buildings would shield some of the enemy drones from detection.

ᑎ ᑎ ᑎ

Business owners in the northwest were quite familiar with Antifa's protests. The riots that occurred after the 2016 election were still fresh in their minds.

With fresh signs of looming unrest, they did what was needed to protect storefronts and hopefully reduce the costs of damage that would be caused by rioters. Windows were covered with plywood and business hours were curtailed. National Guard troops were directed to protect specific targets that were likely to be attacked again. These were sites that inflamed the anarchists and were symbolic of the best that the capitalist world represented.

General Matthews knew that the same targets were once again at risk, and was convinced that in this case, lightning would strike twice in the same place. There was no doubt in his mind that a big national banking conglomerate would be a likely target, as would a major urban car dealership and the well-known and successful coffee house chain of stores.

The Pentagon's supercomputers were busy calculating the

average run time of a conventional drone's battery pack based on its maximum attainable forward speed and various launch points. Once a credible launch point was determined, algorithm-generated maps were overlaid on a single schematic grid that represented the city of Portland. This was used to determine where the armed forces and equipment would be positioned. At the same time, everything had to be fluid and highly mobile in anticipation of the unexpected.

Antifa's first and second waves of drone attacks had a degree of predictability. Now the general's men, linked to their mobile Stryker units and equipped with the MEHEL laser system, were strategically moved from position to position like pawns on a chessboard. These positioning changes were directed by a spy satellite and Predator Drone radar systems.

Half of Antifa's second wave of drones was programmed to attack the federal building. Each drone was designed to precisely move from point A to point Z. It might take the enemy drone two minutes to negotiate the distance of a single city block, depending on its GPS guidance, vs. only thirty seconds to navigate itself to the next block. Each drone's software was its unique controlling factor.

∩ ∩ ∩

Danté had made a grievous error! He just didn't know it yet.

He'd directed the software engineers to code the specific final destination waypoint to also be the detonation spot for every quadcopter and its payload. He wanted perfection – and he didn't want unnecessary casualties. After all, when all was said and done, Antifa shouldn't go down in history as an organization known for killing innocent people.

The first drones dispatched by Antifa pilots were identical, and their maneuvers again provided an infrared signature indicative of a single bogie. From building to building, the drones moved in a synchronized manner before reaching their destination – the federal building. Both were hovering five stories up on the southern side of the building, hugging closely to its exterior and easily eluding the spray of radio waves searching for them. Twenty seconds later, the drones separated, climbing to the top of the building where they again hovered. It was only for ten seconds – and that was their fatal mistake.

"Fire, fire, fire!" a military sniper shouted. Both drones exploded into hundreds of pieces as their C-4 payloads dropped harmlessly to the ground. Troops standing several stories below quickly gathered the unexploded ordnance.

Every drone attacking the federal building was successfully intercepted in a similar manner, except for one, which had veered a little off course because of a programming error. Antifa had apparently done something right by first doing wrong!

The rogue drone flew directly into the building some 30 feet above the main entrance, causing a huge fireball explosion. The building swayed from the shock wave of the exploding C-4, and shattered glass rained down onto the sidewalk and streets below for nearly a minute. National Guard troops scattered out of the way as shards of glass began to ricochet upwards from the concrete before falling back down and breaking into thousands of smaller pieces.

Only two of the remaining Antifa drones targeting the businesses of downtown Portland reached their targets. Again, the reason they made it was a programming error.

The destruction was severe.

Perhaps if the battle had taken place in an isolated desert site, with only three of twenty drones actually inflicting damage, General Matthews would have considered this outcome a success. For him, these results were unacceptable. All of the military's defense systems had been tested in the southwest desert region. But urban drone warfare was an entirely different scenario. He knew there was only one weapon remaining in his arsenal that Antifa's members couldn't foil. But using that weapon required approval from POTUS ... and he needed it now.

In just a few seconds, the general was joined on screen by the Joint Chiefs and POTUS.

ᗌ ᗌ ᗌ

"Mr. President, I need your permission to unleash Recrudesce."

General Matthews waited for what seemed like an eternity before speaking again.

"Sir, I'm not trying to rush you into a decision, but Recrudesce is the only weapon in our arsenal that can fully stop these attacks. I wholly expect there'll be another wave of Antifa drones launched at any moment."

"General, hang on for a minute," the president snapped with obvious annoyance. The general was pushing too hard.

General Matthews knew POTUS was upset. The weapons technology that he wanted to put into play came with multiple expected collateral damages. The president abhorred the idea of using this particular weaponry for that reason. At the same time, the general had a higher level of comfort in using it because no members of his military unit would be put at risk. He was also praying that the majority of Portland's residents would abide by the order of martial law and stay indoors and off the roads.

But he had no way of knowing for sure, as his experience in this type of situation was limited. Prior events were simulations held in a classroom and were totally theoretical. There was no live fire testing or recorded results to his knowledge with this weapon.

The general was wrong. There had indeed been a live fire test of Recrudesce, and the results were almost catastrophic. Unfortunately, his security clearance wasn't high enough for him to be privy to that information.

"Mr. President, I understand the plight you're facing. But sir, right now the folks we're primarily concerned about are the troops who've been here fighting the past few days. Our military didn't start this war, sir, Antifa did! Your priority should be the safety of our soldiers and a victory for the American government and its people! You can worry about criticism from the media until the end of time. They've never been your friend and they're not about to become one now!"

Another thirty seconds of silence followed the general's outburst.

"Mr. President, I'm sorry. I can't wait any longer! I'm going to protect and defend my troops!"

The general exited from the comm-link, summoning his adjutant general. He needed to spread the word down the chain of command that a series of cutting-edge weaponry, consisting of three armed offensive Air Force drones, were about to engage in the battle. Each drone would be equipped with a Recrudesce weapon—a weapon that the military was reluctantly being forced to use.

He gave the initiation order, hoping it wouldn't be countermanded, and knowing that the conflict would soon be over.

It took nearly thirty minutes for the drones and weaponry to get in proper position.

∩ ∩ ∩

Tommy's satellite phone again began to vibrate – almost with a sense of urgency, he thought. "Damn, what now?" he said silently, while turning the phone to shield the message from prying eyes. He stared intently at the display. The text read:

"General Matthews is about to execute electronic HELL!

EMP(s) are about to be unleashed!

This will probably be my last communiqué to you and whatever you do—don't look at the flash!"

Tommy casually moved across the basket, nudging Luke to get his attention and showed him Stan's message. Luke read it, shrugged his shoulders, and gave Tommy a look that said they'd be okay in the balloon. The electronic magnetic pulse disturbances about to visit them would have no impact on the hot-air balloon at its present height. Tommy nonetheless made a throat-slashing motion, indicating it was time to put a halt to the trip. The turmoil going on in the square and the possibility that there'd be some communication issues made the decision an easy one for Tommy. He motioned to Luke to bring the balloon down.

Unfortunately for the two agents, Danté was closely observing their body language during the non-verbal exchange. There was no way he was going to launch his drone at street level. He needed the altitude for the plan to work. Danté also knew how to communicate without using words. He nudged Enrique with his elbow while slamming his right fist into the palm of his other hand. Enrique understood and began to slowly reach for his handgun.

On the ground, the crowd was pressing in on Steven and my shouts of "get away" were largely unheard and fully ignored. A masked Antifa protester dressed in black from head to toe suddenly knocked me from the tether. and the balloon lurched upward at a steep angle. Charles, who was looking at me from the basket above, stumbled sideways because of the sudden jolt. I saw Enrique press the barrel of his automatic into Charles's temple as I turned to regain control of the balloon. I pushed the protester to the ground with my forearm, and when he got back up, he was staring at the end of my gun. Not willing to be shot, he and two of his friends scattered as I regained control of the rope, but it was too late to help anyone in the basket.

By the time Tommy and Luke regained their footing, Charles was prone and face-down on the basket floor. Thirty seconds later, Charles was joined on the floor by Luke and Tommy, both of whom were facing upward.

Danté guarded the three men while Enrique finished assembling the drone that he'd removed from its hiding spot. He gingerly placed the container with the radioactive materials on the basket floor. Tommy was able to see everything that was happening, even as he was plotting an escape. He felt certain Charles was doing the same, but he wasn't as optimistic about Luke's chance for escape.

The propellers were now fully attached to the drone. Tommy watched as Enrique retrieved a mason jar filled with gasoline from his bag and placed the smallest funnel he'd ever seen into a reservoir on the drone. I'll be damned! That drone runs on gasoline! Tommy thought. Enrique next removed the radioactive materials from the lead-lined protective container.

Within seconds, the radiation-detecting equipment on the

military drone circling the sky above the basket began to emit an alarm. The source of the radiation was instantly relayed to the Pentagon and White House, as well as to General Matthews, who wasted no time immediately ordering National Guard troops onto the square. The Portland police department, which had been ordered to take a "watch and observe" stance, now gladly wielded its authority over the riotous crowd of Antifa dissidents. Heads, trunks, and limbs were now being struck by the National Guard's butt end of their rifle stocks and slowly order returned as the rioters retreated. The troops wasted no time pressing toward the location that was supposedly the source of radiation.

Enrique finished sliding the container of radioactive material into the belly of the drone. He primed the small engine, and it quickly turned over. The propellers began to rotate slowly. Tommy's eyes widened as a plume of smoke wafted from the drone. Still in denial Tommy mumbled again, "Jesus, that drone has no lithium battery, it uses gasoline ... what the hell is going on?" Enrique raised the drone high above his head, throttled up the power, and while balancing the machine in one hand, he positioned himself in the basket prior to releasing the drone.

Tommy wasn't sure if the drone had electronic circuitry on it. In reality, it had a virtual navigation system made up of a couple of tiny gyroscopes and could fly by itself for as long as its fuel lasted. When the gasoline ran out, the drone would crash – and that made Danté very happy! His predetermined calculations pretty much guaranteed that the drone would come down very near, if not crashing directly into, the federal building.

Tommy stared intently as Enrique released the drone, and suddenly something caught his attention, out of the corner of his eye. Gazing north, Tommy saw what looked to be a very large bird gliding on the wind in a slow circling path.

"Nah, it can't be," he said out loud.

The gasoline powered drone had been in the air for less than three seconds when the big bird finished its loop and began flapping its wings in pursuit. Tommy lost sight of the bird, but the chase was on!

And in another split second, he and Charles jumped to their feet.

# CHAPTER 71

Charles dove quickly toward Danté's feet to take him down. It was a clean tackle, but not before Danté got off a shot from his gun. Tommy reached Danté at virtually the same time as Charles and finished the job. With both arms extended, he landed squarely on Danté's chest, palms up and knocking him backwards over the rail of the basket, hanging suspended in air. A second bullet was fired into the air without harm to anyone. Tommy was pressed against the rail of the basket, leaving Charles no choice but to release his hold on Danté 's feet.

Tommy and Enrique watched as Danté attempted to fly. His arms began flailing in circles and his legs were pumping as if he was riding a bike. Tommy later told me that it was like watching the scene from the movie Die Hard when Hans Gruber fell to his death from the Nakatomi Tower.

Steven and I watched, our mouths wide open in shock, as Danté plunged head-first onto the square. There was no suffering; death was instantaneous.

Enrique turned away, and in an instant began pummeling Tommy with his fists. Charles jumped into action, grabbing Enrique by the legs. With a quick twist, Enrique was lying restrained on the floor of the basket.

"You murdered him! You killed Danté – he was our leader! I'll find you and kill you!" Enrique threatened, spewing expletives and more threats. Spittle was running down his chin. It didn't matter, though. His words were falling on deaf ears.

Unfortunately, the first shot had found its mark. Luke fell to the basket floor after the bullet hit him squarely in the chest. Tommy was now on the floor of the basket, attending to Luke. He found the entry and exit wounds, pushing and pressing his palm to where the bullet entered. He searched for a pulse on Luke's neck with his other hand. There was none. Laying Luke flat, Tommy began CPR.

With Enrique now handcuffed, Charles began to work the propane controls until the hot-air balloon began to descend. Luke's eyes were open, the pupils constricted. Tommy worked furiously to bring him back to life, but he knew from experience that Luke's odds were slim.

Finally, the basket was back on the ground. Steven and I secured the balloon to the cleats. National Guard troops closed in after hearing Tommy's frantic scream for a medic. Tommy reached for his phone and called Stan.

"Thank God there's a connection," he mumbled to himself as he heard Stan answer. "Stan, Luke was shot and it's not good. Can you get a helicopter out here to the square—fast?" Tommy pleaded.

"Tommy, listen to me! I can't! If General Mathews orders the firing of those EMPs, that helicopter will be hit, and I'll have even more fatalities. Put Luke in an ambulance and pray that an EMP doesn't go off!" Stan ordered.

Tommy's mind was going too fast for his speech center to function properly. "Stan, Stan--"

"I'm still here, Tommy!" Stan answered somewhat impatiently.

"Antifa launched a drone from the balloon! The damn thing is an antique. It runs on gas. And call me stupid, but they weren't too particular as to where it would go. The really bad news is that it's carrying the radioactive payload! Tell me you've got an IR signature on it," Tommy begged.

"We see it, Tommy. We're tracking it!" Stan ended the conversation.

Tommy stared at his phone and shouted, "Well thank you too, asshole!"

This revolution couldn't end soon enough.

As the ambulance pulled away with Luke aboard, the emotional upheaval that had been building inside him for days, first with Danny and now with Luke, overwhelmed Tommy. The fuse had been lit. Tommy looked for Enrique, spotting him 200 yards away, being loaded into a black Suburban for transport to a CIA interrogation site. Tommy sprinted toward the vehicle with Steven right on his heels. Tommy grabbed Enrique by the collar and started to raise his hand to strike.

Steven intercepted Tommy's fist and prevented the possible killing of yet another person. He pushed Tommy to the ground, pinning him there with his arms. "Dad, stop. Please, no more killing!"

Tommy began to cry. He stood, wiped away his tears, and walked over to Enrique.

"Yes, I killed your leader, Danté--or Gabe, as you previously called him! And I'd do it again in a heartbeat if necessary! You'll probably be paroled some day, and I'm begging you, come after me! I want you to try to kill me. In fact, I am demanding that you try. But know this, punk, your odds of success are slim!"

Tommy turned away and headed back to the balloon launch site. "Oh shit. I forgot to tell Stan something!"

"What was it, Dad? I can call him if you want," Steven said.

"I could've sworn I saw an eagle in the sky, just north of where Antifa launched their shitty drone from the balloon. Hell, it makes no difference. Stan said they were tracking the drone."

"It's okay, Dad. We've done all we can," Steven replied, hoping to ease Tommy's mind.

Their part in the Revolution of 2018 was over—maybe!

The National Guard had finished cordoning off the square. Charles and I folded the balloon and stowed it and the rest of the gear on Luke's trailer. That was the least we could do for a patriot. Tommy and Steven had both returned, each with exhaustion apparent on their face. About twenty paces behind them was another familiar face, but I was the only one to notice. I said nothing and just watched as Jerry closed in on the group, with a smile that spanned ear to ear. Sensing someone behind him, Tommy turned around and stared, nearly wordless.

"What! Where the hell?" he finally stammered "How did you …?" Jerry just grinned wider.

"Damn, it was Icarus up there, wasn't it?" Tommy shouted, pointing to the sky and realizing that he'd really seen the majestic bird. Tommy extended his hand and Jerry grasped it firmly, with Tommy laughing hard for a short few seconds. Just as quickly as the laughter started, it ended, as something serious suddenly hit Tommy.

"Oh God, Jerry, Icarus is chasing after a drone that's carrying radioactive materials!" Tommy spoke with heavy remorse. From the look of devastation on Jerry's face, it was obvious he had no clue that Antifa's drones might wreak even more devastation than what had taken place around Mt. Hood.

"C'mon," Jerry shouted as he turned and began running toward his car. Tommy, Steven, and Charles were sprinting to keep pace with Jerry. I was the weak link of the quartet. As Tommy ran, he wondered how Jerry could possibly know the exact spot where Icarus might bring down the drone. As we neared the SUV, Jerry shouted for Tommy to drive while he began fumbling with his smartphone. Steven, Charles, and I climbed in the back seat, all the while listening to Jerry as he commenced barking instructions to Tommy, who was already accelerating at a fast pace.

"You're an idiot," Tommy said to himself. It hit him that Icarus was GPS-chipped. The longer Icarus was exposed to the radiation, the more likely it would suffer a fatal consequence. Radiation sickness was ugly for every life form, not just human beings.

∩ ∩ ∩

Earlier on the square, Icarus had spotted the drone as it was launched by Enrique, standing in the basket of the hot-air balloon. The drone was nearly 500 yards in front of the eagle, but Icarus had an unofficial top speed of 50 miles per hour, and in a dive, that speed doubled to 100 miles per hour. There was never a doubt that the bird would catch his prey. Within less than a mile distance, Icarus had closed in, tipping himself into position to begin his capture dive. The eagle's wings were gliding aerodynamically as easily as an F-14 Tomcat in hypersonic flight. A split-second before catching up with the aircraft, Icarus positioned his legs in front of his body, talons separated and ready to grasp the target.

Icarus's body hit one of the struts that was connecting two of the four props. Even virtual navigation couldn't correct the course deviation after the impact. Icarus pulled the drone down to the ground. Upon landing on firm ground, the bird thrust his body up one last time, grabbed a propeller stanchion and flipped the drone upside down. In a matter of seconds, the gas line was empty, and the three props that were still trying to rotate finally stopped twitching.

The air battle was over, and Icarus intended to guard the prey until his trainer rewarded him for the kill. He had no idea he was being attacked by invisible nuclear daggers.

"Left here." "Take a right." "Make a U-turn; you went too far," Jerry shouted at Tommy.

After a long ten minutes, we arrived at the location Jerry expected Icarus to be and indeed he was. "There's a tarp in the back, Tommy! Grab it," Jerry yelled.

Tommy retrieved the tarp from the trunk, understanding that Jerry wanted it to cover the drone, even though Tommy knew that it would do nothing to stop the radiation emitting from the downed drone. Jerry whistled and extended his arm. Icarus launched into a short flight and ended up perching himself on Jerry's extended arm, patiently waiting for his treat. Jerry rewarded him immediately.

We knew that there was nothing to do now but bide our time.

In less than five minutes, a large black SUV pulled up and several men in hazmat radiation gear got out of the vehicle. They quickly neutralized the radioactive payload, replacing the canvas tarp with a large lead lined wrap. Two more vans quickly arrived. Jerry loaded Icarus in one of them while Steven, Charles, Tommy, and I were told to get into the other. I assumed we were on our way to be decontaminated.

Tommy's phone vibrated once.

"Tell Jerry I said thanks," Stan said.

"Huh?" Tommy asked.

"That drone was headed straight for the federal building. So far there've been no further launches. Damn ... check that! I gotta go; at least twenty more Antifa drones just went airborne! Whatever you do, get the hell out of that car and shelter in place."

And then Stan was gone.

# CHAPTER 73

"Stop the damn van! Stop, dammit!" Tommy shouted in a tone that demanded immediate action. The brakes locked instantly with the smell of burning rubber wafting around us. Tommy opened his door and ran to the front of the car.

"Pop the hood, so we can get to the battery and hurry!"

The driver didn't argue.

"Get me a pliers or a wrench; I need to take theses cables off the battery," Tommy told the driver.

"Don't do that, man!" the driver said emphatically as he reached toward Tommy to stop him.

There was no time to argue. Tommy reached down to remove his stubby revolver from the ankle holster and pointed it at the driver.

"I'm telling you just one time, so you better listen! These cables are attached to the battery. If an electrical pulse of energy, like a bolt of lightning, were to hit this van, I guarantee you that every microprocessor in this vehicle will be fried. Do you want that to happen? It's your choice. I don't give a shit!

The driver nodded, obviously unsure of the right answer.

"Good choice," Tommy said.

At the same time as Tommy was strong-arming the driver, residents in the metropolitan Portland area were hearing the civil-defense sirens sounding a warning that there was a need to take cover. If nothing else, the sirens drove people indoors to shelter

– and to turn on their televisions or radio to find out what was happening.

Tommy had been on the mark. The driver and other occupants of the car heard the recognizable digitally generated voice that every American hears blaring on their media devices when a test emergency warning is issued. The voice was coming through their radio loud and clear, but this time saying:

"This is not a drill!
I repeat! It is not a drill!
Unplug every electrical appliance … that includes computers!
Power off your cell phones and your touch pads!
If possible, turn off the main power switch to your home!
If you are in a car, pull over immediately and turn it off.
Lift the hood of the car and disconnect the battery cables!
When you hear three short siren blasts, it will be safe once again to power everything back up!

This message was repeated over and over, and it was also broadcast on every television network, both mainstream and cable.

Hopefully, people complied. The warning was intended to prevent destruction of computer microprocessors integrated within today's electronics. Such an event would possibly render every electronic device useless.

What the warning didn't say was how potentially serious the situation was. It didn't tell the average American citizen that there were high-level government officials in the Pentagon at that very moment who knew exactly how powerful and destructive an electromagnetic pulse attack (EMP) could be. It didn't tell them that our country's only totally successful response to these Antifa drone attacks could inadvertently cause the death of innocent people.

There was one particular piece of electronic equipment that a small group of unlucky citizens wouldn't be able to turn off or shield, except for a small percentage of the populous that were known as "survivalists." This group of individuals had been preparing for this type of event for years. Most likely they were already tucked away in their thermonuclear bomb shelters.

General Matthews was silently saying a prayer for everyone, as he was still awaiting the president's official go-ahead.

"General, you have my permission to initiate Recrudesce. May God forgive us both for our actions," the president said in a voice filled with remorse.

∩ ∩ ∩

The Antifa pilots controlling the final wave of quadcopters were loyal to a fault. If there was even the slightest inkling of doubt before launching the drones, it was of no consequence. Dante's orders were sacrosanct. More than that, the pilots knew they'd be far removed from the drone's final destination and the accompanying destruction.

After analyzing the flight patterns of the second wave of Antifa drone attacks, the folks at the Pentagon were convinced the third wave would be Zombie-type drones. The only thing holding back the start of the EMP barrage was timing. Those at the Pentagon believed that when the Antifa airborne drones reached their halfway point of battery life, a failsafe notification integrated within each one would signal the beginning of the end. It would signal the last leg … the final apocalyptic surge, of the Antifa revolution.

Tommy's phone was vibrating. Although he should have, he

hadn't yet shut it down. Tommy fully expected there'd be one last request or tidbit of information from his boss. He knew Stan all too well.

"I have an urgent request and need your help. Right now, the mayor and the governor are on the square surveying the carnage. I'm not certain they're aware of the PSAs streaming on television and radio. The governor is in danger! He has a defibrillator!"

"What?" Tommy replied.

"The governor has a pacemaker! When that electromagnetic pulse hits, his pacemaker could stop working. I know you and Danny carried those damn Faraday wraps everywhere you two traveled. If you can get the governor bagged up and grounded, he should have no adverse effects!"

"How soon?" Tommy asked in a concerned voice while unconsciously reaching behind his back, feeling for his his small fanny-type backpack.

"Fifteen minutes, tops, is my best guess! Get going!" was Stan's panicked reply. Tommy didn't know what else to say. He did have the Faraday wrap, but still needed a miracle to get to the governor in time, knowing full well there wasn't a chance in hell that a miracle was going to happen. Lost in thought, Tommy saw a woman in a Toyota 4-Runner rounding the bend and heading quickly toward him. She brought the car a stop and stepped out of it. Tommy approached her and after about fifteen seconds of discussion, it appeared that something was going to happen. He motioned all of us to join with them as he climbed into the driver seat and the woman moved to the passenger seat.

As I got in the back, I glanced up front and realized I knew her.

"Doc, what are you doing, why aren't you ...?" I never had a chance to finish the question. Once the fog of fatigue had cleared from my head, I recognized that it was Dr. Ellie. As we were speeding toward the square, I asked why she was even out on the roads.

"Dr. Becker, Portland may be viewed as bastion of progressiveness, but there's a silent minority that strongly disagrees with that philosophy! I've been driving around all morning in case I came across someone who needed my help. For some reason, I turned onto this road, where I stumbled across you and the rest of your group."

I just smiled and silently thought about my oldest granddaughter, wondering if I could be so lucky as to see her grow up into an adult like this young lady.

It took Tommy less than five minutes from the time he hung up with Stan to get us back to where we'd been earlier. Jumping quickly from the vehicle, he followed Charles, who as a resident of the state, knew what the governor looked like. By now, Antifa protestors had been cleared from the immediate surroundings of the square by National Guard troops. However, they were still outside the perimeter, protesting and throwing whatever debris they could find at the troops.

Before Tommy could stop him, Charles had broken into a sprint. Charles broke through the cordon of troops and police officers and was heading toward the governor. Perhaps he thought that since he wasn't wearing traditional Antifa attire, he'd be safe.

The sound of a gunshot filled the air as I watched Charles fall face-down on the square. Holding her medical credentials up for the officer to see, Ellie responded immediately, kneeling on the ground next to Charles to begin triage.

After also showing their credentials, Tommy and Steven

carefully approached the governor and the security detail surrounding him. Tommy was now carrying the Faraday bag. The officer who had just shot Charles still had his gun out and extended, ready to fire once more. He lowered the automatic weapon, realizing he'd just shot an innocent person. Worse than that, he'd shot one of their own.

Tommy shouted out to the governor.

"Governor, you're in danger! I need to put this around you!" The guards allowed Tommy and Steven through their human security barrier.

"Sir, you have a pacemaker and there's about to be a weapon released that could kill you!"

The look of acquiescence on the governor's face was the only permission Tommy needed, as he and Steven jumped into action. The Faraday wrap reached just to the governor's ankles – and that should be enough, Tommy thought. He grasped the governor under the arms while Steven grabbed hold of his legs. They quickly carried the governor about 20 feet to an open area under a tree, gently laying him down and effectively grounding him.

The guards each had looks of amazement on their faces when suddenly, the bright blue sky burst into a blinding glare of a white-hot sun accompanied by an ear-shattering explosion. Most everybody immediately looked away.

Not one, but three EMPs had exploded.

The cacophony of hundreds of lightning bolts reached our ears, and the first reaction was to cover them. What none of us realized at that particular instant was that the electro-magnetic wave preceded the sound of the explosion. The waves were traveling at the speed of light and had already harmlessly entered and exited our bodies in microseconds.

The EMPs had made their mark in the skies of Portland – and after the EMP attack, seventeen quadcopters fell harmlessly to the ground with their payloads intact. Three, however, had already reached their targets, exploded, and taken their toll.

Tommy checked his phone for an EMP confirmation, but the screen was blank. He punched in his password code. Nothing happened. In the background, he could hear metal scraping against some kind of hard surface; no doubt a vehicular accident was echoing between the buildings. Nearby, a CNN news van came to an abrupt and devastating halt when its electronics shut down from the EMP. The driver was helpless and knocked unconscious when his head slammed hard into the side window. The air bags couldn't deploy, and the window shattered into tiny pieces. His state of unconsciousness was merciful, as the hood of the van hood slammed through the front window upon impact. The driver was decapitated.

Still next to the governor, Tommy and Steven lifted him to a standing position. He was angrily tugging at the fabric of the bag, not realizing that it had saved his life. Cursing a blue streak, the governor promised that heads would roll. "How dare they wrap me in a bag while all hell was breaking loose in my state?" he was ranting. Neither Tommy nor Steven was able to get in any words of explanation, and simply left him with the Faraday bag draped at his ankles.

They suddenly remembered Charles and hurried to his side.

I had just taken over chest compressions from Ellie, who was clearly exhausted. A sense of helplessness was consuming me. If there'd been an ambulance anywhere nearby, the chances of it being operable were nil. After two more minutes of compressions, I could swear I heard the now familiar sound of helicopter rotors.

"Nah," I said to myself.

The sound grew louder and closer when Ellie screamed out, "There it is!" She and I switched again, and in another five minutes Charles and Ellie, assisted by army medics, were whisked away to Portland's trauma hospital.

Over the next five minutes, the number of Antifa protestors dwindled even further on the square. Historians would later write that for all purposes the Antifa Revolution of 2018 ended right then – and with a whimper.

Steven asked, "Was that a nuclear blast?"

# CHAPTER 74

All three of us sat down and rested our bodies against the tree that we'd now forever refer to as the Governor's Tree. Tommy and Steven's eyes started to close, and I really didn't want to interrupt their beginning stages of slumber.

"Guys, wake up! We've got company. The governor is on his way over here!" I warned.

Tommy lurched awake, but Steven was already upright and at attention. With a bit of grousing, Tommy finally managed to stand. The governor stepped up with his hand extended. Tommy grudgingly stuck out his good arm and both men exchanged shakes; Steven and I were next.

"Gentlemen, please tell me that your friend is alive. My personal assistant is truly sorry."

"Governor, we're sorry also! We haven't heard if he's still alive. Of the four of us, he was the only one that is a citizen of Oregon!" Tommy replied. The statement obviously stung the governor, and that was Tommy's intent.

"And before you thank us for saving your life, you need to place a call to POTUS. He's the one that gave us orders to get here and try to save you. I'll give you a chance to share that information with the 'NEWS' folks." The governor nodded, fully understanding the veiled threat that Tommy had just issued.

After the governor was out of earshot, Steven and I heard the word "Asshole" emanate from Tommy's direction.

A black Suburban pulled up to the square, and Tommy slowly began walking toward it. Like sheep we followed. The driver informed us we were being transported to the federal building and Tommy interrupted him. "Young man, wherever our team member, Charles, was taken, that's where we're going. Inform the general of the change of plans." The driver did as asked. Being outnumbered may have had an influence on him, and the SUV changed direction. As we pulled up to the hospital, I blurted out, "This is where they brought Marty."

Charles was in surgery, so Tommy and Steven took seats in the waiting area. I excused myself and went to check on Marty.

As I walked into Marty's room, Lauren stood up.

"Rob, I'm truly sorry for what I've said and done in the past. Marty has been filling in all the gaps of information. I hope we can start our relationship anew."

I was so exhausted and glad everything was over that even if I wanted to be sarcastic, I had no strength to quibble. I kissed Lauren on the cheek and gave her a hug while looking at Marty, who had that expression of "thank you" plastered across her face. I asked Lauren for a few private moments with Marty, and Lauren exited the room.

I spoke first. "Please don't ever leave me like that again. Promise me!"

Marty slid her hand onto mine and said, "Only until death do us part...deal?"

I replied, "Deal."

"Now tell me what happened, because the television news has been sketchy and then the power went out!" Marty asked. For the next half hour I rehashed the turmoil of Pioneer Square. When I was finished, I noticed a slight tear rolling down her cheek.

"What did I say this time?"

"He was responsible for you saving me, Rob. Go! Go see how Charles is doing. Come back later and stay with me tonight, but please go!" Marty stated. I kissed her goodbye and returned to the surgical floor and joined my friends.

∩∩∩

Hospital waiting rooms are the closest thing to funeral parlors. Their only redeeming feature is the presence of a television set. After asking Tommy if there was any report about Charles and his subsequent head shake, I settled in to watch the mainstream news channel's reporting of today's events, while channel surfing each and every one of them. Scrolling across the bottom of all the channels were banners of the day's grim statistics. The dead and wounded numbers scrolled first and then the estimates of damage came second. Amongst those that died were ten individuals with implanted heart pacemakers, victims of the EMP. The news scroll also stated that more of those types of fatalities were expected to be reported in the next few hours. The governor was lucky, I thought.

I began silently saying a prayer for those that lost their lives on this day, when the news anchor began a rant about POTUS employing an atomic weapon to generate the EMP that effectively shut down Antifa's final violent revolutionary thrust. I turned toward Tommy, and he had buried his head in his hands which were slowly transforming themselves into fists. His fuse had been lit! I started to ask him the question, but his son's lips moved quicker than mine.

"Dad, was it nuclear?" Steven skeptically asked.

Tommy desperately wanted to avoid answering but he had

new responsibilities. He was no longer just an elder statesman. He was now a full-fledged parent with a familial obligation.

"Son, it could have been. The little bit that I know about EMPs is, they've always been created in the context of a nuclear weapon. Steven, my job is about preserving our Republic from enemies, foreign and domestic. There are no 'ifs' or 'maybes' in interpreting that responsibility. There were an enormous number of lives saved today because of that EMP explosion. Hell, there may have been multiple EMPs exploded for all that I know, that made it look like an atomic explosion. I just don't have answers right now."

For me, at that moment, I honestly felt like Tommy sounded more like a parent and not a government operative. The look on Steven's face confirmed my opinion. Suddenly I detected movement out of the corner of my eye.

I glanced toward the entrance to the waiting room, wondering if the man standing there might be a source of news about Charles. Tommy sensed the man's presence also and he turned to look. He then stood and advanced toward the stranger, while smiles crossed both men's faces. I stared at Steven, and he also seemed to recognize the man.

"Stan, thanks for coming! Please join us. The only person you've not officially met is Dr. Rob Becker."

I stood, shook Stan's hand, and resumed sitting. He remained standing.

"I had a conference with the doctors and the consensus is that Charles is going to make it but they're not certain if he'll be paralyzed from the waist down. The bullet was a hollow point, and the largest portion of it damaged his spinal cord. Another piece damaged his liver and another fragment collapsed a lung.

He received three units of blood and is resting now. Dr. Becker, if you don't mind I'd like a word with my men." I nodded an okay and the three men moved to a corner of the waiting room out of earshot. I knew I'd eventually find out what was going on so I tried to grab a quick nap.

And then it hit me! I'd totally forgotten about Luke. We all had. I exited the waiting room and headed to the nurses' station. Not knowing for certain if Luke had been taken to the same hospital as Charles, and feeling like an idiot, I stammered as I asked the question.

"Excuse me, is Luke Roberts on this floor?" I quickly followed that question with additional information so as to not be a total fool! "He was a gunshot victim this morning, out on Pioneer Square!"

"Sir, he's up on our ICU floor. That's one floor up. Let me check on his status."

The nurse left and returned about two minutes later. "Sir, Mr. Roberts is currently incapacitated. He was in shock when he arrived here. If you want to go upstairs, feel free to do so." What she wasn't telling me was that the nursing staff upstairs had said they doubted he would awaken in the next few hours. The staff was well trained in HIPAA regulations. I proceeded upstairs and checked in at that floor's nurses' station. I knew I wouldn't be allowed into ICU but hoped I might be allowed a glimpse of Luke and then stop a moment for a prayer. The head nurse directed me to a viewing area and as I rounded the corner, I heard a familiar voice.

"Dr. Becker, if you're looking for Luke, he's over here." My head swiveled left and there Ellie was, once again.

"If I didn't know better, I'd swear you're becoming a guardian angel for our band of misfits!" I stated.

"He's in a coma, Dr. Becker. You might want to reach out with some prayers. Every bit helps, ya know!"

"Thanks," I responded. Ellie allowed me a peek from the doorway, but I saw more monitors and high-tech equipment than I saw of the patient. It wasn't obvious if Luke was going to survive. The thought that it might be weeks before he became conscious again immediately came to mind.

That was the last time I saw Ellie, and I assumed it would be the same with Luke one way or the other.

I returned to join my friends and I prayed for Luke's survival.

∩ ∩ ∩

"The FBI is rounding up as many revolutionaries as possible right now. Your dead hot-air balloon 'flyer,' Danté , was Antifa's leader. And Enrique, he has melted like butter! He is cooperating and we think we've found all the remaining C-4 that was hidden.

"I can't tell you where the Antifa prisoners are being taken. I will tell you they are going to be treated as enemy combatants and will be tried in military courts and not civilian courts. We'll have enough evidence from their documents that we're currently recovering, to indict them for treason. These so-called revolutionary patriots were being funded by specific progressive billionaires as well as foreign countries that want our republic to fail.

"And I don't know if the weapon that generated the EMP was nuclear or not. The television news networks, with the exception of Fox News, and that includes foreign news bureaus, are going full bore with the story that the explosion was an atomic bomb that was detonated in the stratosphere. The target of their wrath is POTUS.

"When I was first employed by the Agency, my father gifted me a laminated copy of a speech given by Mark Twain that he delivered in Connecticut in 1873. It addressed the 'License of the Press.' Let me get it."

I watched Stan retrieve an old tattered wallet from his left rear pants pocket. Then he reached into his sports coat pocket and snatched his reading glasses. Sure enough, he began reading the laminated piece of printed material.

"Twain said: That awful power, the public opinion of a nation, is created in America by a horde of ignorant, self-complacent simpletons who failed at ditching and shoemaking and fetched up in journalism on their way to the poorhouse. I am personally acquainted with hundreds of journalists, and the opinion of the majority of them would not be worth tuppence in private, but when they speak in print...it is the newspaper that is talking and then their utterances shake the community like the thunders of prophecy.

"Gentlemen, our country is being hijacked by the 'Press' or 'Media' if you prefer. Their goals and end game do a disservice to our Founding Fathers and that wonderful document...the Constitution. There's a process for change in our country. That document has survived verbal and written attacks for over 220 years. But now, I believe, there's never been a greater threat to its existence!

"Unfortunately, I must bid you adieu! Steven, if you're ready, the federal judge downtown is waiting to swear you in! I can't think of a greater honor than to have you on board with the Agency. Danny is looking down on you right now, and I know he's just as proud of you just as your father is."

Tommy stood and embraced his son for at least a minute and

shook his son's hand while obviously beaming with great pride. And then he was gone.

Tommy slumped back into the waiting room chair and sobbed. I was in a stupefied shock. Obviously I missed the part about Steven's job offer, I said to myself.

I moved next to Tommy's seat and waited for the proper time to console or congratulate him. I had no idea which one it would be.

HAPTER 75

I t was four months later.

In December, the House and Senate Committees on Intelligence began their investigation into the Portland Insurrection, as politicos were now calling it. Hearings would continue well into the spring of the next year. I had retained legal counsel from the group of lawyers that my son-in-law was a partner with. So far, I had not been asked to appear and testify. If asked, I fully intended to take the Fifth Amendment. I was in no mood to share my thoughts about the darkest moments of my life with anyone else. I still loved my chosen profession and was determined to not embarrass it or myself by publicly revealing how I had tortured another human being.

As expected, the mainstream media continued to focus solely on the possible detonation of a nuclear weapon over American soil.

In February, Tommy hired a new security assistant for Ted. There was no reason a handicapped individual couldn't perform most duties. Ted even provided a van equipped with all the bells and whistles that someone paralyzed from the waist down would need to negotiate the hills of Kentucky. The only thing that Charles lacked in his new job was knowledge about thoroughbreds and the horse racing business.

On this pre-spring day, four of us were gathered at the rail of the track near the finish line at Woodlands Park. Charles had just begun a new security test of the track. Five four-year-old thoroughbreds were led onto the dirt track and into their respective starting gates. The jockeys settled on the saddled horses and tried to calm their steeds. Mike, who was now the track veterinarian, had finished the thoroughbreds' pre-race exams and flashed a thumbs-up to the starter. Mike was my only college friend and partner in the Towers Above endeavor who had no involvement in anything related to the Antifa revolution.

The gates flashed open, and the thoroughbreds were off. The race distance was a mile and an eighth. My guess was that none of the horses would finish.

Holding the binoculars up to my eyes, I looked for and soon saw a hand-crafted quadcopter, piloted by a friend of Jerry's. Ken was positioned well away from the track and was guiding the drone with the use of virtual goggles. I next searched the skies above the track, looking for what might appear to be a turkey vulture. I quickly saw the "bird," while at the same time knowing I was seeing something else.

The horses rounded the bend, streaking into the home stretch, when the drone began its rapid descent to the dirt surface of the track, effectively blocking the oncoming horses. The horse in the lead came to a sudden halt, as the jockey bailed from the saddle irons. Thankfully, the jockey was prepared for this possibility. The other four horses swerved toward the clubhouse side of the track and were quickly reined in.

I knew the entire race was being filmed, so I continued watching the sky as the bird of prey became larger in my binoculars. Lowering them, I watched as Icarus slammed into the drone, bringing it tumbling down onto the dirt track.

With a broad smile, Jerry emerged from the tunnel that

opened onto the track as Tommy pointed his index finger and hand into a gesture that shot skyward. Jerry's assistant, Slade, ran to retrieve the drone from the track as Icarus landed on Jerry's outstretched arm to get his reward.

The test was over – and it had been successful. I had turned away, headed to my car when Mike shouted out to me. "Hey Rob, wait up!" In less than ten seconds, he'd caught up with me.

"Hey, I know the stress you're under, but you and I go way back. There's something else eating at you! C'mon, spit it out, man."

Of all the partners in the Towers Above venture, Mike was the most compassionate. I didn't want to burden him but knew he wouldn't settle for anything less than the truth.

"Mike, it's almost time for our group's annual get-together. I never thought the bond that the four of us have, or maybe I should say had, would be broken. I miss my friendship with Donnie and Mark. I know it's my fault!"

"Keep faith, Rob. I haven't heard the fat lady sing yet," Mike replied.

Mike's comment made me smile. Typical Mike; his glass is always half-full, I said to myself. We shook hands and said our goodbyes before I headed home.

Less than two hours later, I was in the kitchen having a late lunch with Marty. When we finished eating, Marty softly asked me, "Rob, do you have a few minutes to talk?" For me, that usually meant I'd forgotten to do something somewhere in the house drawn from the hubby to do list. Or perhaps she was having flash-backs from the kidnapping again. I knew the therapy sessions she and I were taking weren't coming to an end anytime soon.

"Go ahead, Marty," I said, using a curt tone which I

immediately regretted. She ignored my somewhat nasty demeanor, asking only one question of me.

"Rob, how did our country get to where it is now?

"You're serious, aren't you?" I answered.

"Damn straight I am, Rob!"

My wife is asking me, a guy who got a D in undergraduate sociology, why our country is screwed up, I thought before laughing out loud.

"I hate when you do this, Marty. You always have a way of getting into my head. On the way home, I was asking myself the same question.

"You know, it hasn't been that long since 9/11. On the drive home today, a car passed me that had one of those plastic holders stuck to the window and holding an American flag. It made me think back to 2001 when that was the norm. Seems to me that most every car on the road back then had Old Glory attached, flapping in the wind as the car drove along the highway.

"Patriotism flourished then! It wasn't about New York City politics or blue states versus red states! All those people who perished that day were mostly Americans, end of story. America was enveloped in outrage. How dare terrorists do something that heinous to our citizens – to our brothers and sisters? It was then that I decided if I ever had a chance of owning a thoroughbred, it would be named Towers Above. That would be my tribute in honor of those folks who gave their lives that beautiful September day. And now, look at us! We're at each other's throats. Our patriotism and honor for our country is quickly being replaced with hateful invective thoughts and statements."

I was on a roll, not able to stop my thoughts or the words coming from deep within me.

"Perhaps some of us Baby Boomers screwed things up in how we parented. Our generation's parents were born before the Depression and WWII and they lived through times that were pure hell. They shielded us from their memories of those horrible events. My dad rarely shared anything about what he experienced in World War II. I know my parents, and yours too, promised themselves that their children would never have to go through what they did. Through hard work and real sweat, they were able to keep that promise.

"For the most part, you and I succeeded just as our parents did. We followed that same path, a path that for our generation was less rocky. Then suddenly, a huge boulder fell in front of us and blocked our way forward. That boulder was Vietnam – and many an American was drafted or enlisted to fight in that war. But then a privileged portion of the Boomers began to stomp their feet in protest. They made enough noise to eventually force the US government to abandon its Selective Service requirements. As a result, many children of Baby Boomers and then their offspring, have no sense of national pride, nor do they have an understanding and gratitude for what our country provides and represents. They are entitled, and many expect to be gifted those things that our generation worked so hard to get. They act as if the good life is due them, simply because they are born in the US.

"Sadly, far too many of the younger generation's expectations are to have what we and our parents worked so hard for, without having to expend any physical, mental, or economic effort on their part."

I paused to gather my thoughts, hoping that what I'd been saying for the past thirty minutes made sense – and was helping Marty.

"And so today, many young adults are convinced that they're really special. As a result of our society's overdose of praise, plentiful participation ribbons, and suckling by social media, Boomers have produced a next generation with no understanding that it takes a lot of hard work and effort to be successful and happy.

"The gratification that comes from meeting societal expectations combined with achieving success and happiness in our personal lives are no longer life goals for a large segment of our population. These disenfranchised citizens may not be in the majority, but they're damn close to it! Far too many young adults believe the answer to their misery is to scrap every vestige of America's history and traditions. And that, in my mind, is the definition of a revolution. And right now, Marty, I've moved way past the anger and hatred stage. I have every intention of physically and mentally fighting to preserve our democracy and what our republic stands for!"

I looked at Marty fussing with her iPhone. "You just recorded my rant, didn't you?"

"You know, Rob, someday you need to write a book. What you just said was wonderful." She stood and walked over to where I was sitting and kissed me on the cheek.

"Not so fast. I'm not done! What I really want right now is to reclaim my friendship with Donnie and Mark. They know I'm back home, but I've heard nothing from them."

"Rob, I can't help you with that. Talk to the big guy upstairs. Maybe he'll fulfill your wish!"

I nodded, not telling my wife that I'd been praying that this would happen for well over three months.

# CHAPTER 76

I'm not certain at what age I adopted the philosophy of "If you don't ask the question, you'll never get an answer." With that in mind, the next day I began my first ask with Donnie! His wife Val answered my phone call. I asked her if Donnie would be willing to talk with me. After about five minutes the familiar voice said, "What do you want?"

"Well, for starters, I want to get together with everyone at the track, like we've always done on opening weekend." And I shut up. As I expected, there was a very long pause.

"Rob, Val and I have had some long discussions about what happened this past fall. I owe you an apology. I had no clue as to what transpired with you until I read the news reports in the Wall Street Journal. I'm sorry I let you down with all of that gambling crap. So yeah, count me in, but with one condition. If that guy named Tommy is present, I don't want to sit anywhere near him... no offense!"

I took a deep breath of relief. "Thanks, Donnie. You don't know how much this means to Mike and me. Have you had any contact with Mark?"

"No, Rob, I haven't. But my guess is you'll have trouble getting him to join us. I had no clue he was hip deep in clandestine government business! Good luck even finding him, because I've tried and he has moved. Just shoot me a message about the details Rob. Damn, it's good hearing from you and come on out to the farm. T.A. misses the peppermint shell game. I don't play it nearly as well as you do! Thanks again, Rob; see ya!"

Well, I'll be damned, I said to myself. My next call was to Tommy. If anyone could track down Mark's personal information, it would be Tommy's boss, Stan. Sure enough, inside of an hour, I had Mark's phone number.

With trepidation, I placed the call. I knew he wouldn't answer, because hardly anyone does on a first attempt. I left a message that was soaked in urgency and told him I was going to call every fifteen minutes. Nobody likes their cellphone mailbox filled up. After fifteen minutes passed, I called again. This time I was determined to eat up as much of his voicemail memory as possible. Halfway through my rambling, I was interrupted by Mark's voice.

"Rob, good God you're a pest! What the hell do you want?" I went through the same explanation that I gave Donnie and again I shut up but this time I begged the Lord for a positive reply.

"Rob, there's no way in hell I'm coming! I know that asshole Tommy will be there. That SOB shot off a piece of my ear. Forget it. I've got to go. Goodbye!"

Short, sweet, and saddening were my immediate thoughts. Oh well, three out of four will have to do, I told myself. I refused to dwell on the negative. And besides in ten days, on a Saturday, Woodlands Park was holding their usual celebration devoted to saluting military Veterans. All 'Vets' gained free admittance. It was Ted's intention to also celebrate those of us that had fought in the recent 'Portland/Mt. Hood Insurrection' as many historians now referenced it.

Calypso's and Naucrate's memorial markers were going to be dedicated and Jerry would be present with Icarus. A memorial plaque for Danny was also being unveiled and dedicated while his horse Spike was beginning his first official work day as an outrider horse.

∩ ∩ ∩

Ten days later, as dawn broke, I was greeted by a human voice whistling and immediately after that, there was the sound of one solo ping which indicated I had a message on my cellphone. I glanced at the missive expecting my usual good morning greeting from my middle daughter, but there was no sender's name attached. Whoever the messenger was, they now had my attention. The message read:

YOU THINK IT'S OVER!
IT'S JUST BEGINNING!
TRACK RESTROOM OPPOSITE THE "RIDERS UP" PADDOCK
11:00 A.M. - BE PROMPT!
"OUT OF ORDER" IS DISORDER

I shared the message with Marty, who was supposed to accompany me to the track.

"What do you think?" I asked.

"Well, I think you have an aficionado. You better get cracking; you don't have much time."

Marty could read me like a book. She knew I'd want to get to the track earlier than 11:00 because I'd been challenged, message-wise.

As I rounded the last of the Appalachian foothills surrounding Woodlands Park, I caught sight of the last hot-air balloon rising from the track's infield. It had always been a nice touch to have a balloon festival on opening weekend and as I got closer, I swore the newest balloon had the image of Towers Above emblazoned on it. I eased into the track's parking circle and the valet greeted me with: "Did you see it, Dr. Becker? That new hot-air balloon sure has a great likeness of Towers Above!" I nodded yes, having just received confirmation that Ted had pulled off another sweet surprise, but there was no time for chit-chat. It took no more than fifteen minutes to walk to the restroom.

I opened the door, did a left turn, and found myself staring at two "Out of Order" signs on the first of six stalls. My face flushed as the angst from the previous fall's activities came rushing back to the forefront of my brain's thoughts. I slowly scanned the entire restroom. I seemingly was the only person present and I quickly decided it was time to leave. As I turned to exit, one of the two signs fell to the ground, causing me to pause. Instantly it was followed by a voice coming from one of the multiple stalls.

"Pick it up—please!"

My brain processed the voice and came to an immediate conclusion.

"Mark?" The name echoed throughout the restroom.

"Take a load off and have a seat, Rob!"

The first bathroom stall was locked or jammed shut. I picked up the sign and secured it once again to the door of the second stall, which I entered.

"Raise your feet up, Rob. I've got this!" I assumed he meant I should raise my feet in case someone peeked under the door to see if the stall was occupied.

"Big day for you, Rob. I can't tell you how proud I am of and for you."

What? Huh? were my initial thoughts. He had totally shaken my thought processes as I momentarily forgot what was going on at the track on this day.

"That had to be tough, having to torture that Antifa warrior, huh?"

"If that's what you want—to piss me off—well... you've succeeded, Mark! I don't have time for your shit!" I began wrestling with the door lock when Mark interrupted me again.

"Jesus, Rob, you used to be able to take it as well as dish it. I'm sorry, dude. Sit down, please. What if I told you there's an East Coast version of Wyoming." It took a few seconds to process what Mark had just said when suddenly the door to the bathroom opened and a group of men entered. I braced my feet against the door in case one of the men doubted the sign's message and tried to enter my stall. I wondered if Mark had done the same.

Five minutes passed and again the two of us were alone. I waited for Mark to initiate the conversation since he seemed more in control of the situation at that moment.

"Well?"

"Can we have this discussion outside? There's lots of places we can have privacy! How about we--"

"No, Rob—damn it! Look, I'm the one sticking my neck out here. They probably would kill me if they were to find out that I'm talking to you! I'm giving you a bargaining chip. There's no way they'll call you to testify if they suspect that you know about The East Coast venture and blab about it. Jesus Rob, grab the brass ring!"

"Okay, I'll play along. Where's the ranch located in the Eastern United States? For that matter, what entity or individuals pose a threat?"

"Rob, I'm trying to help out, but for some reason I don't think you appreciate my kindness. This meeting is adjourned!" And with that statement, Mark quietly slipped out of men's room and disappeared into the gathering crowd outside.

It took me a few seconds to realize I was now alone in a restroom stall with an "Out of Order" sign hanging on its door. I slowly unlocked the door and peeked out, making certain that no one else would spot me. I quickly scouted the stall next to mine and discovered how Mark had jerry-rigged the sign to fall off its mount. I started to dial the track's administrative office when another group of men entered the men's room. I bowed my head, avoiding eye contact with anyone and abandoned the phone call.

Ten minutes later I barged into Tommy's office.

"Why do I feel like you just messed with me big time. You had something to do with Mark and that restroom rendezvous, didn't you?"

Tommy hated being peppered with questions, but I didn't give a damn.

"Whoa—Rob, I haven't the slightest idea what you're talking about."

"I asked for your help in getting Mark's telephone number, and you did me one better! You set me up, didn't you!" I countered.

"Rob, I'm only going to say this once more and final time. I don't know what you're talking about!"

I collapsed in one of Tommy's office chairs and buried my head in my hands. My paranoia had peaked, and I realized it was time to shut up.

"Okay, Rob, what did Mark say that has you so riled up!"

"He said there is an Eastern version of a cavalry ranch in one of the states."

"He's right," was Tommy's response.

"What did you say? You mind repeating that?"

"Mark is correct. It's in Virginia!"

"You didn't tell me that," I angrily replied.

"Rob, I didn't get the message from Stan that you were to be included in our intel...." And then he began laughing. "Rob, why don't you go ask Allison for a cup of coffee. Maybe that'll sharpen you up and when you get back, there's someone here that dropped by today to say 'Hey' to all of us!"

I grudgingly followed Tommy's advice but almost decided to leave the office complex. When I returned, Ted ushered me into his office next to Tommy.

"Rob, I want to introduce you to our newest employee. He was up in the Towers Above hot-air balloon this morning. I turned toward Ted's doorway and thought I was looking at a ghost. Standing alongside Tommy was Luke. I sprang to my feet and embraced him.

"Damn, Rob, let the man breathe! He's as thin as a rail."

Tommy was right. Luke's recovery had resulted in extreme weight loss. That's what happens when someone loses a quarter of their intestines via surgery. Tommy suggested we grab some lunch and for a short bit of time I forgot my morning quarrel with Mark. Ted announced that Luke was going to be with us for the entire Spring Meet and that he'd be in charge of a new track experience named Woodlands High Rise. The Towers Above hot-air balloon would bring Luke's tethered ride experiences to the patrons of the park. As we finished dessert, a track plainclothes officer appeared table side and whispered in Tommy's ear. Then he left and Tommy looked at me and said,

"Time to go!"

For the second time on this Saturday, I was heading toward the Riders Up paddock. And then we zagged toward the restroom entrance. Except this time the entrance was cordoned off by police tape. Once inside and past the entrance's left turn, I came full face and was staring at yellow barrier caution tape in front of where Mark had been in hiding just a couple hours earlier. Both out of order signs were askance on the restroom floor. There was a red pool of liquid that seemed to be weeping from the tile, and then the unthinkable seemed to grab hold of me and leave me without a breath!

I looked around the swinging door and I dropped to my knees. "Oh God...no! Oh Lord...no!"

Mark was dead from what appeared to be a self-inflicted gunshot to the head. The nine-millimeter automatic with suppressor attached was in his right hand, and the left side of his head was missing. Tommy, remembering his interrogation from the previous fall, looked at the side of Mark's head that was still intact and then realized it was the other earlobe that he'd maimed. I distinctly heard a "Damn" emanate from Tommy's lips.

The coroner's staff began arriving, and Tommy and I stepped back. Tommy then had a private word with them, and he gently led me slightly farther from the crime scene.

"Rob, tell me again what Mark said this morning."

I paused to catch my wits and then filled him in with the details.

"Rob, I don't need to tell you that this is more than troubling. Whoever killed Mark wanted it to look like a suicide. There's only one problem with that scenario. Mark was left-handed. There's no way he would have been that efficient with his right hand! We call it a 'Vince Foster Hit.' I'm guessing that the DIA finally washed their hands of Mark. It also means that whoever did this probably was watching you earlier this morning. I'm going to call Stan and have him assign an agent to shadow you and Marty until the Agency resolves this situation. There's also another possibility. It's evident that the ongoing civil tension in America is moving beyond its infancy. Antifa thought instigating a revolution would be a cakewalk. If there ever was a junior varsity, they were the perfect example.

"The other thing that's fact is, Rob, you've become a household name. You're a celebrity now, and that means half of America loves you and the other half hates you!

"Even in this state, there's some frightening shit going on. Yes, there's another cavalry unit. You can call it the 'East Coast Unit.' And there are happenings occurring in every state and they're not a coincidence. You just don't hear or read about them.

"That's all the info I can share with you. I've stuck my neck out way too far. I want you to know, and this is me talking personally, I never intended for these scenarios to ever happen. There truly is a level of governance in America that people don't realize exists. And our current POTUS is threatening its existence.

"You better get moving. Today's ceremonies are about to start. Oh, and Rob, didn't I hear you say that you and Marty were thinking about a vacation somewhere?"

Needless to say, the ceremonies became a blur for me. All afternoon I asked myself why I continued to be drawn into extraordinary conflicts. Obviously, people like Mark and Tommy were privy to intelligence that perhaps sixteen other government intel agencies had no, some, or total knowledge of. So what's new with that? I said to myself.

A chill climbed my spine, and that's when I decided it was way past time for Marty and me to get away. Perhaps leaving the continental United States for an extended period of time would help.